"I wouldn't have you were the last man—" Her breath caught in her throat as he nuzzled the side of her neck. He trailed his hand along her belly and down a path to her thigh.

"Weak, despicable cad," she accused breathlessly.

Against her will, she leaned into him, conforming her body to his

Finally he spoke. His mouth was at her ear and his voice was deep and hushed. "I shall give you nothing you don't ask for voluntarily. So you see, my lady, the game is up to you."

She sighed. "Put your knife away, highwayman. You'll have no need of it this night."

He was still. Then, removing the blade from her throat, he tossed the weapon away.

Freed, she pivoted around and began to unbutton his shirt. "Your grace! You shock me!" he mocked.

"I'm an impatient woman, highwayman. It takes more than weapons and promises to satisfy me."

Stepping out of his boots, he asked, "Have you ever been satisfied?"

She showed her teeth in a wicked smile. "Never."

"You are about to put that in the past tense."

She gave him a lusty chuckle. "I admire your confidence. You are most certainly welcome to try. . . ."

THE LAST
HIGHWAYMAN

Katherine O'Neal

BANTAM BOOKS
NEW YORK • TORONTO • LONDON
SYDNEY • AUKLAND

THE LAST HIGHWAYMAN
A Bantam Fanfare Book / March 1993

FANFARE and the portrayal of a boxed "ff" are trademarks of
Bantam Books, a division of
Bantam Doubleday Dell Publishing Group, Inc.

All rights reserved.
Copyright © 1993 by Katherine O'Neal
Cover art copyright © 1993 by Steve Assel.
No part of this book may be reproduced or transmitted in any form or
by any means, electronic or mechanical, including photocopying,
recording, or by any information storage and retrieval system, without
permission in writing from the publisher.
For information address: Bantam Books.

If you purchased this book without a cover you should be aware
that this book is stolen property. It was reported as "unsold and destroyed" to the publisher and neither the author nor the publisher
has received any payment for this "stripped book."

ISBN 0-553-56065-4

Published simultaneously in the United States and Canada

Bantam Books are published by Bantam Books, a division of Bantam Doubleday
Dell Publishing Group, Inc. Its trademark, consisting of the words "Bantam Books"
and the portrayal of a rooster, is Registered in U.S. Patent and Trademark Office
and in other countries. Marca Registrada. Bantam Books, 666 Fifth Avenue, New
York, New York 10103.

PRINTED IN THE UNITED STATES OF AMERICA
RAD   0 9 8 7 6 5 4 3 2 1

For Bill—
my passion,
my inspiration,
my love

THE LAST
HIGHWAYMAN

CHAPTER 1

***

T BEGAN, AS DID SO many of the adventures of her life, with Oscar Wilde. He knocked on the door late one night with his distinctive impatient three raps and tapped his cane as the servant explained that her grace was unavailable.

"Unavailable?" he cried. "To *me*?"

At which point he waved her away with several rapid flurries of his hand and brushed past her through the massive, columned entryway to burst through the door of the salon.

When Christina looked up from her packing, she saw him standing on her threshold with one hand on his hip, striking a dramatic and indignant pose. "Unavailable?" he wailed once more. "My dearest Christina, upon what ungodly assumption do you announce yourself unavailable to *me*?"

Christina laughed. He was an arresting man with the dark, brooding look of a poet and—if one didn't look too closely—the body of an athlete. He was tall and broad, but he took no exercise whatsoever unless forced into it, and he was fond of draping his massive form in a languishing manner across whatever was available—a doorway, a chair, a statue. He was dressed now in a lavender evening coat with a flowing yellow tie. It was his habit to shock London society with his attire and to keep them talking—if not about his clothes, at least about the urbanity of his wit.

The flamboyance of his dress and the brilliance of his

mind proved a heady combination. When he looked at her with those great dark drooping eyes, she sometimes felt that he wasn't seeing her as a person standing before him, but as a symbol that might spark the genius of his work. He was a poet, wit, and dramatist who several years earlier had taken London's literary and social circles by storm. In spite of the ten years' difference in their ages, Christina had befriended him instantly and had helped him reach the pinnacle of his popularity. It was something he never forgot.

She dropped her silk stockings into the open valise and glided across the museumlike proportions of her drawing room to give his cheek an affectionate kiss.

"You wound me, darling. I merely said I was unavailable to visitors. You hardly qualify as a visitor. More as a brotherly sort of pest."

"Then *do* be sure and pass on such information to the help."

"It won't matter after tonight. I shall be long gone from this dreary house. Frankly, for my tastes, it can't be too soon."

Oscar eyed his friend closely. At twenty, Christina Wentworth-Gibbons was by far the youngest duchess in their set. She was a small woman, athletically slender yet with the undeniable curves of a woman designed to set any man's blood to the boil. Her hair was a deep, dusty color somewhere between black and brown, fashioned in elegant rolls and twists about her head. Her eyes were as green as moss in the forest. Her features spoke of her aristocratic breeding: the delicate wrists and hands, the long neck, the complexion as flawless and creamy as the finest pearls. Her face was refined, with high patrician cheekbones, a narrow nose, and eyebrows that arched as gracefully as the wings of a butterfly. Though it wasn't the most beautiful face in London, the animation of her features—haughty one moment, meltingly sensual the next—and her dramatic sense of style were so striking that one could easily mistake her for a beauty. She presented herself as the most bewitching woman ever to grace the earth—and you believed her.

She was dressed in an enchanting gold-embroidered

green velvet gown that hugged her womanly curves. When she walked, flounces of white lace peeped from beneath the gown as it flowed about her legs. Oscar thought it was just like Christina to be clad in nothing but a petticoat underneath her dressing gown. It was something they had in common, this love of shocking society with their clothes.

She was surrounded by trunks and the last few remnants of clothes to be packed. She went back to her task, folding a wisp of an embroidered silk nightgown into the top of a trunk.

"You haven't been the same since the death of the Duke," Oscar commented, still watching her with a keen eye.

"Did you expect I would be?"

"Certainly, I didn't expect you to plunge yourself into mourning over an admittedly unloved husband, and then dash off to God knows where without so much as a fare-thee-well."

"If I've neglected you, I apologize. Truly I do, Oscar. You've been a dear friend through these awful times, and for that I'm grateful."

In a hushed voice, he said, "I hadn't noticed these times as being so awful."

"They have been for me."

He crossed the width of the room and picked up a feathered slipper in his violet-gloved hand. "Where are you off to? France? Perhaps some fresh blood will bring back that beloved sparkle to your cheeks. A little slumming in the back alleys of Paris, perhaps? I might even be persuaded to join you."

"And what would I find in Paris? Nothing but the same tiresome fops who seldom do anything adventurous, but who fancy themselves libertines of the highest order. Soft men. God protect me from soft men! Once—just once—I should like to meet a man who's worthy of me. Or at the very least, who can keep up with me."

"That, darling, is a tall order, indeed."

She smiled at him. "Oh, Oscar, I'm so tired of it all. I've known men enough in my life. Yet none of them could even hold a candle to *you*. Which, forgive me, darling, is saying precious little."

"Many thanks. You never told me where you're off to."

"Egypt. I fancy a cruise down the Nile."

"How ever did you come upon that particular choice?"

"By a process of elimination. England is too confining. I've done everything I can think to do in London, most of it scandalous. I long to travel the world, to escape the same dreary people, embarking on the same empty round of parties, balls, and pranks. I've already traveled Europe extensively. So Egypt seems as good a choice as any for escape."

"You shan't like it."

"Whyever not?"

"Darling," he said outrageously, "I can tell you on certainty that every last man in Egypt has tucked within his trousers the most *diminutive* John Thomas. Not your sort of place at all."

"Oscar, really! Don't be absurd."

He put his hand to his heart. "On my honor."

Christina gave an insouciant shrug. "It's all academic. I'm through with men in any case."

"You? Through with men? Better give up breathing. You, dearest, are a woman who was made—if not exclusively for men—at least for sinful pleasures."

"Then I shall wilt like a picked bloom. Do try to understand. I'm so disgusted with myself, so tired of the frivolity of the Marlborough House set, that Egypt, with its ancient mysteries, is most appealing."

"So it's the Prince of Wales you're running from?"

"And why not? Every time I see him, I think of poor Wynterbrooke. I can't help but reproach myself."

"You were a good wife to Wynterbrooke, in your own way."

"You must be joking! I cuckolded him, made a fool of him. When all is said and done, I suppose I killed him, too."

"Christina! Precious! You're breaking my heart. Enough of this maudlin self-pity. Come along, my brooding little pet. We're off to Mott's."

"Mott's, in my present state, is the last place I care to be."

"Nevertheless, it's my farewell wish. God only knows what wretched fate may befall you in the wilds of Africa. The very least you can do is leave me with one parting night of debauchery to remember." He rummaged through the dresses on the settee. "Here," he said, handing her a striking gold-and-black gown with a plunging neckline. "This should do nicely."

She looked at the gown dangling from his hand. Her instinct told her to turn him down. But it was, after all, the last time she would see him for some time. And he *had* been good to her through the hard times of the Duke's death. Why not indulge him one last time? Maybe it would do her some good. Perhaps as she had done numerous times in the past, she could forget herself in the stylized diversions of the most notorious and elegant sin club in London.

CHAPTER 2

$\mathscr{B}$Y THE STANDARDS of the day, the woman was exquisite. With lush blond curls and a rounded face, she might easily have been mistaken for an innocent. But she was painted and powdered to give her the look of wicked sophistication that had become the establishment's trademark. Her lips were moist and red, clearly defined. Although Mott's catered strictly to the aristocracy, Kettie Swindell's fame had spread, and her lips were famous even in the provinces for the thoughts they inspired in men's minds.

By now, she was scantily clad in a mere wisp of a petticoat, corset, and black stockings rolled to just below her knees. At Oscar's request, she was performing her notorious striptease, an act that had gone far to further the reputation of her mouth. As she slipped out of each piece of clothing, slithering it along the ample flesh of her bosom and arms, she ran her tongue along the contours of her lips, pursing them in expressions that suggested various acts of love. It was a shocking display, one that rarely failed to make men hard and impatient. The first time she'd seen the show, Christina had been as enthralled as the men. But tonight, it all seemed rather silly. Far from feeling her blood stir, she had to fight the overwhelming impulse to laugh.

They were in a private room upstairs from the main ballroom. There was a rounded, padded stage in the center of the room with several plush chairs scattered about its perimeter. This particular chamber was decorated in shades of rose and gold, but the colors were shadowed by the dim light of the flickering candles.

Besides Oscar and Christina, the room contained four other regular patrons. One of them, the young Sir Weldon Markham, had attached himself to them the moment they entered the hall. Sir Weldon had long been thwarted in his desire to bed Christina and, having heard the rumors of her imminent departure, could hardly believe his eyes when she appeared on the arm of his friend Oscar Wilde. Lean and blond with a reddish-blond mustache, he affected the bored sneer of the fashionable "swell." Tonight, though, as he ignored the infamous stripper and fixed his attention on Christina, he had the leering look of a man who was hopeful of a last-minute reprieve. The other swells were casting equally hopeful glances in her direction. The Duchess of Wynterbrooke's reputation was well established within these walls, and one never knew whom she might choose to share for the night.

It wasn't unusual for women to accompany men to such a place. For years, the great beauties of London and even Paris had come to Mott's Dancing Rooms to see and be seen by the cream of the Marlborough House set. Many of them were kept women, mistresses of wealthy men. Some were high-class prostitutes. A few, like Christina, were titled women in their own right. Albert Edward, son of Queen Victoria and himself the Prince of Wales, had set the precedent by bringing his own mistresses since the 1860s. In the ensuing twenty years, it had become a notorious but discreet playground of the Prince's fashionable friends.

Christina had found the place amusing on more than a few occasions. It was ruled with exaggerated propriety by the white-waistcoated owner Freer, who screened his clientele as scrupulously as he might guard admittance to the Crown jewels. He was proud of the distinction of his guests, and was careful to keep the riffraff out. Thus, it was a place where a lady of Christina's station could go to escape the rigid conventions of Victoria's virtually nonexistent court.

But tonight, Christina was finding little of her usual diversion. Oscar, who was attuned to her moods, could see at once that she was ready to bolt.

He motioned to a man who stood discreetly in the shadows, who in turn opened the door, poked his head out, and gestured. In a moment, a red-haired woman named Bonnie entered and beamed at the assembled group. At the sight of her, Kettie lounged back onto the padded stage and spread her arms out to the newcomer. Bonnie wasted little time in getting to work. She'd been given the sign that the audience was restless, and might be lost if the momentum didn't improve.

Bonnie was slimmer than her partner, but still possessed a healthy amount of flesh. Men liked their women robust, and Mott's was careful to cater to the fashion of the day. She stripped down to corset and stockings and knelt over Kettie, keeping her backside to the audience and giving them a view of her molded buttocks and smooth white thighs. Then she leaned down and kissed Kettie on her legendary mouth.

There was a general murmur from the men. Encouraged, Bonnie pulled aside the barrier of the petticoat and brought her mouth to Kettie's breast. When she removed it, the red of her liprouge left a mark on the swelling nipple.

Christina felt a hand at her shoulder. Turning, she saw the eyes of Sir Weldon burning into hers. All around them, men were stripping off their Bond Street suits to have a go at the women writhing in mutual ecstasy before them. But Sir Weldon found them to be of little interest except to hope the sight of them might make the Duchess feel more tenderly disposed toward him. He brought his face closer and lowered his voice for her ears alone.

"Might a gentleman hope for the favor of a farewell kiss?"

She knew well enough that it wasn't a farewell kiss he had in mind. She'd rebuffed him before, but tonight it didn't seem to matter. She'd drunk enough champagne at Oscar's instigation that she was losing her will to resist. What difference did one more man make at this point, anyway? She put her finger to his chin and leaned forward to kiss him.

It was all the encouragement he needed. Starved for her attentions for so long, he sprang upon her like an unleashed tiger. He took her face in his hands and kissed her madly, then let his fingers wander to the cleavage that had so tantalized him from the moment he'd seen her step into the room. He took her breast in his hand, paused as if waiting for the expected rejection, then crushed it in his eagerness to explore the promise it held. Soon his lips were nibbling at the folds of her gown, and he was reaching behind to unfasten the back of her dress.

Suddenly, it was enough. Her distaste for the scene drove the once-welcome fuzziness from her brain. All at once, she felt ravaged by the excesses of her life. A senseless marriage at an early age to spite her parents. Another loveless marriage to an old man for his title, a celibate marriage that had lasted three short months before he'd died. Three months during which, to punish herself, she'd caroused—discreetly, of course—with any man who caught her fancy. The only requirement the Duke had asked of her was her sparkling presence at his side on the odd occasion when he ventured out of the house in St. James's Square. She'd thought it all a grand joke on herself, until the scandal had killed him, and she was left with his title, his money, and a heartful of remorse. Suddenly, her life seemed shabby and meaningless. The price of her self-punishment—the taking advantage of a kindly old man—had been too much to pay.

She shot to her feet, ripping the back of her gown out of the randy knight's hand. "My apologies," she murmured, although all but Oscar and Sir Weldon were too engrossed to hear. Then she tore from the room and out into the glare and ruckus of the balcony overlooking the grand ballroom. There, a discordant quartet played for the dancers below.

She stood grasping the rail, watching with dispassionate eyes the swirling of the dancing couples as she gasped to regain her breath. She felt the place closing in around her. She wanted nothing more than to be home. Home, where she could try once again to shed tears for her poor, dead Duke. Perhaps this time she would succeed.

She turned to the stairs, prepared to make an inconspicuous exit, when she heard a woman's scream. All at once, it was bedlam below. Dancers scurried to the far corners of the room, women shrieking and pulling up the voluminous folds of their skirts. Halfway down the elegant staircase, Christina stopped to observe the scene and saw immediately what the fuss was about. There must have been two hundred or more rats darting about the polished floor of the room.

In a far corner, one of the swells howled and raised his arm in triumph. Soon, it was clear that the rats were a practical joke, one of the many perpetrated in these halls. The men began to laugh while the women still screamed, and soon the story was circulating of how the Marquis of Hastings had paid the rat-catcher twenty guineas to produce full-grown sewer rats and set them loose on the dance floor.

She was about to continue on her way when a burst of laughter, louder than the rest, halted her steps. She looked across the room to see the Prince of Wales doubled over in hysterics as he slapped Hastings on the back. No one enjoyed a practical joke as well as the Prince, as long as it wasn't aimed at him. Seeing him, with his portly frame stuffed into one of his many dinner jackets, Christina's heart constricted. She wished now that she'd listened to her instincts and avoided Mott's at all costs.

She hurried down the stairs, hoping to escape unnoticed. But in the midst of a guffaw, he glanced up, caught sight of her, and hastened to cut her off at the front door.

He stood, awaiting her patiently. He had dark gold hair thrown back like a lion's, and a neat, close-trimmed beard. His evening suit was of the utmost quality, yet the vulgarity of his appetites was evident in the bulge of his stomach and fleshiness of his jowls. Still, he carried himself with an air of dignity that said at once that this man was destined for the throne of England.

"Ah, Duchess," he greeted her. "We had heard that you'd abandoned our paltry pleasures."

It was a struggle to look him in the face, but she made a supreme effort. "Unfortunately, the cost of my return has been dear."

He stiffened. With a lowered voice, he said, "I had hoped that on the eve of your departure you might be more—civil."

"Have I been uncivil, Highness?"

"Dammit, Christina, you've been uncivil since the day you left my bed!"

It was true. She'd captivated him initially because she, of all the women in England, hadn't groveled for his attentions. The Prince was known to take whatever woman caught his fancy. He preferred married, experienced women whose husbands were to recognize the honor done them and consider their cuckolding a pleasurable duty. The Duke, like other husbands, had looked the other way, but Christina was decidedly unimpressed. She had graced the Prince's bed, but her barbs had shown her contempt for his common intelligence. To even the score, he'd snubbed her in public, then within her hearing, made vicious implications to his friends. The scandal had threatened to ruin her socially, for those the Prince of Wales snubbed were similarly ignored by society. Anyone rejected by Marlborough House might just as well leave England. Christina hadn't cared for herself, but the Duke had suffered miserably, and the strain had finally killed him.

It was only the Prince's unwarranted fondness—and fascination—for Christina that had saved her from disgrace at his hands. She was everything he'd come to admire in a woman: intelligent, witty, daring, unafraid to express her own mind, a woman who conducted her life at a breathless pace while still maintaining the outward decorum of a lady. She was also considered a great beauty, and her sexual appetite surpassed his own. She was wholly uninhibited, and displayed a passion for life that was mesmerizing.

But she wasn't interested in him.

He didn't know why she'd finally succumbed. But once she had and he'd tasted of what she had to offer, he found that he could hardly do without it. He'd made a mistake that he hadn't made since Lillie Langtry: he'd fallen in love. While Christina's indifference maddened him, it also made her irresistible to him. He'd hoped to call her to heel by humiliating her publicly. But it hadn't worked as he'd planned. She hadn't crawled back to him with a more submissive—and grateful—attitude. She had merely walked away. So what could the poor man do? He had to allow her back into the set. He could hardly face the thought of losing her completely. But by then, her husband had died, and she'd made it clear that he was the last person she would ever seek out again. He had learned the hard way that the Duchess could hold a grudge.

She gave him a cool look. "It wasn't my intention to be uncivil," she told him. "In fact, it wasn't my intention ever to see you again."

He was angry now. "I could have you in chains for speaking to me so!"

She gave him a cynical smile. "You tried that once before, Bertie . . . remember?"

He blushed. In an effort to humble her, he'd inflicted on her every sexual deviation he could think of. Still, blush as he did, he couldn't help wishing for such an opportunity again.

He was saved a reply as Oscar and Sir Weldon rushed to their sides. They bowed to the Prince, then Oscar, sensing the tension, grumbled, "Bloody rats. It took us a good ten minutes just to cross the floor."

Nearby, Freer was reprimanding Lord Hastings. "Really, my lord, these practical jokes just cannot be permitted."

Hastings was far from chastened. He laughed as the swells bounded about on hands and knees in a frantic effort to retrieve the rodents.

"I'm leaving," Christina told Oscar. "You stay and enjoy yourself."

"My dear girl, you don't expect me to allow you to run off home alone!"

"Certainly I do. Whyever not?"

"Haven't you heard?"

"Heard?"

"About the marauder, of course!"

She stared at them. Every one of them was nodding his head seriously. "Come, gentlemen, surely one practical joke for the evening is enough."

"But it's no joke, my dear. There *is* such a hooligan."

"Really, Oscar. Is he to jump from the shadows and thrust fingers in our sides, demanding our valuables? Like the time we dressed as pickpockets and rifled the watches of our friends on Derby Day?"

The Prince was looking at her intensely. "It would seem the Duchess's descent into her ridiculous mourning has isolated her from the latest news."

Oscar put his hand to his forehead. "I'd forgotten! You hadn't heard! How remiss of me not to keep you better informed."

"Let us not forget that our Christina was away on the Continent for so long. You only returned long enough to marry and bury your Duke, didn't you, dear?"

There was a veiled derision to the Prince's tone that angered Christina. "Is anyone going to tell me what it is I don't know?"

Markham did the honors. "In the last year or so, we've been plagued by a fiend so cunning that he's escaped every attempt to apprehend him."

"What sort of fiend?"

"It's hard to know, really. He robs trains, if you can imagine, and has been rumored to be responsible for half a dozen acts of sabotage in the last few months alone. They call him the Brighton Bandit, for it was at Brighton that he first struck. He takes in quite a lot of plunder, from all accounts. What he does with it, God only knows."

"He robs trains?" Christina repeated. "How does he do it?"

"Various ways. Once he and his men sat on horseback upon the tracks with black kerchiefs covering their mouths and noses and waited for the train to stop. Then they calmly leapt on board and relieved the passengers of their valuables at gunpoint. Other times, he's merely appeared out of the blue and without so much as a fuss, taken every last farthing without the conductor's ever knowing what had happened until it was over. A thorough search of the train turned up nary a sign of him. They speculate that he jumped from some bridge or other onto the *roof* of the train, and entered from the caboose. It's the damnedest thing, really."

Something clicked in Christina's head. "Oh, yes, I did hear something. Mother was going on about some train robbery, but I didn't listen. I thought it was a prank. It's difficult to tell these days."

"Particularly," Oscar retorted, "where your mum is concerned."

"It was no prank, you may be certain of that."

"Actually," said Oscar, studying his nails, "this ruffian is all the rage. Young girls swoon, and men are sharpening their skills with pistols in preparation for a confrontation. I hear Hastings is threatening to ride every blasted train hoping for one clear shot."

Markham bristled at his mimicking tone. "Not everyone is as enchanted as Oscar would have you believe. *Lady* Hastings was on one of those trains, and she fainted dead away at the sight of him. She said he made the most indecent suggestions. She says he *tortures women*. In point of fact, she called him a cad!"

"How," asked Oscar, "could she have heard his indecent suggestions if she fainted at first sight of him?"

Christina was hardly listening. "Robbing trains," she murmured. "Fancy that. It's like something from the American West."

"If he just robbed trains, it would be one thing," said the Prince, who'd puffed up progressively during the course of the conversation. "But the blackguard has gone too far."

No one explained, so Christina prompted them. "Well?"

Sir Weldon shifted uncomfortably. The Prince turned red. It was left to Oscar to expound. "The thing is, he seems to have set out on a sort of vendetta against His Highness's especial friends."

"A vendetta!" she cried. "My, this *is* interesting!"

"For some reason, he's been personally picking on those who are known to frequent Marlborough House."

"Picking on them?"

"Robbing them, dear. In their coaches. On the roads of London. In the dead of night."

Like a highwayman, she thought. But in the 1880s? There had been no highwaymen since the twenties. "But surely, he can't get away with such a thing. The police—surely Scotland Yard—"

"We have every available man on the case, naturally," said the Prince. "But the wretched fellow has succeeded in eluding them all. He slips in and out of London like a phantom. Right under our noses. We can't for the life of us figure out how."

"I shall tell you how," Oscar said. "The knave is obviously a meticulous planner. London is a city built on reason and logic. The man *defies* logic and does the unexpected."

"Ridiculous nonsense," Markham scoffed. "Obviously, he has friends in town who shield him. Who and why, we have no idea. He hasn't allowed us to know his motives, so we can't predict the pattern of his crimes. But have no fear. He shall trap himself one day, and then we'll have him. Criminals always do."

"The Queen is outraged, naturally," moaned the Prince. "Quite an embarrassment." It was no secret that Victoria thought little of her wayward and scandalous son, even blamed him for her husband's death, and left him completely out of any decision-making process in the running of the government. That these robberies seemed connected to him was further instigation for her disapproval.

"But who is he?"

"We haven't the foggiest."

"There are rumors, of course," Oscar said pointedly. "Some say he's some disgraced nobleman or other."

Christina looked at the Prince. "Why, Bertie, surely you haven't enemies you're not aware of?"

He squirmed. "The worst of it is, popular opinion is divided. Some say he's a villain, but others swear he's quite cultured in his dealings. Lady Starrington was held up by him only last week, and she hasn't stopped speaking of him since. In the most *glowing* terms, I might add."

"I should think it treason to *glow* about so notorious a political criminal," said Oscar wickedly. "Particularly one who only two days ago shot Lord Hampton in the arm." It was a veiled barb, for Christina's sake. The Marquis of Hampton was one of the Prince's best friends.

"No!" cried Markham. "I hadn't heard!"

Oscar paused for effect. "Some say he's more than a fallen nobleman. *Some* say he's Lord Wycliffe."

"He can't be," snapped the Prince. "Richard is long since in his grave!"

Oscar shrugged expansively. "I only repeat what I hear, Highness. I can't be held responsible for idle gossip."

Christina was watching closely. For an instant, when Oscar had mentioned Lord Wycliffe's name, she had caught the flash of fear in Bertie's eyes.

"Well, well, well. Could it be," she asked with a deceptive innocence in her eyes as she stared straight at the Prince, "that there exists in all of England one real man? A man so brave that he has no fear of the social power you wield like a cleaver? That in itself should prove quite a novelty."

Oscar saw at once that she'd offended the Prince and belatedly stepped in to deflect mischief. "That said, you are not to be allowed to traipse about the streets alone. I shall accompany you and see you safely to your door. Now, say good-night, dear. We must get you home in time to get plenty of rest." To the Prince he added, "She has an early train to catch, you know."

"I shall come along, if I may," Sir Weldon announced.

Christina shrugged and, without saying good-bye as she'd been instructed, headed out the door. "Come along if you must. If all you say is true, I shall need more than Oscar to protect me from the brute."

As Oscar was helping her into her sable coat, she whispered, "Who, pray tell, is Lord Wycliffe?"

Oscar looked about to make sure no one could hear. "The Earl of Wycliffe. I don't know all the story, for it was before my time. I wouldn't know anything except that Hastings, while in his cups one night, spilled the truth. Do you remember hearing of that nasty business about ten years back when Sporting Joe Aylesford wanted to duel with Lord Blandford over the stealing of his wife?"

"Of course. Bertie talked them out of it. He won't tolerate public scandal."

"There was a time when he wasn't so scrupulous with his reputation. When he was willing to risk everything."

"Oscar, what *are* you talking about?"

"Lord Wycliffe, dear, is the man the Prince of Wales killed in a duel!"

CHAPTER 3

$\mathcal{L}$ONDON OF THE eighteen-eighties was the London of Gladstone and Disraeli, of Whistler and Anthony Trollope, and, of course, of Queen Victoria. Dickens had been dead for a dozen years, yet his spirit lingered on, and enthusiasm for his writings reached unprecedented bounds. It was a regimented world of afternoon teas and cucumber sandwiches, of horseback riding along Rotten Row with stiffly clad ladies riding sidesaddle and top-hatted gentlemen paying court. It was the city of the English renaissance. It was the very center of the world, the empire on which the sun never set, whose provinces stretched to the four corners of the earth.

But there was a predictable dark side to this London as well. Soho at night was a decidedly seedy place. It was alive with lights and sounds, with gentlemen wandering the streets seeking forbidden pleasures, with painted women sashaying through the crowds, eager to provide the means. With over a hundred thousand prostitutes in the city of London alone, competition was fierce. Bobbies looked the other way as high-class whores in bright silks ambled along the Haymarket, and "under-fifteens" thronged Piccadilly Circus. The streets were jammed with casinos, gambling dens, "dance halls" and "introducing houses," pornographers, and even a publisher of obscene sheet music. It was London after dark—the London that had sprung up from rebellion against the Queen's puritanical dictates, and with the wholehearted encouragement of her son, the Prince of Wales.

It was a London Christina knew well. It was also the city, the pervasive frivolity of it all, that she was fleeing. After the aborted "fancy show" and her confrontation with Bertie, she felt soiled. It was a familiar feeling these days, one of not being able to wash herself clean. Because of this, she insisted Oscar and Markham drive her home in an open buggy.

"I wish to feel the clean air on my face," she said by way of explanation. The men could only shrug. May evenings could be brisk, but the Duchess was known for her whims. They couldn't know that she hoped the chill air on her face would cool the shame burning in her cheeks.

They drove through Soho and skirted Trafalgar Square on their way to St. James's. Oscar took the reins. Christina was dying to question him further about Bertie and Lord Wycliffe, but Oscar had warned her not to speak in front of Markham. The Prince's duel was a well-guarded secret, and it wouldn't do for him to hear that Oscar had been bandying the story about town.

"Markham's not one to trust with secrets," he'd whispered.

"Markham's a fool," she'd agreed.

Before moving on, he'd given her a wicked grin. "You, on the other hand, are not. You're wise to steer clear of the poor besotted knight. Aside from being a fool, he's no more well-endowed than an Egyptian. Take it from one who knows!"

So Christina stewed while Markham produced a booklet from his pocket and, from the lights of the street, began to read aloud.

"You can't believe what I've discovered," he pronounced, hoping to impress Christina with his resourcefulness. "It's a guide to the sinful pleasures London has to offer. I've heard tales of these pamphlets in common usage among the swells in the fifties, but this is the first I've seen. I found it in one of father's old trunks. Can you imagine? Every fancy lady worth mentioning at the time is expounded on in these pages. Here, do listen."

Christina pulled her sable coat closer about her and leaned her head back on the seat. The breeze ruffled her hair as they wound their way through traffic, with horns sounding and carriages occasionally screeching to a halt as a drunken pedestrian darted in front.

"It's quite hilarious, really. 'Miss Maria Bolton is a six-foot Amazonian with firm, plump, and white breasts, which when they rise and fall, paint the exuberance of the soil in the most expressive terms. She walks singular genteel and is supported by beautiful legs.' Oh, my! Listen to this. 'In duets, she performs her *tongue* and *voice* full as satisfactory as when it emits the shrillest note. She performs her part with admirable skill and dexterity, and in such cases chooses the *lowest* part.'"

"She sounds charming," Christina said lightly. "Shall we let you off?"

Oscar laughed as Markham put the book in his lap and pouted.

"Oscar," she added, "do let's drive through the park. These streets are so tiresome."

Although her eyes were closed, she could feel Oscar's grin. She knew he understood that it was darker in the park, and would render the reading of such nonsense impossible.

Oscar turned west on Piccadilly toward Green Park, and onto the Broad Walk. From there, he would cut east toward St. James's.

Soon, the cacophony of street traffic dimmed to a distant hum. Christina was silent, keeping her eyes closed, breathing deeply of the fresh greenery. The clip-clop of the horses' hooves on the cobblestones was an unexpected comfort. Oscar was content to allow her privacy, but Markham, unused to her brooding, was uncomfortable. He began to chatter.

"Do you know why Green Park, of all the parks in London, has no flowers? It's said that Queen Catherine, knowing Charles the Second stopped off here to pick bouquets for his mistresses, ordered the flowers dug up."

Christina sighed.

Suddenly, as they turned the corner, Oscar jerked the buggy to a halt. Christina was flung forward. She was about to reprimand her friend when the change of mood alerted her. It was unearthly silent. Even Sir Weldon had stopped his gossiping and seemed to be holding his breath.

Straightening, she opened her eyes and looked about. At first, she could see nothing. But Oscar's gloved hand crept over and took hers in a cautioning grip. As her eyes adjusted to the dark, an image formed before her that at first seemed like a mirage.

He was silhouetted against the night, sitting tall and straight on a giant horse. There was a pistol in his hand and a wide-brimmed hat upon his head. The cape on his shoulders fluttered slightly in the breeze. She could see none of his features, for the trees filtered the moonlight and sheltered the carriage from the lights of the city. But she knew who it was before he uttered a word. And, she thought, she was right. Cast in the shadows, he looked like a highwayman from another age.

"Wh-who goes there?" quailed Markham.

The stranger's voice was soft and low, a deep voice that was filled with just the slightest trace of laughter when he spoke. "A friend of the Prince," he said with exaggerated courtesy. "At your service, sir." And, sweeping off his hat, he gave a deep bow.

As he was doing so, Markham reached into his pocket, and a moment later, a gunshot shattered the stillness of the night. He apparently missed, for the ruffian flung his hat at the young knight. Markham ducked, and two other men raced from the shadows to overtake him and wrench the pistol from his hand. In the struggle, one of the criminals boxed his ear. They wrestled him to the ground, where the same man tied his hands behind his back. The other retrieved his master's hat and passed it to him while holding a pistol on Oscar and Christina.

"That was foolish," said the leader. "I trust your friends are not so shortsighted."

Oscar stood slowly, jiggling the buggy with his weight, and spread out his hands in a conciliatory gesture. "I am a poet, sir, not a marksman. If we battle, we must do so with wits."

The intruder chuckled. "I should look forward to matching wits with you, were I not so pressed for time.

Another night, perhaps. For now, I must ask you to step down and suffer the same indignity as your friend. A self-proclaimed wit paired with even so unworthy a marksman may cause trouble for me that I'd rather not endure."

One of his henchmen jerked his head, and Oscar reluctantly stepped down and allowed himself to be tied in a prone position. Christina remained seated, collecting herself. Strangely, after the first gunshot, she wasn't frightened. Her cool mind raced, deciding the best approach. If she could bluff her way through this, she could leave and send help. He wouldn't expect her to defy him.

"You, too, my lady."

She didn't move. Instead, she used her most seething hauteur to catch him off guard. "I most certainly will not. Moonlight may disguise the finer qualities of my frock, but it cost me more than I'll wager you make in a year of pilfering. I have no intention of spoiling its shimmer by lying about in the wet grass." She looked with contempt at the two men who were doing just that. "If you gentlemen had any pride, you'd refuse as well."

Oscar looked up with a facetious grimace. "I find, dearest, that a pistol in my ribs is grand inducement."

"In any case, Lord—Scalawag, if you're not content, you'll simply have to shoot me."

Markham, aching from his mistreatment, hissed, "Hush, you fool! He'll strip the bloody rag from you and barter it for ammunition."

Raising her chin, Christina looked the outlaw in the eyes and said, "I should like to see him try."

The stranger's teeth flashed in a grin. "Once again, I shall have to forgo such—pleasures for another evening. In light of your refusal, however, I am forced to frisk you for weapons. With your permission, of course."

She stepped from the buggy with regal grace and spread her arms wide. Without removing her gaze from his face, she dared him. "You wouldn't be the first."

From the ground, Sir Weldon groaned.

As the moon shifted, she saw the flash of astonishment in the masked criminal's eyes. If he'd intended to dismount and conduct the search himself, he changed his mind. At the jerk of his head, one of his men came forth and hesitatingly patted her down beneath her sable coat.

"She's clean, Captain," he said in an Irish brogue.

"Relieve the lady of her valuables."

Before the man could move, Christina removed the gold bracelet from her wrist. "It's all I have, I'm afraid, and a paltry piece at that. And Oscar's as poor as a church mouse. For all your efforts, I fear you'll go home tonight with little to show."

"Have no fear, my lady. The night is young." With another gesture from him, his henchman removed her sable coat.

She shivered in the night air and eyed the coat longingly. But she wouldn't allow herself to dwell on her loss. She must stay focused and determined if she was to do Oscar any good. And Markham, too, of course.

"Well, then," she said, "if our business is settled, I shall take the buggy and go home to bed. It's been an exhausting evening, and frankly, my lord, the novelty has worn off."

She picked up her skirts and without hesitation climbed back into the buggy, taking up the reins.

"You're not going to leave us at the mercy of this madman?" Markham cried unthinkingly.

Christina shrugged. "If you men intend to pander to this ridiculous sport, by all means feel free. I, for one, have an early train to catch, and I have no intention of spending the night in the park." She looked at the robber. "I shall give my word not to report this till morning, if it appeases you. That will give our brave Markham a chance to cool his heels. And Oscar is always ripe for a bit of adventure. We shall laugh about this, Oscar, in days to come. My lords, I bid you adieu."

With that, she slapped the reins, and the horse lurched off toward home.

One of the men made a move to follow, but the ruffian raised a restraining hand. "It seems the lady wearies of your company, gentlemen," he said with a hint of amusement in his voice.

"Don't think for a moment," Markham threatened, "that you'll get away with this indignity. The Prince of Wales himself will hear of this!"

Everything stilled. The two associates cast assessing looks at their leader, who seemed frozen on his restive steed. When he spoke, his voice was hushed, yet throbbing with excitement. "The Prince, did you say?"

"Don't doubt it. We've just left him at Mott's not a half hour since. That lady you just robbed is the Duchess of Wynterbrooke, and an intimate of the Prince. The moment she arrives at Wynterbrooke Hall, she'll have word sent out of this abomination. Rest assured, sir, the Prince will have you cut dead to avenge the lady's honor."

"An intimate," the bandit repeated thoughtfully. "That, gentlemen, puts a new light on the subject. Bobby, Toby, check the knots on those ropes. I shouldn't care to have these gentlemen escape with undue haste. I require time to—remedy my mistake."

He reined his horse around and tipped his hat to the men. "My thanks, lords, for your generosity. I hope to meet up with you again, some lonely night."

"Where are you off to, Captain?" asked one of his men.

Again his teeth showed in a grin. "Why, Wynterbrooke Hall, of course!"

CHAPTER 4

THE RIGORS OF the evening had left Christina feeling drained. She entered the mansion and crossed the wide hall to the grand salon. Her heels rang out on the tiles in the oppressive stillness of the house. Without turning on the lights, she crossed the length of the floor and went for the bell-pull. She wanted nothing more than to go to bed and forget this night, but there was the matter of Markham and poor Oscar tied up in the park not two miles away.

As she reached for the velvet rope, there was a rustle of brocade. She stopped. A shadowy figure stepped from behind the drapes. Her hand convulsed open, and the bell-pull slipped from her fingers.

"You must forgive the intrusion," a familiar voice said in the dark. "I was deprived of your company too soon." His voice was a strange mixture, coaxing and mocking all at once.

"How did you get in here? There are gates outside, and a courtyard. Not to mention Scotland Yard, which, I'm told, combs the streets nightly in your pursuit."

"Come, Duchess, you wouldn't have me divulge professional secrets?"

So he knew who she was. Markham's work, no doubt. "What do you want of me?" she asked in a hushed voice. In the open air, she had felt no fear of him. But here, in the intimacy of her home, she was alarmed. Her hand had fallen short of the rope that would summon her butler. She glanced at it, wondering if she dared pull it, wondering if he'd notice. As if reading her mind, he strode toward her with a sweep of his cape, and she stepped back.

She heard something scrape against his boot, then a light flared from a match. He glanced about the room, spotted a gas lamp on a nearby table, and stepped over to turn it up. As the warm yellow light spilled in a small pool, he shook out the match and looked around.

Without answering her question, he walked about the long chamber, noting the rose-color marble Corinthian columns that graced the corners, with their bronze capitals and metal acanthus leaves sweeping outward like fans toward the ceiling. His eyes scanned the ceiling, ornately painted in varying shades of rose, gold, and green in depictions of mythology inspired by Raphael's loggia in the Vatican. A circular painting of Diana dominated the center of the ceiling, with smaller likenesses of Hercules and Apollo at either end of the room.

The room never failed to impress even the most cultured and ostentatious of her friends. The walls of the salon were covered in striped rose-and-gold coverings of watered silk. The furniture was Georgian. Every piece of it was a collector's delight. The Duke had not been one to scrimp on his pleasures, and his house reflected his lavish tastes.

As the intruder surveyed the place with a leisurely eye, Christina in turn took the opportunity to study him. He was in his late thirties, she would guess, and not at all the rough, pockmarked, crude villain she'd expected when she'd first heard of him. Instead, he was tall and lean, and desperately handsome. His hair beneath his hat was midnight black. His eyes behind the rakish mask were a grey-green that sparked like flint as he moved about the room. He had the prominent cheekbones of an aristocrat and firm, sensual lips that grinned at her from across the massive length of the hall. She thought of Oscar's words: *Some say he's some disgraced nobleman or other. . . . Some say he's Lord Wycliffe.*

"Is it necessary to shout?" he quipped.

"Only on occasion. You haven't told me why you're here."

He gave her an assessing stare. "Have you ever wondered where a thief of the night goes, once his plundering is completed?"

She hesitated. "Once, I think," she answered, her voice steadier now. "As a child, before I drifted off to sleep."

His glance fell on the trunks and shifted to the unpacked clothes on the long rose settee. "I thought you might enjoy the satisfying of your curiosity."

His words were as gracious as if he were offering her tea. But his meaning, diamond hard, was clear. He was kidnapping her.

"Then I suppose," she murmured with affected cool, "my train is to leave without me."

"My apologies, of course. The Duchess of Wynterbrooke is too valuable a fish to throw back into the pond. Particularly with the Prince of Wales at her beck and call. Although I can't say I sympathize with your choice of friends." His voice hardened as he said the last, and she detected the note of a sneer.

The implication galled her. "So you know of me."

"Everyone knows of the Duchess of Wynterbrooke. You're as notorious as I am."

"If you had better manners, you might refrain from mentioning my—notoriety."

He grinned, showing perfect white teeth. "I might." He moved toward her, untying a black kerchief from his neck. "I shall have to blindfold you, I'm afraid."

"Naturally. I wouldn't want you, in your panic that I had seen too much, to feel obliged to—dispose of me unduly."

"Perish the thought, my lady. I only offer an invitation."

"In that case, it has been a trying night, Lord Highwayman. I don't suppose I could persuade you to wait until I've had some sleep?"

He frowned at her. "Highwayman?"

"A romantic notion, perhaps. But what better to call a

thief of the night who robs the Prince's friends on dark London roads? Am I to be allowed my sleep?"

He stepped before her, so close that she could see the stubble of whiskers on his jaw. She felt his hands at her shoulders, strong as steel, felt herself being turned so that her back faced him. Her heart began to pound as she cast a last, wistful look at the bell-pull.

"I'm afraid not, Duchess. I shall have to offer you a bed myself."

A sliver of silk fluttered against her face, then was brought to cover her eyes. Christina laughed.

"Then I must warn you that you will find difficulty in meeting your goal. Romantic notions or not, my days of gracing the bed of rakes are behind me. Such a pity. I'd come to that conclusion only just tonight. What is it they say, highwayman? Timing is everything? Had you been one day sooner in your escapades, you might have found me a more willing partner. As it is, I find myself steadfast in my resolve. But if it amuses you, you are, of course, most welcome to try."

His fingers, fastening the knot behind her head, paused. He hadn't meant to offer such an invitation and was shocked—she could feel it—at her suggestion. Then, quite suddenly, he chuckled deep in his throat.

"Thank you, Duchess. I shall keep it in mind."

He'd had the foresight to bring her sable with him. He held the coat to her shoulders, and she fumbled to slide her arms into the sleeves. "Don't you shackle your prisoners?" she asked, taunting him. "Or do you find blindfolding to be sufficient?"

"Quite sufficient, considering that you'll be riding before me on my horse. Should you succeed in jumping off, I shall merely double back and trample you with the obliging beast's hooves. He should enjoy that. He hasn't trampled a duchess in some time."

Again, amusement tinged his voice, but she sensed a serious edge to his words. She had no doubt that he intended to prevent her escape at all costs. Blindfolded, it was easy to feel the panic clutch at her throat. The band at her eyes served to emphasize the helplessness of her position. She tried to think. *Don't antagonize him. Lull*

*him into a false sense of security. Then, when he least
expects it, make your escape.*

"Am I to have clothes where we're going?"

"My men are short on my heels. They'll retrieve your
trunk for you."

"How obliging of you, Lord Highwayman. Perhaps
I'm to have my holiday after all."

He didn't reply. Then she felt his strong arms at her
back and knees. She was swung into his arms as if she
weighed no more than her fur. They crept out through
the window into the cold night air. This time, he went
through the front gate. When it squeaked, he paused,
waiting for the expected alarm. But all was silent, and he
moved again and helped her onto his horse. Christina
took the mane in her hands as she felt him climb up behind her, felt the heat of his body pressing against hers.
As he put his arm about her, holding her tight, she
cursed her unsuspecting servants and resigned herself to
her fate.

But as he urged the horse into a walk, careful of the
sound of its hooves on the bricks, Christina was afraid. It
wasn't that she feared what he might do to her. She was
so battered by her regrets that the thought of rape or dis-
figurement or even death hardly scratched the surface of
her despair. No, it wasn't death she feared. It was dying
with her conscience in tatters. She'd lived her life reck-
lessly, hardly giving a thought to the consequences of
her actions. Now, feeling broken by those consequences, she could remember nothing but missed op-
portunities. Once—just once—she wanted to do
something real. Something meaningful. Something to
make up for all the misery she'd inflicted.

Minutes later, he kicked the horse into a canter. They
clattered through the back streets and out onto the open
road. At first, Christina listened stiffly for any telltale
sound. The sound of someone spotting them and calling
to her. The sound of pursuit. Always, there was hope.

"You might as well relax, Duchess. We've a long ride
ahead."

The very nerve of his suggesting that she relax made

her tense. But soon, her fatigue began to numb her brain. Her recriminations blended with the rhythm of the horse's hooves. Before she knew it, she'd leaned back against his shoulder and dozed as the stallion galloped through the night.

CHAPTER 5

$\mathscr{C}$HRISTINA AWOKE MUCH later to find herself lying on a scratchy straw pallet on the floor. It was pitch-black, but there were noises of shuffling and scraping and occasional hammering coming from below. Her mind was numb with fatigue. For a while, she couldn't remember where she was or what had happened. She was stiff and disoriented. Then she remembered. Mott's. The ugliness with the Prince. The drive home with Markham and Oscar. And *him*. The rogue who had followed her home and taken her to ride horseback through an endless night. She didn't remember being put up here to bed. She must have been exhausted by that time, and he must have carried her up without her knowledge.

Her hand flew to her bosom. She was fully dressed in the same black-and-gold ball gown. If he'd taken liberties—and she doubted he had—he'd had the consideration to clothe her afterward. She looked around, trying to adjust her eyes to the darkness.

By feeling her way around, she ascertained that she was in a contained room with some sort of machinery rising through a circular hole in the wooden floor. To the side was a rickety twisting flight of stairs. These she descended, careful to gather her skirts into her fist, holding on to the wobbling rail as an anchor in the gloomy depths. The machinery she'd noticed loomed like a gnarled tree in the center of the room. She caught the glow of a light from a far corner. Following it, she crept halfway down a stone staircase. She gasped. Below, as she squinted her eyes against the light, she could see four men heaping riches into wooden boxes and nailing them shut. The plunder was mind-boggling, littered about every corner of the room. There were jewels and gold, silver platters and tea services, expensive pistols, and every description of gold and jeweled cigar cases. One corner was reserved for ladies' finery, silken gowns and shawls, fur coats and muffs, elaborate ivory fans and pieces of toilette sets: boxes, perfume carafes, brushes and combs of ornately molded silver. She recognized Lady Starrington's prized silver tea set, which had been in the family since the time of Henry VIII, and which was to be a wedding gift for their daughter.

Something moved behind her. "Come to help, Duchess?"

She jumped. He was so close that she could feel his chest against her back, feel his breath at her neck. Without a word, she squeezed past him and returned to her loft. She was too stunned to think of a retort, too unsure of her position to know how to react. Tonight, she would simply stay out of his way. But tomorrow—tomorrow she would get her bearings, and then he'd regret his high-handed treatment.

The next morning, the sun awakened her as it slanted through one of the small windows. It took her a moment to remember the night before. When she did, she recalled as well her resolve to catch her captor off guard. Putting a hand to her head, she felt that her hair was tumbling in tangles. She remembered his promise to bring her trunk, but the loft was empty, so she removed the pins and ran her fingers through the thick mass, smoothing it as best she could. Then she shook out her dress and descended once again to the lower floor.

In the daylight, it was obvious that she was in an abandoned mill. The machinery she'd noted the night before was apparently used to grind flour. It was old and rusty now, but still held a certain charm. She looked it over as she walked down the stairs, but halfway down, her eye was caught by some movement across the room.

There, two men were rifling through her trunk, tossing her clothing haphazardly about the floor.

She rushed down, swooping upon them like a protective mother hawk. "What *ever* do you think you're doing!"

The men looked up. One was young, small, impish, with cherry red cheeks and freckles. The other was older, white-haired, and bent, with a weathered face and suspicious blue eyes. The younger triumphantly held up a diamond bracelet. "Why, we're lookin' fer valuables, naturally."

Christina shoved him aside and searched the contents for her jewelry case, which he'd opened and left lying at the bottom of the trunk. It took her a moment to find what she was after, a triple row of exceptionally matched black pearls. She swept them up and moved away with a huff. "You may have whatever else you fancy, but I forbid you these."

She reached up and fastened them about her slender neck.

The younger man put the bracelet to his neck and mimicked, " 'I forbid you these!' Well, la-dee-dah. I'd forgotten we're in the presence of a lady." His voice was thick with some back-country Irish brogue.

Christina might have retorted, but the door opened just then and her captor entered, his black hair damp as if he'd just had a bath. Unmasked, he was devilishly handsome in the early morning light. His clothes were simple—just a white shirt open at the neck and black pants tucked into knee-length black riding boots—but the quality of the material and workmanship were impeccable. The severity of his clothes made the jaunty aristocracy of his bearing seem more rakish than it had the night before.

He took in the scene with one swift flick of his grey-green eyes.

"Ah. We're having a party, I see."

"Her highness isn't amused by the proceedings," the young one retorted.

Their leader looked her over, taking in the sleepy look of her, the black hair tumbling about her shoulders, the flash of green eyes, the stubborn, affronted tilt of her chin—and the priceless Wentworth pearls gleaming at the planes of her throat. "I daresay her grace will adapt in time."

He bent over a small stack of books the men had discarded. They were her eternal favorites, *Wuthering Heights, Jane Eyre* . . .

"Are you a devotee of the Brontës?" he asked.

She blushed as if he'd found her out.

"So the scandalous Duchess is a romantic at heart. I'd wondered."

She found her voice with difficulty, so violated did she feel over the dissection of her personal things. "When had you wondered?"

"When you called me a highwayman."

"It takes little imagination to liken you to a knight of the road."

"Still, you're the first who has."

He handed her the books. She opened her mouth to thank him automatically, then stopped herself. She'd be damned if she'd thank him for the return of her own possessions. He saw her reaction and smiled.

"Lookee here, Cap'n."

Bobby held out a necklace. It was made of diamonds, fashioned in the three feathers that were the symbol of the Prince of Wales. Bertie rarely gave women expensive jewelry, but he'd been mad with desire in the early days when she was still resisting him, and had the necklace made up for her as enticement. It was a measure of his madness that he'd chosen a symbol so easily recognizable by anyone who happened to see it.

Abruptly, the Captain's mood changed. He took the necklace and stared at it for some time. When he looked at her, she was startled by the contempt she saw in the depths of his eyes, by the flash of some raw hatred. It stung her, for she despised the necklace and would happily pay him to relieve her of it. The blaze of his eyes spoke of an assumption of devotion to the Prince that sickened her. Still, her pride kept her silent. Her degradation at the hands of the Prince was none of his business. She would volunteer no such information unless he asked.

But he said nothing, merely pocketed the necklace and turned away.

She felt insulted by his abrupt dismissal of her, and because of it, assumed an imperious tone. "Are my clothes to be seized?"

He glanced at the men. "All through here, Cap'n," the elder man assured him.

"Bobby." He jerked his head toward the loft, and they piled her remaining things back into the trunk and the young one took it above.

"Was there anything else you required?" he asked her.

"As a matter of fact, I came down to see if you'd brought my toiletries. As you neglected to, I shall trouble you for a mirror—if you have one amidst your plunder."

"Toby will oblige you, I'm sure." He motioned to the older man, leaving no doubt as to his expectations.

Toby promptly stomped down to the basement, grumbling, "So now 'tis a bleedin' handmaiden I am, is it?"

They were alone in the room. She sensed his attention in the sudden hush and looked up at him. He was watching her with a slightly cocked head and a narrowed eye, as cool and arrogant as any prince, assessing her with a disinterested glare. As he walked toward her, his boots sounded on the stone floor. He put his hands to her shoulders. She backed away, her gaze held captive by his, but he took a step, closing the gap. Her mind whirled, trying to stay one step ahead of him, but not yet knowing what to expect. She sensed in him an anger as deep, as fearsome, as primitive as a primeval forest.

When he spoke, his voice was low and impersonal, yet it wounded her because she sensed in it the same loathing of her that she felt for herself. "I'll have those pearls now, my lady."

Her fingers crept reluctantly to her neck. The pearls. She should have known. He'd made her feel small and vulnerable with the penetration of his gaze. She wasn't accustomed to feeling that way with men. It broke down her defenses as nothing else could. Tears stung her eyes as she looked pleadingly up into his.

"They were a gift from my father," she whispered. "They're the only thing he ever—"

Suddenly, she realized she was pleading. His brow arched as he watched her intently, waiting for her to finish. Reddening, she said gruffly, "Oh, hang it. What difference does it make?" She turned abruptly so that his hands slid from her shoulders, and stood with her back facing him. With shoulders erect, she waited for him to take them from her.

He did. His hands at her neck were strong, yet he brushed her skin with a tenderness that surprised her. "You may content yourself with the knowledge that they go to a worthy cause."

"Whores for your bed, no doubt. Well, these should fetch you some dainty flesh for some time to come."

She'd forgotten her vow to catch him off guard. Instead, she'd allowed him to throw her so off balance that she'd almost confessed to him the secret longings of her soul. She was left shaken by the experience and was relieved when Bobby returned from upstairs and Toby came in with the mirror. He handed it to her sourly. She took it, turned it over in her hand. It was silver, circular with a handle formed like two vines tied together in a reef knot. "I'm impressed," she commented, recovering herself. "Rather a fine specimen of Roman silver. Mined from Stiperstones, I should think. It could very well date back from A.D. 100 One quite similar was found at the Roman ruins in Shropshire. It should fetch upwards of a thousand pounds on the open market. Although, of course, you'd do better to donate it to a museum."

She walked off to her loft, but as she was climbing the stairs, she glanced back to see the men exchange impressed looks with their leader.

After fixing her hair and changing into a spring green dress with rose piping and a high neckline, Christina went outside into the fresh morning to explore her surroundings. She carried with her two biscuits that were left for her on the table, chewing them as she moved thoughtfully about. She found herself in a small clearing surrounded by trees. The building she'd vacated was, indeed, an old mill. It was a small, vertically rectangular building, gently gabled on top to form the shape of an A. The bottom half was fashioned from local stone, the top from wood. To the right of the building was an old water mill made of oak. Three men, including Bobby and Toby, were working on the mill, Bobby digging the yellow clay from beneath it, while the others worked at the spoke with wrenches and picks. A rivulet wove a path to the waterwheel, then meandered down the hill through the woods below. Wildflowers dotted the clearing, leading gaily to the tangled recesses of the woods. It was bright with filtered morning sun, and alive with the chirping of birds.

A hundred paces off from the mill was an old hammer forge. The floor and walls were built from slabs of stone, while the meager half-roof was timbered. It was open in front. An old furnace, anvil, and tools cluttered the left corner, while the horses were tethered at the right. A small boat was tipped up to rest on its side.

The Captain was bent over the back foot of his horse, prying off a shoe. In the daylight, she could see that the horse was a black stallion of magnificent quality. Odd. She'd spent half the night clinging to this horse's mane, yet she'd never seen him until this moment. The stallion must have recognized her, for it nickered and shook its head as she approached.

By now, she'd rediscovered her ambition and reminded herself of her purpose. She affected a cool yet interested attitude as she stood watching the outlaw.

"You have a charming little hideaway. It's quite enchanting, really."

The shoe came loose, and he dropped the horse's leg and stood, looking about him with a critical eye. "I'm glad you think so," he said mildly. "I chose it for its charm."

She surprised him by laughing.

"Feeling better, Duchess?"

"Quite. It's amazing, isn't it, what a bite of food can

do for one's spirits? It was most thoughtful of you to leave me breakfast."

He frowned as he tossed aside the bent shoe and took up the tongs and sledgehammer to pound out another. The hammer clanged against the iron, discordant in the morning stillness. He wore a ring on the small finger of his left hand, and as he repositioned the shoe, it flashed gold in the sun. "You mustn't credit me so," he commented. "It might go to my head."

When she only smiled, he looked at her more closely as he worked.

"Am I to take it you've forgiven me for the pearls?"

She stiffened. "I should like to buy them back from you, if I may."

"Sorry, Duchess. Your trunk was searched, remember? The amount of coin you carry wouldn't cover the cost of the clasp."

"I have other money. Quite a lot, actually. The Duke left me a sizable fortune. You saw for yourself the house in St. James's. It's only the beginning. I've a cottage in Haworth, a villa in Spain, a sheep farm in Australia, an emerald mine in Africa—"

He waved her to silence.

"You're not impressed? Most people are flabbergasted by the immensity of my holdings. I should think a common thief might find *something* to interest him."

"As you carry none of them on your person, I hardly see how your holdings—immense or otherwise—can benefit me."

"I shall send you the money."

He flipped the shoe and began to bang away at it. "Are you asking me to trust you, Duchess?"

She sighed, realizing how ridiculous her proposition sounded, even to her.

He changed the subject. "Your reputation doesn't speak to a love of quiet things. In which case, we've some amusement for you come nightfall. We're shipping off the booty—that which you saw us packing up before dawn. You can add the experience to your list of adventures. And if you're very good, we might even let you help with a load."

It wouldn't do to show any unwarranted interest in his plans. She looked around, took a deep breath of the fresh, country air, and said, "Actually, the tranquility of the country better suits my present mood. May I have a look about?"

He stopped his hammering and eyed her suspiciously. She smiled her most guileless smile and raised a hand in the air. "I shan't run off, on my word."

After a brief hesitation, he gave a short distinctive whistle with an upward lilt. Toby looked up from the waterwheel and caught the jerk of his master's head. Sulkily, he dropped his wrench and limped off after her.

She followed the course of the water down the hill and through the woods. It was clear that the place was isolated. She doubted if there were any people to be found for miles around. She walked through bluebells and crocuses and turned her face to the sun. It must appear that she was simply out to partake of the morning's enjoyments. Doing a half-turn, she looked back at the grumbling Toby and smiled.

"It must be dull for you, accompanying temperamental ladies on their morning strolls. I do apologize for the necessity."

He looked surprised, then shrugged as if embarrassed to be spoken to in such a kind manner.

The hill led to a meager bowl of a valley, and that to the edge of a cliff. Standing at its precipice, she looked out upon the sudden green expanse of the English Channel. Her eyes scanned the coast. She was at a point where the coastline jutted in toward land, forming a natural shelter from prying eyes. A ship could easily anchor in the small harbor without being seen.

She guessed by the landscape that they were in Sussex. East or West, she couldn't be sure. But it hardly mattered. All she had to do was head north from the shore and find her way to the main London road. There, she could find an inn along the way and be directed to the local constable, who could come back and flush out this den of thieves.

Then she could be off to Egypt as planned.

She studied her surroundings for a few minutes more before heading back. A plan was forming that she was certain would distract her captor long enough for her to make her escape. And if what he'd said proved true, it appeared as if tonight would be the ideal time to try.

CHAPTER 6

*I*T SERVED HER purpose to be sociable, so she dressed for dinner in a white silk voile gown with silver trim and a tempting but modest neckline, and joined the men downstairs for dinner. Earlier, she'd bathed in the icy river with a lookout who'd vowed to keep his back turned but who, she suspected, had taken a peek now and again. Now her skin glowed and her hair shone with a brilliance that made up for her obvious lack of jewels.

After the simple fare of fish and potatoes, the Captain spread out his ledgers on the round, scratched table by the fire and set to work as the men dragged boxes up from the basement and carted them outside. Restless, but forced through necessity to be patient, Christina took her sable and settled upon it on the floor before the fire, leaning back against the stone wall to skim *Wuthering Heights* and periodically watch the outlaws work. It was easier to watch than read, for Bobby and Toby were carrying on a running conversation with little thought to her comfort.

Bobby was explaining why he'd left his wife to work with the Captain. " 'Tis a crime, but the wives of our family have always been a curse. They berate us poor men so, night and day harpin' on our poor heads, till what's a self-respectin' man to do, but seek employment elsewhere? Anything would be an improvement, so it would."

Without looking up, Christina said, "It doesn't speak

very highly of the men in your family, that they can't satisfy their women."

This shut Bobby up. He cast a baffled look at Toby, wondering what to think. He'd never considered the matter in quite that light before.

"The Duchess has her point," Toby agreed. "If yer women was happy, they'd be quieter, I'm guessing. What manner of man is it lets his womenfolk push 'im around?"

The Captain, his elbow on the table, put the back of his hand to his mouth to cover his smile.

"Well, 'tis hardly the point I was makin'," Bobby grumbled. "There's an old Irish saying, so there is: 'Better the fightin' than the loneliness.' So it was I came to fight with the Captain. Give me the life of the renegade any day. The open air, the thrill of the hunt, the darin' escape. Now *that's* the life for a man!"

Christina bent one knee, placed her other calf across it, and examined her silver slipper with a disinterested air as she twisted her foot to and fro. "Your next trip out, do something useful and pilfer some Madeira, why don't you? Then, at least, I should have something to do."

Bobby and Toby looked shocked, but the Captain merely bent his head lower over his books.

The two men picked up the boxes of loot and carried them outside, closing the door awkwardly behind them. They were gone for some time, leaving Christina to assume they were taking the boxes down to the Channel.

She watched the man at the table diligently copying figures from torn scraps of paper into his ledgers. "It's a rather odd life you lead, highwayman. Holed up in abandoned shacks, dealing with thugs. You're obviously a man of some culture. I should think you'd find it tiresome, living like a fugitive."

He glanced up at her with serious eyes. "Has it ever occurred to you that I have my reasons for leading the life I do?"

"Certainly. We all have our reasons for what we do. But what possible reason could you have for the torture of innocent women?"

"Is that what they say I do—torture women?"

"Repeatedly."

"And how do they say I do that?"

"Oh, any number of ways. But now I've met you, I've formed my own opinion."

"Such as?"

"Looking at you"—which she did—"I should say that you torture them with your—how shall we put it? Masculine charms."

He saw then that she was teasing him. "If you don't mind, I have a great deal of work to do before the night's entertainment." With that, he went back to entering his figures in earnest.

She watched him for some time, tilting her head this way and that. After a few moments, he asked, without looking up, in an exasperated tone, "Is there a reason for this penetrating scrutiny?"

"I was trying to determine," she mused, "if I find you handsome."

He gave her an arch look. "You'll be sure and let me know, won't you, when you've reached your conclusion?"

"Oh, undoubtedly."

"I can hardly wait to hear the verdict." He sounded as if he couldn't care less.

"Do you always behave in this indifferent manner with the women you kidnap?"

He flashed her a smile. "Not always."

"Ah! You've intrigued me. You must tell me all about your escapades. Of the female variety, I mean. You'll find I'm an avid listener."

"Some other time, Duchess. When I've nothing better to do."

"I wonder."

He looked up again, with a trace of annoyance. "What?"

"If all those other women found you handsome."

He gave her a mysterious smile that intrigued her more than anything he might have said. "Is this how the infamous Duchess of Wynterbrooke amuses herself? By ferreting out the debauchery of strangers?"

"It's all I *can* do anymore. I've sworn off debauchery

for my own sake. I find it's not as satisfying as it once was."

He cast her a sly look. "Such a pity. It appears that I've come into your life too late."

She gave him a delighted smile. " *Now* who's being naughty?"

"Given up debauchery, have you?" he said dryly.

The smile dropped from her face. "Sorry," she said, making a study of her toe. "Force of habit." When he chuckled, she challenged, "You don't seem very shocked by my confessions of an ill-spent past."

"Well, I'd hardly be one to cast stones."

She viewed him with renewed interest. "Indeed? You really *must* tell me all about it some rainy afternoon."

"I thought you'd given up your life of debauchery?"

"Well, that hardly means I can't learn from the experience of others. One has to have *some* thrills in life, even if they *are* vicarious. I should dearly love to know your secrets. I'd imagine you to be quite the—rogue with the ladies."

"Since I'm stuck with you for the time being—and since we've already well established that you've given up your pleasures—it would be safe to assume that I've given up mine for the duration, as well."

"Why, you surprise me! You *are* a gentlemen, after all!"

"Don't count on it, Duchess."

She leaned back into the sable and eyed him languorously. "Highwayman, you almost make me want to change my mind."

He looked up and met her eyes. "You're a strange woman, Duchess."

"Indeed?"

He got up and went to the hearth, where he stood with his back to her, his elbow on the mantel, his knuckles against his forehead, staring into the fire. "You exist in a world where women marry for titles, where logic dictates the order of the day, and self-gratification the excesses of the night. It's a sterile life by any definition, but a world in which your class moves without thinking, and is satisfied, more or less. Yet you're different. You read the Brontë sisters, and see in a common thief the splendors of the highwaymen of a different century. In short, you're a woman in rebellion against her time. You live in a world that is the very antithesis of romance, and yet you secretly long for little else."

She was so stunned by his insight that she could hardly think of what to say. She had meant only to taunt him, but something had passed between them that shook her deeply. She stood up, no longer content to lounge idly by the fire. "Have you a point to make?"

"Yes, Duchess, I have. I understand your longing for romance. But don't, by God, look for it in me."

She whirled around and stared him in the eyes.

"You'll be sadly disappointed," he added.

She was saved a reply when the men burst into the room. They were accompanied by a big brute of a man, wearing a striped shirt and a sailor's cap. When he spoke, it was with a harsh American accent.

"Well, I'm back, Christ protect me, and none too happy about it. Give me the stuff, my man, and send me on my way. The feel of land beneath my feet turns my stomach sour. Oh." He reached into a pack and tossed a stack of softcover books on the table. "Here's them cowboy books I promised."

Then he noticed Christina, who had backed against the wall at the offensive smell of the man. "And who's this? You didn't tell me we had company, boys. Maybe I'll just reconsider and let you fellas load up yourselves whilst I while away a happy hour or two."

In spite of her brave talk, the man frightened Christina. She was known for her adventurous spirit, but men never dared to speak to her with such blatant disrespect. She lifted her chin and was about to retort in anger when the Captain tossed a log into the fire and its blaze distracted them.

"The Duchess is a guest of mine," he said quietly, but with a deadly ring that brooked no argument.

The brute curled his lip. "Duchess? Well, hell, lady, I didn't mean no disrespect. You can't blame a fellow for trying, when he comes off six weeks at sea and spots a looker like you his first step off the boat."

"I'm sure," said the Captain smoothly, "that there was no offense taken. Was there, my lady?"

Christina fought hard to keep her plan in mind. Nothing must tip her hand. Swallowing her anger, she answered coolly, "None whatsoever. So long as it doesn't happen again."

The American's quick glance flitted from the Captain to Christina and back again. Understanding cleared the lust in his eyes. "Yours, is she?" he concluded. "Well, why didn't you say so?"

Christina could easily have spit fire, but the Captain ignored the comment completely. He moved to the table and picked up a list, which he handed to the American. "Here's your inventory. Now, let's have no delay in the loading, shall we? There's the threat of a moon, and we'd not like to stretch that fine neck of yours on the gallows."

"Goddamned right," cried the brute, fingering his fleshy throat.

The Captain cast his cool glance back at Christina. "Care to come, Duchess?" He cloaked it in the form of a question, but she recognized in the steely voice the tone of command.

"Aren't you afraid I might see too much and report your operation?"

He gave her a careful perusal in which she felt herself stripped bare of any pretense. "Not especially," he replied.

She wondered what he meant. But it would further her plan to see them safely involved in the loading, so she nodded and let him take her arm and lead her outside.

They picked their way through the dark woods, with the Captain conferring quietly with the American. She was puzzled by what she overheard, phrases like, "it's slow, getting troops," and "the shipment was appreciated, but more are needed." But the truth was, she wasn't paying close attention. Now that the moment was almost upon her, she was surging with energy, and a flutter of nervous excitement. It wouldn't be long now, and then she would be free.

When they reached the cliff, she could see the vaguest outline of a ship's sail out in the harbor. It was so faint, it might have been a dream. Below, men were loading boxes onto a small boat and, when it was full, rowing it out to the ship. She watched them push off, thinking that her priceless Wentworth pearls were among those boxes. She'd never forget the courage her father had displayed in giving her those pearls over her mother's staunch objections—or the awful reason why he had. It was the only thing he'd ever done for her, the only thing he'd ever given her himself. All her life, those pearls had represented a romanticized link with her father that had never really existed. The highwayman was right to call her a romantic, she thought wistfully. But how, on such a short acquaintance, had he known?

The American bounded down the cliff, and the Captain stayed behind to help her down. The sand was slippery, and halfway down, she slid, tumbling into him. They lost balance and fell, rolling to the bottom. She could feel the sand in her neckline as he landed on her, crushing her breath from her lungs. Her skirts were everywhere, caught beneath her and between them, exposing her legs to the night air. She moved to slide from beneath him, but stopped when she realized how still he was, lying atop her.

She looked up and caught the faint gleam of his eyes in the darkness. His hand came up to brush the hair from her forehead, and his thumb lingered as if with a will of its own, stroking her skin. She could feel his breath on her face, and her heart skipped a beat. His lips were so close that all he had to do was lean the slightest bit and press them against hers. The appalling realization hit her that she wanted him to.

But he didn't. With an effort, he pushed himself away. He held his hand out to her. She took it and allowed him to pull her to her feet. His hand was warm. She could feel his pulse in his palm, beating as hard as hers. She held the hand a moment and looked up into his face.

"Why didn't you kiss me?" she whispered. "You wanted to."

She could still feel his racing pulse, but his voice carried a lazy, insolent tone. "Because I don't kiss naughty little girls bent on romance. I'm not that brave."

She was rebuffed, insulted, as he'd intended. With a forced show of dignity, she snatched her hand from his. "You must look again, highwayman. I'm not so little."

He chuckled suddenly. "I have no doubt of it, my lady." Then he headed off after the men.

She watched for a while more as he resumed his conference with the sailor and the empty rowboat was brought in to be filled once again. When she deemed the time right, she wandered over and made her apologies.

"I'm dreadfully tired," she told him. "The lack of sleep last night, no doubt. Could you spare a man to escort me back to the mill?"

He cast a glance out to the ship, then back again. "Not now. If you'll wait half an hour—"

"I'd really rather not, if it's all the same. Please, don't disturb yourself. I shall find my way back with ease and fall into the sleep of the dead, no doubt."

"You do that," he said, before turning back to his men.

Back at the mill, she hurriedly donned one of her riding habits and pulled on her boots. Then she gathered up her fur and slipped silently down the stairs and out into the night.

It was a simple matter to saddle one of the horses, but her heart pounded and her fingers trembled at the thought that one of them might whinny and give her away. The bridle was more difficult, for the horse was still chewing at the remains of its grain and it resisted the bit. Finally, she'd pried it in and fastened the headstall to her satisfaction. Feeling a tremendous relief, she turned to get her coat and came up against the blade of a knife at her throat.

CHAPTER 7

"GOING SOMEWHERE, DUCHESS?" the Captain asked.

She backed up against the stone wall of the forge, but he followed, keeping the sharp blade perched against her neck. He was so close that she could feel the hard contours of his body pressing into hers. Her breath was coming fast now as her mind raced. She could outsmart him, but she couldn't overpower him. She swallowed, and the motion of her throat lodged the knife deeper into her skin.

"How did you know?" she gasped.

"A number of ways. You never asked why I kept you here, or for how long. I've never once known a woman who wasn't curious about her fate."

Damn! She hadn't thought of that. She lifted her chin with a show of bravado. "Well?" she demanded. "Are you going to slash my throat? Cut off my ear?"

He ran the knife along her neck in a ruminative manner. "Frankly, I can think of more interesting things to cut."

His voice was at her ear, muffled and intimate, yet hard as steel. Putting a thumb to her throat, he moved the knife and cut away the top button of her habit. She shivered. In the distance, she heard the men heading back for the mill. She took a breath to cry out, but he replaced the knife and pressed himself against her in a menacing way.

"I wouldn't. They'd just assume that I was doing what I'm doing, and leave me to my spoils."

She was shaking uncontrollably. "You won't like it," she warned in a croaking voice. "I'm dead inside. I can no longer feel anything. You might as well vent your lust on a sack of meal."

He cut away the second button. "Is that why you spent the night vexing me? To show how impervious you are to desire?"

"I merely meant to distract you, to keep your mind from my escape."

He cut away the third button, opened the bodice with the point of his knife, and lowered his lips to her neck. "You did a fine job of—distracting me, I must say."

She found courage enough to taunt him. "I've overestimated you. I wouldn't think a man like you would have to resort to rape. As promised, you disappoint me."

He ignored her. One by one, the buttons were severed to fall on the stone floor. He undressed her slowly, as if he had all the time in the world, tossing each piece of her clothing aside.

When she was naked, he turned her so that her back was to him. He rested his left arm around the front of her shoulders so that the knife once again lay across the hollow of her throat. Bending, he kissed her shoulder, felt her shiver against the night air. With his right hand, he stroked her belly and moved up to cup the mound of her breast. She swayed, and her breath became labored.

"You're a weak-livered coward," she moaned, "forcing your attentions on women who have no interest."

His hand moved to the other breast.

"I should die of shame, knowing I had to force a woman at the point of a knife," she continued.

He brought his lips to her ear. Her breath caught in her throat as he nuzzled the side of her neck.

"I wouldn't have you if you were the last man—"

He trailed his hand along her belly and down a path to her thigh.

"Weak, despicable cad," she accused, but her voice was breathless now.

His hand found her between her thighs. His lips, at her shoulder, curved into a smile as he realized she was wet. He continued to stroke her with firm, insistent fingers that knew instinctively where to probe. Against her will, she leaned back into him, conforming her body to his. She rubbed against his hand like a cat against a post.

Finally he spoke. His mouth was at her ear, and his voice was deep and hushed, yet ruthlessly hard. "I've never raped a woman in my life," he informed her, his breath warming her ear. "I have no intention of starting now."

"You make a poor showing of your good intentions," she retorted in a voice crackling with passion.

"I shall give you nothing you don't ask for voluntarily. So you see, my lady, the game is up to you."

Having stated his intentions, he moved his mouth once again to her shoulder. He kissed the satiny skin, making his way with infinite leisure down the quivering flesh of her arm. His hand, meanwhile, had buried itself in her, exploring with feathery strokes as he awaited her reply.

She sighed and dropped her head back against him. "Put your knife away, highwayman," she directed. "You'll have no need of it this night."

He was still. Then, removing the blade from her throat, he tossed the weapon into the half-roof so that it landed in a far beam with a twang.

Freed, she pivoted around and began to unbutton his shirt. "Your grace! You shock me!" he mocked.

"I'm an impatient woman, highwayman. It takes more than weapons and promises to satisfy me."

Stepping out of his boots, he asked, "Have you ever been satisfied?"

She showed her teeth in a wicked smile. "Never."

"You are about," he informed her, "to put that in the past tense."

She gave him a lusty chuckle. "Well," she said with a shrug, "I admire your confidence. You are, most certainly, welcome to try."

Any other man might have been intimidated by her challenge. He showed no sign of such quaverings. Taking her shoulders in his hands, he pulled her to him very slowly, so that her breasts just barely touched his chest, until—slowly, slowly—she could feel every rigid contour of his frame.

He kissed her with the same exquisite languor. His lips were firm, and they moved over hers with practiced ease. She'd expected force. Instead he was giving her seduction. He seemed to be moving in slow motion, luxuriating in each touch, each kiss, each moan of pleasure that escaped her throat. As his hands stroked her body, igniting the long-dormant flames, he tasted of her mouth with a leisure that was devastating.

Soon, it became unbearable. Her body, denied since the ravages of the Prince, was alive with passion, with hunger, with need. She pressed herself against him, urging him on to more expedient matters. He smiled against her lips, but refused to take the hint.

She wrenched her mouth from his, gasping. "An odd way you have of satisfying a woman, I must say."

He only grinned. "If you're displeased, my lady, we can always call a halt—"

"Blackguard!" she accused.

Bending, he put a hand at her knees and one at her back and swung her up into his arms. She could feel the play of his lean muscles against her naked skin. Taking her around the horses, he laid her down in the hay and continued his languid ministrations, tasting of her flesh as one might partake of the delights of a buffet. He kissed her lips, ran his mouth along the point of her chin, played with a nipple until it was hard against his tongue. All the while, his hands roved over her, finding—with astonishing speed and accuracy—the places that made her wild with desire, then backing away and exploring some more.

Restive beyond endurance, she grabbed hold of his hand and thrust it back between her legs. She could feel the ring on his small finger brush cold against her burning flesh. He caressed her expertly, and she felt the first flutterings of the wave that would carry her to release. She gasped and parted her lips, anticipating the rush.

Instantly, he drew his hand away. With one fluid motion, he was atop her, his hands pinning hers to the ground on either side of her. She could feel him hard against her and moved to help him enter. But he lay still, anchoring her to the ground with the weight of his body. His hand gone, his body motionless, her climax slipped away from her, melting before it had begun.

Devastated, she let out a whimper and sought out his face in the meager light of the rising moon.

"What kind of game are you playing, highwayman?"

"No game, Duchess. I simply prefer to enjoy my pastimes at a more leisurely pace."

"This *particular* pastime is over."

She tried to free herself from beneath him, but he was too heavy. She couldn't budge. He let loose her arm, and his hand found the curves of her body once again. He lowered his mouth to her breast and heard her groan.

"I think not," he said against her skin.

Once more, he brought her—with unendurable deliberation—to the brink of bliss, and once more snatched it from her just as she had the taste of it in her mouth.

She let out an agonized cry. "Damn you for the wretch you are. You speak of satisfying me, then leave me dangling from this precipice. If it's your intention to kill me, then be done with it. I shall retrieve your knife for you myself. But for God's sake, man, get me off this bloody cliff and allow me to either soar with the falcons or fall to my death below!"

He affected surprise. "Why, Duchess, you shock me! Are you telling me you *want* me?"

"Yes, dammit," she ground out through her teeth. *"Yes!"*

"Well." He grinned. "Why didn't you say so in the first place?"

He kissed her again, but more forcefully this time. Suddenly, the man came alive. His hands, finding her, were masterful and sure. When she was ready again, her blood boiling in her veins, he entered her with a swift thrust that forced an anguished cry from her throat. He found his rhythm, and her breath flew from her in gusts. She sought his mouth with her own and clawed at his back as her heart pounded in her head and her senses toppled around her like a shower of falling stars.

She arched up to meet his thrusts, driving him deeper and deeper still. Sensing her need, he brought her slender legs to rest on his shoulders so that he filled her to the very hilt. She tottered on the brink between pleasure and pain. It was the most exquisite torture she had ever known. Needing something to hold on to, she reached up with her hands and grabbed onto his hair. She pulled him down toward her, felt him fill her more deeply still. He wasn't gentle. His thrusts were savage, fueled by a primitive force that more than matched her own. She found his lips with her own and kissed him greedily, moaning her rapture into his mouth as her breath became one with his.

When her climax came, it was all the sweeter, all the more electrifying for having been teased and denied before. Every cell within her seemed to burst into an endless splash of color and light, swirling her within its midst as she tumbled—ever so delectably—back to earth.

They lay locked in each other's fevered embrace, shattered by what had passed between them. Each was left drained beyond reason. Each felt the impossibility of movement. And each was stunned—and a little alarmed—by the intensity of their union. What had begun as a game had ended as a revelation, and neither could think of words to express their realization of its impact.

Their bodies were hot and damp. The Captain rolled off her, and for an instant her hand darted out, bent on keeping him at her side. He sensed it and paused, but when he turned around, she had shut her emotions behind the mask of her closed eyes.

He settled down flat on his back, threw one arm across his forehead, and stared at the ceiling.

Christina, jarred by the experience, could still feel the shocks reverberating through her body. When she thought of him slamming into her while her legs spanned his shoulders, her heart pounded once again within her breast. She took a shaky breath, wishing he would speak and set the tone.

She wasn't accustomed to this feeling of unease. Usually, after making love, she gathered up her clothes, gave the fellow a quick kiss on the nose, and set off into the night for home. Tonight, she had lost any such inclinations. She wanted to talk to him about it, to confess to him what had happened. She wanted to tell him that he had made her feel true passion—true emotions—for the first time in much longer than she could remember. Maybe the first time in her life. And, God help her, he had freed her from the vile memory of the Prince.

But she didn't even know him. How could she profess to him such vulnerable truths?

Soon, because something must be said, he cocked his head toward her and raised a mocking brow. "Satisfied, my lady?"

It wasn't how she wanted this to end. But he had set the tone, and she felt compelled to follow. She pushed herself up and, standing, began to gather up her ruined clothing. "Well enough. For now."

She slipped into the sable, covering her naked limbs. Then she looked back, caught his eye, and raised a delicate, aristocratic brow. She gave him the faintest trace of a secretive smile and said, "Well, highwayman, one thing is for certain."

"What's that, Duchess?"

"You, sir, are no Egyptian."

CHAPTER 8

THE NEXT MORNING, Christina dressed with a new sense of excitement. Her fingers trembled a little as she buttoned her gown, and her heart fluttered strangely. She chided herself for her foolishness, but the truth was she couldn't wait to see the Captain, to see the first unguarded look in his eyes when he saw her. In spite of his feigned indifference of the night before, she was experienced enough in the ways of men to know that he had been as rocked by the experience as she.

She dressed with care in a lovely blue-and-white morning dress that reminded her of a summer sky. It seemed appropriate, for she felt—ridiculously, she told herself—that this morning was the start of something new and fresh and wonderful in her life. She felt, without knowing why, that it *was* the start of her life.

She waltzed down the first few steps, wanting to sing. Halfway down, she spotted the men sitting at the table over biscuits and coffee. The Captain looked up, caught sight of her, and gave a crooked little smile. It was more like a sneer, as if he could read her mind and knew the pains she'd taken to look pretty for his sake. He sat back in his seat, brought his arm up to hook it at the back of the chair, and watched her with a derisively amused air.

"Good morning, men," she called gaily. "And a most glorious morning to *you*, my lord."

She danced over to him, dropped gracefully into his lap, and moved to kiss him. Before her lips could touch his, he stood abruptly so that she was left grappling for balance, and turned his back on her, taking his cup to refill it with coffee.

It infuriated her. She was left standing there like a silly fool. Like a schoolgirl, gushing over a teacher who barely knew she existed. She couldn't believe it! No man had ever made her feel so absurd, so absolutely muddled, in all her life. She recalled her happy expectations and damned herself for the dupe she was. For once, her unerring instincts into the designs of the opposite sex had failed her. Miserably. Embarrassingly. He hadn't seen a new beginning in what had passed between them. He had used her, just as the Prince had. Just as *she* had used men.

The outlaws were staring at her. She could feel their eyes boring into her, feel them absorbing her shame. She straightened her shoulders, assumed her duchess stance, and looked them collectively in the eye with the grace and dignity of a queen. All at once, they remembered urgent business they had outside. They scrambled to their feet, shoved the last bits of breakfast into their mouths, washed it down with a quick swallow of coffee, and ran from the room.

The Captain had turned and was watching her closely.

"Last night you weren't so niggardly with your affections," she reminded him in an injured tone.

"Last night was last night."

"How very astute of you to make such an observation."

Her sarcasm didn't faze him. Rather, he seemed to find it entertaining. "Did you sleep well, Duchess?" he asked in a conversational tone.

"Exceedingly well, thank you. And you?"

He gave her a sardonic grin. "Like a lamb."

"Of course," she added, "I did toss and turn halfway through the night. Thinking back on it, I daresay I wasn't quite as satisfied as I'd supposed."

The Captain chuckled and tossed a bit of biscuit into his mouth, watching her as he chewed.

He was making her decidedly uncomfortable. "Just

why is it exactly that I am here—Captain? For your private amusement?"

"You will be the first to know the answer to that."

"When?"

"When I've decided it myself."

She sensed that there was no use arguing. To divert her mind from her questionable fate, she eyed the meager fare. "Is your breakfast always so unimaginative?" she asked coolly. "Are there no crumpets? No fruit? No tea?"

"We 'knights of the road,' as you so charmingly dubbed us, lead a simple life. Too simple, I take it, for the tastes of the nobility."

It was her turn to study him. She may well have misread his intentions, but she was never wrong when it came to a question of breeding. Her mother had taught her from the cradle to follow the grand old family tradition of snobbery. If she had rebelled, it didn't alter the fact that she could spot a nobleman in the dark. Whoever this highwayman was, he'd been born an aristocrat. Yet he always spoke of the nobility with a jeer in his tone. Even the way he called her "Duchess" set her teeth on edge. It was as if he accused her every time he spoke her name. It stirred the guilt she felt at having married poor Wynterbrooke for his title, and for having left him with such a sorry bargain for his pains.

But she was no longer in a revealing mood. She would withhold her observations, just as he was withholding . . . what? What was it she wanted from him? He was a stranger. A common criminal. A man to be feared. Yet, strangely, she didn't fear him.

"I should think you would dine in style, what with all the riches you've accumulated. My pearls alone would feed you at Grosvenor Hotel for a lifetime. Assuming, of course, that you dared show your face."

"Your pearls go to better use than the filling of our bellies. Now, if you're hungry, eat. And I'd caution you to enjoy it. It's the last meal you'll be served. From now on, you'll be expected to cook your own food."

"Cook! I'm a duchess! I don't cook."

"You do now."

"I don't know the first thing about cooking. I wouldn't know how to go about it. Why, the last time I tried it, I set myself afire!"

She was taunting him, rubbing his nose in his manufactured image of her, but he refused to take the bait. He flung the remains of his coffee into the fire to douse it. "Then I'd say it's high time you learned."

True to his word, he came back upriver a little past noon with a saddlebag full of fish. She'd been outside enjoying the sun when he pitched the bag into her lap. "If you can't cook, you can clean them."

"Clean them?"

She unstrapped the leather and lifted the flap, then closed it back again. "These are fish."

"Clever, Duchess. You'll make a cook yet."

"I haven't the faintest idea of how to go about—"

"Practice on a few. You'll get the hang of it."

"This is absurd!"

He gave her an unrelenting look. "You don't clean them, Duchess, you don't eat."

Taking a knife from his boot, he flipped it so that it landed point down in the grass before her. It was the same knife he'd used the night before to cut the buttons from her habit. The sight of it sent an unexpected thrill through her, made her remember with alarming intimacy the smell and taste of his sweat, so hot and manly against her tongue. Hating herself for remembering, and despising him for his rejection of that memory, she looked up and met his eyes.

They were mildly amused. "What's the matter, my lady? Is the adventurous Duchess of Wynterbrooke afraid to try something new?"

He didn't think she could do it. Well, she'd show him just how capable she was.

"I want it noted that I'm doing this under protest."

"It's noted."

She picked up the knife and turned her back to him. When he was gone, she sat cross-legged and gingerly pulled out one of the fish. It was cold and slimy, and she dropped it to the ground. She shuddered, but braced herself. It couldn't be so difficult. She eyed the fish—who seemed to eye her back—and tried to imagine what it might look like on a plate. The thought of cutting into it made her stomach churn. She'd never stopped to think before where food came from. She'd never had the need.

She felt a presence beside her and looked up to see a man they called Michael squatting beside her. He was young, lank, and dark with odd, protruding, bulldog eyes that blinked convulsively. "Here, I'll show you, mum," he said in a soft voice, looking over his shoulder to make sure he wasn't spotted.

He took the knife, wiped it on his pants, then proceeded to cut off the head. This he tossed aside. Then he cut the fish up the middle, gutted it from bottom to top, pulled out the intestines, and threw the mess into a pile with the head. He finished by scraping off the scales with the knife, wiping it again on his pants, and presenting it to her with a prideful grin. It had taken little more than a few seconds, but Christina felt she must have turned green watching him.

"It's our secret, now. It wouldn't do to let the Cap'n know I'd helped." He winked at her, then rose and ambled off, looking back at her with a shy smile.

She sat looking back and forth between the saddlebag full of fish and the rubbish of guts in the pile by her side. *Simple*, she thought. *I can master this*. But she couldn't help wishing she'd kept her mouth shut and pretended she could cook.

Later, when she had but two more to complete, the Captain came by to take a look. A lock of her hair had fallen in her face as she worked, and she'd pushed it back with a dirty hand and left a streak of blood on her temple. The blue-and-white dress was splattered. She had a badly butchered pile of fish in front of her, and was wielding the knife as if she'd never held one in her hands. She looked up and gave him a rueful smile.

"I shall ruin my *entire* wardrobe at this rate."

He laughed. He squatted down before her, resting his forearms on his bent knees. "I doubt, my lady, that you've ever looked more beautiful."

It was so unexpected that she blushed.

"Just think," he added, "with what satisfaction you will sup tonight."

Hours later, in the cool twilight, she sat on the grass with the men before a campfire, eating her fish with her hands. She wore the same splattered dress, although she'd thought to wash her face and fix her hair. The men, watching the gusto with which she ate, nudged each other and grinned.

"I daresay this is the most delectable fish I have ever tasted," she declared.

"It's because they're so fresh," Bobby said, wiping his mouth on his sleeve.

"It's because of my meticulous cleaning of them," she corrected.

The Captain chuckled. "You have a wicked way with the knife, Duchess."

"But not nearly as wicked as yours."

His mouth twitched. The others showed renewed interest in their fish.

That night, the men set out on a raid. The Captain came into the room just at dark, wearing the black clothing of his trade—the cape, the gauntlets, the mask over his eyes, the wide-brimmed hat on his head. He was pulling on a glove as he spoke rapidly to Toby, leaving his instructions to have Christina watched. He looked quite dashing, and Christina was hard-pressed to concentrate on her reading as he moved about with the energy and fire of a man about to put his life in danger.

"Just what do you expect me to do here, while you're traipsing about the countryside?" she asked.

"Talk to Toby. Read your book. I don't care what you do, so long as you stay put."

It didn't speak too highly of his opinion of her

chances of escape that he left the oldest and most feeble of his men to guard her. As if he read her mind, he added, "Toby may look frail, but step one foot out of this building and you'll soon learn the mettle of the man."

He was too busy, really, to think of her. He went outside, and she could hear in his voice the crisp air of command as he went over his plans with his men. Her heart beat faster at the sound of it. Suddenly, she envied him. She envied them all. They would mount their horses and gallop off into the night to God only knew what adventures while she paced the room and tried to read sentences that danced across the page. It was insufferable to have been born a woman, and to get left out of all the fun.

She hadn't been left out, though. In London, she and Oscar had made up for her femininity by devising all sorts of escapades meant to sneak her into the hallowed domains of men. They'd staged their own versions of pranks and adventures to while away the hours before dawn. Some of their diversions were legendary, such as the time Christina had dressed as a man and she and Oscar had picked pockets on Derby Day at a popular dance hall. But none of those adventures could hold a candle to what these men did on a nightly basis. Suddenly, she wanted more than anything to go along.

"We won't be long," the Captain informed her when he'd returned. "We've word that one of the Prince's closest friends it traveling by train to Dover. You may know him. Lord Plimpton."

The Earl of Plimpton. "I know him well. It seems I'm in for a comparatively dull evening. I don't suppose you'd take me along?"

"For what? So you can escape when my back is turned?"

"No," she said mildly. "Because I hate the Prince as much as you do."

He turned and looked at her as if for the first time.

When he stood staring at her, saying nothing, she added, "I shouldn't mind seeing Plimpton beg for his life."

She was telling the truth. Plimpton had participated in one of her more humiliating experiences with the Prince. To think of the things she'd submitted to at their hands brought a flush of rage to her cheeks. He saw it, but still said nothing. Her confession had unsettled him as much as her earlier realization of his hatred had her.

After a moment, he went to the basement and returned a minute later with a small pile of books in his hand. "If you're in need of amusement, you might try these."

He tossed them into her lap, then tipped his hat and disappeared into the night.

As the clatter of horses' hooves disappeared into the distance, Toby gave her a toothless grin and put a pot of coffee on to boil.

"Want some?" he asked.

"That awful concoction? I'd rather drink water, even. Wherever did you acquire the horrid recipe?"

"Cap'n picked up the habit in the Americas."

"The Americas? Was he there?"

"For a few years, aye."

"Tell me, Toby. Why do you call him Captain?"

"He used to captain our ship, once upon a time."

"What sort of ship?"

He would say no more. "Ye'll be askin' the Cap'n your questions, mum. 'Tis bad enough I'm left behind as a wet nurse to yer grace."

Defeated, she looked down at the books in her lap. They were penny novels bound in heavy paper, all with stylized depictions on their jackets of scenes from the American West. One showed cowboys shooting at Indians from behind a rock ridge, another a homesteader holding a rifle to an apparent outlaw who had his hands in the air. They had quaint titles like *Bad Day at Lonesome Ridge,* and *Gunman of Grey's Gulch—or—The Desperado's Revenge.*

"How truly odd," she murmured, flipping through them. It was the very last thing she'd expected to find when the Captain had handed her the books. His speech, so refined, had the distinctive inflection of an Oxford man. She'd assumed the books he'd given her were volumes of poetry. Lord Byron, perhaps, and Lord Tennyson. But penny dreadfuls?

She lifted the next book and stopped cold. So this was the source of his inspiration! There, on the cover, was a colorful drawing of an outlaw gang, kerchiefs over their faces, pointing guns at a locomotive. The engineer, like the outlaw on the previous cover, had his hands held high, and there was a look of terror on his face. The title read, *The James Gang—or—Mighty Jesse Rides Again.*

CHAPTER 9

$\mathcal{B}$Y THE TIME the men returned, she'd read the entire book.

"Haven't you moved?" the Captain asked when he came in.

She looked about her in a daze. It was after midnight, yet the time had passed with remarkable speed. "I suppose I haven't. As it happens, I've had a fascinating evening after all, reading all about the brigand Jesse James." She stretched the tired muscles in her back. "I know little about the American West, but I confess to being intrigued. Tell me, highwayman—why did you loan me these books?"

"For your amusement, naturally. Why else?"

"It wouldn't be, perhaps, that you hoped to further my understanding of you?"

"I care not, Duchess, whether you understand me or not."

"I wonder."

He was dirty, his face streaked with some sort of black grease. "You should smudge your face every time you go out," she commented. "It adds to your air of menace."

He rubbed his cheek, looked at the dirt on his hand, then loosened his kerchief, wet it in the nearby bucket, and scrubbed his face with it.

"Were you successful?" she asked.

He was saved a reply when the others came bursting in, carrying leather bags full of goods. "What a haul!"

Bobby cried. "We can rest our weary bones for a week!"

"And did Plimpton beg suitably?" she asked.

"Like a brat of seven."

"I wish I'd seen it."

They plunked the bags down on the table, and Bobby opened them, rummaged through, then turned to Christina with a grin. "Look what we brought, my lady."

He held out a bottle with a Spanish label.

"Madeira!" she cried. She jumped up and took it from him. "Bless you, my man. Where *did* you come upon it?"

"It seems while I was relieving the passengers of their valuables, my men were raiding the dining car." The Captain spoke sternly, but there was a glint of amusement in his eyes.

"And that's not all we got," Bobby continued. He began to pull staples out of the bag, counting them off. "We've some tea, and crumpets, and marmalade, and caviar—"

"Caviar! Let me at it!" She took it from him, unscrewed the jar, dipped her little finger in, and took a taste. "Beluga. I *am* impressed. Did you bring all this for my sake?"

Bobby blushed. "Well . . ."

"Then I'm honored. Men have gifted me with many things, but never have any risked their lives that I might dine in splendor. Come, you must join me. Do let's feast to celebrate the night's success."

"Success?" The Captain looked at her oddly. "That's an uncommon choice of words, coming from someone we so recently robbed. I should think you'd empathize with the victims, not the spoilers."

She was licking her finger of more caviar, and she paused, reflecting. "It is odd, isn't it? Perhaps reading about Jesse James has influenced me unduly. I do enjoy a good time, though, and I can assure you the fun is had on your end."

Toby had opened the wine and brought out a pewter goblet. The others were carting the bags of spoils down to the basement.

"Only one? Won't you join me?"

He cast a glance at his leader, who was removing his cloak and draping it across a chair. "Uh, no, my lady. 'Tis late. Another time."

Disappointed, she watched them spill out the door as though running from some threat. She looked at the Captain suspiciously, but he was busy stoking the fire.

"Will you join me, at least?"

He looked back at her, then nodded once. "Very well."

Taking a wooden tankard, he poured the wine while Christina opened a tin of crackers and sat at the table. "Have you your knife handy?"

He laid it on the table. It was large, but she was able to use it to scoop caviar onto a cracker and hand it to him as he sat. "A very useful tool, this knife," she said mildly.

"It has been known to be of use."

She took a sip of the wine, then sighed. "Heaven!"

He tasted his, then took another cracker from her and popped it into his mouth. They ate in silence for a while, looking at the fire. Christina broke it presently, asking in a soft voice, "Captain?"

"Yes, Duchess?"

"What *are* your plans for me?"

He considered this a moment as he chewed. "I intend to ransom you back to your parents."

Quite unexpectedly, she began to laugh. She threw back her head and put a hand to her chest, and he stared at her as if she'd gone daft.

"The joke is on you, highwayman," she said when she could talk. "They won't pay."

"I—beg your pardon?"

"They won't pay, I tell you. Not a farthing."

"That's absurd. What sort of parents would let their only daughter die at the hands of a renegade rather than pay for her safe return?"

"*My* parents." She sipped her wine, then asked, "How did you know I was their only daughter?"

"Everyone in England—everyone on the Continent, for that matter—knows the doings of Derk and Sasha Wentworth. You can hardly escape knowing of them.

King and queen of the theatrical stage. It's no secret that your mother inherited the title of Marchioness of Northampton from your grandfather, then married a common actor and gave him the title of Marquis. How the scandal was overcome by the brilliance of their acting so that even the Queen breaks her isolation on occasion to frequent their plays. How they are wealthy beyond their desires. Notorious for their public battles, and equally public reconciliations. And you, their treasured daughter, who at the tender age of—nineteen, wasn't it?—married a worn-out old duke and set London tongues awagging. . . . These are the fairy tales of the middle classes, Duchess. What do you mean, they won't pay?"

She stood up and took a turn about the room. "Since you know so much about my illustrious parents, I'm surprised you haven't heard the rest. Although, come to think of it, I'm not. They take careful pains to present to the world the image they wish to uphold. Part of that image is the falsehood that they are doting parents. They were once, but not to me. You see, highwayman, my parents have never been overly fond of me. I was a rebelliously troublesome child and have grown into a happily immoral woman."

"Immoral, perhaps. You'd know that better than I. But not so happily, I'd venture."

She refilled her glass and drank it down. "Are you a philosopher as *well* as a renegade?"

"You were telling me why your parents won't meet my demands."

"So I was. It's all quite simple, really. I had a twin sister. You might have heard of her. Elisabeth."

"She was an actress as a child. She died."

"Yes. She was my dearest friend. I loved her devotedly. So did my parents. She was everything they could have wanted in a daughter: lovely, charming, kind, generous. But most of all she could act. She had the gift of both my parents, the very best of them rolled into one breathtaking package. Even when she was ten, when Elisabeth stepped on the stage, you knew you were in the presence of greatness."

"I remember. I saw her once."

So he'd been a patron of the theater once. She gave him a pained look. "She was the only other actress Mother wasn't jealous of. How could she be? She was a *reflection* of Mother. Everyone who saw her remarked how glorious it was that Mother had made Elisabeth into such a star. She was Mother's creation, you see. Every moment my parents had to give was spent rehearsing with my sister. It was the three of them, the magnificent Wentworths. What plans they had!"

"Just where did you fit into those plans?"

"I did what I could. I learned to sew at an early age and became the finest costume designer I could. I made all their costumes, and I became a master at makeup so that in my own way, I was indispensable to them. I set all my energies to the task, and it wasn't long before I was dressing them for all their productions. But it wasn't the same, you see. It was as if I were the help, and they the stars. Which, of course, was the truth."

She looked up and noticed him watching her intently. "Mother never expected, nor did she care for having, twins. From the beginning, I was a nuisance to her. Twice the work, twice the aggravation. It was only that special, unspoken bond between twins that transcends love that kept me from hating Elisabeth for receiving everything my parents denied me. And for not receiving what they—"

She took a breath. She was treading dangerous ground now, skirting along topics she never spoke of to anyone—even Oscar, who had no patience for childhood traumas. What was it about this bandit, she wondered, that inspired confession? Given half the chance, she felt herself capable of pouring out the whole miserable story, the harsh reality that was the terror of her youth. Something about his manner, his seeming interest in her words, his quiet acceptance of all she was saying, tempted her to spill secrets she knew she didn't dare confide. Ugly, brutal secrets that had ravaged her soul. Perhaps it was his unabashed lack of judgment that made her want to pour her heart out to him. But that could be a lie. People had tried—or pretended—to accept her wholly in the past. But in the end, when it really counted, when the real Christina that was locked inside a broken heart had shown a corner of her face, they had let her down. For her own sake, for her own protection, she assumed a less personal tone.

"Well, she died, as you've said. Influenza, they told us. You can imagine our horror. It was as if the tender soul of our family had died with her—what little tender soul we ever had. I, being her twin, felt that half of me had died with her. For years, I didn't know where to look to find myself. She had always known my pain and suffered with me. She never even had to tell me. In the middle of a rehearsal, she would look at me and I would *know*. Suddenly that was gone. It was as if—"

She was doing it again. Soon she'd be stripping her soul naked for his perusal. The old defenses came to her aid and hardened her voice lest he feel more pity for her than she'd intended. "Sooner or later, we had to go on. We had to start living once again. Mother did so in the only way she knew how. She tried to coax me on the stage. She wanted me to replace Elisabeth." She paused, remembering. "I tried. I did, really, for a time. I suppose in a way I thought it would bring her back to me as well. I used to pray for Elisabeth's spirit to come to me and give me what I required to succeed. She didn't need it anymore, that gift of hers that had brought my parents so much joy. I used to think if I could concentrate hard enough, she'd come to me and tell me what to do. But she never did. It was soon painfully evident that I had inherited none of my parents' gift. Oh, I had a flair for drama in life—how could I not?—but whatever it is that makes a person appear larger than life from the seat of a darkened theater, I didn't have. It was disastrous. The harder I worked, the more demanding Mother became. I began to rebel, because I could see what was happening, where she couldn't. The result was inevitable. At the delicate age of thirteen, I appeared with them in *Hamlet*. As Ophelia, no less! I was abominable. Not just bad, but a public embarrassment. Mother never forgave me."

"Surely you exaggerate."

"If you knew my mother, you would know that she's the consummate actress. Nothing is more important to her than the stage. From her own warped point of view, it was a bitter blow. Her last hope to mold me into whatever it was she wanted me to be."

"I met your mother once, years ago."

"Did you? Where?" It distracted her, for it was the first clue he'd given to his identity.

"No probing, Duchess. As I recall, she spoke in glowing terms of her daughter."

"In public, she does, naturally. But she never got over the fact that I wasn't Elisabeth. I never could forget that she wanted me to be. We don't speak of her now, but her ghost haunts us still. My parents and I were never close, but after that travesty, whatever bonds we had were severed. Once they could see that I wasn't up to snuff, they ignored me. Sent me off to boarding school, and lived the gay life of bachelors, bringing me home when they needed me to fashion their costumes and little else."

"You must be handy with a needle, then."

"I am unsurpassed."

"Go on."

She couldn't help wondering if he was really interested. He seemed to be, yet he was so enigmatic in his manner that she couldn't be sure. He was certainly listening intently, but could he be allowing her to ramble merely as a means of finding out what he wanted to know? For all she knew, her confessions meant less to him than her presence—or conspicuous lack of it—in his bed.

"At fourteen, I married a poor sod just to see if I could capture their attention." *And I've told you this*, she thought, *to capture yours*.

He raised a brow, infuriatingly detached.

"The unfortunate lad was an accountant, and too dreary for words. His name was Mortimer. He was much older than I was, of course. A dreadful bore. But I thought if I married the chap—well, to be truthful, I suppose I thought I'd cause a ruckus."

"Did you?"

She looked at him closely. He was watching her with cool deliberation, as if carefully mulling over everything she'd said. Still, his eyes showed none of the ardor she was accustomed to seeing when men looked at her. It was discomforting. It was downright baffling! Had she suddenly lost her powers? The one thing she'd always been sure of was her power over men. She'd taken her frustration over her lack of affection from her father and turned it into a rebellious, brittle charm that when turned on men made it impossible for them to remain in the same room without falling in love with her. Even Oscar—who was presently engaged to a woman as a way of disguising his lack of interest in that species— was half in love with her in an artistic sort of way.

But what of this Captain who kept everything—his thoughts, even his identity—to himself? Having bedded her once, was he suddenly indifferent? How could he be? She watched him for signs. He must be interested! She hadn't imagined what had happened between them! Yet he sat listening with a dispassionate interest, from all outward signs emotionally unmoved. His self-possession challenged her, raised her more outrageous instincts. She adopted a more theatrical tone in the telling of her tale.

"Would you care to know what my illustrious parents said when I told them—at the tender age of fourteen, mind you—that I'd married? Mother, struggling to contain her relief at no longer having me underfoot, said, 'Have you? Darling, how amusing. You must name your first child after me.' Then father said"—here she lowered her voice in a parody of her famous father—" 'What do you mean, her first child? Her first child will be a boy, and she will name the *little monster* after me.' "

He smiled, and it encouraged her.

"To which Mother replied, in that wonderfully theatrical sneer of hers, 'The child will most certainly *not* be a boy. I won't have one in the house. Filthy things. He'll spoil my Louis Quinze.' "

"What did you do?"

She shrugged expansively. "I filed papers to divorce him. What else was there to do? Mother was ready to hush it up—God forbid there be *another* family scandal! Even though she herself had been divorced twice by then. Then he saved me the trouble and died in a carriage accident. So I set out on my own campaign to break the hearts of my parents, just as they had broken mine."

"And did you succeed?"

"You have to care for someone before you allow them to wound you. My parents have never cared for me, and I've resigned myself to the fact that they never will. Oh, Father tries on occasion. He gave me those pearls you stole, even when Mother threw such a tantrum. They were the only thing of value in his family, and Mother was wild to have them. But for once, he ignored her wishes for mine. She divorced him because of it, before—after another husband had come and gone—she finally consented to have him back. But on the whole, their affections have been precious little and for public consumption only. I should think it would be convenient to have you do away with me once and for all."

"You can't mean that."

"I mean it sincerely. Not only would you, in one bold and most *theatrical* stroke, rid them of a troublesome embarrassment, but you would also provide them with that which they love more dearly even than acting."

"Which is . . . ?"

"Publicity. Not to mention the sympathy it would garner from around the world from their admirers. Just think how they would flock to the theater where Mother, always the show-woman, would bravely set aside her mourning to play the part of a bereaved mother. In actuality, it could be said that by disposing of me, you would be playing right into my mother's hands."

He frowned at her, but was silent. Could he be serious in wanting to ransom her? Could he really turn her over without a qualm?

"Why are you telling me this?" he asked quietly.

"Perhaps for the same reason you loaned me your books."

He was silent, considering her reply.

"Well?" she demanded. "Have you nothing to say?"

"I think your mother isn't the only show-woman in the family."

"Very well. Send off your ransom demand. Shall we wager on the outcome?"

"Don't trouble yourself. I've already taken everything I want from you."

She looked up and met his steady gaze. There was no rancor in his eyes, just a straightforward rejection. "You must," she said softly, "be a very *satisfied* man."

At this, he laughed. "You'd best stop tempting me, my lady. You could end up in a great deal of trouble."

"Trouble is no stranger to me, Captain. You might even conclude that I have thrived on it. Now, as to that wager. If my parents send the requested money, I shall cook you and your men dinner. A real dinner, mind you. I shall do what I must to learn to cook it well. I shall dismiss the servants, and you may all come dine at Wynterbrooke Hall."

"And if they don't pay?"

She grinned slyly. "Then you will take me along on one of your escapades."

"Oh, no."

"It won't be my first. I've played pranks with Oscar in every corner of London and half of Paris. But none quite so—" She searched for the word.

"Dangerous," he supplied.

Her eyes sparkled. "Exactly."

"Far too dangerous to take along troublesome young ladies bent on defying their parents."

"It isn't merely my parents I'm hoping to defy."

"Who, then?"

"Let's just say I have my *own* grudge against the Crown."

"The Crown *Prince*, perhaps?"

"Perhaps."

"I won't take you, no matter what the reason."

"Why not? Are you afraid?"

"Of you? Or *for* you?"

"Of what I might do."

"Now, there's a consideration. I should imagine no one ever knows *what* you might do next."

"Because I won't, you know. Give you away. I shall give you my word of honor. I only covet the adventure."

"Why this *particular* adventure?"

"Because I'm so beastly tired of it all. The endless round of parties and country homes, the incessant chatter, the pranks, the dishonesty, everyone talking behind everyone else's back and sleeping with everyone else's mate. Then going to church the next morning and pretending to be pious and behaving perfectly charmingly to their faces. The dandified fops who pass for men—"

"And the Prince?"

"Most especially the Prince. Suddenly, it all seems so sordid, and I can't abide it another minute. I want to scrub myself clean every time I'm around Bertie and his cronies. I was on my way to Egypt when you sequestered me, to escape it all. But the idea of turning it around on *them* for a change—of doing something really honest and unexpected—well, really, it's irresistible. Don't you see?"

He was grinning. "Oh, I see. I have to confess that I find it equally irresistible."

"Then you'll do it."

"It's all academic. I shall send my man out with the ransom demand tonight, and within the week, I shall have my money and you—my little would-be adventurer—will be packed off for home safe and sound."

She extended her small hand. "It's a wager, then."

After the briefest hesitation, he took it. His hand was warm and large clasped over hers. The fingers were long, artistic—the hands of a gentleman roughened by work. She thought of those same hands stoking the embers of her desire, and swallowed. Surely he felt the spark as well!

"You will lose this wager," she predicted.

He grinned again, enjoying the challenge. "We shall see."

"Only—"

"Yes?"

"Only, *do* ask for a large amount of money, won't you? Something excessive, I mean."

"So you'll be assured of winning?"

"No. So my parents will see that someone, at least, puts a substantial value on my life."

He was quiet, still holding her hand. When she glanced up, she saw the surprising look of empathy in his eyes.

"I shall ask for ten thousand pounds," he told her quietly. "Will that satisfy you?"

She smiled with genuine pleasure. "To begin with," she said.

CHAPTER 10

SHE SPENT THE week preparing. Anything she could contribute, she did. She became proficient at cleaning fish. She brought in wood for the fire. She befriended the men; the older Toby with his gruff, complaining exterior, and the young, sensitive Michael with the lank frame and shy, bulldog eyes. She cut through Toby's disapproval by proving what a fast learner she was at everything he taught her, and complimenting him on his ability to teach. When she found that Michael was a reader, she loaned him her copy of *Wuthering Heights* and offered to discuss its merits when he was finished over tankards of Madeira. He read every word and said to her most astutely when he was done, "There are times, your grace, when this Heathcliff reminds me of the Captain." She didn't tell him so, but secretly she was pleased.

She convinced the Captain to allow her to go for long rides in the country with Toby by her side.

"Why are you doing all this?" he asked.

"Because when the time comes, I want you to know I can handle myself. You won't have to slow your pace for me. I shall prove to you that even a duchess can be of benefit to a highwayman."

"I'm not a highwayman," he corrected.

"A mere formality."

When the answer came, she thought she was prepared. She'd built up her time on horseback so that she could easily stay hours in the saddle. She'd planned carefully the conditions she wanted to set as part of her participation. And she'd earned the respect of the men with her quick assessment of what their pilfered treasures were worth. She could tell them to the ha'penny what any item would bring on the open market, and often who it had belonged to.

Bobby rode back into camp late one afternoon. The men had been tinkering with the waterwheel, trying to get it to work, and Christina was laughingly offering suggestions. She stood, brushing off her skirts, and watched as Bobby rode over to the Captain. She noted at once that Bobby's face was lacking its usual clownlike enthusiasm. He reined his horse and simply shook his head. There would be no ransom paid for the Duchess.

She slipped away before anyone could notice, following the riot of wildflowers along the river and out to the cliff. There she sat down, dangling her legs over the edge, and looked out across the choppy expanse of the Channel. She'd expected the reply, but she realized now that some small part of her—some remnant of that lonely little girl—had hoped it would be otherwise. She'd hoped her parents would surprise her, just this once.

Some time passed. The sun began to slip down over the horizon. A cool breeze blew in to ruffle her hair. Still she sat, thinking back over the years, thinking of the humiliations she'd suffered at her parents' hands. It almost broke her heart to recall the final, negative shake of Bobby's head. But she wouldn't cry. She hadn't cried since Elisabeth's death, and she wouldn't do so now. She'd vowed never to cry again.

It was almost dark when he joined her. He stood for a moment, looking at the straight, proud line of her back. Her shoulders were erect, and she sat with the unthinking grace of her station. But when he sat down beside her and she looked at him, he saw in her eyes the agony she'd sought to hide.

She lowered her lashes, masking the pain.

"I didn't believe you," he told her.

"No one ever does."

"Their position is that you're better fixed than they,

and can arrange for your own ransom. It seems they have little doubt as to your ability to handle yourself in such a situation."

"That, I suppose, is meant as consolation."

He looked out at the deep grey water churning like a sea of slate.

"I shall pay you your ten thousand pounds," she promised presently.

"You don't need to do that. I only asked it for your sake."

"It's only money, highwayman. It means precious little to me."

There was a heavy silence in which she dismissed his presence and dove into the sanctuary of her own thoughts. Needing to speak, he contemplated the sea for some time, choosing his words with care.

"I've led a hard life, Duchess. I'm not accustomed to thinking of others and what they might need. If my men are troubled, they keep it to themselves, and I do the same. We work together for a common cause, and we don't let personalities interfere."

"Have no fear, my lord. I shall not obstruct your well-ordered world."

"You mistake me. It has occurred to me that you might—need more at this moment than I'm accustomed to giving."

Her eyes, flashing on his face, showed him he was right.

"I'm rather inept at the comforting of women. It's not something that comes up with any regularity."

She smiled a little, touched by the sweet awkwardness that she'd never have guessed of him. "No. Your reputation speaks to other things," she agreed.

"Perhaps if you were to tell me what you need—"

She wanted more than anything to be held. Simply held, as a father might hold a child he esteemed dear. But how could she, with all that had passed in her life, admit such a simple thing? How could she confess her longing after his previous dismissal? She'd been rejected by her parents already. It was enough for one day.

She lowered her eyes to stow the wistfulness she knew they'd reveal.

"I see," he muttered thoughtfully. "Well, then, I shall have to use my own resources. I've led a lonely life these many years. I find when I'm feeling the most— assailable, that the thing that suffers most is my sense of touch. At such times, I recall what it's like to be held by someone who cares."

Someone who cares. Her gaze flew to his face, showing too much of the hope that suddenly fluttered in her heart.

He gave her a self-conscious grin that was more charming than anything he'd offered to date. "So by your leave—if I might—"

"You're asking my *permission?*" She couldn't believe what she was hearing. Not after he'd held a knife to her throat and threatened rape!

He took her hand in his. He twined his fingers through hers, then stroked her knuckles with his other hand. There was nothing sexual, nothing threatening, in the gesture. It was, remarkably, just what she'd wished for. Comfort. Solace. Nothing more.

She looked at him tenderly. Seeing the gratitude in her eyes, he released her hand, put his arm about her, and held her close. "Come, Duchess. Cry if you wish. I should like to think I'm good for something in this miserable world."

"I never cry," she said, rigidly.

"Don't you? How odd. I do." Amazed, she shifted away and looked at him. He pulled her back so that her head rested once again on the broad expanse of his chest. "Or I used to," he added. "I've had nothing for a long while that I cared enough to weep *about.*"

"Then we're alike, you and I."

He was quiet a moment. Then, in a soft tone, he said, "I know what it is to be shunned by family. I sometimes think it's the most debilitating humiliation one can suffer. It matters not what you do, what you prove to the world at large. Family, in the end, is always the last to accept you. The last to applaud your deeds. I learned long ago that the secret to staying sane is not to care. Or if you do care, not to expect what they can't give."

"You're right, of course. But that's the trick of it, isn't it?"

"Sometimes the cruelty of one's relations is a gift unto itself. It makes you angry. Angry enough to pick yourself up from the ashes of their malevolence and do the impossible as a form of—retribution. You don't earn their love or respect any more than you ever would have, but you've accomplished something you might not have otherwise. Perhaps, in the end, it's a small price to pay," he said.

"I suppose you're right. Channeling your emotions into your art, as Oscar would say."

"A difficult thing, when you're chapfallen."

"I dream of the day when I can show my parents I'm made of stiffer stuff than their sorry opinion of me would warrant," Christina said passionately. "The trouble, of course, is that up till now, they've been quite right in their assessment. I haven't found my channel, as you have. Sometimes I hunger for it so, I can taste it on my tongue."

"Aye," he said with a faraway look. "I've tasted of the same brew."

He withdrew his arm from her. In the silence, they experienced a sudden embarrassment, a disentanglement of their emotions that was born of soul-confession.

"Thank you," she said presently. "It helps tremendously to feel that someone empathizes with my plight. I rarely have the luxury of pouring my heart out to a *sympathetic* ear."

"I understand the plague of being locked away in the cell of your own mind."

"It's a pity for a man such as you to be so lonely."

They exchanged a look. In Christina's eyes was an offering, in the bandit's a wary comprehension. Abruptly, as if this were territory he'd rather not tread, he deflected the subject to her.

"Just out of curiosity, who would be your heir, should I carry out my implied threats and dispose of you?"

"Are you asking if my parents are hoping you'll kill

me so they can collect on my estate?" She smiled. "I have left every penny to Oscar. Don't think it doesn't infuriate them. But it keeps Mother civil to him, which is something, since she used to treat him shabbily. She has some twisted notion that she must keep Oscar content. I suppose she's hoping he'll take pity over her should I die and give all the money back to what she considers is its rightful place. Namely to her."

"What are the chances that he will?"

She grinned then, splendidly. "Absolutely none. It's my one consolation, that if something happens to me, Oscar will oblige me by spending every penny of my estate on food and wine and paintings right beneath my parents' noses!" She laughed gleefully, her earlier gloom dispelled.

"You disdain money. How—in your present state—do you feel about adventure?"

In her sorrow, she'd forgotten their wager. "I'm to go?"

"I'm a man of my word."

She took a deep breath and smiled. "Thank you. I shall always remember it."

"I still say it's a dangerous proposition, taking a woman on a mission."

"In all you've heard about the Duchess of Wynterbrooke, did you ever *once* hear that I was helpless?"

"Not once."

"Well, then?"

"Then I'd suggest you get a good night's rest. We ride tomorrow."

CHAPTER 11

$\mathcal{D}$URING DINNER, THE Captain went over the details of the job.

"I want it simple. No chance for slip-ups with the lady present. She'll dress in some of Bobby's clothes and stay mounted and well back in the shadows with Toby as protection. I want no opportunity for her to be recognized as a woman and thus endangered."

The men ate in grim silence, avoiding her eyes. She supposed she couldn't blame them if they resented taking a woman along. According to Toby, they'd been sailors once, and she recalled hearing some sailors' superstition against taking a woman to sea. Likely they carried this fanaticism to their missions. She could understand it, but she'd be damned if she'd pander to it.

"Actually," she said when the Captain finished speaking, "I had another idea."

Their disbelieving eyes turned to her as one.

"I'm a thorough planner, Duchess. Which accounts for why we've never been caught. No further ideas are needed."

"You rob trains, do you not?"

The Captain nodded.

"Well, I was thinking. Why go to the trouble to flag down the train in the dark? You and I could pose as husband and wife. That way, we would be on the train, and at the appointed time, you would simply need to walk to the front, put a gun to the engineer's head, and have him stop the train. The men could embark, and the whole thing could be accomplished with a minimum of fuss."

The men exchanged startled looks.

"I told you, I don't want you recognized."

"I shall wear a heavy black veil. I'm supposed to be in mourning for Wynterbrooke, remember? I have one that shows nothing of my face, as well as a black funeral frock that will be perfect. And I'm a master at theatrical disguise. I've made my father look every nationality known to man. Most convincingly, I might add. We could devise a mustache, put you in a bowler hat and bumbershoot—with a woman in mourning on your arm, who would suspect you?"

He was chewing reflectively.

She pressed her advantage. "Five minutes before the appointed stop, you could excuse yourself, go to the washroom, change your clothes—we shall be carrying a small valise to make it look authentic, after all—and no one need be the wiser. In the panic of the situation, I shall simply drop from the train, where your men will have horses waiting. It's quite brilliant in its simplicity, really, and I shan't be forced to miss out on all the fun."

Toby snorted. Michael blushed his embarrassment. Bobby ate as if he'd been starving for a week and refused again to meet her eyes.

The Captain tore into a chunk of bread and surprised them all by saying, "It just might work."

"Captain, you can't seriously think to use the lady—"

"She's right. Who would suspect it? Who would remember it? I shall play a dowdy aging middle-class gent whose only thought is to get home to hearth and hounds. It simplifies matters immensely."

"Not to mention," Christina added with a twinkle in her eyes, "the fun of queuing up to buy a ticket, knowing all the while your intentions. I should imagine by now they'd have police scouring the stations for you. You could slip onto the train right under their noses."

He regarded her with a look of admiration. "Yes. I admit I'd thought of that. Things have become too routine for my tastes of late. I'd fancy flaunting my intentions under the authorities' noses."

"But the danger, Captain—the lady—"

"If it gets too dangerous for the lady, we shall simply allow her to remain on the train and continue to its destination. From there, she may catch the next express for London."

Christina clamped her lips tight. She had no intention of being kept on the train, but it wouldn't do to contradict him. Not when things were so beautifully going her way.

"You shan't be sorry," she promised. "I shall spend the night devising an absolutely flawless makeup. Undetectable, even to your men. But I shall need some supplies."

"Bobby can go into town tomorrow," the Captain decided. "Have a list made up for him in the morning. It's settled, then."

Everyone nodded, but it seemed to her that they were still stubbornly grim, as if there was something they weren't saying.

"Good. Now let's go over it again. Step by step."

Christina used burnt matches and cat's hair to give the Captain bushy brows. She made deep creases along his eyes and forehead, then painted a mustache on him that was so realistic, a person would have to step on his toes to detect the forgery. Finally she took ash from the hearth and streaked his hair with grey.

"You can wash everything off easily enough in the washroom, if you care to," she said, handing him the Roman mirror to inspect her handiwork.

He did so with a critical eye. "Yes . . ." he murmured. "With the clothing, it might just work."

"With the clothing, you'll look three decades older than your years. I told you, I'm an expert. I know what I'm doing."

She leaned over and touched up the inner corner of his mustache. It was an intimate process, bending over him, running her fingers along his face as their breaths mingled. More intimate, in many ways, than their love-making had been. The curve of his lips was firm and strong. Pressed together in his impatience for her to finish, they constantly drew the attention of her eyes. She was a shameless woman, she thought, in spite of her great resolve. With all that was going on, she couldn't help but remember the feel of those lips against her earlobe, against the hollow of her neck. . . . Since the night of her aborted escape, he hadn't come near her. Many nights she'd lain awake thinking of going to him. His touch against her skin was too sweet not to experience it again, one last time. But memories of his rejection of her the next morning kept her rooted in her bed, alone and dissatisfied, tossing the night away. She wondered if, sleeping under the stars as he did, he ever wished for her to come to him.

She moistened her lips and looked up to find him watching her.

"I could give you a goatee, if I had my father's makeup kit," she said with regret.

"You've done enough. I doubt my own mother would recognize me."

He handed her the mirror, then stood and went into the basement to change. In the main room, the men were preparing, pulling on boots and gloves, checking weapons and ammunition. Christina, dressed in the crisp black satin of mourning, held the veil up to the lamp for the thousandth time to make certain she couldn't see through it.

"Nervous, my lady?" Michael asked.

She took a deep breath. "Nervous? Not really. But terribly excited."

Michael smiled, but the others exchanged covert looks. Well, let them sulk, she decided. She'd change their minds soon enough.

The Captain's voice came from below stairs. "Are you ready?"

Christina put her hands to her mouth and fabricated the blare of a trumpet. "Make your entrance, my lord."

When he walked in, even the most cynical of his men stopped what they were doing and stared. He was dressed in a tweed suit, wearing a bowler hat and carrying an umbrella. To disguise his height, Christina had fashioned a small bump in the back of his jacket, which, when he bent, using his umbrella as a cane, made him appear the very essence of a rheumatic, twisted old man. He wobbled across the room, taking small, deliberate steps and shaking the umbrella as if his hand barely had the strength to hold it. The transformation was remarkable. No one would guess his true age.

As the men gawked, Christina went to him and put the wire-rimmed spectacles on his nose. She stood back, looked him over, then walked around him, taking in every detail of his appearance.

"Well?" he prompted.

She beamed. "You'll do quite nicely, I should think."

"Land's sakes, Captain, I wouldn't know you," cried Bobby.

"Don't forget the voice," Christina reminded.

"Ah, yes, the voice." He took two more steps forward, looking as though he might fall forward at any moment, then screwed up his face and asked in an aged, whispery rasp, "Might I trouble you, sir, for a ticket to Dorset for my wife and myself?"

The men let out squeals of laughter, and Christina clapped her hands together. "Derk Wentworth could not have done better!"

"Are the things ready, my dear?" he asked in the same voice.

She opened the valise. Inside were his riding clothes, hat, gloves, cape, and pistol with extra ammunition. She held up a jar. "Lather this over your face liberally, then wipe it off and wash your face. With your hat and mask, no one will suspect you to be the old man. Toss everything back into this bag when you've changed, and leave it by the door to our coach. I shall pick it up on the way out."

"Then we're set, are we?" he said, still playing the old man.

They nodded.

He straightened up, assuming his normal voice and demeanor. "Good. Then let's off. You men know where to meet us. If the train doesn't stop, you'll know some-

thing went wrong. Go to town and find out what it is."
He gave them a piercing look. "Discreetly, of course."

"Aye, Captain."

He picked up the valise and headed outside. Toby helped Christina onto the horse they'd brought for her. Obviously, he'd been given private orders to look after her.

The Captain grabbed hold of his stallion's mane and with one quick movement, flung himself into the saddle.

Christina laughed. "You look so incongruous, dressed the way you are, sitting upon such a steed."

His horse was restive. He let it dance in a circle, then drew up to her. "All right?"

"Couldn't be better."

"I shall tell you this once, Duchess. Keep your mind on the job at hand. Just ride along with me. If we get separated for any reason, remember—you escaped, you don't know who we are, and you never saw my face. Is it clear?"

"Quite."

"Good. Then all you have to do is keep your mouth firmly closed and endeavor to keep pace. For, doubt me not, Duchess. You lag behind, and we shall abandon you to your fate."

She had no doubt from his tone that he meant it.

"Put your fears to rest, Captain. You'll not abandon me as easily as you might think."

CHAPTER 12

A PATROLMAN SAUNTERED across the tile floor of the train station, swinging his nightstick. He wore the blue uniform and high, rounded hat of the bobby, and he whistled a sketchy tune as his gaze slid over them before moving on to the next passenger in line. She glanced toward the platform, where another policeman was watching with a more careful eye.

A newsboy sat slumped in a corner, his hat pulled down over his eyes, more interested in sleeping than in selling papers. Beside him the news slate showed the headline in a childish chalked scrawl:

BRIGHTON BANDIT KIDNAPPING
DUCHESS STILL MISSING

The Captain took a copy of the *London Times* and tossed the coin into the tin. The boy winked awake and retrieved the lavish payment gratefully, never realizing it was the bandit himself who offered it. "Many thanks, gov'na."

As they stood in line, Christina continued to stare at the policeman. She felt a hand of steel at her elbow. Turning, she saw the Captain's eye, behind the spectacles, giving her a hard assessment. It added to his danger that he couldn't know what to expect from her. She decided to set his mind at rest.

"I do wish they'd hurry along, Frederick," she whined in a tearful voice. "It is so trying, all this traveling at such a time."

She held a handkerchief in her hand, and she reached beneath the veil to dab at her eyes as if she'd been crying. The hand dropped from her elbow.

"If you'd like to be seated, my dear . . ." he offered in his feeble voice.

"No, no. I'm quite well. And look, we're next."

They stepped up to the window, and the Captain held out the shillings in his gloved, shaking hand. It seemed to take a full minute for him to move it across the window and drop the money into the cashier's palm. Christina looked over her shoulder to see that the first patrolman had moved away.

"Would you care for some assistance, sir?" the cashier asked. The man was obviously on his last legs, and the weeping woman seemed of little use.

"Why, that would be most kind," the old man surprised her by saying.

She shot him a sharp look through her veil. He ignored her.

The cashier motioned for a young page, who came running up to help. "Care to take my arm, sir?"

"Thank you, lad. God bless and preserve you."

He shuffled along so slowly on the arm of the boy that Christina grew impatient. In her agitation, she wanted to be on the train, away from the prying eyes of the police. At the same time, walking past them and watching as they dismissed the old man and grieving woman gave her a thrill she'd never experienced. She could barely catch her breath.

When the page had settled them on the train and put the valise above their heads, the old man fumbled in his pocket and drew out a shilling, pressing it laboriously into the boy's palm. "Buy something nice for your mother, son."

When he was gone, and they were alone, she hissed, "A fine time to be offering gratuities, when you're preparing to rob the passengers of every last farthing."

"An old man likes to show small kindnesses to those who assist him," he croaked. He didn't criticize her, but she felt chastised just the same. He had no intention of stepping out of character, and she must follow his example. The coach was filling up, and there was no telling who might overhear.

As the train pulled out of the station, he shook out the *Times* and began to peruse it through the spectacles, reading about himself and clucking his tongue periodically as an old man might do who disapproved of what he was reading. "My, my," he murmured when he'd read some more. "My, *my*."

Christina felt a wild impulse to laugh. She read the piece over his arm, brushing her shoulder against his companionably. The reporter described her in great detail and reported that her parents were in such a tizzy that they'd *nearly* canceled their performances. But being the troupers they were, they'd decided the show must go on for the sake of their loyal audience. The Prince of Wales was said to be frantic, lambasting the bandit and promising all sorts of dire consequences for the man once he was caught. Oscar Wilde was quoted as saying he had no doubt the bandit would realize soon enough that the Duchess was no one to trifle with, and once she'd worn him to a nub, he would send her back to spare himself the undue anguish of being continually whipped by the tongue of such a formidable woman. It seemed everyone in London was expressing an opinion on the subject. In the meantime, the Wentworths' production of *Macbeth* was raking in the profits, and the police were combing the countryside for the missing duchess.

The train thundered through a tunnel, and in the ensuing clatter, the Captain put his mouth to her ear and said so that only she could hear, "I hadn't noticed being unduly whipped by your formidable tongue."

She, in turn, put her lips against his ear and replied, "If Oscar only knew the tongue-whipping I should *like* to give you."

It was a blatantly sexual remark, and he took it as such. As the train shot out of the tunnel, he met her eye and the corner of his mouth turned up in a grin.

The train picked up speed, and the miles began to chug away behind them. Occasionally, her companion would turn the page of his paper with a shaky hand, or make a comment about what he was reading. "Did you know, dear, that Mrs. Allenby won top honors at the flower show for her roses? If it hadn't been for the loss of our dear Harriet, we might have done the same."

Each time he did it, her tension mounted. Yet she was required to play her role, so she patted his gloved hand and murmured, "Next year, dearest."

Mostly, she watched him read and let the churning of the wheels pound a rhythm in her head. What a cool customer he was! Her knees shook at the thought of what was to come. She began to believe that he was as relaxed as he appeared. But when the conductor came by to retrieve their tickets, she noticed that the Captain watched him with a keen eye as the man moved along, collecting from each passenger. He took the opportunity to study the people in their car to determine who among them might be a threat. She did the same. There were a few couples present, the women dressed in dreary spring-weight woolens, the men in broadcloths and tweeds, but mostly they were stodgy-looking men returning to their wives for a long weekend in the country. Christina realized for the first time that it was Friday. She'd lost track of the days, but she understood now how meticulous the Captain's planning had been. Working men returning to their wives on a Friday evening were bound to be carrying extra money and perhaps a few baubles to soothe their lonely spouses.

They made several stops before heading out into the open country. Each stop was an agony to Christina. She kept expecting the car to be searched at any moment. Although he appeared to be engrossed in the *Times*, the Captain was really keeping a sharp lookout for her. If she shifted or seemed restless, he would invariably reach over and take her hand. To anyone else, it might seem a gesture of comfort. But Christina felt the iron in his grip.

Soon, she began to squirm just so he would take her hand again.

All too soon, it was time to move. With a casual air that stirred Christina's admiration, he used the arm of his seat to push himself up on wobbly legs, wrestled with the valise, then cupped her chin through the veil in his unsteady hand. "I won't be long, dearest," he croaked. He bent over her as though to help her hear, and in doing so cast a glance beneath his arm to make sure no one was paying any undue attention. When he was satisfied, he gave her a last look, then hobbled with the help of his umbrella toward the washroom.

The conductor came back through and rushed toward him. Christina's heart stopped.

"Here, sir, allow me."

He took the old man's arm and guided him to his destination. The old man's head bobbed up and down as if he couldn't control it. "So good of you," he mumbled. "So good . . ."

The conductor moved on.

Christina took some breaths and talked to herself. *This is what you wanted. You can't back out now.* She was nervous suddenly. She wished she'd thought to visit the washroom herself, before it was too late.

They'd purposely chosen the first coach on the train. That way, given luck, the Captain could change and slip up front without being noticed.

She watched her fellow passengers to see if anyone was looking toward the washroom. Most were reading, and some had settled back to sleep. One younger couple was giggling softly as the young man spoke in his wife's ear. She felt the lurch of her heart and looked away.

In a matter of minutes, she caught the flash of a black cape. It happened so quickly, if she hadn't been looking for it, she might have missed it completely. So it had begun. She glanced toward the doorway of the coach. On the floor was the small valise, with the umbrella lying by its side. She took a breath and sat up straighter in her seat.

Suddenly, the train lurched to a stop. She heard the pounding of hooves outside, then Toby leapt from his horse, opened the door, and was in her coach in an instant. She would never have thought him capable of such agility. But she knew that down along the line of the train, other masked men were boarding other cars with pistols in their hands, just as Toby had.

For the first time, she fully realized the danger of their position. Including the Captain, there were only five men. Not nearly enough to position a man in each coach. If one of the outlaws turned his back for an instant, an armed man could sneak in from the next coach and shoot him before he had time to notice. It explained the unexpected alertness in Toby's darting eyes. Enemies could be lurking in every dark corner of the train.

It wasn't a moment before the Captain came in, pushing the white-faced engineer before him. He was dressed again in his black costume, and every trace of age had been wiped clean from his face. His hat hid the grey ash in his hair, and his green-grey eyes glinted through his black silk mask. He moved briskly, tossing his cape over his shoulder. No one could possibly mistake him for the old man.

The passengers had long since panicked. Some stood, some screamed, some tried to open locked windows and couldn't. Christina could almost smell their fear in the air. She moved aside to make sure the Captain could pass. He didn't once look her way.

He stood with the gun at the engineer's temple, waiting patiently for silence. Soon enough, arrested by his presence, they quieted down and stood quaking, looking at him with fear-widened eyes. The young woman was crying, and the man had his arm about her shoulders.

"I thank you all for your attention," the Captain said in a deep voice that bounced off the walls of the coach. "You may have assumed by now that this is a holdup. If so, you are correct. I shall ask you for your belongings, and then I and my men will be gone, to trouble you no more this night. If you comply, you will all reach your homes safely. If not——" He shrugged expansively. "I'd hardly care to hazard a guess as to the consequences."

He jerked his head at Toby, who moved off in the direction of the next coach. The Captain extended a leather saddlebag. "You'll be good enough to remove your jewelry, your watches, your cigar cases, anything that might be of value, and place it in the bag. Cash is always welcome. Mind, I have a fair idea of what each of you is carrying on your person, and I count honesty, in these cases, as the highest of virtues. Do be sure not to disappoint me, won't you?"

He passed the bag around, and one by one, the men tossed their valuables into it. The couples were more perverse. They argued, wishing to hold on to something that had belonged to the family or some token that held sentimental value.

The young man handed forth the usual goods, then turned to take a seat. "Not so fast, my fine lad," the Captain said. "Surely a gentleman with so—sweet a companion has something tucked away? Something you might have planned as a surprise for the lady, perhaps?"

The man gave a startled look. How had the fiend known? His eyes darted to his bag above the seat, and the Captain pulled it down and opened it with one hand. There was a small box tied with a peach bow. He took the ribbon in his teeth and pulled it loose as the young man fumed before him. His gloves made it difficult to retrieve what was inside, but at last he succeeded. It was a small porcelain figurine, a woman with loose blond hair that resembled the man's bride.

"It was for her birthday," the young man said in an angry, accusing tone.

The Captain held it up close to the young woman's face. Her eyes shone as they looked gratitude at her husband, and a tear spilled onto her cheek. "Oh, Charles! It doesn't matter. It was such a beautiful thought."

"Well," Charles mumbled, "you said you'd always wanted one."

After a brief hesitation, the highwayman took the woman's hand in his. She flinched at the contact, and Charles bolted upright, ready to fight. But the outlaw ignored him. He placed the figurine in the lady's hand and said, "You may have your present, miss, with a fool's blessing."

For the first time in years, Christina thought she'd cry. He moved on. A plump woman in her forties bemoaned the loss of her cameo brooch, hoping for a similar concession. The Captain merely extended his black gauntlet toward her, put a finger to her fleshy chin, and raised her face to capture her eyes with his own.

"Come, good woman," he addressed her in a silky tone. "Looks such as yours need no trifle to adorn them."

The woman flushed beneath his gaze and happily gave him the brooch.

Watching, Christina felt an uncharacteristic surge of jealousy. Ninny that she was, she'd imagined he spoke only to her in that faintly flirtatious way.

For the most part, the passengers were too scared to put up a fight. But Christina noticed the eyes of the engineer moving constantly in search of some way out. He was responsible for the train, and it was his job to die defending it, if he must.

After collecting from all the passengers, the Captain at last turned to her. "And you, my lady," he asked in what sounded to her ears like a more intimate tone. "Have you nothing for me?"

It startled her. She hadn't thought that he would ask her, but of course he must. She stammered, trying to think. "I am in mourning, sir. I carry no valuables at the present time."

"Come, come, my lady. Even a woman in mourning carries *some* possession worth notice. In your bag, perhaps?"

She carried on her arm a small black velvet bag. At his nod, she hesitantly opened the silky ropes and looked inside. There, nestled deep within the folds, was the same gold bracelet she'd given him the night he'd first stopped her in London.

She was so surprised to see it that she jumped. But she realized in that instant why he'd eluded the authorities for so long. He left nothing to chance. No detail was too small. She withdrew the bracelet and handed it to him.

"I was robbed once before," she said. "It seems I am to be forever relinquishing my valuables to thieves of the night."

"Only if my luck holds, my lady."

Something dropped in the back of the car. The Captain wheeled about with the reflexes of a cat to find the young woman sheepishly picking up her figurine. "It didn't break," she assured him, holding it up so he could see.

Christina felt her heart had stopped for good. But in the next moment, she saw something that he did not. In the commotion, when the thief had turned his back, the engineer had lunged for the nearest seat and grabbed onto a large metal trunk. This he was lifting high to crash down upon the Captain's head.

Christina wasted no time. She leapt for the umbrella on the floor and thrust it into the man's back. "I wouldn't try it, sir," she cried. "My aim at such a distance is indisputable."

Thinking she had a gun at his back, the engineer slowly dropped the trunk to the side. Triumphantly, Christina looked up to find that the Captain had turned back again and was glaring at her with the fury of hell blazing in his eyes.

"You little minx," he growled beneath his breath.

He grabbed her arm and shoved her toward the door. Then he raised his pistol and smashed it across the engineer's head. The man's eyes popped open, then he slumped to the ground with a groan.

The Captain turned his pistol to the coach, scanning it to take in each and every passenger. "Would anyone else care to play the hero?" he demanded. "I find, in my present mood, that I should be happy to oblige."

No one moved. "No? Then I thank you for your time, and bid you all a good night."

Christina picked up the valise and prepared to jump from the train. She could see the horses in the distance. The Captain whistled once into the night, and almost immediately, his men began to pour from the train and race swiftly for their mounts. It was prearranged that Toby would bring her horse to her so she could mount just as quickly and be off into the night. But when he came, he was towing only the stallion. Had her horse run off in the confusion?

The Captain leapt from the coach onto the back of his steed. He came around to her, and she picked up her skirts to better mount behind him. But instead of helping her up, he stood in his stirrups, lifted the veil from her face, and threw it back over her head. Then he took her jaw in his fist and leaned forward to kiss her hard on the mouth.

"You've played your part to perfection, your grace," he told her in a booming voice the passengers were certain to hear. "As promised, in return, we most happily render your life."

She stared at him, dumbfounded. "You wouldn't dare—"

His hand tightened on her jaw, cutting off the words. Then he dropped it, took the valise, yanked the reins, and put heel to his horse. The stallion gave a half-rear, then bolted off into the night. The men followed close behind.

Looking around, she saw passengers running to their windows to peer like specters into the night. As the horses thundered away, the victims turned and stared at her with horrified eyes.

"She's that duchess!" one gasped. "The one they kidnapped!"

She had to grasp the doorway to keep from falling. He was gone. He'd left her. She couldn't believe it.

The conductor rushed in just then, and the passengers began to babble the story. He stepped over the stirring engineer and went to peer at Christina solicitously.

He'd left her, she kept thinking. *How could he do it? How?*

The conductor's lips were moving, but she couldn't hear the words. She didn't know what he wanted. She didn't know what was in store for her. She didn't even know that she cared. She knew only that he'd left her alone on this, the most exhilarating night of her life. And that the image of the highwayman, his cape flying behind him as he dashed off into the night, would live in her heart forever.

CHAPTER 13

IT WAS LATE, and the party was in full swing when Christina arrived. She hadn't been at all certain that she'd go, but at the last minute, she'd given in to the pressure and resigned herself to her responsibilities. It had been a week since her return, and she'd holed herself up like some wounded dog, refusing to see anyone but the police. The note she'd received from her mother earlier in the evening had decided her that the time to put aside her despondency was upon her.

"You've had a trying time, and no one knows it—or sympathizes with it—more than we," Sasha Wentworth had penned in her elaborate script. "But really, Christina, how long do you expect your father and myself to fend off the barrage of questions that our friends will inevitably ask? The scandal is regrettable, but as it has happened, it is your duty—yes, your *duty,* girl—to make the best of a poor situation. By locking yourself away, you raise questions that are best left unuttered. I hoped we had reared you better than this. Your friends wonder at your weakness, when you've never shown the slightest tendency toward such a trait in the past. As your mother, I fear I must demand that you set aside this nonsense *immediately,* and join us all in Norfolk for the week's end."

It enraged Christina that her mother should make such a show of sympathy. Perhaps she really believed that she had her daughter's best interests at heart. But Christina knew what awaited her, and she dreaded it more than she had ever dreaded anything in her life. Still, her mother's words made sense. She had done what she could to throw the police off track. But if people began to wonder about her state of mind, to wonder why she was grieving more deeply now than when the Duke had died, she might give herself—and the highwayman—away. In her own perverse way, Sasha was right. It was Christina's duty to reenter society and put on a brave show. Her duty to *him* . . . whoever he might be.

Even with her mother's warning, though, she wasn't prepared for what met her in Norfolk. She entered the country estate of her friend, Lady Wilton, to find it ablaze with lights and music. When she presented her card, the butler's eyes flicked to her face before he stiffly announced, "Her grace, the Duchess of Wynterbrooke."

There was a gasp. Although the music played on, the dancers stopped and rushed to her side. She felt herself being swallowed by a sea of people, powdered and perfumed and dressed in finery that glittered like jewels. Everyone was talking at once, and her friends fought to embrace her. The spaniels, who were always allowed in the ballroom, yapped and leapt about in circles at her feet. Only when Lady Wilton herself pushed her way through the crowd did they settle down enough for their hostess to be heard.

"Christina, *darling,* you did come! I *am* thrilled, absolutely. But don't you look divine! We were so worried. We tried and tried to see you, but that beastly majordomo kept turning us away!" She was a dainty blond woman, a few years older than Christina, very pretty in a fragile sort of way.

Everyone began to speak at once. They moved as one rushing entity as Lady Wilton guided her honored guest into the center of the ballroom. She waved her hand impatiently, then called to the orchestra, "*Do* stop playing, won't you? I can't hear myself think! Now, darling, you must tell us all about it—every *detail*, mind you. And we shall listen with bated breaths."

Christina looked about at her hushed, expectant friends. She saw true concern in their eyes, but looking more closely, detected the same fascination she herself had always felt when there was scandal in the air. Their eyes gleamed with curiosity, revealing their desire to hear the worst even as they rejoiced in her safe return. They wanted to know if the rumors were true, that this experience had broken her. She swayed a little, and was caught by a masculine arm. Turning, she saw Oscar Wilde shoving some gentlemen aside to make more room for her.

"Oh, Oscar," she said, and went into his arms. It was the first time she'd felt any joy at being home.

"How are you, pet? Up to snuff? You can't know how concerned we've all been. Concerned? Terrified, more like it. I canceled two stops on my speaking tour to rush back when I heard you'd returned."

His kind, droopy eyes gave her the courage she needed. She smiled and answered with a playfulness she didn't feel, "Now, Oscar, really, you should know it takes more than a common desperado to get the better of me."

There was another gasp, and all at once everyone began to laugh. "I knew it!" Lady Wilton declared. "Didn't I *tell* you our duchess would put that brigand in his place!"

"She did." Lord Wilton nodded energetically. "She said, 'I'll wager that bandit has his hands full with our Christina!' I heard her myself."

"Well, you're back home safely, in the bosom of your friends, and we're thankful for that."

"But come, darling, tell us *all*! We've been reading about it in the papers for the last week. Is it true the bandit forced you to help him rob that train?"

They hurled their questions at her, and she gave the same well-rehearsed answers she'd been giving the police for a week.

"Couldn't you have allowed the engineer to knock him out? Surely it wasn't necessary to *aid* the blessed fellow in his crime!"

"He threatened to kill me if I didn't comply. Naturally, I had no choice."

"Did he really kiss you right in front of everyone?"

Lady Wilton asked. "How perfectly dreadful! I don't know where you find the courage, dear. I should faint *dead away.*"

It continued like this for several minutes, each with his own question and concern, each vying for her attention. She answered automatically, but she was wishing inside that she'd never come. She looked about at all the greedy faces, and felt like an alien in her own circle. It astonished her. She'd been devastated, locked away in her house in St. James's, longing for the highwayman, wanting to go to him, yet having no idea of how to go about it. She'd spent the week pacing her room, telling herself there must be a way to find him. But she had no real idea where the camp was located. And there was always the possibility that she'd be followed if she tried to find it. Finally, she'd been forced to face the hopelessness of her situation.

But she'd always expected that once she faced reality and went back out into society, the routines of her life would soothe her, and she'd forget about the Captain, with his cool, piercing eyes and his daredevil sense of adventure that matched her own. What she hadn't expected was this awful pain in her heart, this pain that mocked her and her friends, and made her whole life seem even more of a sham than it already had seemed.

As she was feeling her most vulnerable, her most overwhelmed, the crowd began to part, and she looked up to see her parents standing before her.

They were as famous as any actors could be in such times. Their faces were known far and wide. Looking at the tall, striking features of Derk Wentworth, the elegant long hair—now salt-and-pepper grey—thrown back from his forehead, the protruding brow, the strong, passionate lines of his mouth, she felt herself a child again, longing for his love. When he looked at her, she felt the power of his gaze, the deep green eyes, the force of his concentration that had made him one of the greatest Othellos of his—or any—time.

Beside him, Sasha Wentworth was diminutive. It was always a surprise to those who saw her on the stage to realize—upon meeting her—how tiny she really was.

Her face was small, with delicate features reminiscent of Christina's. Her hands were tiny, as were her wrists, and her feet. She was dressed to perfection in a bronze-color satin gown that highlighted the autumn coloring of her hair. While Dark was dashing—even at his age, you could see him cavorting about the stage, brandishing a sword—he by no means eclipsed his wife. Her presence, while different, was every bit as commanding as his. Looking at them, it was difficult for the eye to settle. They seemed, by virtue of their existence, to be continually stealing the spotlight from one another.

No one but Christina noticed the look in their eyes. It was a look that always came upon them on first seeing her, because Christina looked so like Elisabeth. Always there was a leap of joy and hope, like a fire bursting into flame, and then when conscious realization set in, the flame was doused as surely as if it had been drowned in water, and disappointment took its place. Christina had learned to expect it, and to understand that her physical presence was a cruel reminder to her parents of the daughter they'd lost.

But they were actors first and foremost, and they masked their feelings in a show of bravado and parental concern. They stood beaming at her, their arms outstretched. They scooped her up, clutched her to them, and gave each of her cheeks a noisy smooch.

"My dearest daughter!" Sasha exclaimed. "I feared I'd lost you to that madman!"

Christina froze in her arms. "But not enough to ransom me back," she murmured softly.

"Pshaw! We knew he'd never harm you. Why pay out good money, when all that was needed was to call the ruffian's bluff? It has worked beautifully, as you can see. We never thought for a moment that he'd actually *dispose* of you."

Derk said, "But tell me, dearest. The ruffian didn't *really* confiscate the family pearls?"

"I'm afraid so, Father. Although I offered to ransom them back. I'm so terribly sorry. You know they meant the world to me."

Oscar put his mouth to her ear and whispered, "Apparently, they meant the world to Derk as well. He asks after the pearls, but not after his daughter's welfare."

"If you'd given them to *me*," Sasha reminded Derk bitterly, "they would be the *family* pearls yet."

"We were just speaking of your daughter's harrowing experience," Lady Wilton intervened. "Tell us, darling, is it true the brute actually *bought* a ticket and stepped onto the train like any other passenger? With you at his side?"

"Yes. It's all quite true."

"I hear his disguise was incredible."

Sasha angled a look at her daughter. "Was it indeed?"

"They say you'd never take him for less than seventy."

"Remarkable! However did he do it?" She stared harder, suspicious now.

Christina was beginning to realize her mistake in coming. The last thing she wanted was to talk about him now. In all the confusion, she would likely jumble her stories and give something away without realizing that she had. She decided her best defense was to slip into her Duchess of Wynterbrooke persona, and behave as they expected.

"Must we discuss it?" she protested. "Really, wasn't it enough to have to live through it? I was under the impression that I was to find sanctuary here tonight. Was I mistaken?"

They were appalled, but they couldn't very well insist.

"Well, of course, dear," Lady Wilton said, recovering her composure. "We are, naturally, at your disposal. Miriam is with us, all's the pity, but what could we do? She's ill, insisted on coming along. I've forbidden her to come down on pain of death, though, so not to worry."

Christina looked at her mother, who was watching her closely. The way Cynthia Wilton spoke of her daughter reminded Christina of her own mother's indifference. She didn't like the sharp look in Sasha's eyes. The woman was shrewd and could often see through Christina's defenses. She must be careful.

Lady Wilton didn't notice. She continued talking in a conspiratorial tone as the group around them began to disperse. "The servants have been sent to bed, so we may cavort to our hearts' delight. We shall help you forget the entire sordid affair!" She drew Christina aside and whispered, "I've heard the most dreadful stories about the man. About the things he's done to women. He didn't . . . ?"

They were interrupted by the butler's announcement. "His Royal Highness, the Prince of Wales."

Christina shot her friend an accusing look.

"Well, really, darling, what could I do? He was at Sandringham for the weekend, and left specific instructions that I was to inform him if you turned up. One cannot ignore an order from the Prince, after all."

Bertie descended the short flight of stairs as the crowd of people bowed down before him. He ignored them all, moving his portly frame in a dignified line headed straight for Christina. He wore the dinner jacket he'd made famous. His mouth twitched beneath his mustache as he looked at Christina, so regal and resplendent in her emerald finery. When he came to her, he extended his hand.

She put hers into it and, because everyone was watching, dropped into a curtsy.

"You're looking well for your adventures, Duchess," the Prince pronounced stiffly. "We trust your health doesn't suffer?"

"My health up till this moment has been exceptional, Highness."

He gave her a frigid look. "And what news have you of our Brighton Bandit?"

"Nothing that hasn't been repeated in the press over the last few days."

He couldn't hide his disappointment. Everywhere, people were whispering. He knew well the rumors that were circulating about the identity of the thief. But he couldn't very well come right out and ask in front of everyone. He'd hoped Christina would save him the trouble. But as usual, she stubbornly refused to give him any satisfaction.

He looked at Sasha with all the hauteur he could summon, addressing her in a lowered tone. "I must speak with you, Madam, about your deficiencies in teaching your daughter her proper manners. Perhaps, together, we might remedy the situation before it is too late."

To the others he blustered, "Well, it hardly matters, does it? We've doubled our efforts, and you may rest assured the brigand will be brought to heel forthwith."

He moved on, and when he was out of earshot, Sasha turned on her daughter. "See what you've done! You've offended him once again."

"Good. Maybe then he'll leave me alone."

"Perhaps you may afford to anger him, but I cannot. You're a fool, Christina. Any woman in her right mind would give her eyeteeth to be mistress to the Prince."

Christina raised a brow. "Indeed, Mother? Then by all means, take my place in his bed."

She excused herself and headed upstairs. She was shaking. She couldn't imagine spending the rest of her life in such senseless conversation. But what was there left for her? She'd been shown something else— something so wondrous, she'd hardly guessed of its existence—only to have it cruelly snatched away.

Oscar caught up with her at the foot of the stairs. "I've been dying to have a word with you. I can understand your reticence where the others are concerned, but you really must satisfy my curiosity."

"Oh, Oscar. Not you, too."

His usually drowsy poet's eyes blazed with a carnal light she knew too well. So he was sexually excited by the thought of being ravished by a bandit, was he? That—in spite of their friendship—made him the most dangerous of all.

"Oscar, not now . . ."

"Very well. Just answer me this. Is he or is he not Lord Wycliffe?"

"That's something," said a voice behind her, "I would like to know as well."

She turned to find a man of middle age with reddish hair and mustache. He wore evening clothes, but of inferior quality, and his shoes were scuffed, marking him as a working man.

"I beg your pardon?" she asked.

"Forgive me. We haven't been introduced. I'm Inspector Worthington, Scotland Yard."

Christina sighed. Oscar made her introductions. "The Duchess of Wynterbrooke, Inspector. And I, naturally, am Oscar Wilde."

"I've told the police everything I remember, Inspector."

"Perhaps, but I should like to hear it for myself. Surely you've heard the conjecture about the bandit's identity."

"I know little about the speculation, and less about Lord Wycliffe. I never knew the man. From what I've heard, he is dead. I can't imagine how the story got started in the first place."

"Lady Starrington knew him. She thought she recognized him."

"You mustn't forget, Inspector. The fiend is a master of disguise."

"I knew him as well." Sasha joined them with a smug smile. "He was Edward and Bridget Wycliffe's only son. I remember Lady Wycliffe well. She was a legendary beauty, in her time. All the men were after her. Her son Richard inherited her dark looks. He was quite a dashing fellow, as I recall. Dark, brooding eyes and an air of command. Quite the wit. Although, after his return from Ireland, he did little but pull pranks with the Prince, chase after women, and bury himself in his cups."

Christina's heart sank at the uncanny description. But she said, "In that case, the bandit cannot possibly be Lord Wycliffe. I've said before, he was a light-complected man with blondish hair. He looked, in fact, a great deal like you, Inspector."

The policeman turned red. He was receiving more criticism for having let the blasted fellow escape repeatedly than he cared to admit. The Prince had brought him to Norfolk for the weekend to personally put pressure on him to speed up the proceedings. With His Highness's pronouncement that they would capture him soon, Worthington was feeling that pressure keenly. The implication that he might *be* the bandit was hardly appreciated.

"And his men?"

"Ten that I could count."

"And the woman?"

"There was a woman with them," she lied. She didn't know why she'd done it, except that in the first hours of her freedom, she'd been hoping the Captain would change his mind and come get her again, and she could ride at his side. Now she was stuck with the story. "I never heard her name. She had red hair that flowed loose, and she wore a mask. I never saw her clearly." In truth, she'd manufactured the woman solely from her imagination.

He was about to ask another question when she put up a hand. "Inspector, I'm really quite exhausted. Could we speak in the morning, perhaps?"

Lady Wilton, walking by, gave Christina a knowing look. "Yes, Inspector, do let the poor girl alone. She's had an ordeal. She must rest."

She took Christina aside and whispered, "I've put you in the blue room, your favorite. And the Prince is in the red."

Christina stared at her. Cynthia thought she was making excuses so she could sneak off to Bertie!

"It was his request," Cynthia said simply.

No one knew better than Christina what that meant. Cynthia Wilton was famous for her weekend parties in which she placed everyone discreetly in bedrooms that would easily accommodate their wanderings. If the Prince was in the red room, it meant he planned to pay her a call before dawn.

On her way to her room with a cup of cocoa, she paused before an open door. Inside, Cynthia's daughter, Miriam, was propped up in bed reading a fairy tale.

"Aren't you supposed to be asleep?" Christina asked in a teasing tone.

"Your grace! I was hoping you'd come. I kept my door open just in case."

"Of course I came. Did you doubt me?"

"Well, what with all the excitement and all . . ."

"Here." She set down the cup of cocoa. "I believe you need this more than I."

The child looked ill. Her blond curls hung lifelessly, and there were dark circles under her eyes. "I prayed for you when I heard the news. Did you feel my good wishes?"

Christina stroked the child's hair. "I think I did. Thank you."

"It's awful when you're gone. No fun at all. No one else comes and talks to me the way you do."

"I remember what it was like to be a child, wishing I were allowed the festivities."

"It isn't just that. You're so good to me—to everyone, really. I missed you terribly."

Christina kissed her. "I missed you, too, lambkin."

"Everyone kept saying, 'Poor Duchess. It must be frightful.' But I knew better."

Christina's hand paused. "What's that, darling?"

"I knew you couldn't be having the awful time they said you were. Not someone like you. Why, I wagered with myself that you would be having the most fun of all."

"You mustn't say that to anyone . . . understand?"

"Of course not. Do you think me a goose? Besides, who'd believe a child? But do tell me. Was it wonderful? Was *he* wonderful?"

Christina thought back to the moment on the train when she'd seen the engineer turn on the highwayman, when she'd thought his life was in danger. She recalled her thrill at having thwarted the engineer. She could still see the fury in the Captain's eyes, feel the hard, parting kiss on her lips.

"Yes," she admitted with shining eyes. "It was wonderful." It was wonderful to admit it, to finally say it aloud.

"I knew it."

Christina put her finger to the girl's lips. "Our secret, yes?"

The girl beamed. "Of course. Perhaps someday I might find someone like him to take *me* away from all this. Even if it *is* just for a week."

Christina could hardly speak. Miriam was so much like herself as a girl. It pained her to think of those awful times, so she shook her head to clear it. "Someday," she promised, "someone wonderful is going to come along and take us both away."

"Do you think so?"

Christina nodded. "Not at the same time. You may have to wait longer than I. But someday . . . yes. I believe it."

She tucked the child in and kissed her again and headed quickly for her room.

She combed out her hair, dressed in a lace nightgown, and fastened her green-and-gold dressing robe over it. Then she went out through the French doors onto the stone terrace to look out over the gardens, to breathe the fresh night air, and to wait for the Prince.

As she stood in the moonlight, her mind reeled back over the week she'd spent at the hideaway. She could see it all so vividly. The abandoned mill, the wildflowers streaming out from the river, the churning green of the Channel. She could hear in the breeze the whispered voice of the highwayman. *I've never raped a woman in my life. I have no intention of starting now.*

But what of the Prince? He would come expecting her submission. Would he be content to be put aside like so much rubbish? Would she, having lost everything, have the will to resist?

She heard his voice behind her. "You've put me off successfully, Christina, but the time of reckoning is upon us."

She wheeled around. "Hush! Do you want the world to know you're here?"

She ushered him inside and closed the French doors. A single candle burned at the side of her canopied bed.

In the darkened room, the Prince took her wrist in his hand and pulled her close. "I've been toyed with enough, my dear. Now, I demand to know the truth. *Is he?*"

Still steeped in her thoughts, she couldn't think what he meant. "Is he what?"

"Lord Wycliffe. Is he?"

"How could he be? You killed him, I'm told."

"I thought I had." He frowned, trying to remember. "Yes. I did. I shot him. He was dying. *He was dead*, damn it all."

"Then you may rest assured."

"Rest? Lady Starrington swears on her mother's grave that it was he! How could it be? Is the fiend so diabolical that he can rise from the grave to haunt me?"

"Why this desperation, Bertie? You've never been a man to worry needlessly. It's quite out of character."

He tightened his grip on her wrist. "He hated me, I tell you. He would have killed me. It was only a lucky shot that saved me. I shall never forget the fury of those eyes. If he's alive, he will kill me, I'm certain of it."

"What did you do to him that he should hate you so?"

He looked into her eyes and saw hatred blazing in their depths.

"Don't look at me so. Have I treated you so poorly that you'd turn from me?"

"You treated me despicably. You treated me worse than your whore."

"Did you expect less? From your reputation, I assumed you'd welcome such advances. You welcomed others into your bed, and then you spat on me. If you were wounded, Christina, you brought it on yourself."

She knew it was true. "Perhaps that's why I hate only one person more than I hate you, and that is myself."

Pity filled his eyes. "Come, dearest," he pleaded. "Can't we start anew? Come. We shall forget all that's passed between us. Kiss me, Christina. Come, just one more time."

He kissed her, but she pushed him away and wiped her mouth with her hand. "The Queen is right in her opinion of you. You *are* a fool!"

He raised himself up to his full height.

"And if I were to command you as your future king?"

"Then I should be as much a traitor to the Crown as your Lord Wycliffe."

He was still for many moments, breathing hard. Then he turned on his heel. "You shall regret it, Christina. Mark my words." Angrily, he left the room.

She felt shaken by the entire experience. It had taken all her will to fight him when all she wanted was to lie down and be left in peace. She felt numb. With the single exception of her brief talk with Miriam, she'd felt nothing for over a week. She shed her dressing gown, crawled into the sheets, and closed the heavy curtains about the bed. It was cozy inside, her own private retreat. She lay back in the pillows and sighed, feeling the tension seep out of her body.

Suddenly, the French doors crashed open. She sat up. The doors banged softly against the wall in the breeze. So he was back, she thought. She wasn't to find her sanctuary after all.

She sat waiting and pulled the covers up about her breasts. "So help me, Bertie, if you force me again, I shall—"

The curtains at the foot of the bed were thrust apart. But it wasn't the Prince. Christina's gasp filled the quiet room. For there, silhouetted in the moonlight, his hair blue-black in the silver light, was the Captain. He looked as feral as a panther standing there, waiting to pounce, and his eyes were hard with fury.

"*Again?*" he snarled.

CHAPTER 14

SHE RAISED UP on her knees, and the bedclothes fell around her. In doing so, she caught her nightgown beneath her knees, pulling the lace bodice tightly against her breasts.

He moved to close the windows, but was back in an instant. "Is anyone welcome?" he asked, his voice low and dangerous. "Or just those of royal blood?"

Her gaze darted to the door. The Prince could possibly change his mind and return at any moment. But then, the Captain must have thought of that as well. Perhaps, as it was with her, the danger was the thrill.

He pulled the drapes around them, enclosing them in a world all their own. She said nothing as he moved with feline stealth across the bed, so that he knelt before her. He was so achingly handsome that her breath caught in her throat.

Taking her flowing hair in his hands, he pulled her roughly to him. "Did you enjoy your little rendezvous? Tell me, Duchess, is the pampered Prince more pleasing the second time around?"

She didn't bother to answer. His breath as he spoke mingled with hers, and she caught a whiff of brandy.

He was talking again, in that same dangerous tone, holding her face in his hands.

"Did he make you shiver as you're doing now? Did he make you tremble at his touch and cry out his name? Did he kiss you like this?" He kissed her, blindingly. "Or touch you like this?" His gloved hand moved to her breast and crushed it. Then, impatient, he gathered the delicate lace in his fingers and with a single jerk, rent it in two. Her naked breast was bared to the air for only a moment, before his hand covered it again.

"Or this?" He ripped the gown down the middle and thrust it aside. Then he circled her waist, her back, her buttocks, with his masterfully roving hand.

"Or this?" His voice was but a breath at her ear as his hand rounded her belly and moved between her trembling thighs. He removed it a moment, took the leather gauntlet in his teeth, and pulled it off. When he found her again, his hand was bare, and he could feel her, wet and ready for him.

She cried out softly, her lips parted, and slipped her arms helplessly around his neck. Her mouth sought his, and she moaned as he kissed her with fierce, insistent force.

His hand left her satin skin to tug at the fastenings of his clothes. His boots dropped with a thud to the floor. Then she felt him, hard as unsheathed steel, find and tease her so that her flesh seemed to scream at him to ease the sweet agony of her desire. She fell back into the bed, and he tumbled atop her, ravaging her mouth with a hard, irresistible passion that took her breath away.

He ran his hands along the inside of her thighs, parting them as he raised her calves to rest upon his shoulders. Then he entered her with a single, barbarous thrust. Losing control, she reached up and clutched his fine, proud head between her hands, pulling him down to devour his lips in a greedy kiss. He was so strong, so utterly different from any man she'd ever known. He was so deep inside her that, forgetting where she was, she gasped aloud at every merciless thrust.

"Tell me, Duchess. Does your Prince make your body beg for him, as it does for mine?"

Wild with passion, she still refused to deny his allegations. Instead, in a softly amused yet panting voice, she said, "I'll say one thing for you that I can't for poor Bertie."

"What's that?" he growled, increasing the power of his thrusts.

"You, highwayman, know how to make an entrance."

She'd meant to amuse him. He stilled, looking down into her eyes, and she felt keenly the absence of the exquisite pain and pleasure he'd been inflicting on her flesh. Then he grasped her head in his hands and lifted it so that she was forced to look at him. His mouth just a fraction from hers, he said distinctly, his voice sounding in her ears like the roar of the stormy sea, "You're mine, Christina. I don't intend to share you with anyone again."

Her heart burst with joy. "How," she asked him, "could there—ever again—be anyone but you?"

He kissed her again, hard but with a matchless tenderness.

"I'd despaired of ever seeing you again. How could you leave me? How?"

"Maybe I wanted to test you. To see what you might do."

"To see if I would give you away?"

"Perhaps."

"Who are you, highwayman?"

He put his lips to her neck. "Who do they say I am?"

"Richard Wycliffe."

The name hung in the air. He paused a moment, then continued kissing her skin. "Lord Wycliffe died some years back, as I recall."

"Some say he didn't. Some say he's come back to wreak his vengeance on the Prince."

"And if I were him?"

"If you were . . . then I should love you all the more."

He stopped kissing her and looked into her eyes.

She put her fingers to his lips, and he sucked them into his mouth. "I must call you something," she prompted softly.

Still, he stared.

"If I were going to betray you, I'd have done so by this time. You know that to be true."

He took her hand in his and turned it, kissing the palm. "Yes, my lady. I know it."

"What shall I call you then?"

It was a moment before he answered. Finally, he said, "Call me Richard."

"Richard," she whispered, tasting it on her tongue. She smiled. "Richard. Richard." She couldn't stop saying it.

"It's been a long time since anyone called me by my name."

"Then make me say it. Make me—as you suggested—cry it out in passion. Love me, Richard, and I shall whisper it to the heavens. For your ears alone . . ."

CHAPTER 15

THE NEXT MORNING, she announced to her friends that she was embarking for Egypt after all. They did their best to dissuade her. Not only would they miss her, but her recent adventures had heightened her glamour. Her reluctance to elaborate lent her a tantalizing air of mystery. It was clear that she had been through an ordeal, but that next morning, her face seemed all aglow. When she was present, the air felt electrified in a way it hadn't since Lady Crawfton had left society to marry a cobbler some three years before.

"You mustn't fuss," she scolded them. "I have earned my holiday, and shall have it. As to my recent adventures, you'll have to wait to hear. Perhaps I shall write my memoirs someday, and divulge all the sordid details."

Those sordid details were enticement enough for Oscar to accompany her to Dover on the train. He sent her maid away and spent the entire trip trying to extract from her the true particulars of her capture. He wheedled, cajoled, and when that didn't work, resorted to blackmail.

"I know things about you that you wouldn't want another soul to hear," he teased. "It would be a pity to have to spill the milk at this late date."

"Perhaps. But don't forget, Oscar, I know equally smutty secrets about you—secrets I'm sure your little bride-to-be would find most distressing. Your penchant for boys, for starters. And I *don't* mean your desire to father children."

He paled. "You wouldn't!"

"Certainly not. No more than you would divulge confidences of mine."

He shook his head regretfully. "You're an outlaw woman, Christina."

At this she laughed. He didn't know how close he'd come to the truth.

He insisted on seeing her to her stateroom. There, as her maid Gladys attended to the trunks, he tried one last time.

"I know there's something you aren't telling me. I know you, pet, and don't forget I was a victim of the bandit myself. And a hot-blooded fellow he seemed to me."

"You would know, of course."

"And you wouldn't? *Kindly* don't insult my intelligence. Come, what is it, dearest? Did the swine ravish you in the wilds? And if so, how *dare* you keep from me the details! Really, Christina, I had thought us the best of friends. You've said so on numerous occasions."

"You are my dearest friend. But my stay with the outlaws was mostly uneventful."

"I don't believe it. There never was a moment with *you* present that was uneventful. Something happened whilst you were away—something so dreadful, so highly charged with drama, you dare not breathe it even to me. I warn you, darling, I'm determined to discover what that might be."

"You have a poet's imagination, that's the trouble with you. Now do be a dear and cart yourself off this ship before we sail and I am forced to listen to your pleadings all the way to Egypt."

She kissed him and shooed him down the galley, then stood on the deck to make certain he was gone.

Ten minutes later, the Duchess of Wynterbrooke's maid—dressed in a brown woolen cape with her hood over her head—descended the gangplank as the last of the ship's warning whistles blasted the air. She was carrying two large carpetbags. When the steward offered to assist her, she declined, but thanked him for his offer. After seeing her mistress off, she explained, she was

heading for her own well-deserved holiday with rela-
tives in France. She would be gone most of the summer.

That said, she left the wharf and headed up the main
road. From there, she angled off onto a series of side
streets until she found herself quite alone. She looked
up to see a horseman picking his way toward her.

"You weren't followed?" he asked.

"Who would follow such an unassuming maid?"

She threw back her hood and smiled at the Captain.
He, in turn, leaned down, swept her up, and gave her a
kiss. Before their lips had parted, they were giggling.

"Oscar called me an outlaw woman," Christina told
him gleefully.

His eyes flicked over her. "Well—an *outlaw's* woman,
at any rate."

He took her bags, dropped his foot from the stirrup,
and reached down to help her. Putting her foot in his
stirrup, she took his arm and swung herself up behind
him.

In the act of picking up the reins, he suddenly
checked himself, pivoted in the saddle, and stared at her
a moment. Putting his hand to her cheek, he rubbed her
cheekbone with his thumb while his gaze roamed freely
about her face.

"Richard—"

"Hush." His fingers moved to her mouth. "Let me look
at you a moment. I'm not certain I believed this day
would ever really come."

His hand slipped into her hair, and he kissed her hesitantly, as if expecting her to vanish under his touch.

"We'd best go before we're detected," he said reluctantly, still watching her. "The men are close by, waiting
in the woods. We've an extra horse for you there."

"Let the bags have the horse," she told him. "I prefer
snuggling up to you."

He turned his back with a smile. She put her arms
about his waist and held him close, savoring the feel of
him. Then he kicked his horse into a canter, and they
clattered away over the cobblestones and out of town.

•   •   •

They spent the afternoon down the hill from the hideout, along the banks of the river. He lay on his back, his arm thrown across his eyes to block the sun, and she lay at an angle from him with her head upon his chest, glancing through a small Gaelic dictionary she'd spotted at the mill. It was peaceful there, listening to the ripple of the water and the warble of the birds. A peaceful respite from the men's animated chatter because of her return.

"This Irish seems a strange language," she commented. "I speak English, French, Italian, Spanish, and Greek, yet I can't seem to pin down the pronunciation." She flipped another page. "Oh, here's a perfect word to describe me. *Fiaran*. To leave home in a huff, to go awandering. How simply delicious!"

He took the book from her and tossed it aside. "Enough studying," he announced.

"You'll offend your men. I suspect they left it there for me, after the loan of *Wuthering Heights*. I must say it was sweet of them, to want to share something of themselves with me."

"You've won my men over," he told her, idly picking wildflowers and placing them in her hair. "No woman has done so before."

"They know I have a good eye for stolen goods."

"They know their captain is enamored of you."

There was a sleepy, sensual look in her eye as she smiled at him. "Are you, indeed?"

"Do you doubt it?"

"I should be a fool to doubt it now, when you've risked so much to have me at your side."

"I'd risk that and more just for the feel of you." He ran his fingers through her hair to muss it, continuing a path to her neck, her shoulder, along the length of her bare arm. Then he lifted her hand to his mouth and kissed her fingers one by one. "Do you know what it's like to have you touch me?" He flattened her palm on his cheek and guided it over the angular planes of his face. "I haven't been touched enough in my life. My parents were distant to me, crippled by their own failings. My mother lived in her own private prison. She didn't have the wherewithal to sufficiently suckle a child. And my father—" His tone turned bitter. "He was a soldier who never expressed feelings of affection. I had no one to teach me the delicate art of touching and being touched."

"And when I was touched—"

"What, love?"

"It was . . . horrible."

He waited for her to explain. When she didn't, he went on in a lighter tone. "Then we both have much to learn. But I warn you, it will take time. And practice. A great *deal* of practice."

She rolled onto her side and looked down at him with dancing eyes. "I'm certainly willing to help. In fact, I shall gladly touch you till the end of time. But tell me . . . since you seem to have the cure so close to hand . . . where, pray tell, should we begin?"

"What about here?" he suggested, guiding her hand over him. "And here . . . and here . . ."

Soon they were laughing as she fought to touch places he restricted from her eager hands. She won out in the end, opening his breeches and pulling him out into the afternoon sun. There she revered him with heartfelt kisses and caresses, nibbling her appreciation as he swelled beneath her touch.

"This fellow seems accustomed enough to such sport," she observed, giving him quick feathery licks as she spoke. "From the ease with which he accepts this, I should say it was *other parts* of your body that were neglected."

He chuckled in spite of himself. "Would you care to know what I love most about you?"

"I wasn't aware you loved *anything* about me. Is this a confession?"

"Your mouth, Duchess. I love your mouth. I love the wicked words that come tumbling from it with scarce a thought. You're the only woman I've ever met who could match wits with me."

"Oscar says the same thing," she announced saucily, before taking him once more between her lips.

He gasped. "But unlike Oscar," he continued in an increasingly guttural voice, "I have a deep appreciation of your mouth's *other* talents."

"Oh? For instance?"

"Delicately speaking, you're a deliciously oral woman."

"Oral . . . as in precision of speech?"

"Put more succinctly—"

"I wish you would."

"I love the willingness of your mouth to wander about my person without—favoritism of any kind."

"And what exactly does that mean?" She was enjoying teasing him. She knew damned well what he meant.

"It means you don't seem to care *what* you put in that luscious mouth of yours—which pleases me no end. But tell me, Duchess. Did your mother not warn you not to put strange things in your mouth?"

She fondled him with unabashed delight, gliding her tongue along his shaft in a long, slow, moaning swipe. "What," she asked, "is so strange about this?"

Her hand joined her mouth and soon he could speak no more. As he erupted beneath her, his hand shot to the back of her head. She took all of him, never pulling back, relishing his pleasure as if it were her own. When he was finished, he collapsed his head back in the grass and spread his arms limply out to his sides.

"My God, you're good!"

"Been touched enough for one day, have you?" she teased, wiping her mouth on the back of her hand the way a gunman might blow at a smoking gun.

He took a few minutes to recover, then swiveled his head and looked at her, pensively this time. "Now that I've got you, what shall I do with you?"

"I've been thinking about that."

"Oh, no."

"You mustn't groan. My idea in regards to the train was a smashing success. Toby tells me you made away with a remarkable amount of goods."

"It's not your ideas that make me groan. It's the unpredictability of your behavior along the way. Your daring is something I admire as much as your lips. But the trait that I so revere also gives me a cold fright. The thing I truly love most about you is my greatest liability."

"Meaning?"

"Meaning you might very well have got us all killed with that little stunt."

"Putting the bumbershoot to the man's back?"

"Precisely."

The mood changed so abruptly that she needed a moment to adjust. She leaned into the stream and took a drink from its rushing, icy depths. Still reeling, she glanced back over her shoulder at him and said, "Surely you can't be serious!"

He was buttoning up his breeches. "By doing so, you made yourself conspicuous when I gave strict orders that you were to remain unobtrusive. I had kidnapped you only the week before. Did you think they wouldn't know who the woman with me was?"

"I attended to that, remember? I told the authorities a woman rides with you. I should think you'd thank me for the job I did with the police. Leading them astray with a false description—"

"Did I neglect to thank you?"

"That engineer was going to ambush you, in any case. Would you have me let you die to save my reputation?"

"You endangered your life and the lives of my men."

"Yes. And I saved yours."

He met her gaze, then pulled her down to lie in the crook of his arm. "What *am* I to do with you?"

"I shall tell you. I've an idea that's so daring, so utterly reeking in perfection, that even you will see the inevitability of it."

"And what is that?"

"We shall rob Bertie."

He stilled. "Rob . . . ?"

"Steal directly from the Prince of Wales. In disguise, naturally. I've brought some things that will render us unrecognizable. And I know his schedule down to the last minute. He never varies it. Paris in the spring, back to London for early summer, Cowes for yachting, Homburg for the cure, Scotland in autumn for shooting, then back at Sandringham in Norfolk for Christmas. I can even tell you which weekend he will spend with which friend. He lives off his friends, you know. Never has enough money of his own to support his pursuit of pleasure. Since Victoria refuses—and rightly so—to give him any authority, he masks his frustration in a frantic attempt to spend his friends' money and enjoy every depravity life has to offer. Why, he even borrowed thirty thousand pounds from me to pay off his gambling debts! He won't be carrying much money on his person when we stop him. But then, we're not after money with Bertie, are we? Just think, Richard, of the fun of taking his purse as all the while he's struggling to see if you *are* who he thinks you are. It's absolutely irresistible."

"Yes," he murmured, staring off into the distance. "Irresistible."

"And I shall have my revenge upon the wretch once and for all. I should enjoy smiling to myself every time I meet him henceforth, knowing that I lifted his purse without his recognizing me."

"I have to admit I enjoyed my disguise the other night. I'd never thought of it before, but I find it appeals to me."

"You see? I have much that I might contribute. More than you know."

His tone softened. "You contribute more than I can express. But robbing the Prince . . ."

"You can't seriously tell me *that* doesn't appeal to you!"

"Oh, it appeals to me enormously. In fact, I'm ashamed I haven't thought of it before. But understand, Christina, if we do this, it's to be looked upon as a highlight of my career. It will take meticulous planning, and we can leave nothing—absolutely nothing—to chance. In fact, it will be the most dangerous job we shall ever pull."

She could hear the mounting excitement in his voice. "Then we shall do it."

He looked at her. "I'm not certain *we* shall do anything of the sort."

"Please don't disappoint me by becoming stodgy at

this late date. You can't leave me out of it. Not when it was my idea."

"Can't I?"

She took a steadying breath. "Now *you* understand this, Richard, and understand it well. I'll be *hanged* if I shall pace the floors of this mill one more night while you and your men go romping off to wild adventures. Particularly when they involve the Prince!"

" 'I'll be hanged,' " he warned with a twinkle in his eye, "is not a phrase we use in this camp."

"And 'I'll stay home' is not a phrase I shall use. Ever!"

"What an interesting choice of words, Duchess. Do you consider this your home?"

She rolled onto her stomach and looked down at him. His eyes were narrowed green-and-grey slivers in the sunlight.

"Tease me all you like. Only tell me I might go. You shan't regret it."

He regarded her closely a moment. "Have you no moral qualms about what I do?"

"Qualms? About pilfering Bertie of his pocket change?"

"No. About robbing people of their possessions."

She thought about this. "I suppose if you were stealing from the poor, I should have strong objections. If I thought someone would lack food for the table because of you. But as far as I can see, you steal from those who can well afford it. I have friends—second and third sons of noblemen with no birthright to inherit—who make a game of living beyond their means without ever paying their debts. I can't see that that's any different. And God knows, you don't spend the money on yourself. A good pair of riding boots and an exceptional steed is all the extravagance you seem to have allowed yourself. I can only assume you have a noble reason for doing what you do."

"I've told you before. Burden me with no such romantic notions."

"Then what *do* you do with your plunder?"

He grimaced.

"Well . . . ? Here's your chance to prove me wrong. By all means, if you can, burst my romantic image of you."

"We . . . send the goods to America, where they are sold for cash and used to provide—things of use for those in Ireland." He was clearly uncomfortable.

Something her mother had said registered now. Edward and Bridget . . . "You're Irish, then?"

"My mother was Irish. My father—" He broke off for a moment. "My father was an English earl."

"He met your mother in Ireland?"

"He was in Ireland to squelch the rebellion."

"I see. So now you *help* the Irish by stealing from your father's people. I scarcely see what you would call noble, if not that."

He stiffened. "I'm no Robin of Locksley, if that's what you mean."

"Robin Hood could scant do more than you. Robbing from the rich to help the poor."

"I assure you, my motives are far from altruistic."

"What are your motives, then? You seem bent on shattering my illusions, yet you've told me nothing that would do so. If you mean to frighten me away, I warn you. You shall have to do better than this."

He thought it over. "No. I'm not ready to tell you. I think if you knew, you'd demand to be taken back to St. James's Square. I'm not ready to relinquish you just yet. Having gone to all this trouble to fetch you, I'd like you with me for a little, anyway."

She softened her voice. "I shall be with you longer than a little."

A deep sadness clouded his eyes. "That, love, is something I don't dare hope for."

"Richard, I wouldn't have come if I had any intention of deserting you at this juncture. I may, as you attest, be unpredictable, but I am loyal to the last battle. I demand an opportunity to prove it."

He considered. "Before I take you on a job as important as robbing the Prince, I shall have to test you first. See if I can truly trust you."

"Anything. I shall do anything. And I shall prove to you that I can carry my own."

He ran a hand along her temple. "We shall see."

They were quiet for a moment. She bent down and kissed him because she couldn't help herself. "My mother remembers you. In fact, she had more glowing things to say about you than she's ever had for me. How dashing and handsome you were. How devastating to the ladies. That sort of thing."

He grinned. "You make it difficult to hate her."

"Give me time. She also said you were once a friend of Bertie's."

Once again, she felt his withdrawal. "Yes," he admitted finally. "We were once the best of friends."

"He must have done something horrible, that you would spend your life spiting him."

He said nothing.

"I know because I hate him, too. He did the one thing no one else has ever done: he made me feel ashamed of myself. I understand that you hate him, only . . ."

"Only . . . ?"

"Only, I have to wonder why."

He sat up, pushing her away. With his back to her, he said, "Tread softly with your questions, Christina. There are things a man is dread to reveal."

This was quite a blow, coming as it did on the heels of his earlier intimacy. "Even to the woman he loves?"

"Even so."

She was hurt, but she swallowed it with difficulty. He had said he was testing her. He would tell her his secrets when he was ready, when she'd proven the worthiness of her trust. No one knew better than she how the Prince could wound, even as he loved.

She straightened her shoulders. "Very well, highwayman. It's to be business between us, is it? If you want to test me, why not do so at once? If you want a nice— haul, do you call it?—I have an idea that will not only warrant you a great deal of money, but that will, I daresay, satisfy your sense of adventure as well."

It was a moment before he turned to her, and when

he did, the anguish was wiped from his face. He looked at her with hooded eyes before moving on her and lowering her with his weight to the ground. Pinning her there, he asked, "When, Duchess, did you ever get the idea it was to be business between us?"

CHAPTER 16

As ALWAYS, THERE were five or six young boys from which to choose. Those Lord Malverton dismissed would be sent away, disappointed, for another week. If they were particularly anxious, they'd be allowed to stay in hopes of another customer. But on busy Saturdays, Lord Malverton was generally the only candidate. Other gentlemen with such proclivities scattered their visits throughout the week, when there was less likelihood of their specialized tastes being discovered by mutual friends.

Madame Bignourcy's house in Chelsea was constantly looking for new prospects on Saturdays, for Lord Malverton craved variety above all else. The Madame herself sorted through them beforehand, then displayed her finds for the earl in a private back room just off the servants' stairs. There were two among tonight's bunch that he fancied. One, a particularly young lad, had sandy hair and lean, spare hips. The other, older but no less appealing, wore a cap and walked with a decided swagger. His features were delicate—almost as dainty as a girl's—and his sharp eyes were a brilliant forest green.

The sandy-haired youth appeared nervous, while the fellow with the cap seemed particularly eager to please. This was hardly remarkable. Lord Malverton came to Madame's weekly to quench his thirst for young boys, and he paid the lads—and Madame—exorbitant fees. Youths often fought to win his favor, knowing the money they pocketed would feed their families for months to come.

The choice was difficult. While the green-eyed lad had a come-hither look in his eyes that would tempt Moses himself, there was something utterly mouth-watering about the snake-hipped lad's nervousness. The Earl loved initiating boys into the world of his making. It gave him such a wonderful feeling of accomplishment!

He was a man of fifty years with a most substantial girth, not tall, with pink fleshy cheeks, silver curls, and muttonchops that nearly connected at his chin. He was known far and wide as a gourmand, and as such was an especial friend of the Prince, who enjoyed little more in life than a fabulous rich meal. The Earl circled the youths, waddling a little as he walked, caressing his thick lips with his tongue as though perusing a banquet table piled high with puddings.

At length, he chose the inexperienced boy. With a short jerk of his head, he guided the youth up the back stairs before him. As he was closing the door on the rejects, something happened that had never transpired before, and that caught him—and Madame—completely unaware. The green-eyed baggage had the audacity to come running after him, tugging on his coattail! "You don't want him, gov'na," he cried in a high-pitched Cockney voice. "He can't satisfy you the way I can."

The Earl turned his grotesque frame and stared at the lad. Madame rushed forward in a swirl of French perfume and pulled at the boy's shoulders. "How dare you, you leetle ruffian. I shall expel you from my establishment *sur-le-champ*!"

Lord Malverton looked down his nose at the presumptuous pup. "Had I wanted you, my impertinent lad, I would have said so in the first place."

Madame pulled at the boy's arm again, but he broke free and ran up the stairs behind the Earl. "But might I interest you in . . ." He reached up and whispered in the astonished Earl's ear. Slowly, Lord Malverton's face changed from outrage to one of intense interest. The scamp had just offered to perform his most favorite— and most shameless—erotic act. The Earl studied the boy's face with a puffing out of his fleshy cheeks, and raised a hand to Madame Signourey.

"I find, Madame, that I have chosen hastily." With another short jerk of his head, he scooted the first lad back down the stairs. As he passed, the boy shot a look of hatred at the young interloper.

The winner tugged once again on the Earl's coattail. "Wouldn't you like to give him somethin', gov'na? For the disappointment, I mean. 'Tis a cruel disappointment, losin' out on the likes of you."

"What the devil?" The Earl took out a half crown and flipped it to the first boy, who caught it and, fearful that he might change his mind, raced down the stairs.

"I apologize, my lord," said Madame. "This is *most* irregular. This scapegrace will be punished suitably."

"Let's wait on the punishment, shall we? Until I ascertain whether or not the disruption was worth the trouble."

The youth turned and stuck his tongue out at Madame before scampering up the stairs behind the Earl.

The room was elaborately decorated in deep blue and gold. Christina, dressed as the young scamp, had been in such places a dozen times before. But never Madame Signourey's. This was a specialty house that dealt only in the most taboo perversions, anything the bored aristocracy might dream up to while away their evenings. Madame was particularly famous for her set of twin girls who engaged in incestuous foreplay for the amusement of certain honored guests. Though Christina had never been here before, she'd heard all about it from Oscar, who had also told her the most intimate details of Lord Malverton's tastes. It was because of these stories that she'd known the right enticement to offer.

She put her hands in her back pockets and swaggered about the room, looking it over with a cocky eye. "Right fancy place you've got, gov'na."

"Beg pardon?" He was undeniably distracted, watching the youth move about with a sexual confidence he'd seen only in the world's most skilled courtesans. "Oh, that. Well, it's hardly my place, is it? Now, what was it you were saying . . . ?"

"By your leave, let me disrobe you, m'lord."

Now that she'd fought for her place with him, it was strictly a matter of killing time before the highwayman could burst through the door and attend to the lifting of Lord Malverton's considerable purse.

She stripped off his clothing with care, taking her time about it, yet teasing him enough that he never lost interest. "You're an interesting lad," he commented, watching. "Almost as frail as a girl."

"There's nothin' frail about me, gov'na, as you'll soon see."

It was difficult, undressing him. Like the Prince, Lord Malverton was of a girth that gave testament to his goodly appetites. Christina could not have spanned his waist with her arms if they'd been twice as long.

But soon enough, he stood before her naked and hairy. She cast a covert glance at the door. Nothing yet. It was rather a sticky situation. She was loath to go too far, and the Captain was likely to have his own ideas about what was appropriate and what was not. She suspected he might view her "participation" as being beyond the call of duty.

"On your knees, lad," the Earl suggested.

Slowly, she dropped to her knees before him. He moved toward her and Christina sat back on her heels.

"Is your bark better than your bite?" the Earl asked. "I warn you, lad, I shall pay for nothing save what I was promised."

"Then why waste time with this?"

It seemed to the Earl that the lad's voice had altered slightly, but he was in such an aroused state that he scarcely gave it a thought.

Christina stood, took his hand, and led him to the bed. There, with a playful grin, she bent him over so that he was facing the bed, supported on his hands. This provided her with a generous view of his backside. Again, she cast a glance at the door.

Before she could move away, he began to grope between her legs. Suddenly he gurgled and threw himself around so that she was thrown back from him.

"You! You have no pecker at all! Why, you're a—"

Just then the door opened. A tall man with curling brown hair and freckles, dressed in an ill-matched suit and a bowler cap, poked his head meekly into the room. He recoiled at what he saw and said in a meek voice, "I'm so dreadfully sorry. I seem to have found the wrong room."

The look of horror had frozen on Malverton's face. "Well, off with you, bloody cur, to find the right one!"

Instead, to the Earl's amazement, the intruder stepped inside and closed the door behind him.

"That's no way to speak in front of a lady, my lord," he said in a deep and deadly voice.

As the Earl, fully naked and feeling at a distinct disadvantage, was digesting the sudden change in the man's voice, the meddler stepped over to the counterfeit boy and took her elbow in his hand, helping her up.

Then he moved with a swiftness that was mind-boggling and put a pistol to the Earl's temple.

"Why—" sputtered the Earl, "why you're that Brighton Bandit, are you not?"

The Captain bowed with a flourish. "At your service."

"And this—this—"

"Lady?" Christina supplied, looking up from rummaging through his pants.

"Who are you, you harpy? You had me fooled right enough."

The bandit put an arm about the Earl's throat and jerked it hard, choking him. "I shall warn you once again, Lord Malverton. Take care in how you address my lady."

"Lady!" spat the Earl, in spite of the tightening vise of an arm. "If you'd like to know what your *lady* was about to do before you came in—"

Enraged, the Captain raised his pistol high to bring it down on the Earl's head. Anticipating this, Christina went to him and put a hand to the gun to stop him. She looked into Lord Malverton's eyes.

"In answer to your question, *gov'na*, they call me . . ."

she thought quickly "... Fiaran. And you're right, my lord. I am no lady. I should dearly love to see your tongue cut out and strung upon a pike. You'd find precious little satisfaction with your fresh striplings after that, I'll wager."

She went to the chiffonier, shuffled aside some corsets, and brought out a pair of silk stockings. One she twisted and slipped into his mouth, knotting the gag with a savage tug. The other she used to tie his hands behind his back. Then she fetched two more stockings. The Captain shoved the Earl back into a chair, forced him to spread his knees so that he was exposed to anyone who might come to his rescue, and used the stockings to secure his fleshy ankles to opposite legs of the chair.

Christina took up the velvet bag into which she'd placed the Earl's valuables, and tossed it to the Captain.

"A hearty thanks for the contribution, lord," he said with another bow. "I can't admit to enjoying the view, but it's been a most—*enlightening* evening."

He pocketed the loot and stuck his head out the door to check the hall. Christina backed out of the room, giving the Earl a jaunty salute and affecting the Cockney accent once again. " 'Ave no fear, gov'na. Your secret is syfe with me!"

She would have run, exhilarated, down the stairs, but the Captain's hand at her arm restrained her. Casually, as if they were satisfied customers, they descended the stairs and headed for the front door. They had to walk through the parlor where Madame's girls paraded themselves before the pampered swells. Christina paused. "A pity," she whispered, "to allow all the rest of those riches to go to waste."

"The secret of success," he whispered back, "is knowing when to quit."

An hour out of London, in the midst of a gallop, the highwayman reached over and took her reins in his fist, pulling her up beside him. The horses, caught off guard, stumbled into each other, but the Captain held tight to the reins and soon they were stopped.

Confused, Christina looked askance at the men who were loping off into the night. "Let them go," he said. There was a note in his voice that made her shiver.

He led her off the road, deep into the woods. Then he stopped and peered at her through the darkness.

"Just what was it you were doing to my lord Malverton when I made my auspicious entrance?"

She laughed. "Is that all? I thought it was something serious."

"I am quite serious."

"Well, I didn't do it, did I? Only gave the impression I would. Besides, it suits your purposes that I'm considered not quite a lady. Would you have them suspect that a duchess rides with you?"

"What—*exactly*—was it you didn't do?"

"I don't know that you'd want me to tell you," she said coyly. "It's one of the most intense sexual experiences known to man—or woman, for that matter."

"I think, given the circumstances, that I'm entitled to know."

She looked back at him a moment, then dismounted. "Very well. Step down," she said.

"I beg your pardon?"

"Come along, Captain. Step down here."

He dismounted. She went to him and began to unbutton his pants. He caught her wrist in his hand.

"What are you doing?"

"Do you care to know what Lord Malverton wished me to do?"

"You know I do."

Their caper had excited her greatly. She stood on her toes and put her lips to his. "Then, my lord highwayman, do stop your fussing and allow me to show you. That is, *if* you're game . . ."

CHAPTER 17

❧

$\mathcal{T}$WO MORNINGS LATER, when Bobby brought the London papers, Christina was infuriated to see their escapade wasn't mentioned.

The Captain gave her a droll look. "Given the nature of the crime, you'd hardly expect Malverton to confess it, would you?"

"But it's such a pity! It was so inventive. You'd think they'd give us credit for originality, at the very least."

He smiled. "I daresay you've inherited a craving for publicity to equal your parents'."

"That's a despicable thing to say!"

"True, nonetheless."

Since coming back to the camp, Christina had unpacked her things and put them in the loft, but she slept with the Captain. He had fashioned a shelter of branches downriver from the mill, deep in the woods. That way, if anyone were to find the camp and attack, he could sneak upon them from behind and thwart their efforts. At first, Christina thought he was mad, sleeping, as he did, virtually under the stars. But after the first restless night, she came to love the open air, to appreciate the endless night, to cherish the time spent lying snug beneath the branches in the highwayman's arms. In time, she even grew accustomed to the sun in her eyes, awakening her at dawn.

"Fancy the Duchess of Wynterbrooke," he'd said the first night, "sleeping in the hay, and in the arms of a hunted criminal, at that. What would people say?"

She'd looked him in the eyes and told him solemnly, "I've done many more ignoble things than this, my love. In fact, sleeping in the arms of this particular criminal is the first thing I've done for quite some time that has made me feel . . . clean and . . . whole."

He'd gathered her in his arms and held her close. "That a woman like you," he'd said in a haunted voice, "could love a rogue like me . . ." He'd woven his fingers into her hair. "At times . . . it feels like a miracle. At others . . . it's too frightening even to contemplate."

When he was like that, she just held him close, waiting for the panic to subside.

Now they lounged about their little shelter in the mid-morning fog, scanning the papers and drinking coffee and tea. In the days they'd been together, they'd affected an easy, loving affinity, and they were enjoying each others' company immensely. "What's next?" she asked, putting away the disappointing papers and lying back in their bed of straw.

"Oh, I was thinking we could go out on a few jobs. Something simple. Just to get you initiated. I shall be planning for the Prince, and would prefer to put my head to suitable use. Not wasting it on . . ."

"Rehearsal?" she supplied.

"Exactly. I shall count on you to be a good girl."

"I shall be the *best* girl you've ever had, highwayman," she teased. "But I don't yearn to dress as a boy. It's rather tedious, once it's been done, and I've done it quite a lot. Not to mention unattractive."

"Malverton seemed to find you attractive enough."

She ignored this sally. "I've an idea for a costume I should like to make. In fact, I brought along everything I need. It's simply a matter of taking the time to create it."

He was amused. "You thought of everything beforehand, did you? Tell me, was it when you saw me standing at your bed in Norfolk that you commenced your planning?"

"No, love. I had other things on my mind at that moment."

"Say my name the way you did that night."

"Richard," she whispered.

"The way you say it is like a sexual advance." He sucked her upper lip into his mouth.

"I thought we had work to do," she reminded him.

"So we do." Nibbling her lip with his teeth one last time, he reluctantly forced himself away. "Make your costume, then. I shall require a few days of planning in any case. Dare I ask what you plan to masquerade yourself as?"

"I think you dare not, actually."

"Then you may surprise me. Incidentally, *Fiaran* . . . you've called yourself by a verb. *Fiaran,* as you may recall, means *to* leave home in a huff and go awandering."

"Oh, I did, didn't I? Oh, well. Too late now."

"Not exactly. It's clear Malverton isn't talking."

"No, but I like my *nom de plume* the way it is. I never was one for conventions. Since I possess the temerity to cast myself as an outlaw woman, I shall call myself by a verb if I bloody well choose."

His eyes were gleaming. "I always did appreciate a woman with a mind of her own."

She stretched over and kissed him on the jaw. "Good thing, I'd say."

The weather turned gloomy, with periodic fogs and afternoon rain. It was just as well, for they had no jobs planned, and they would need the rest. The Captain and Christina saw each other only at night. She stayed in the loft and sewed all day while he sat in the shelter, with a canvas tarp on top to keep out the rain, and planned the jobs ahead.

By the time they were finished, the men were restless. They'd had enough of playing whist for matches and wanted some action. Even when Christina taught them baccarat—which they considered a scandalous game— they soon tired of it and spent hours looking out the window, waiting for a break in the weather.

On the fourth day, they were rewarded. The sun broke through the clouds, and in the course of the day, the muddy roads began to harden.

It was time to go. The night of their first ride, Christina came down at the last possible moment, dressed in her costume. It was made of a deep purple lightweight wool to ward off the chill of the night, so dark that it was almost black. She'd chosen the color purposely to thwart the Prince. Purple was considered the color of royalty, to be worn only by the royal family.

The outfit consisted of a tight-fitted jacket and a slim split skirt that would allow her to ride astride a horse with ease. The neckline, front, shoulders, and sleeves of the jacket were intricately decorated with black braid and strips of jet beads, so they swirled when she moved, catching the eye. Her boots were black suede with jet tassels peeping provocatively out from beneath the short hem of her skirt. The costume hugged her body like a second skin, accentuating in a most sensual way her bosom and the flare of her hips. In a day of wide bustles, it was unheard of to see so much of a woman's natural curves. She'd completed the disguise with a flowing red wig and a wide-brimmed, feathered hat that slanted rakishly over her right eye. Covering her eyes was a purple mask, exotically embroidered with jet beads, so that her eyes, shaded as they were, took on a mysterious and captivating depth.

The attire was hardly the fashion of the day, but she was accustomed to the theater, and delighted in the stagey feel of it. She spread her arms and took a turn before the men.

"Great day in the mornin'!" Bobby cried out in the astonished silence of the room.

"Holy Mother of God," Toby echoed.

Michael was speechless. The Captain was giving her a fierce frown.

"I shall have to pop the eyes of my men back into their skulls," he drawled. "I do hope you've thought of a way to keep their minds on their work."

"I have," she said breezily, pulling on a pair of black-tasseled gloves. "If they pause to think what you *assume* they are thinking, you will simply have to kill them."

The men cast appalled eyes at their Captain. He, in

turn, gave them a sardonic grin. "Yes," he murmured. "That, I imagine, should be incentive enough."

They went on a series of routine jobs over the next week, robbing trains, holding up coaches outside of London, crashing a boat cruise of youngbloods from Oxford out for a bit of sport. The primary goal was to acquaint Christina with every conceivable situation that might occur in their robbing of the Prince. In every case, Christina made her presence known, but a warning look from the Captain served to keep her in line. She was conscious of the need to be on her best behavior. If the Captain was forced to worry, she knew he would withhold his permission to go on the one job in which she most longed to participate.

Still, they acquired a number of goods on these outings, and more cash money than was their norm. Christina teased the Captain about being his good luck charm. "You will have to keep me with you forever, at this rate," she quipped.

But he only grew grimly silent when she spoke of the future.

It wasn't long before the papers were as full of stories about her as they were about him. The *London Times* called her "The Bandit's Bride," and *Society in London*, one of the best-informed sources of social gossip, carried a sketch of her under the headline: BRITISH BELLE STARR.

The execution of the jobs, as well as her growing notoriety, excited Christina profoundly. She thrilled at reading of her exploits in the press, at mulling over the speculation as to whom she might be. Her costume was remarked upon, and her legend grew with each printing. Her beauty, it was said, had a bewitching quality, one that lured men into a spell so that the Brighton Bandit might more easily perpetrate his crimes.

"It would seem," she told him one day, "that I am indispensable to you."

"So it would seem."

It was a sunny afternoon, warmer than most. They sat at the edge of the river, dreamily tossing bluebells into the water. The men had fixed the waterwheel so that it turned in the river by the mill, squeaking and splashing pleasantly up the hill. Christina listened with a faraway look on her face. She was in a thoughtful mood.

"Those books you gave me," she asked him. "Those penny dreadfuls. Remember? Where did you come upon them?"

"In America."

"Were you there long?"

"Four or five years. Enough to learn a thing or two."

"How to rob trains, for instance?"

"For one instance."

"Toby said you used to captain your own ship. To Ireland?"

"Yes."

"From here, then to America, then on to Ireland?"

"In my younger days."

She could tell by the clipped tone that she was treading on dangerous ground. She switched tactics.

"Did you enjoy America?"

"Very much. Particularly the West."

She said nothing, watching him, waiting for him to offer more.

At length, he began to speak. He told her of his travels across endless prairies, of mountains unsurpassed in all the world, of pioneers who gave up hearth and home for an uncertain future and a dream. He told of meeting men she'd never heard of, untamed men with names like Bat Masterson and Kit Carson and Billy the Kid. And he spoke of Indians forced onto reservations, and buffalo killed not for their meat but for their hides. Of the forgotten bones of men and beast littering the great wide plains.

"It was the space I relished," he continued, looking down the long corridor of his memory. "The sense of freedom. No one asked questions about where you came from or who you were. No titles. No pretensions. A man proved himself by his deeds, and not his family name."

She was so moved by his eloquence that she felt she could see in her head the things he spoke of. Still, she teased gently, "Such talk, coming from the Earl of Wycliffe."

He gave a snort. "Even if they knew I was alive, I daresay they'd rescind the title. Not that I'd miss it. But an enemy of the Crown could hardly be expected to take his seat in the House of Lords."

"Your quarrel, it seems to me, is not with the Crown so much as with the Crown Prince."

"My quarrel is . . . complicated."

She took his left hand in hers and fingered the ring he wore on his small finger. It was an old Irish coin, mounted in gold. "You always wear this. Even when we make love. I can feel it cold against my skin when you touch me. Where did it come from?"

He picked more bluebells, but said nothing.

"It's a woman's obviously. Should I be jealous?"

"Don't be absurd."

"I hardly think it absurd to wonder about whose ring you wear on your finger, when you won't so much as utter her name."

"It doesn't matter. It was a long time past. It's nothing to concern you."

"Everything about you concerns me. Don't you know that?"

He dropped the flowers in the river and watched them float away. "Yes. I suppose I do."

She threw back her head, looked at the sky, and took a deep breath of air into her lungs. "We should marry, you and I," she said unexpectedly.

He leaned back on one elbow, watching her but saying nothing.

"We could think up some story to expain why you've been doing all this—something to please Victoria, who has little respect for Bertie anyway. And we could apply for dispensation and have you dubbed a duke in my husband's place. There are precedents, certainly. It has a rather nice ring to it . . . Richard Wycliffe, Duke of Wynterbrooke."

"Like your father?"

"It would hardly be like my father, who was a commoner when he met Mother. Certainly, I would have no reason to throw it in your face, as Mother does. I scarcely care for the beastly title anymore. I coveted it only to make Mother jealous."

"Yet you desire that I be a duke."

She laughed. "It does all seem rather silly, doesn't it? But what do I care for my duchy? I shall be a countess happily. Christina Wentworth-Gibbons . . . no, Christina Wentworth-*Wycliffe*. *Countess* Wycliffe. It's not bad, really. I would take a demotion in rank—to be with you."

"There's an old Irish saying, 'If you want praise, die. If you want blame, marry.' "

"The Irish, it would seem, have old sayings for every conceivable situation."

"And what would we do, you and I? Settle down to raising our pigs and mending our fences and planting our spring crops—?"

"With me? My dear man! Now who's being absurd? We should—travel the world. I haven't seen half the places I'd like to. America, for one. You could take me to see your beloved West. I should like to meet some cowboys and saloon-girls and such. See for myself if this Wild West you've painted so vividly for me really exists."

He was watching her with lazy amusement showing in his eyes. "You fancy cowboys, do you?"

"Rather. Now that you mention it. I should like to see *you* in a sombrero and spurs."

He laughed. "You read those books, I see."

"Every last word. In fact, if you've more, I should like to see them. They're fascinating reading, really. Though without the depth and emotion of *Wuthering Heights.*"

"Naturally."

"Shall we, then?"

"What?"

"Marry. I married one husband for spite and the other for a title. It might be fun to marry for love for a change."

She'd said it offhandedly, but once said, the words echoed like birdsong in the early summer air. She lifted her eyes to his and felt his gaze burn into her own.

"We'll never marry," he said, more quietly than the whisper of the wind.

"Why?" she gasped.

"You must try to understand. I have no confidence in my ability to love you truly and well. I have, in fact, no reason to believe I can love at all."

"I don't believe that, Richard. You've done a splendid job of loving me thus far. Either that, or you're a better actor than both my parents put together."

She could see his struggle to find the proper words. "Much as I might long for it, the thought of the closeness we might share—should I allow it—is a frightening prospect. I've hurt women before. Worse than I could ever tell you. The truth is, I've hurt everyone I've ever known. I find that the thought of wounding you is more than even *my* black heart can bear."

"Nonsense, Richard. Have you a wife stashed away somewhere? It's the only excuse I shall accept."

A shadow of a smile crossed his face. "No, my love, I've no wife—stashed away or otherwise. Do you fancy me a Rochester to your Jane Eyre with a mad wife locked away while I promise home, hearth, and children to you?"

She was silent for many moments, her eyes cast down. "I can't have any children," she confessed hesitatingly, as if it were a long-buried secret. Distracted from his own dark brooding, he waited for her to explain. At last she did so, her face etched in pain. "It was why the Duke married me. He was in his seventies, and his wife had died years before without leaving him an heir. He knew why I married him. He knew I didn't love him—I had told him so quite honestly before the nuptials. But I vowed to him to be a good and true wife. I didn't know why he was marrying me. If I gave it any thought, I supposed he relished the idea of a young and popular wife on his arm."

She paused, closing her eyes and rubbing her temple to ease the sudden stab of pain. "He didn't tell me until our wedding night. He came to my bed, loved me with all the tenderness he had to offer, and then—beaming, mind you—told me he hoped we'd conceived a child. I wanted to cry. But I couldn't. All I could do was watch his face crumble as I told him the truth. I never would have married him if I'd known, I swear, title or no. I offered to annul the marriage, but he was a gentleman and refused. He said he'd made a bargain and he intended to abide by it. If I would accompany him on his infrequent outings so that he might be proud of me, I was free to do whatever I chose, as long as I was discreet. Proud of me, he said! I thought I might die of shame. I wanted to, certainly. Every time I looked into his eyes, I couldn't help but think how I'd destroyed this poor, dear old man's last hope for a child."

"That's when you set out to—"

"To acquire my scandalous reputation? Yes. That's when. Only it never worked the way I'd intended because, of course, everyone else was doing the same thing, and as far as all the snobs and swells were concerned, since I was now a duchess, I could do no wrong. But every time I dallied, I sought to punish myself. I took my pleasures and turned them into retribution. But it was never enough, because I still had to look into Wynterbrooke's eyes and see what a selfish and mindless fool I'd been. That was the real punishment. Until Bertie came into my life and helped to kill the poor man with his abuse."

She pulled up a handful of spring grass, then flung it angrily away. "Now you know."

"Why can't you have children?"

She'd known he was going to ask, and she'd been dreading it. Even though it came from him, she felt devastated by the question. Explosive, sick insecurity welled up inside her. It was something she'd never told anyone—not even Oscar. Nor could she bear to remember it now. Even her love for the Captain couldn't chase away the horror of the memory.

"I'd rather not discuss that, if you don't mind. It's not that I don't—"

She stopped, realizing how useless it all was. It's not that she didn't—what? Trust him? Love him enough to tell? How could she explain it? She longed for him to divulge his secrets, but when it came to this—the thing that had haunted all her days—she couldn't oblige him. Embarrassed, she put her face in her hands.

He was still for a long time. Somewhere, a lark sang and the warm wind rustled the leaves of the trees. Presently, he reached over and took her chin in his strong hand, forcing her to look at him.

"I don't need you to give me children. Or marriage. Or your damnable title. I just need you to be here with me now—while you can."

"But for how long, Richard? For how long?"

He looked off into the distance, away from her questioning eyes. "I'm a wanted man, Christina. For as long as it lasts."

CHAPTER 18

*I*T WAS GENERALLY agreed that Christina's presence in the camp was having an astonishing effect on the Captain.

"Whatever do you mean?" Christina asked when this fact was put before her. She was in the midst of one of her many Gaelic lessons, with Bobby, Toby, and Michael laughingly correcting her pronunciation. She hoped to surprise the Captain by learning how to speak the language.

" 'Tis the enjoyment he's havin'," Bobby tried to explain. "He's a tortured man, the Captain. I'd venture he had nary a day's amusement till your ladyship joined us. 'Twas a lonely and dirty job, no doubtin' it."

"That first night in Green Park he didn't strike me as a man grimly bent upon his work."

"Well, he's a flamboyant type, the Captain. He can't help the way he be, but he found little satisfaction, I'll warrant ye that."

"What he's tryin' to say," Toby supplied, "is we've been with the Cap'n these many years, and we've yet to see him happy. Till now, that is."

"Are you saying," Christina asked with a smile, "that I make him happy?"

"Well, now, it ain't *our* lovely pusses."

"That I have put the fun back into his work?" she pressed.

Bobby was grinning, but Toby, older and more attuned to human nature, was thoughtful. " 'Tis a dangerous thing," he muttered, "for an outlaw to be too happy."

She was reminded of his assertion several days later when the Captain dropped into his seat and stretched out his long legs, propping his boots upon the table. He clasped his hands behind his head, leaned the chair back so that the front legs came off the ground, and sat grinning at her as she sipped her tea.

"Well!" she exclaimed. "To what do I owe *this* cheerful mood?"

"Care to have some fun?" he asked.

She sat upright. "We're to rob Bertie!"

"Presently. But I fancy a masquerade first."

She looked at him suspiciously. "You're up to something dreadful, I can tell. Well, do be quick, man! Don't keep me floundering in suspense."

"Is it not true that the Cavendishes hold their annual masquerade ball on the thirtieth of June?"

"It is, in fact, one of the highlights of the London season."

"And is it not further true that the Prince of Wales is invariably a guest at this spectacular affair?"

"It is."

"Tell me . . . when does he arrive?"

"Late. Never before eleven. He insists on being the last one there, in order to make his entrance. Everyone's expected to ensure their arrival beforehand."

"Is it likely that he might arrive early . . . say at ten instead?"

"If he did, it would throw the Countess—and everyone else—into a dither."

"It might be fun at that. Does the Prince dress for the ball?"

"He never dresses, always comes as himself. Although he particularly loves to try and guess who's who beneath the masks. Why do you ask?"

"Because I should like you to disguise me as the Prince."

It was a moment before she could digest this. "As the Prince?"

"Exactly. So that not even Victoria herself could detect the difference. Can you do it?"

"If you're asking if I'm capable of it, I believe so. For Othello, I completely reconstructed Father's face, giving him a protruding brow and a great hulk of a nose. God knows I have every inch of Bertie's face emblazoned on my memory. But if you're asking if I think I *should* do it—"

"Actually, I'm asking nothing of the sort."

"What exactly would be the purpose of this deception—I'm afraid to ask."

"Are you?"

"What?"

"Afraid?"

She searched his face a moment. "Of you showing up at the Cavendishes' masquerading as the Prince of Wales?"

His eyes lit at the prospect.

"My God, you're courageous!"

He grinned. "Stop flattering me and tell me your opinion."

"It's frightfully dangerous. You should have to fool people not only with your looks but with your voice and demeanor as well. You will have to play your role in the true sense of the word, by *becoming* the Prince. If anyone should suspect, I'd hate to think what would happen."

He screwed his face up in a good imitation of Bertie and, looking down his nose, cried, "What! No lobster? Egad! What *has* this wretched world come to?"

"That's good," she admitted thoughtfully. "You sound like him. You'll need coaching, though; it's a bit hammy."

"Then you're convinced I can pull it off?"

"It's possible. If I coach you night and day. But it isn't just the surface mechanics that concern me. You should have to pretend to know people who will be looking to you for favor. It wouldn't do to be overly friendly to those with whom the Prince is displeased. How long has it been since you've been in society?"

"A good five years. And before that, I was in Ireland."

"Things have changed in five years. What with the influx of the monied classes into society, there are more members than ever before. There are bound to be people you've never met or even heard of . . ."

"I've thought of that. It isn't a consideration."

"The masks will help, of course. And they don't allow the dogs in the ballroom, which is a real blessing. They'd be sure to growl and give you away."

"I shall merely make a game, as you suggested earlier, of guessing who is beneath which mask. Things can't have changed too much. As I recall in my drinking days with the Prince, if he inquired about a lass's identity, he received nothing less than the full life's confession and her more than eager willingness to make—or keep—his acquaintance."

His words left a sour taste in Christina's mouth. "No," she conceded. "Things haven't changed that much."

"Then?"

"It's terribly daring."

"And as such . . . ?"

"As such, I adore it. Only, if you're caught—"

"I shan't be caught."

She studied him a moment, the fine, bold, handsome lines of his face that she would have to bloat and redden to make him look like the Prince. "Does it not unnerve you a little to reenter society after so long an absence?"

"Unnerve me? No. If it weren't for the fun of the masquerade, and the thought of the look on the Prince's face, I can't say, however, that it would strike me as a particularly pleasant prospect."

"Why not? I mean, I know why I dislike society at this stage. It reminds me too much of a past I'd rather forget. But I'm not certain I understand your grievance."

"You said it yourself. Society is more of a sham than ever before. It used to be that the aristocracy decreed themselves the country's betters, and more capable than anyone else to run the country. My father, your Duke— they were all a part of that society because they were the ones with seats in Parliament. Balls used to be little more than political meetings in fancy dress. Now, with the Prince's influence, the emphasis has shifted. It's not government they revere now, but money. Every Tom, Dick, and Harry with enough capital to squander is allowed within the ranks."

"It's true," she agreed. "All it takes to crash into society these days is enough money and ambition. My husband's dukedom was passed down through seven generations. Nowadays, dukedoms can be bought if one has the money to purchase enough land and throw enough parties. Why, remember the Grenvilles? I hear they bought up most of Buckinghamshire in the early century in order to gain themselves a dukedom, only to crash into financial ruin once they had achieved it."

"Soon enough, it won't matter. The aristocracy is a doomed race."

"Doomed?"

"A dying breed, just as the Indians are. And do you know the instrument of the aristocracy's death? The railroad. The great leveler. Once, the aristocracy rode about in coaches befitting their station. You could tell at a glance who was who, and the masses were suitably impressed. For a while, it looked as though the railroad might continue the tradition. It used to be that a young noble could order a special train so as not to rub elbows with the 'riffraff.' But these days, the trains wait for no one, noble or not, and a duke is forced to ride in first class side by side with a prosperous merchant. It's changing the way this country thinks about their so-called betters, that they can hop on a train and enjoy the same luxuries—or lack of them."

"And so you chose that same instrument—the railroad—to wreak your vengeance."

"Just so."

"You've made me feel rather sad."

"Why?"

"I don't know why exactly. Except that you're talking about everyone I know. My family, my friends. I should hate to think of myself as living amongst the dead. Or worse, being one of them."

"Pay attention at the Cavendishes'. Take a good look this time. Look at the plump, overfed, atrocious women in their drab finery who have little to say except to mouth platitudes. 'Isn't the weather warm? Wasn't the punch divine?' Listen to your grand lords and see if they ever speak of anything important. Or even interesting. They're so inbred that they're beginning to resemble one another. Look at the greed, the corruption, the unabashed lack of moral fiber. They're so proud of the orderly way in which Victoria's empire is run. No war. No chaos. They have their clubs, their committees, their estates, their routines. You said it yourself once. They go to church on Sunday, then spend the rest of the week chasing after other people's mates. Take a hard look, Christina. Then you tell me if this is a race you'd have survive the test of time."

"But it's your race as well."

"Only half. I have no quarrel with my English blood. Only with what the aristocracy do with their privileges. Simply put, they're bored and boring. They have money and position, but they no longer hold the reins of power. They're being replaced by manufacturers and men of money, and few of them even realize it. They give themselves such airs, but there isn't one of them that has a tenth the sophistication that I see possible in you."

"And what, exactly, do you call sophistication?" she asked.

"The ability to see others' points of view. And to learn from them."

She was silent for a moment. Richard had never before spoken so seriously or at such length.

"Very well, I shall endeavor to see your point of view while at the Cavendishes'. In which case, we had better get to work. We've precious little time, and a great deal of work at hand. I shall have to send Bobby to London for supplies. Being one of those spoiled aristocrats you so disdain, I can't, after all, be expected to accomplish a miracle on country goods," she finished, a teasing smile on her lips.

·   ·   ·

The Cavendish ballroom was ablaze, as it was every year, with sparkling chandeliers. Sumptuous music, enough steaming food to feed an army, and guests decked out in gaudy and outrageous finery filled the room. No fewer than twelve footmen were there to greet the guests, a sign of true affluence. These footmen, it was well known, were chosen for nothing more than their height (six feet) and the shape of their calves, which must look spectacular in the striped leggings that were part of the Cavendishes' peach-and-gold livery. Since there were no other qualifications, except for greeting the guests and showing them to their carriages later, footmen were notorious for their drinking, and already some of them were swaying noticeably on their feet.

Christina entered nervously a little before ten to the familiar aroma of the Cavendishes' famous tea roses. She'd taken pains to hide her identity. She'd padded her bosom and wore a crimson velvet gown that hugged her bodice enticingly and molded itself along her breasts, her ribs, her wisp of a waist, then flared out in a wide bustle to fall gently at her feet. The top was sleeveless, the straps of the gown fashioned by strips of paste diamonds the size of robins' eggs. These jewels glided over her creamy shoulders and rounded the low back of the gown. A scattering of the brilliant gems throughout the folds of her skirt created the illusion of the twinkling of stars as she moved. She wore an ice blond wig piled high about her head and laced with similar paste diamonds, and a crimson-and-white mask with smaller diamonds framing the exotic wings of a butterfly that fanned out into the tendrils of her hair. As she handed the butler her crimson-and-ermine cape, she felt the eyes of the crowd on her. She waltzed through them, disguising her walk, bowing mysteriously then gliding quickly away before anyone could engage her in conversation.

Along the way, she heard snippets of gossip. "Velvet? In summer? Why, how inventive!"

"She looks for all the world like a fairy princess!"

None of the women present had been as inventive as she. Her gown was elegant, romantic in its conception, simple yet dramatic in its styling, and more French than English. As she looked about the ballroom, she saw a drab lack of imagination. Many had come as historical figures, Cleopatra, Marie Antoinette, and Joan of Arc being favored. Their costumes were either dull and lacking in imagination or fussy and far too opulent, and the women were squeezed into them, speaking breathlessly the way a lady does when her corset is too tightly strung. The men were little better. They came as French courtiers in powdered wigs or as medieval English knights. A particularly corpulent gentleman was dressed appropriately as Henry VIII. Three separate lords, she was amused to see, had come in costumes similar to the highwayman's—black cape, gloves, hat and mask, although they lacked the dash and innate sense of stylish simplicity that she so admired in the Captain. While original and daring in her own designs, she had never been overly fond of fussily dressed men—Oscar Wilde not withstanding.

The smell of roses mingled with the scents of perfume, of roasted venison, of syrupy strawberry tarts. The music wafted through the hall, soft enough that guests could hear themselves speak, yet lilting enough to encourage the dancers who swayed and dipped their way across the floor. Christina circled the murmuring crowd, trying to catch bits of conversation from behind the masks.

The women spoke in hushed tones, neither very witty nor lively as they discussed their usual subjects:

"Wasn't the river *gushing* last night? Simply gushing!"

"Isn't her gown exquisite? I must know her dressmaker."

"How sad it is that his lordship's cold is no better."

Others were discussing their children or their roses, some food, their health, or seasickness, which they genteelly called *mal de mer*, in such a serious, sensible way that Christina moved on, too bored to linger.

The men, when not voicing the customary political platitudes—"How rousing the Prime Minister's speech was!"—were more interested in sport. Sport was a duty to be taken with the serious devotion of war. The months spent in London for the season were torture to the English country gentlemen to whom fox hunting, polo, and pigeon shooting were the active pursuits of their lives.

Christina, of course, had grown up among all this, but she'd had the added excitement of the theater. She'd expanded her knowledge with serious reading. And she'd generously bestowed the benefit of the doubt upon her neighbors and friends. Because she was intelligent and educated, she'd endowed them with the same qualities. Now, recalling the Captain's words, she had a sinking sensation that he was right in what he'd said. They did look to be an overfed, overspoiled lot with little to occupy their minds or their time. It was, perhaps, the reason Christina was so popular. She stirred them up with her intellectual sense of fun, made them feel alive for the short time she was in their presence. The qualities she'd attributed to her friends were simply, she could see now, reflections of what she herself had to give.

It was a decidedly depressing thought. For it made her realize more than ever that if it weren't for the highwayman, she'd have nowhere to go back to.

The clock struck ten. Suddenly, the trumpets blared and the butler made his announcement. "His Royal Highness, the Prince of Wales."

A gasp swept the room. Never had the Prince been known to arrive at such an hour! The nobility, cloaked in their finery and hidden behind masks as they were, were nonetheless thrown into a panic. It wasn't customary. What were they to do? They were still bustling about it when the Prince made his entrance.

Christina looked up and stared at the overstuffed, flaxen-haired, bearded Prince, noting with satisfaction that no trace of Richard Wycliffe was left open to detection. She had done her job superbly. Still, all at once her heart was hammering in her breast. She could almost taste her fear. She tried to calm herself with the knowledge that she had managed what she could. Now it was all up to him.

CHAPTER 19

*H*E WAS DRESSED with meticulous care, in the height of evening fashion. This was a crucial point, for the Prince was known for his demanding taste in and fondness for clothes. Anything less than the best and latest fashion would have given the secret away.

He handed his top hat to the butler without so much as a glance, but kept his white gloves on. His hands—long, slender, strong as flint in contrast to the fleshiness of Bertie's paws—were impossible to diguise, and thus it had been decided to avoid any opportunity for recognition.

It was a moment or two before the crowd could settle itself and adjust to the startling revelation of the Prince's untimely arrival. As they did, those seeking favor rushed forth to bow or curtsy and exchange pleasantries. The Captain had spent tireless hours rehearsing his role, and he did those hours justice now. Gone was the flamboyance, the boldness, the wit. Greeting the throng, he exuded just the proper touch of quiet dignity, a trait the Prince was known to favor as befitting his station in life. He could carouse with the best of them, but would always retreat into the royal dignity that he considered separated himself from other men. Watching him, Christina's heart swelled with pride. Bertie could not have played himself as brilliantly as the Captain was doing.

She looked carefully to see if anyone might be suspicious. Far from it, they were throwing themselves at him in a pathetic attempt to please. Once, an older lord had bankrupted himself and allowed the Prince to make a complete fool of him, and when asked by Bertie if he didn't mind, was heard to say the fateful words, "As Your Royal Highness pleases." Since then it had become the catchphrase of the day. Anything Bertie wanted, these people would rally round to provide.

As if reading her mind, he requested a glass of wine, and one young swell dressed as Lancelot scurried off to oblige. When handed the silver goblet, the Prince raised it high and with a solemn and rather dull stateliness, toasted the health of his friends.

Christina was keeping a careful eye on him when another young noble, dressed as a page and obviously less engaged by the Prince, asked her to dance. It was the last thing she cared to do, but she dared not protest and make herself conspicuous, so she relented

He took her in his arms and began to spin her around the room. As they danced, she looked back over her shoulder, attempting to keep the Captain in her sights.

"You're the talk of the ball," her partner told her.

"Hmmm? I beg your pardon?" She was barely listening.

"I say, you're all anyone can talk about. Rather like Cinderella, what. Every man here begs to know the identity of such a divine creature."

Belatedly, she realized he was talking about her. "Oh!" she gasped, tearing her mind back from the Prince, who was chuckling quietly within a group of admirers. She lowered her voice to a breathless whisper. "Then you must call me Cinderella, by all means."

His arm tightened about her waist. "Mightn't you entertain me with a confession?"

She flinched in his arms. "Confession?"

"As to your real name. I should carry it to my grave—or at least till midnight, when we all unmask."

He was much too close. She tapped his chest with her crimson-gloved finger to move him away and chuckled low in her throat. "You shall have to wait longer than that to make your discovery, I fear."

There was barely time for his disappointment to register before another man took his place. For the next few minutes, one man after another lined up and tapped the one who was dancing with her on the shoulder, bowing his apology for dragging him away. There were young men and old, most recognizable by their voices, their jewelry, or their scents. Lord Darton smelled perpetually of lemons, and Sir Roger spoke with a lisp. Every one of them followed the same routine, cajoling her with various enticements if she would only reveal her secret. As more wine was consumed, the enticements grew increasingly more suggestive as their hot, shellacked breath consumed the air. She was invited to the terrace, to the drawing room, to take a stroll in the gardens. Each she treated with as much mysterious silence as was possible, all the while undertaking to keep her eyes on the Prince.

She had a moment of horror as one young man, obviously proud of his abilities on the dance floor, whirled her about so that she came virtually face-to-face with Oscar Wilde. He was weaving his way through the dancers in an attempt to reach the refreshments. Dressed in a parody of his beloved ancient Greeks, he carried a lily drooping in his hand. It was a Jersey lily. Christina stiffened at the sight. The lily had been the trademark of the Prince's ex-mistress Lillie Langtry. She had since gone on to become an actress in her own right, touring the world and leaving brokenhearted lovers in her wake. Although Christina uncharacteristically despised the woman who had taken society by storm and considered herself Christina's rival for Bertie's affections, Oscar would insist on singing her praises.

Someone stopped him right in her path and asked him about the topic of his present speaking tour. This impromptu question launched Oscar into one of his favorite speeches. "Modern pictures," he said, striking his lecturing pose, "are no doubt delightful to look at. At least, some of them are. But they are quite impossible to live with; they are too clever, too assertive, too intellectual. Their meaning is too obvious, and their method too clearly defined. One exhausts what they have to say in a very short time, and they become as tedious as one's relations."

Inwardly, Christina groaned. At this rate, he would be there all night. Hastily, she excused herself from the arms of her partner and made her way across the room from her friend. Even in the throes of eloquence, he was sure to recognize her, and she couldn't take that chance. Not tonight. Not with so much at stake. So she hurried away and, to her dismay, found herself cornered with a group that was paying homage to—of all people—her mother.

Although Sasha was the smallest woman in the group, she was without a doubt the most commanding. She was dressed as Desdemona in the very costume Christina had fashioned for the role. She wore a long white wig with a gold headband and gold sandals on her feet. The costume was daring, meant only for the stage. It was typical of Sasha to wear it to a party, where, naturally, it would be remarked upon. She was masked, but her famous voice was unmistakable.

"But you aren't serious!" one woman was crying. "Can you get away with such a thing?"

"I don't see how we may be prevented," Sasha said in a superior tone. "It's done. We open within the month."

"But what will the Prince say?"

"What *can* he say?"

"A great deal, I've no doubt," said one man. "After all, this bandit has made a plague of his life for the last year. I should think the very idea of your glorifying him on the stage should gall His Highness no small bit."

"I should think just the opposite," predicted Sasha. "In fact, I should think the fact of thousands of people watching the reenactment of his crimes night after night should be a great inducement to the authorities to bring the beast to justice. Furthermore, I deeply resent the notion that I should try and *capitalize* on the brute. He did, after all, molest my own dear daughter."

"But what roles will you take? Does the bandit molest you in the play? Forgive me, darling, but I can't see you as a victim in this thing."

"A victim? Good heavens no! Derk, naturally, plays the bandit. *I* play his accomplice," she announced.

"His accomplice?"

"This mysterious woman who travels with him. This Fiaran—although who would call herself by such a name, I'm sure I don't know. I'm told it's Irish. One can never tell about the Irish, can one? But I shan't spoil it for you by revealing the plot. For that, you must come and see for yourselves. And just wait till you see the costumes! My dears, I have never been so scandalously attired. A pity poor Christina is off boating down the Nile. I daresay she would have enjoyed taking part in this production, and wreaking a bit of revenge for her treatment at the bandit's hands."

"What are you calling it?"

"*The Bandit Bride*. Isn't it divine? Oscar Wilde helped us with the play. Well, after all, he too was accosted by the man. Just wait till you hear the dialogue he's concocted for us. Derk and I are producing it ourselves. We shall make an absolute fortune! I do believe we shall run for a year!"

By now Christina was seething. It was bad enough that her mother was exploiting her lover in order to increase her fortune and her fame—but she was, albeit unknowingly, playing the part of Christina as well. And with Oscar's help!

"Madam, I protest!" said a man in the group. He was masked, but Christina immediately recognized the voice as that of a former prime minister.

"Protest?" cried Sasha. "Upon what grounds?"

"Upon the grounds that you are, by producing such a travesty, contributing to the romanticization of crime. Why, it's little better than the 'Newgate School' of writing, which the critics have decried for so long, which turns the criminal into a dashing, romantic figure and distorts the true facts out of all proportion."

"Don't be absurd, my lord. You know perfectly well that one can find a critic to support any preposterous point of view. Why, there are those critics who count our old friend Charles Dickens's *Oliver Twist* amongst the Newgate School of novels."

"And he protested that indignation with his dying breath. He told me himself, 'In *Oliver Twist*, I have drawn my criminals in all their deformity, in all their wretchedness, in all the squalid poverty of their lives; to show them as they really are, forever skulking uneasily through the dirtiest paths of life, with the great, black, ghastly gallows closing up their prospect, turn them where they may.' I shall never forget it. He felt strongly that he had stripped the very glamour from crime. While you, madam, I don't doubt, endeavor to glorify it by portraying your hero as—"

"As the audience would like to see him, and as I have been told—by those who have come upon him—that he is. If truth is to be told, then it will be told to the best of our ability in this play. If we prevaricate, then let the brute come forth and tell us so," Sasha said with dramatic emphasis.

There was general laughter. Christina, able to bear it no longer, turned away, only to see the false Prince coming toward them.

Her first reaction was to sneak away. But it was irresistible, his coming upon such a group which, of all in the room, was equipped to spot a fabrication. Sasha prided herself on being able to detect an actor from a hundred paces. And the minister was well known for his powers of observation. Even as Christina's breath caught in her throat, the defiance of it thrilled her.

When they saw him, the conversation came to an abrupt halt as they bowed and curtsied in turn. The Prince bent over the ladies' hands and gave a curt bow to the gentlemen. "As always, I'm at a disadvantage on such an evening," he greeted. "Do allow me to indulge in the pleasure of guessing your identities."

"You're most welcome to try, Highness," said Sasha.

"Oh, but you cheat me. You, dear lady, are unmistakable. Who would not recognize the first lady of the English stage?"

Sasha preened under the unexpected praise while Christina bristled. As if sensing her discomfort, the Prince turned to her.

"And who," he asked, "is this bewitching creature?"

They hadn't spotted her, but now they turned and stared. She felt the heat of her mother's gaze and wanted to back against the wall. From behind her, the page who had first asked her to dance came up and made the reply. "No one knows, Highness. She calls herself Cinderella. We've been trying to ascertain the truth all evening."

"Perhaps if she would consent to a waltz, I might have better luck," suggested the Prince.

Suddenly, Christina wanted to laugh. Suddenly, she was having a wonderful time. To dance with her lover in full sight of her mother, and Oscar, and every other friend she had in the world . . .

"As Your Royal Highness pleases," she said with a graceful curtsy, careful to maintain her whispery tone. He extended the back of his hand in the same regal way Bertie did, without questioning that the woman to whom it was offered would take it without hesitation. Christina did so, and as they moved away from the group, she heard her mother ask, "Who, indeed, is she? And *where* did she get that garish gown?"

It was too much. Christina began to laugh, in spite of her awareness that all eyes were turned their way. The Prince took her casually in his arms, and together they began to move to the music.

"If you don't stop laughing," the Captain warned, "you will do the Prince's reputation more good than harm. The eyes of the room are upon us. Everyone will wonder what His Highness could be saying that so enchants such a lovely maiden." His hand beneath the glove was virile, his arm at her waist sure and possessive.

"Aren't you wicked! Do you always tempt fate so spectacularly?"

"Always."

"You make me tremble. I never thought I should say this about our friend the Prince, but tonight, he brings to mind any number of the most passionate ruminations."

"Now who's being wicked?"

"I find I can't forestall it. The thought of us dancing in public—under everyone's noses! And of them knowing tomorrow who we are and why we're here. I find that, bloated as you are, I can hardly keep my eyes from you."

"Then I shall warn you to caution. Don't forget, Cinderella, why we're here. The time escapes. I intend to cut it down to the last possible minute, but I shall need your help. I'll not have you turn to a pumpkin when I need you most."

"You've only to command me. I shall do anything you ask of me." The words were innocent enough, but there was a sensual undertone to her voice that implied a different sort of willingness.

"Wayward vixen. Stay with me for a few minutes more."

He'd meant for her to stay focused on his plans, but she deliberately misunderstood him. "Have no fear, Highness. I intend to remain with you much longer than that."

"Then listen to me. The timing could mean the difference between life and death. I want you at the windows from here on. Any gentleman who requires your presence on the dance floor is henceforth to be disappointed."

"Ah! So it's jealousy that prompts this tempting of late!"

"Jealousy be damned. Are you listening?"

"With bated breath, darling."

"Stay by the windows. At my signal, open them wide and race out onto the terrace. Bobby will be waiting in the garden with the horses. If for any reason I'm not beside you, you're not to wait. Is that clear?"

"Why don't we leave now? I can suddenly think of much more exciting things to do than play out this charade."

"Just a bit more, love, and we shall."

She looked up at him, trying to detect his face beneath the makeup. "You're up to something. I can feel it. Why is the timing so crucial?"

"Can I not tend to business without a barrage of questions?"

"Not if I'm to be part of it. No. On second thought, I

think perhaps you're right. Perhaps it's better not to know. If what I'm thinking is true . . ."

"Don't think it, then."

So it was true. "Very well . . . I shan't."

In that moment, the music, which had seemed little more than a background hum, took on a life of its own, floating through her like an unforgettable fragrance. Her senses were heightened. She could feel the floor beneath her slippers, feel the vibrant strength of his arm at her back. She could smell the greasepaint, see the readiness in his eyes. Her body tingled with her awareness of them, and their position, and their danger. She'd never wanted him more. It was all she could do to keep from touching him, from kissing him, from tasting his flesh. She looked up at him, and from behind the mask that hid her eyes from everyone save him, she let her love for him shine through.

"I adore you, do you know that? I've never loved a man before. It's the most bewilderingly joyous feeling I've ever known. I find that I can scarcely contain my pride in you, or my delight at being by your side. You were so very right in everything you said. About these people, this world. There's nothing for me here. Not after knowing you."

He swept her with a gaze that was a strange mixture of grateful tenderness and a tortured despair.

"Then I've done you no favor."

"I forbid you to say such things. And I can, you know. Don't forget, I outrank you. Even if you do look so damnably like the Prince. My God, but I long to strip off this padding and run my tongue along your belly—"

He checked her abruptly. "Hush. Here comes the Inspector. Remember, now . . . the windows. If you do your part well, I may consider your proposition."

"Oh, Captain!" They stopped dancing, and she curtsied low. "I thank Your Highness for his kindness."

He bowed over her hand. "The pleasure, I assure you, was mine." Then he turned to Inspector Worthington as she moved away. "Ah! Inspector. Just the man I was hoping to see. What news have you for me of this bandit?"

The Inspector glanced about to make certain no one was listening. It was clear from the animation of his eyes that he was feeling heady with confidence. "I believe we've come up with a plan to flush him out, Highness. One I'm sure you'll approve."

"Do tell, Inspector."

"We're to set a trap for him."

"A trap? How ingenious."

"Yes, we have every confidence in the plan. We shall bring him out into the open, where my men will be waiting. They will outnumber his, and the result will be inevitable."

"You intrigue me. What's your plan, Inspector?"

"He seems fond of trains. As you know, Lord Yarnbrooke's sister is being married in Dover over the weekend. We thought to post an announcement in the press stating that his lordship is visiting his sister and taking with him as a wedding gift the emerald necklace that belonged to Marie Antoinette. If ever there was a bait sweet enough to tempt the bandit, this is it."

"Interesting. Did it really belong to the late queen?"

"Humph! How should I know? He claims so, but every fish in the brook holds the same claim, doesn't he now? In any case, the necklace is a magnificent piece, and should draw the ruffian. Naturally, Lord Yarnbrooke will be replaced by one of my men, and the rest of the passengers will be special agents to Scotland Yard."

"Naturally."

"Then you approve?"

"Approve? I applaud your confidence in divulging the plan to me, Inspector."

"Well, naturally, sir."

Just then, there was a commotion at the entranceway. The butler, it seemed, was having words with one of the guests. Lady Cavendish herself went forth to hush the disturbance, only to stop dead in her tracks and squeal her horror. For there, in the doorway, was yet another Prince of Wales.

The trouble had started when the confused butler couldn't decide whether or not to make a second announcement. The ball was a masquerade, but after all, it was heinous to assume that someone would come costumed as the Prince. And if so ... who was the *real* Prince?

Groups of guests wandered over to see what the fuss was about, only to come up short in a similar reaction to the Countess's. A shocked silence swept the room. As one, the guests turned and stared at the man they had assumed was their Prince, and then back again at the newcomer.

"What goes on here?" asked the latter, and real, Prince. Then he spotted the impostor, who was inching his way backward toward the open windows. "Good God!" he gasped.

The impostor gave a rakish grin and offered a jaunty salute. In his best regal voice, he called, "You're late, Highness. We started without you." Then, without skipping a beat, he turned to his hostess. "My apologies for this hasty retreat, Countess, but I feel assured you'll understand. You will have my thanks in the post for a most entertaining evening."

Christina was standing by the windows, her heart beating so rapidly that it had immobilized her. Everyone else in the room was in such a state of shock that none had yet thought to move. The impostor took quick advantage of the situation by heading for the windows with a speed and agility that further startled the crowd because of his apparent bulk, taking the mysterious lady's elbow in his hand, and steering her out the windows to the terrace. There, he leapt over the balustrade and helped the lady climb over. Her skirts caught for a moment on the stone, but he yanked them loose and helped her onto the horse that another man had brought.

By now, the crowd had come to life. The Inspector, red-faced with shame, rushed to the windows, shouting orders for the capture of the impostor. By the time they reached the terrace, it was too late. The three riders had cantered off into the night.

The Inspector could feel the noose closing around his throat. "After them, all of you," he bellowed. "Any gentleman who can ride. I want them caught, do you hear? Tonight! Now, off with you."

There was another moment in which the gentlemen exchanged horrified glances. "Any gentleman who could ride" included every English gentleman up to the age of seventy. They were proud of their horsemanship, even manic about it, but it was hardly their intention to leave the comforts of one of the parties of the year to go traipsing through the countryside in the dark in search of God only knew who.

Still, the Prince was fuming, and it wouldn't do to insult him by refusing. With one word, His Highness could destroy social positions they'd worked for years to attain.

So they rallied, horses were brought round, and the costumed aristocracy mounted up and rode off in hot pursuit. As he was exiting the ballroom, the shamefaced Inspector paused before the Prince to express his heartfelt apologies. "We shall have him in your hands tonight, Highness, you have my word!"

"Worthington," spat the Prince, "you worthless pup! What are your assurances to me?"

After which the Inspector retired to his borrowed horse and swore under his breath that this bandit, whoever he was, would be forced to pay dearly for this humiliation.

CHAPTER 20

$\mathcal{J}$UST OUTSIDE OF town, the Captain gave the order to pull up. "I want the lady kept out of danger if at all possible. We shall split up. You men take the south road and try to head off the pursuers. Under no circumstances are you to lead them to the camp. We shall head for Wayburn Hill and meet you later."

No time was squandered on questions. Already, they could hear the dogs close behind. The Captain came up beside Christina and motioned for her to mount behind him. She did so, and he tossed the reins of her horse to Toby. "Take the mare. If they get too close, let her go. It will distract them for a few moments and give you precious minutes that you'll need. The dogs will complicate things. Cross water whenever possible to throw the scent. Go quickly now, and Godspeed."

Christina gripped his shoulders, as his waist was now too ponderous for her arms. They leapt off into the night, and she could hear the others heading away. The ride through the darkness was a blur. They raced through the trees, down hills and across meadows, all the while being fiercely pursued. If some had followed the men, a goodly number were still close behind the one horse. Christina knew she should be frightened, for if ever they'd been close to capture, it was now. But she couldn't bring herself to doubt the Captain. She couldn't conceive of him in anything but a triumphant situation. She didn't believe he could be caught. Her faith in him and his abilities was so great that she began to laugh, and the sound of it carried with the wind.

"What, pray tell, can amuse you at this tender moment?" he called back to her.

"I just thought of our fine country gentlemen in their tights and masks, racing through the night to fetch a phantom. I almost wish it were daylight, so I could witness the sight."

She didn't know where they were going, and she didn't care. It was glorious, dashing for their lives, splashing through streams and jumping fallen logs that threatened their path. She leaned her cheek on his back and felt the flexing of his muscles as he maneuvered the steed over the riotous terrain.

She hadn't thought to retrieve her cape, and she began to shiver from the bite of the wind. Moving closer to him, she tried to absorb his warmth. She could still hear the dogs, howling as they ran. Once, she thought she heard a gunshot, but she felt dislocated from the reality of the evening, and couldn't be sure. All she could feel was the exhilaration of the chase.

Presently, they passed a series of estates. "Hold tight," the Captain warned, before kicking the stallion over a fence. Christina nearly lost her balance, but the thought of the consequences—of what he would think of her—made her hang tight. They galloped across a field, scattering startled horses in their midst, and up a gravel drive to a barn. He rode directly inside before swinging his leg before him and sliding down in front of a startled older groom.

"Why—why, Your Highness!" the man gasped.

The Captain had nearly forgotten his disguise. "No, Bern, it's the Captain. We've need of sanctuary. Take care of the horse, if you would."

"Why, Captain, sure thing. You'd best hurry along, if that's your pursuers."

The Captain helped Christina down and led her to the back of the barn. There, he brushed aside the hay in the far stall to reveal a trapdoor, which he yanked open. The entire floor of the stall opened up, and she could see the slope of a tunnel underneath. They hurried down, running through the dampness as they heard the groom bring the lathered horse in behind them.

The dark tunnel led to a similar trapdoor in the house. "You'll like this," he said quickly. "One of Wayburn's ancestors was a highwayman. He built this tunnel to protect his identity. Wayburn, sympathizing with us, loans us the use of it when the occasion arises."

"How terribly fitting."

"You would think so, I suppose."

He helped her up. She found herself in a small room large enough only to hold the two of them. It was tall and narrow, and dark as soot. By now they were out of breath, and their panting echoed off the brick walls. "What is this?"

"We're behind a false chimney. From the front, it looks like an ordinary fireplace. But it hasn't been in use since the highwayman's time."

"Except, of course, by *this* highwayman."

They could hear voices outside over the barking of the dogs as the pursuers questioned the groom. No one was home, they were told. Lord Wayburn was at the Cavendishes' party himself. Still, the men insisted on searching the premises. One of them thought he had caught sight of a horseman jumping the fence down the hill.

The front door was opened, and the sound of boots echoed through the empty rooms. They ran to the back of the large house, evidently flinging open doors and searching behind furniture before moving on to the next room.

"Can they find us here?" she whispered.

"It's doubtful."

She smiled her satisfaction. "Splendid."

She found his face in the dark and reached up to kiss him. His breathing had calmed somewhat, but she felt his start of surprise.

"Don't be foolish," he warned.

Her hand wandered down the front of him, and she found him, hardened by the excitement. "You can't fool me," she whispered. "You're just as excited by all this as I."

"They could find the trapdoor at any moment. I can't guarantee—"

"I ask for no guarantees."

"This isn't the time or the place—"

"Hush, Highness. I've been mad for you all evening. I can wait no longer. I want you now."

"Now? With our would-be captors stomping about?"

"Now. While there's still a chance of discovery."

It was the very danger he sought to warn her against that made her blood boil. She was so hot for him that she felt she couldn't wait another moment. Her breasts were throbbing, and her loins were screaming for his touch.

"They won't hear us if you're quiet. Let us see how well you can contain your passion."

"Ah! I must have misunderstood you. Is it the *containment* of my passion that you're after?"

Fumbling about in the padding, she opened his trousers and reached to touch him. His breath caught harsh and sharp in his throat. She caressed him teasingly, fondling him as he grew like an uncoiled serpent beneath her touch.

"Christ, what a woman!"

In the house beyond, the footsteps were moving closer.

His hands moved to pull her tight against him. She went to him, kissing him with equal voracity. He clamped his lips to hers and shoved her back against the wall. Without taking his mouth away, he waded through the mounds of skirts, as impatient now as she.

When he'd pushed them aside, she slipped out of her silk drawers and he brushed up against her, hard and insistent. The door of the room beyond burst open. A brigade of booted men came stomping into the room. The Captain paused. Christina took her mouth from his and placed it against his ear, whispering in the smallest voice, hoarse with passion, "Don't disappoint me, Richard. Once—just once—allow me to enjoy making love to the Prince."

She guided him inside, then wrapped her legs about him and urged him on. As the men stormed through the room, banging furniture aside, he thrust her back against the wall with a madness that matched her own. In no time, they were ready to explode. Sensing it, the Captain kissed her again, deeply so that no sound could escape her lips. They cried their release silently into each others' mouths as beyond, the noise of the men's search fanned the flames and mixed, like a symphony, with the frenzy of their passion.

CHAPTER 21

"WHERE DO YOU imagine your friend Wayburn is?" she asked when it was quiet and the men had finally gone.

"Leading the other party astray, no doubt. Pity there aren't two of him."

"I wouldn't say that. I haven't had such fun in years."

She kissed him, then reached up to pull off his beard. "I've tired of kissing Bertie. I want my highwayman back. Let us shed this disguise and head for home."

His hand caught hers in a grip that halted her movement on his face. It surprised her. She detected an intensity that wasn't apparent in his soft tone.

"Not yet. I've one more thing to do this night. If you'll wait for me here, I shall fetch you directly."

"Here? Wait for you *here,* in this musty chimney?"

He smiled. "You didn't seem to mind it a few moments ago."

"That was when I was driven to madness for wanting you."

"Then think pleasant thoughts of me till I return."

It was useless to argue. She sensed a core of stubbornness that perplexed her. He wouldn't say where he was going or when he would return. Only that she must stay behind this wall regardless of who might come along, and that she was to open the trapdoor only to him.

She had no way of knowing how long she waited in that cramped cubbyhole of a room. It might have been an hour, it might have been two or three. She must have dozed, for when she opened her eyes, she smelled the faint aroma of greasepaint and knew he was there.

"Is it you?" she asked because her brain felt numb.

He lit a candle. "That depends on who you think I am."

He was still dressed in his Prince's clothes, but they were rumpled now. Although his words had the same mocking ring as usual, she detected a serious edge to his voice. "What's happened?" she asked, alert at once.

He didn't answer. He'd brought his own clothes from his saddlebags and was pulling out the padding from beneath the massive shirt. "We shall have to burn these later. It won't do to leave them here and chance trouble for Wayburn if someone finds them. You're shivering. Here."

He put the huge dinner jacket over her shoulders. She was watching him intently, too absorbed to put her arms through the sleeves, so he did it for her, as if she were a child. He didn't once look her in the eye.

"Something's different about you," she said.

"Is it?"

"Won't you tell me?"

"Don't you think we should be off if we're to get home before dawn?"

She relented. He obviously wasn't going to tell her now. Perhaps after he'd rested. She was suddenly exhausted. The excitement, the fevered pitch of their passion had left her depleted of energy. Perhaps he was feeling it as well. Except that he didn't seem tired. He seemed . . . distracted.

They rode through the night in silence. The carefree, exalted mood of the chase was gone, to be replaced by brooding from the Captain and concern from Christina. She wondered if something had happened that he deemed too frightening to tell her. For the first time, she began to think about the others. She and the Captain had escaped, but what of the rest?

"Are the men all right?" she asked.

"As far as I know."

She might as well not have been there, for all the attention he paid her. Again, she rested her cheek on his back and tried to doze, but she felt distanced from him for the first time, and she didn't understand why.

When they arrived at the hideout, the horses were back and the camp was still and dark. They went into the mill, and the Captain stoked up the fire and laid on another log. Presently, the log burst into flames, lighting the room.

Christina had been standing by the doorway, watching him. He pulled off his beard and wig, the artificial forehead, the nose, the chin. Then he reached into his saddlebags to retrieve the cold cream, lathered his face, and removed every trace of greasepaint. He washed in the bucket, then straightened up to dry his face. When he turned to her, wiping the back of his neck, his hair was damp, but it was black again, and his strong, lean face looked to her more handsome and dear than ever before.

"Have you nothing to say to me?" she asked softly.

He studied her for a few moments, as if trying to decide. Then, wordlessly, he fished in his saddlebags once again and withdrew something, which he tossed carelessly onto the table. In the fire's light, she could see that it was a silver brush. A beautiful, Danish silver brush with long, light hairs in its bristles.

She looked at it as if it were a deadly thing. Without taking her eyes from it, she muttered, "It's Princess Alexandra's. Bertie's wife's."

"That's right," he said, speaking for the first time in hours.

"You went back to Marlborough House. Of course. Dressed as the Prince you—went to Alix's bedroom and stole her brush."

"Right again."

"But you always tempt fate, don't you? So it wouldn't be enough just to take a personal possession. You'd want to see her. To know if she'd recognize you. If you could fool her. What better opportunity would you have? The Prince was likely off supervising your capture, making himself feel useful. And if he happened to return, what concern was that to you? You would simply fling yourself out the window, and would leave with the satisfaction of knowing the Prince had seen you with his wife. Dear God, Richard." She picked up the brush with shaking fingers. When she looked at him, her eyes blazed her fury at his betrayal. "Tell me, how long were you with the Princess? Did you brush her hair for her? Did you ravish her the way you did me that first night? The future Queen of England? Did she suddenly thrill to the Prince's lovemaking just as I did earlier?"

He turned away, saying nothing, so she threw the brush and hit him in the shoulder. He wheeled around and crossed the distance between them in three savage strides. "Stop it," he growled, bringing her up against the door. He took her hands and pinned them back with his own, flush against the wood. "I'll have no more of this."

" *You'll* have no more of it? And what about me? Am I to sit back and wait while you—"

His hand crushed her mouth. "Don't say it."

She bit his hand and wrenched her mouth from his hold. "Not saying it doesn't change it."

"You're rather harsh with your accusations—a woman who ran off with a criminal."

She felt crushed. For a moment she couldn't breathe. The silence was heavy, broken only by their heaving breath. "Do you deny it?" she challenged. "By all means, highwayman, have your say. The court stands before you, waiting for you to bend it as you will."

She met his eyes, and there was something cold and forbidding in their depths. She felt, for the first time since meeting him, that he was a stranger to her. It terrified her more than anything they'd done, or any risk they'd taken.

"Tell me it isn't true," she pleaded.

His gaze raked her face with icy indignation. All the arrogance of his breeding showed in the flare of his nostrils, in the proud and haughty tilt of his jaw. "I shall concede nothing." She felt herself go limp with relief. But in the next moment, as if purposely, he destroyed her illusions. "Nor shall I deny it."

She let this settle a moment, fighting to gather the shreds of her pride. "Just tell me one thing. Why would you do it? Why would you think of doing it? What has

Bertie done to you to make you hate him so much that you would harm poor Alix because of it?"

Again, he said nothing, but his fury burned in his eyes and he had to clench his fists to keep from lashing out. His control infuriated her.

"Bastard!" she cried. She slapped him hard across the face. "You bloody bastard. I don't even care if it's true. But I don't even know you! You profess to love me, yet you keep from me the secrets of your soul. I don't understand you. I don't understand what you're trying to do. I don't know why. I would walk on hot coals to the ends of the earth for you, yet you can't even trust me with your heart. Do you think I've said this to any other man? Do you think I'd allow *any* other man to make of me the fool that you've made of me this night?"

"I've made no fool of you."

"You went from my arms to Alexandra's! Just as Bertie did. Damn you to hell, Richard Wycliffe!"

"And if I told you it wasn't true?"

"I should hate you. Because I wouldn't believe it."

"Then believe what you will."

She was quiet for a moment, gasping for air. "You're a stranger to me. There's something hard and ruthless in you that I've never seen before. I don't know why you seek the Prince's destruction, but I do believe one thing. You will stop at nothing—and will spare no one—until it's achieved."

"That's right, Duchess," he growled at her. "Did I not warn you not to pin your romantic hopes on me? I'm a dead man, Christina, capable of no compassion when it comes to wresting my revenge. You wonder that I don't reveal my heart? It's because I *have* no heart. My heart was eaten away long before this time."

"As was mine. But you changed all that for me. You taught me to feel again. Let me do the same for you. Let me help you," she pleaded.

"It's too late. You came into my life too late."

"I don't believe that." She took his hand and pressed it to her heart. "Do you feel that? Feel it beating with love for you? You did that. Whatever it is, it doesn't matter. Whatever eats away at you, let it go for a time. Let me love you. Let me heal you. Let me do for you what you've done for me."

"Don't you think I would if I could?"

"Say you'll try. Richard, please . . ."

There was a rap on the door. He was still holding her flat against it, and she jumped at the intrusion. "Cap'n?" came a male voice from outside.

Christina looked up into his eyes. "Tell him to go."

He glanced at the door.

"Tell him to go, Richard."

He arched a brow.

"Please."

"Cap'n, sir?"

He glanced from her to the door and back again. Then, without taking his eyes from hers, he said, "Another time, lad."

There was a heavy stillness on the other side of the door before they heard the reluctant shuffle of footsteps moving away.

"I'm warning you, you've taken on a lost cause."

"I don't believe in lost causes. As long as there's life, there's hope. I shan't give up on you while I've one breath left."

He pulled her to him and clutched her close. Then he kissed her hair, breathed in her fragrance, and held her as if he would never let her go. "If only I could share your belief."

"It doesn't matter. I've belief enough for both of us. Someday you'll see that I'm right."

He moved back and took her face in his hands, looking down at her desperately. "Understand, my love, that what you said was true. I have a mission. And like it or not, I am willing to sacrifice anything that I must in order to accomplish that mission."

"Anything, Richard?" she asked. "Even me?"

CHAPTER 22

─────────────────

ౌ⁣ఞఞ⁣ౌ

$\mathcal{T}$OBY WAS MISSING. The last anyone had seen of him, he was leading Christina's mare as ordered, following close behind the others. It was nine o'clock in the morning before the Captain, having had precious little sleep, was told the news.

"Why wasn't I informed sooner?" he demanded.

Bobby looked at the ground. "I tried to tell you earlier that he hadn't returned, Cap'n."

Earlier. When he had sent him away. The Captain closed his eyes.

"Perhaps he stopped off somewhere, as we did, to hide," Christina suggested.

As one, the men slanted resentful looks her way.

"Could be, I suppose," Bobby grumbled, averting his gaze. It was clear that he thought her theory half baked, and was only being polite.

This sudden change in attitude startled her. From the first, the men had accepted her as one of their own. Bobby joked with her and listened to her fanciful tales of her travels. Toby was teaching her to speak Gaelic. And the unobtrusive Michael was reading her written accounts in her journal—carefully screened by Christina first—of their escapades with an appreciation that she found enchanting. Now a tension crackled in the air that she felt certain was directed at her. It hurt her, because she didn't understand it. She'd felt so much a part of them, yet suddenly she couldn't comprehend anything about them. Or their Captain.

Their leader recovered himself momentarily. "If he isn't back by now, it means he's run into trouble. Bobby, take the train into London and see what you can learn. Discreetly. I want details. Check the papers, see if any late editions carry the story of last night's escapades. If so, bring them." He looked at Michael, lank and dark with the protruding eyes that blinked compulsively. "Mickey, go along as backup. The rest of us shall lie low and wait for news."

The men scattered without another word, but their mood was sullen.

"What do you suppose has happened?" Christina asked the Captain.

He gave her a dispassionate look. "We shall find out soon enough."

It was dusk before Bobby and Michael returned.

"They've got 'im," Michael announced, pale and grim-faced.

"Where?"

"Newgate."

The men exchanged uneasy glances. Once, the very thought of Newgate Gaol was enough to put the fear of God into even the most hardened criminal heart.

The Captain sat at the table and put his hand to his brow, thinking.

"It isn't as bad as all that," Christina said, hoping to lift their spirits. "Newgate isn't the horror it once was. They rarely even use it as a prison anymore, except for cri— for people awaiting trial."

Bobby turned to her with a look of ragged bitterness in his eyes. "They've tortured him."

"That's absurd! England is a civilized country. We live in a modern age. The reformers have put an end to all that. We no longer torture prisoners, nor do we hang our thieves. Only murderers. The worst he can expect is life in prison."

"Tell that to Toby!" Bobby cried. His voice rattled, and he seemed on the verge of tears. "Like it or not, *my lady,* your fine civilized English jailers are just as we speak torturin' the poor man to get information out of 'im. The Prince has made it clear he wants the Captain found any way he can. What's one bandit or another to him, if he gets what he wants? Toby's an old man, for the love of Christ. 'Tis no tellin' how long he can stand up under the lash. Or worse."

"You're right, of course," the Captain said, his steady voice the one anchor in the groundswell of emotion. "We must retrieve him at once."

There was a stubborn silence from his men. He looked at them with an arched brow. "Well?"

They shuffled their boots, put their hands in their pockets, and tried to keep from looking at Christina.

"If you've something to say, out with it."

Still, they refused.

Christina could no longer bear the tension. She knew very well they were silent because of her presence. "I shall leave you," she said, touching his arm as she passed him.

She'd hardly closed the door behind her when she heard Bobby's high-pitched voice whine their grievance. "'Tis well enough to fetch poor Toby from the clutches of the English. But he shouldn't have been pinched in the first place."

The Captain's voice was menacing in the face of this mutiny. "Meaning?"

"Meanin' he was caught due to foolishness. 'Twas a frivolous thing we did last night. It brought us nothin' save the capture of one of our own. Ever since the lady's been with us—"

"Careful, lad," she heard the Captain warn.

"Well, it has to be said, dammit all. If it weren't for her and her bloody disguises, you'd never have thought up the silly prank in the first place. Ever since she's been with us, we've been off our mission. Now, Captain, I understand well enough that you've a grudge against the Prince. But we've a higher goal here, or are we mistaken? What of Ireland? Have ye forgotten what we're fightin' for, man? Has your madness for the Prince made ye forget what we set out to do?"

"Ireland and the Prince are one and the same to me."

She couldn't listen anymore. She heard the Captain's voice, angry now, as she moved away, but she didn't bother to linger. She didn't understand their mission, but Bobby's meaning was clear enough. The men blamed her for Toby's capture. They thought she was leading them astray.

Presently, the Captain came down to the shelter they shared, where she was waiting.

"We're going to fetch Toby," he told her brusquely as he began to gather his things.

"I shall be ready in a moment."

"You're not going."

"You don't expect me to sit around here while you go off and rescue him, do you?"

He flipped open the barrel of his pistol, checked it, then closed it again and took up a box of bullets. "That's exactly what I expect you to do. I can't risk taking you along."

"Risk what, highwayman? My safety? Or the favor of your men?"

He shot her a steely look. "I haven't time for this. Isn't it enough that I must answer to my men for my actions? Must I answer to you as well?"

She stood and faced him. "Take me with you. Please."

"I've already said no. I can't tell what's going to happen. This is no simple task we take upon ourselves. There's no telling if we'll even return."

"If something happens to you, don't you think I'd prefer to be there, so I could know? So I could help?"

He came to her and gripped her shoulders with his hands. "If I'm captured, you'll be more use to me on the outside. If I'm killed, it won't matter."

"Won't matter!"

He took her chin in his hand. "Christina—do you love me?"

"You know I do."

"Then do this thing for me. Stay here and wait for our return."

In the end, she relented. She watched the men ride off without her, feeling sick, helpless, and alone. Her fear and worry over Toby was compounded by the attitude of the men. It hadn't occurred to them that she was every bit as upset about this turn of events as they were. She felt heavy with responsibility. Worse, she was not allowed to share in their grief. At the first sign of trouble, they'd tightened their ranks and excluded her. They'd gone off without her to do a man's job, resenting her and thinking her frivolous.

She couldn't sleep. For hours, she paced the mill, locked away with her thoughts, her recriminations, her fears. The lack of sleep the night before, and the emotional upheaval, left her feeling battered, but she couldn't force her mind to rest.

It was late when they returned. She ran outside to greet them. The Captain was holding someone before him on his horse. "Is it Toby?" she asked.

"In a manner of speaking."

The men dismounted and went over to help the old man down. As they did, he screeched in agony, and Christina's heart caught in her throat.

"Careful with him, lads," the Captain warned. "Take him to the loft. I'll be up directly."

They moved off, and again Toby cried out in pain.

Christina took the Captain's arm as he dismounted. "Thank God you're back. I've been so worried. But there are only three other men. Where's Michael?"

He paused a moment and met her gaze. "Dead," he said.

She froze, and he moved beyond her, up toward the mill. She thought of the hours she and Michael had spent together in the meadow as she wrote in her journal, then passed it on to him to read. How he, shyly, would make suggestions to aid in its authenticity. How they would discuss a point endlessly before agreeing on a change. How his reading it compelled her to write in a more stylized and entertaining way. She could see his eyes light contentedly as he read a particularly effective turn of phrase.

It was many moments before she could move. Dead. The word kept echoing in her weary brain. As it did, it took on a distorted quality, like a written word that, when stared at long enough, begins to look misspelled. Dead. Dead. Poor, quiet, unassuming Michael was dead. . . .

When she could manage, she followed them into the mill and climbed the stairs to the loft. The men had stripped off Toby's shirt and were cutting away the leg of his trousers. When she moved closer, she could see the hideous slashes on his back and chest, deep and red, and caked with dried blood. Some of the welts had stuck to the shirt as it was peeled off and had started to bleed again.

Bobby rushed past her and tromped down the stairs. When he returned, just moments later, there was a jar of salve in his hands. The Captain was bent over Toby's leg, pressing it gently. The old man was unconscious, but even the slightest pressure made him squeal.

"It's broken," the Captain said.

"Mother of God, 'tis his good leg, too. Bloody bastards!"

"I shall need some flat boards for splints. And something to tie them with."

"Will rope do?"

"I'd rather not. It might rub."

"I have something," Christina said. She went to one of the carpetbags she'd brought with her and retrieved a petticoat. When she handed it toward Bobby he just stared at it as if he thought her daft.

"You can tear it in strips, for bandages."

Bobby ignored it completely, turning his back on her. The Captain, sensing the tension, looked up.

"That should do nicely. Tear it up for me, will you?"

He handed her his knife, then went back to inspecting Toby's mangled leg.

When she was done, she laid the strips of petticoat beside him and went to Bobby, who was doing a poor job of spreading the salve as the others held Toby up. Every time Bobby touched Toby's back, the older man bellowed.

" 'Tis breakin' me heart, Cap'n," Bobby cried.

Christina put her hand on the jar. "Here, let me help."

The men turned to look at her, and she felt blasted back by the coldness in their eyes. Bobby spoke for them, and she could hear his struggle to maintain an even tone in front of the Captain. "Thank you, m'lady, but you've done enough already."

Stricken, she stepped back and watched them tend their friend alone.

It seemed the awful ordeal would never end. Toby screamed as the Captain set his leg. The men shivered as he was laid back in the blanket-covered straw, which rubbed into his welts and made him whimper in his sleep. He was as pale as moonlight, and his face was contorted with his pain. Feeling helpless, Christina went downstairs and poured some of the Captain's brandy into a tankard. She took it upstairs and, ignoring the men's glowering, lifted Toby's head and helped him drink. It was a slow process, as he was still unconscious. She had to fill his mouth with brandy, then entice him to swallow. The men watched, feeling vulnerable now that there was nothing else to do. Bobby quietly broke into tears.

"Go on, lads," the Captain said gently. "There's nothing else to be done this night. Go get some sleep."

"I'll sit with him, Cap'n," Bobby offered, wiping his face. "You've more of a need of sleep than the rest of us."

"I shall sit with him," Christina announced.

They looked at her blankly. It hadn't even occurred to them that she would.

"We can't allow you—" Bobby began.

"You've had a much more strenuous evening than I. You're all exhausted. I shall sit with him whether you agree or not, and I'll hear no argument about it."

She'd used her best duchess tone of authority, one that was never questioned. When the men looked to the Captain, he jerked his head for them to go. Morosely, they left, feeling as banished as Christina had earlier.

"I'm sorry for the behavior of the men," the Captain said presently.

"Well, it isn't your fault, is it?"

"Neither is it yours. I shall speak to them tomorrow."

"It's quite all right. They think I killed their friend Michael with my foolishness."

"But," he said, reading her mind, "they don't stop to think he was your friend as well."

"You can hardly blame them. Given the circumstances, I might feel the same."

"You're not blaming yourself?"

"Perhaps I am."

He sat back on his heels and looked at her closely, noting the paleness of her face, and the tight line of her mouth. "Forgive me," he said gently. "Once again, I'm taking care of business and not giving a thought to how you might feel."

"I imagine you think I killed him, too."

"Then you imagine wrong. The men knew the risks when they hired on with me. The possibility of death or capture is our constant companion. They've grown complacent. They're superstitious. They thought me charmed because I'd eluded capture for so long. They don't understand the level of planning that goes into these things, or the risks."

"But you do. And you assume those risks for them?"

"If necessary. I'm sorry to lose Mickey. But we're lucky we didn't lose more."

Once again, she felt chilled by the calculating way he was able to look upon such things. "I shouldn't count my blessings too quickly, were I you. Toby may not last the night." She took a damp cloth and sponged his face.

He put his hand on hers, halting it in midmotion. "Thank God for your being here, in any case. Things would look considerably blacker for me if you weren't."

How, she wondered, could the same hands that slaughtered men stroke her so tenderly? She had no wish to convey her feelings, so she turned back to poor Toby instead. "I can't believe they did this to him, Richard. It makes me feel ashamed."

CHAPTER 23

***

For TWO DAYS, Christina nursed Toby tirelessly, refusing to leave his side. She dozed when he did, and jerked awake when he moaned. Bobby made some broth, which she fed to the patient at regular intervals. But in spite of her dedication, the men refused to thaw. They still blamed her for Toby's condition—and worse, for Michael's death.

In truth, she was too tired to notice. She was vaguely aware of comings and goings, of the men riding in and out of camp in search of news. The day after Toby's rescue, Bobby brought back the papers, which were full of stories of the bandit's impersonation of the Prince. Lady Utterton had recognized the cape Christina left behind as having been made from the ermine stole the bandit took from her two months before. And Lady Cavendish reported that she had received a thank-you note in the mail from the bandit, just as he had promised. The note was now at Scotland Yard, being carefully scrutinized for clues as to his identity. The Captain had left the note with Wayburn to post.

Two papers decried the fact that Inspector Worthington of Scotland Yard had actually spoken to the impostor and inadvertently revealed his trap with the headlines WORTHLESS WORTHINGTON—BANDIT ELUDES CAPTURE and, further reflecting the Prince's views, WHAT IS WORTHINGTON WORTH?

Once, the outlaws would have laughed at their grand joke. But that was before Toby was taken. Because of their evening's prank, a man had been killed, and Toby might never recover from his beatings. The men were right to call her frivolous, she thought. But the worst of it was that she had enjoyed every minute of it. And she knew that, given the chance, she would do it all again.

The day after that, she found a copy of the *Times* crumpled beside the hearth. She was so weary, she could hardly keep her eyes open. But when she shook out the page, the headline gripped her like a hand at her throat. THREE GUARDS KILLED IN NEWGATE BREAK—BANDIT'S AC-COMPLICE AT LARGE!

Hurriedly, she read the story of how the guards, in the middle of the night, had been overpowered and, when they fought back, were killed, two of them shot and one knifed to death. In true stiff British tradition, the details were cloaked in euphemisms, but as she read, she could see it all in her mind's eye. She recalled the Captain's words: *I have a mission, and I will sacrifice anything to achieve it*. Despondent, she let the paper fall into her lap.

She wasn't sure how long she sat there before the Captain came in. He glanced at the paper in her lap, stopped, then went on to pour himself a cup of coffee.

"Like some?" he asked.

"No, thank you. Why didn't you tell me you'd killed three guards?"

"Things have been busy around here of late. There hasn't been time for idle chitchat."

"I see. You consider, then, the taking of three lives to be an idle matter."

He came and took the paper from her, setting it aside. "It was necessary. They would have killed poor Toby with their torture. Surely you can see that?"

She sighed. "Yes. I suppose I can. Only I can't help wishing that we could go back, before that night, and do it all again. Differently, I mean."

He took her hand and helped her to her feet, then kissed her forehead. "You're tired. You've barely rested for days. Go sleep. I shall look after Toby."

She was so exhausted that she could feel every nerve in her body tingling. His voice seemed to ring and throb

in her ears. And through it all, she saw the headline—
THREE GUARDS KILLED—and heard his words—*It was necessary. Surely you can see that?*

"Yes," she said, feeling as if she were floating in water.
"Perhaps I shall."

She declined his offer of help and wove her way
across the meadow in the afternoon light. It was a surprise to see that light, cloud-filtered as it was. In her
mind, shut up in the loft as she was, it had seemed perpetual night.

Once she reached the shelter in the woods, she fell
upon the pallet where she'd shared so many nights with
the Captain and fell instantly asleep.

It was dark again when she awoke. She felt dull with
sleep, and her head ached. She'd had little rest, for her
dreams were haunted by nightmarish visions. She saw
the Captain as the Prince, and she went to him joyously.
But when she kissed him, she realized he was really
Bertie. His wife, Alexandra, stood behind him, brushing
her hair. She smiled a satisfied smile and said, "You'll
never know the truth." Then the Prince turned and shot
a guard at the door, and she realized he'd been the Captain all along. He turned to her and said, "It was necessary. Surely you can see that?" Through it all, she was
nursing Toby and was powerless to do anything about
the events that were spinning out of control.

When she awoke, she was drenched in perspiration.
She wished it were still light so she could clear the cob-
webs from her brain. She felt dejected, and for a moment she wondered why. It must be the dream, she
thought. Then she remembered all that had happened in
the last few days. It hadn't been a dream after all.

She heard a horse tearing into camp. Pushing herself
up, she stumbled through the night toward the forge that
served as a barn. Bobby was talking excitedly. She could
hear his voice, but could barely make out the words.

"I've been to Wayburn's, Cap'n, and heard some
news. He says there's a new shipment of—" His voice
dropped, and she couldn't hear. She moved closer and
caught the words, ". . . a secret . . ." and "hardly guarded
at all, since no one knows about it . . ."

"When are they set to be shipped out?" the Captain asked.

"Tomorrow. So it's tonight or never, sir."

"Yes. I see what you mean. But what of Toby? Are the men up to it after all that's happened?"

" 'Tis me own opinion, sir, that the men would insist upon it."

"Then we shall do it," the Captain pronounced. "Perhaps I might restore some of their good graces." There was a faintly teasing note in his voice, and Christina wondered that, after all that had happened, he seemed so unchanged. She didn't feel the same at all.

She joined them then. "What are we planning?" she asked. "Another job so soon?"

The men froze. Bobby shuffled uncomfortably, then muttered, "I'll pass the word, Cap'n."

When he'd gone off, the Captain turned to her and put an arm about her shoulders. "Did you sleep?"

"I think so. Although I wish I hadn't. I feel worse for it."

"That will pass, I don't doubt. Perhaps some brandy to soothe your nerves."

Suddenly, she hated the way he was speaking to her. It was as if she were a child, and he were being careful to protect her. "Richard, what's afoot tonight?"

"Nothing much. We just have to go out for a while. We won't be gone long, I shouldn't think."

"Oh? When do we leave?" she asked with a sinking feeling, because she already knew what he was going to say.

"Not we, love. I need you to stay with Toby. I shall leave Frank with you, in case you need help moving him."

"Then let Frank stay and nurse Toby, and allow me to go along and help."

"You'll be more help to me here."

She recognized that unrelenting tone. "What you mean is you don't want me there."

"If you insist."

"And what is it you intend to do that I can't come along and help?"

"Nothing amusing, I guarantee you. You won't be missing a thing."

"As if I could think of amusement at such a time. I never expected you to treat me this way—like a helpless female who might get in your way. I thought you knew me better than that."

"It's precisely because I *do* know you that I'm asking you to stay."

"Asking—or ordering?"

"As you will."

She turned on her heel and headed toward the house without another word. She was so furious with him, so deeply disappointed, that she didn't trust herself to speak to him.

When she opened the door to the mill, the men were in conference. "Just out of London, on Cutter Street, by the docks," Bobby was saying. "I'm to go arrange for a boat now."

He stopped abruptly when he saw her, and the men nodded and moved away. They said nothing to her, extending their silence of the last few days, but their spirits seemed to have picked up. Some of the old excitement was back, yet she sensed a heightened urgency. They'd been angry and restless, and suddenly they had a channel for those feelings. Bobby left, and the others set about fixing the meal, so Christina took a bowl of broth up to Toby. But all the while she was feeding him, she kept wondering what was so important that it had to be done tonight, and why —suddenly—she was not allowed to know their plans.

The more she thought about it, the more resentful she became. She fumed about it while the men were below eating, discussing their preparations too softly for her to hear. When the Captain came up to say good-bye, she barely acknowledged him. She was too furious, felt too betrayed by his lack of trust. She couldn't shake the feeling that, in spite of the Captain's casual words, something serious was transpiring, and the men didn't want her to know about it.

As she heard them ride away, she decided to do something about it. She would be damned if she'd sit here one more night and wait for the men to return. Once and for all, she was going to find out what was going on—what serious business it was the men thought they should be doing, and why they felt she had distracted the Captain from his goals.

She called Frank in and asked him to sit with Toby until she returned. Smiling secretly as she descended the stairs, she thought that he would have a long wait. She went outside and crossed the distance to the shelter. There, she hurriedly stripped off her clothes and donned her purple costume, assuming once again the mask and identity of Fiaran. She dropped a pistol into the deep pocket of her skirt. Then she took Frank's horse and ever so quietly led him through the woods so as not to be heard. As she mounted, she recalled Bobby's words. *Just out of London, on Cutter Street by the docks.* She knew the area. There was nothing there but warehouses and factories. What, she wondered for the hundredth time, could possibly be the attraction? And why the need for such secrecy?

She kicked up the horse and headed for the London road, determined to find out.

CHAPTER 24

HE FOUND THE horses tied on the warehouse side of a two-story brick building with a sign out front that read MASTERS AND SONS. When she found the door, it was unlocked and she quietly slipped inside.

She saw them at once at the far end of the cavernous warehouse stacked high with long wooden boxes. There, before the loading dock, the Captain was holding a gun to the head of a nervous, elderly guard whose white mustache trembled along with his lip. A shock of thin hair stuck up from the back of his head as if he'd been surprised sleeping in his chair. The outlaws, with their kerchieves up over their noses, were lifting boxes from the stacks and heaving them into a wagon just outside.

"What are you to do with these?" the guard asked.

The Captain grinned. "I'm glad you asked, old man. We hear your cargo is the latest model, and that these boxes were meant for the troops in Ireland, to replace the old. As a means of squelching the rebellion, I don't doubt. We've a better idea. We fancy delivering them into the hands of the rebels themselves, where they might be put to better use."

"You're devils, is what you are!" the guard cried.

"So we've been told."

Christina, dying to know what was in the boxes, looked around for a clue. To her right was a stairway leading to a catwalk high above. Thinking to gain a better view, she crept up the stairs, careful not to make a sound.

From high above, she could see all about the building, but it proved to be little help in detecting what was transpiring below. Whatever the factory produced, the goods were safely boxed up, apparently ready to be shipped out the following day.

She settled in to wait.

"Let's have some fun, shall we?" the Captain asked. "I'll tell you what, old man. When the authorities ask you, tell them the Brighton Bandit has struck a blow for Ireland. The Prince is so keen to know who I am. Let's see what he can make of that."

A chill swept through Christina. She didn't understand what Bertie had to do with the Captain's mission in Ireland, but she knew well that reckless tone. It was as if he wanted the Prince to know who he was, and was deliberately leaving a trail.

"They'll stop you afore you land this load in Ireland, I'll warrant you that," the guard predicted.

"Shall we bet on it? I should enjoy coming back to collect my due."

The color drained from the guard's face.

"Never fear, old man. There are no English where these are going."

"Blast you! I hope they blow up in your face!"

It seemed a curious remark, but before it could register, Christina saw something from her vantage point that the others could not. Bobby had gone deeper into the warehouse to collect some of the further boxes. Behind them, a young man was sneaking up behind him with a gun in his hand. She wasted no time in moving noiselessly down the stairs. Not thinking what she might do with it, she drew the pistol from her pocket and crept up behind the man.

"I should drop that if I were you," she warned him softly.

He wheeled around. He had the bluest eyes she'd ever seen and a handsome, boyish face. She'd startled him, but when he saw that she was a woman, he checked his impulse to shoot and glanced about. Grabbing onto the edge of one of the boxes, he shoved it so that it fell to pieces in front of her. Bobby whirled. He'd been loading boxes, and his pistol was in his belt. As the young man raised his own gun, Christina leapt over the shattered box and took his shoulder in her hand. She pulled just as the gun went off so that his aim was deflected and Bobby was shot in the arm. The young man pushed Christina out of the way and raised the gun again. She knew in that instant that he would kill Bobby. Without thought, she pulled the trigger. The gun blasted in her hand, sending her reeling back so that she tripped and fell over the broken box. The young man clutched his chest, then his gun dropped from his hand as he fell hard to his knees, and slumped forward with a strangling gurgle onto the floor.

Bobby, holding his bleeding arm, was staring at her. "Holy Mother of God!"

The commotion distracted the Captain. In that instant, the old man saw his opportunity and took it. He grabbed for his captor's gun. With the rapid reflexes of a hunted man, the bandit fired, and after a moment, the old man, too, fell to the floor.

The Captain turned and saw her then. Stepping over the old man, he crossed the room and squatted down before the body. He turned it over, felt for the pulse, then let his hand slip away. He looked over at Christina, who sat staring at the brilliant blue of the young man's eyes.

"Saints preserve us," Bobby whispered. "She's done killed 'im."

His words penetrated the fog in Christina's brain, and she looked up to find, much to her surprise, a look of respect and awe radiating from Bobby's eyes. *He respects me,* she thought incredulously, *because I killed a man.* The words vibrated within her. Killed a man . . . killed a man . . .

Only then did she understand what she'd done. She had taken a man's life. She looked at him, lying twisted on the cold, hard floor. He couldn't have been much older than twenty-one. A pleasant-looking young man. In an earlier day, she might have fancied him. She'd danced and dallied with many such decent young men. She'd even married one. The thought of it turned her stomach. This young man must have had a mother and a sweetheart—perhaps even a wife.

One of the Captain's men, Harry, joined them, loosening his kerchief. "The old man's alive, Captain, but 'tis anyone's guess if he lasts the night." When he saw the scene before him he paused. His eyes flicked to Christina and back again. "Oh, Jesus."

"She saved me life," Bobby said, as if he still couldn't believe it. "He shot me once and was movin' to kill me, so he was."

Christina suddenly became aware of the pistol in her hand. She dropped it as if it burned her and heard it clatter against metal. Looking down, she saw that she was sitting in the ruins of the broken box, and that its contents were scattered all about her. She began to shake.

The Captain was watching her closely, waiting. She looked up and met his eyes. "Rifles," she said. "I killed a man so you could smuggle guns into Ireland?"

"Leave us," he told the men. "Finish the loading. There's no telling who might have heard the shots."

They didn't move. They stood gaping at Christina as if they'd never seen her before.

"Go," the Captain commanded sharply. This time, there was no disobeying. They shook themselves from their spells and left to finish the job. On the way, Harry tied his kerchief to Bobby's arm.

The Captain turned back to Christina, whose horrified gaze was still fixed on his face.

"You killed a man because if you hadn't, Bobby would have been killed. No more and no less."

She couldn't look at him anymore. She couldn't sit there, feeling the accusing blue eyes of the man she'd killed glaring up at her. She put a hand to her mouth. "I want to leave."

"We will, momentarily. First, we must finish the job."

"The job!" she cried. "It's a horrid job. You should be damned for doing it!"

He stood abruptly, his body stiff with rage. "Too late, Duchess. I was damned long ago."

• • •

The Captain and Christina rode back alone. Bobby and Harry were to take the arms to the waiting boat and from there, sail to Ireland. Before he left, Bobby took her hand and thanked her for saving his life. She simply turned away. Days before, his rejection had stung her. Now, his admiration appalled her. She wanted nothing to do with them. She wanted little more, in fact, than to forget this night had ever happened.

When they reached the camp, Christina walked ahead to the mill. Frank was steaming by now, frantic at her disappearance. The moment the Captain stepped into the room, he defended his own actions.

"It weren't my fault, Captain. She snuck off, right enough. Under me own nose. If I'd had a horse, I could've tracked her down. But as it was—"

"Leave us," the Captain interrupted.

Frank looked shocked.

He amended his tone. "It's not your fault. It's late, lad. Go get some sleep."

Frank seemed confused. "All right, Captain, if you say so. Toby's better, I think. He spoke to me a time or two."

"Thank you," When Frank had finally left, he turned to Christina. She was staring into the fire, her mask in her hand. "Now you know why I didn't want you along."

"I can be hanged now," she said dully. "For murder."

"No one knows it was you. I give you my word they'll never know."

"I shall know."

"Well, you can't say I didn't warn you."

"Oh, no, Captain. I certainly can't say that." She turned on him with angry eyes. "You may ease your conscience by assuring yourself that you gave me adequate warnings. What you didn't see fit to do was trust me with the truth. You told me you sent things to Ireland. Fool that I was, I thought you meant food and clothing—medicine, perhaps. It never once occurred to me that you were using the money I helped you steal to buy guns. Tell me, have you an army of your own that you're supplying?"

"Of sorts. We're endeavoring to raise one."

"In Ireland?"

"And America."

"I see. You're Fenians. Of course, it all makes sense now. You steal from the British aristocracy, then send the goods off to America, where I imagine they're sold and the money used to purchase arms. In the meantime, you try and recruit Americans who might be interested in your cause. Any takers?" she asked harshly.

"Not enough."

"That man who was here the night after I came, the American. He must take your goods to America, collect the money, purchase the arms, then sail them to Ireland, and then back here for another round. You used to do it yourself—in your younger days, as I recall."

"Until I realized the great need we had for money. And I saw that I could be more useful here."

"By stealing from people like me. Well, it's all very pretty, I must say."

"I never promised that life with me would be pretty. Quite the contrary, as I recall," he said.

"But you never told me why. If only you'd told me— been honest with me—I think I might have stood anything, except your excluding me. But finding out the way I did!"

"I'm sorry you had to find out at all."

"Did you not think I had a right to know?" Christina asked.

"I don't know. I suppose I knew how you'd feel, and sought to delay the inevitable as long as it was possible. I was selfish enough not to want to lose you at such an early date."

"You mightn't have lost me at all, if you'd only confided in me."

"Ah, Duchess. Don't tell me that after all that's happened this night, you still believe in fairy tales?"

"I don't know what I believe anymore. I only know I can no longer stay."

She saw the flash of pain in his eyes. "Do you imagine you're the only one who suffers here?" he rasped. "Do you think I didn't know, every agonizing step of the way back, what you would say? Do you think I didn't torment my brain trying to think of an answer that would make any sense? That would convince you to stay? In spite of the fact that I know it's impossible, that I've known it since the first day I saw you. I, who have the uncanny ability to plan *anything* down to the last detail!" His voice crackled with an emotion that was quite unlike him. She saw this, saw the anguish in his eyes, saw the look of pleading that she knew was the very nemesis of his hard-won pride. It should have moved her, but it didn't. She turned her back. He came up behind and squeezed her arms, resting his forehead on the back of her head.

"So you'd leave me, would you? Would it influence you if I told you what a difference you've made to my life? That supplying guns for a cause was once my reason for existence, but now it's you? What if I told you I'd wanted you from the first moment I saw you? I wanted you so badly, I'd have put a knife to your throat and taken you by force if I had to. And after—when it was so much more than physical between us—what if I confessed to you how it scared me? How it was the first time in my life I ever really wanted something I was afraid to lose."

"Stop it!" She turned from him, flinging him from her. They stood staring at each other, breathing hard.

Pinning her eyes with his, he pressed on with a relentless will, spilling things he'd never had the courage—or the drive—to say before. But his tone was soft now, almost a whisper in the aftermath of his heat.

"Would it even matter to you if I said I could no longer live without you? That losing you would be the darkest moment in a life already black with pain?"

She put her hands to her face to escape the desperate look of love that flared in his eyes. "Once," she said tonelessly, "I'd have thrilled to hear you say it. But it's too late. I've waited too long, and it comes as compensation for too much." She dropped her hands and faced him again. "I don't understand you. I don't know how you can do what you do. You're a monster. You kill people without conscience, and you provide others with the means to do the same. How can you live with yourself?"

His gaze had slowly hardened as she spoke. He came close with a haughty tilt to his jaw and looked her in the eye. No longer was he the ardent lover, bent on keeping his woman by his side. He was a man who could turn her blood cold by the stark, lifeless look in his eyes. "I was trained to kill at my father's knee. I learned my lessons well."

He sounded so bitter that she wondered if she'd ever known him at all. Abruptly, as if looking at her was too much for him, he turned his back on her.

"What will you do?" he asked.

"Go to Dover. I should like to be alone for a bit. I shall wire my maid in Egypt to return to England, and when she does, we'll go back to London."

"And after that?"

"After that, I haven't a clue. I only know that I've done a despicable thing, and that I must learn to live with it."

"And without me."

"Yes, Richard. Without you."

"Then by all means, break clean," he said coldly. He left her then, going down to the basement. She was so caught up in her grief that she scarcely noticed his absence. When he returned, he was holding a black velvet pouch. He took her hand and put the pouch in it.

"I imagine you'll want to sleep in the loft. In the morning, I shall have Frank escort you to the train. That is, if you haven't changed your mind."

"I shan't change my mind. There will be no happy ending for us, highwayman."

He took her chin in his hand and bent to give her an angry kiss. "There was never any hope of a happy ending, my love. Only what happiness we could borrow—or *steal*."

When he'd gone, she opened the pouch to find inside the jewels he'd stolen from her. Every piece was there, including the diamond bracelet, the Prince of Wales necklace, and her cherished black Wentworth pearls. She thought of her father and mother, and all her friends. She thought of the life she'd be returning to, and the one she was leaving behind. *What will you do?* he'd asked. There was nowhere to go, nowhere that she belonged. These jewels were all she had to show for her many years of searching for a home. Feeling sick and timeworn, she dropped to her knees before the fire and brought the priceless pearls to her cheek.

CHAPTER 25

OPENING NIGHT OF *The Bandit Bride* was to be one of the highlights of the London season. News of the bandit had reached a fevered pitch. Every other day it seemed that he was spotted in a different part of England, pilfering with renewed zest. His impersonation of the Prince had particularly captivated the public. His daring was made more fascinating by the awareness that it had made the Prince and Inspector Worthington look foolish. The bandit had bested the authorities, and England laughed secretly behind its hand.

But another dimension was added when, shortly after the breakout of one of the bandit's colleagues from Newgate, an old man at a munitions factory was found lingering between life and death. "The bandit's sending arms to Ireland," he managed to say before he died. This information, coupled with the cold-blooded death of a young boy and an old man at the bandit's hands, put an entirely different complexion on the subject.

Suddenly, the Brighton Bandit was no longer viewed as a devil-may-care purloiner of the aristocracy. His crimes took on a fresh menace. At once, it was clear that what they'd been taking for a scamp of a railway thief was indeed a dangerous political criminal who wasn't above the murder of fellow Englishmen to achieve his objectives. The press began to refer to him as the "Traitor." Even Queen Victoria, shut away at Balmoral as she was, began to take an interest in the arrest of the "wretched fellow."

The news was a blow to Derk and Sasha Wentworth, who, believing the timely and romantic subject of the bandit to be a gold mine, had invested a fortune of their own money in the play. For a time, it began to appear as if the shock and horror of the public on hearing of this turn of events would keep them away.

This feeling was compounded when, not a fortnight before the opening, the Bank of England was bombed and the ghastly deed was attributed to the Traitor. No one was killed and only two men injured, but the country nevertheless reeled at the news. It wasn't so much that Irish anarchy was a new topic worthy of comment—it had, naturally, been going on for hundreds of years. More precisely, the English public preferred the legend of the dashing criminal-of-the-night to the reality of a man who bombed innocent people for the tiresome Irish cause.

Ticket sales dropped off, and people queued up to demand their money back. Sasha, in hysterics, ordered the doors closed to the public to give them time to reconsider. Even as she was assured that it would be to no end, she held out a last desperate hope. A failure of this magnitude could wipe out everything she and Derk had built up over years of constant and diligent work.

It began to look as if the play would, indeed, flop until the most unexpected event turned it around: the Duchess of Wynterbrooke returned from Egypt.

If Christina was hoping for some peace and quiet upon her return, she was sorely disappointed. She was met at Victoria Station by a contingent of her friends, and was allowed hardly a moment's solitude afterward. Everyone wanted her. She must go to this party, be guest of honor at that dinner, accompany friends to St. Paul's on Sundays, ride in Rotten Row in the mornings, take tea in the afternoons. Evenings, she went to the theater or the symphony before moving on to midnight suppers in friends' salons.

It was, in short, much the same life she'd left just months before. But there was a difference. She hadn't counted on the renewed interest in the bandit to embroil her in speculations about him. Because of her kidnapping at his hands, she found herself once again to be a woman of intrigue. Rumors flew behind her back. Every imaginable atrocity was said to have been committed against her while she was in his camp. While acquaintances were more delicate in their questioning of her, they openly speculated about what she *wasn't* saying—trying to read that funny little look that crept into her eyes when the bandit was mentioned. When she entered a room, she could feel the whispers, and she knew very well that the subject would be abruptly changed by the time she joined the group.

She tried to talk about it as little as possible, but there were times when it was unavoidable. Inspector Worthington was a constant nuisance, searching for any new information that might lead him to the bandit and help him to redeem himself in the Crown's eyes. Because the Captain himself had seemed to want to advertise the fact, she confirmed that his gang were Irish Republicans. This statement made the headlines and even prompted some favorable response from pro-Irish factions in the British government. Later, when asked for details at a party, Christina said she knew little about their politics, but confirmed that the bandit did, indeed, seem to have a grudge against the Prince of Wales. What it was, she couldn't know. To her dismay, the comment was overheard, and it, too, made the papers. After that, she refused to say anything. But once again, her silence backfired, as it created an undue aura of mystery that made the matter all the more spellbinding. While people were still stunned and appalled by the enormity of what the bandit was up to, Christina's association with him made him more intoxicating than ever before.

The worst of her humiliations was the growing awareness that her presence, and the speculation about her experiences with the outlaw, had brought about a resurgence of interest in her parents' play. Christina's comment about the bandit's grudge against the Prince unleashed conjecture as to the Prince's reaction to the production. Would he attend? At first, it was assumed

he wouldn't, but rumors began to circulate stating that
the Prince considered himself above such petty nonsense and would, indeed, be present. This prompted a
deliciously juicy expectation, as everyone knew about
Christina's affair with the Prince, and his continued feelings for her in spite of her rejection. That, added to the
fact that the Duchess's parents were the ones exploiting
her misfortune, caused tongues to wag gleefully. Suddenly, sitting in the Lyceum opening night and watching
the reaction not only of the Duchess but also that of the
Prince of Wales became irresistible. In an afternoon, the
opening was sold out, as well as performances five
months in advance.

Try as she might, Christina could not avoid attending
the opening without either causing an open scandal, appearing to be a spoilsport, or giving her true feelings
away. So she donned her finery, sat in eighth-row center, and watched as her parents dredged up memories
she was trying desperately to forget.

It was a nightmare. The parts that were true were bad
enough, but the fabrications were calamitous. The bandit
was seen as a drunkard and a womanizer, a man whose
lust for women equaled only his appreciation for fine
gems. He was a ruffian, uncouth and untamed, a boy of
the streets grown into a man of desperation. His woman,
the bandit bride of the title, was of equal measure. Wild
as the sea, she was an Irish gypsy whose lusts matched
her lover's and who happily, after a shared life of crime,
swung by his side. The image of the final scene was
done in silhouette, a man and a woman swinging from
the gnarled oak at Tyburn Hill, hand in hand.

It upset Christina deeply. As absurd as the play
seemed to her rational mind, the image of Richard hanging from a tree was like a flame to her heart. She'd done
her best to forget him. She'd given herself every justification for leaving him behind and pursuing her old life.
But sitting in the dark with the eyes of the audience
upon her, she wanted nothing more than to hasten from

the theater and the all-too-real prediction of her lover's fate.

It was all she could do to rise on steady legs and smile into the piercing rays of the house lights. In the lobby, the crowd that pressed toward her seemed cloying. The play, from all accounts, was a smashing success. The audience had laughed and cried as was intended, and had vicariously been afforded the pleasure of seeing their number-one enemy hanged. And everyone, it seemed, was *dying* to express an opinion to Christina.

"Your father played the bandit so dashingly that it all but broke my heart!"

"Wasn't Sasha splendid? So wild and fierce, she nearly took my breath away!"

"I daresay I found myself sympathizing with them, although they were so slovenly and . . . well, *Irish*."

Nearby, Oscar Wilde was taking his bows as co-author of the play and expounding on his own outrageous brand of philosophy. "Extraordinary thing about the lower classes in England," she heard him say. "They are always losing their relations. They are extremely fortunate in that respect."

When he spotted Christina, he excused himself from his new wife and circle of admirers to rush to her side.

"Darling!" He took both her hands in his. "I've been off on another of my beastly lecture tours through the provinces. Only just arrived this afternoon, or I'd have come to see you sooner. How are you, sweet? Satisfied with your travels?" He lowered his voice. "Were the Egyptians all I promised?" he added wickedly. "Or should I say, as *little* as promised?"

She pulled him through the crowd to a more secluded corner and turned on him. "How dare you speak to me, after this shameful display!"

He was dumbfounded. On the heels of the audience's praise, her hissed accusation stung him more deeply for its unexpectedness. His soulful eyes blinked askance at her as his hands tightened on hers. "Why, my dear, what *ever* do you mean?"

"Isn't it bad enough for Mother to make a mockery of my life? Must you aid and abet her?"

"Would you kindly stop shrieking at me and inform me what you're babbling on about? What have I done that's so shameful?"

She wasn't shrieking at him, but her tone implied that she would if she could. "I'm speaking of the fact that you actually helped Mother in the writing of this piece of filth."

"Piece of filth? As a critic, darling, your manner leaves quite a lot to be desired. The audience seems rather taken with it."

"The audience doesn't know the travesty of the truth that it is. I find it highly offensive, and the fact that you helped with it a betrayal of our friendship."

This was serious. While Oscar skirted controversy at every turn, he was underneath his witty barbs a kind-hearted man who hated to hurt his friends' feelings. He shifted uncomfortably and answered in a defensive huff. "Well, after all, how was I supposed to know you'd be offended? It's just the sort of subject that might have captivated you, in other days. For all I knew, I was doing you a favor. I actually fancied us having a laugh or two in our cups afterward."

Of course he had. How could he know the hurt he'd inflicted on her?

He was watching her closely. "But then, if the play is, as you say, a travesty of the truth, you can't say I didn't give you ample opportunity to set me straight. I seem to recall grilling you on the subject all the way to the coast. If there was any truth to tell, that would have been the time."

If there was any truth to tell ... The truth, and her conscience, was nagging at her so that she felt she could no longer keep it inside. She felt a wild, impulsive need for confession. She had killed a man, yet here she was, as if nothing had happened, attending the same balls, the same parties, the same unending rounds of plays. Except that this play had stirred embers she was hoping to extinguish. She'd made her decision, now she must live with it. She was determined to do so. Then why did it hurt so much to think of Richard?

And why couldn't she repress that awful, final image of him swinging by the neck from a tree?

Oscar's soft voice broke into her thoughts. "You seem unduly distressed, dearest."

He recalled her conspicuous condition. People were watching them, hopeful of a bit of scandal. Across the room, the Prince was greeting friends with as much grace as he could muster. But when he looked her way and caught her eye, she could see the flash of humiliation in his. She also saw the need for confrontation. It wouldn't be long before he found an excuse to make his way over to her. Tonight of all nights, she couldn't face it.

"I don't want anyone else to notice my—distress. Oscar, would Constance mind if you took me home, do you think?"

He glanced back at his new wife, a tall, attractive blond woman dressed in the Pre-Raphaelite folds Oscar favored. "Mind?" He sniffed. "What matter if she minds?"

In the coach, she leaned back and listened to the horses' hooves on the cobblestones. The rhythm soothed her at first, but soon her ruminations took on the same rhythm, so she found no peace.

"Did you get my letters?" Oscar asked, to ease the silence. "I can't say you were the most exemplary correspondent—not having written me once."

Christina's maid Gladys had, on her return, presented her with a stack of letters from Oscar, which Gladys had collected in Egypt and kept for her. "I received seven letters from you, to be exact. I shall save your letters and pawn them in my penniless old age. By then you'll be known worldwide for the erratic genius you are, and your correspondence should be worth a few farthings at the least."

"I am known worldwide at the present, thank you. Or at least, in the parts of the world that count. Now tell me, pet, why so glum?"

So prompted, she broached the subject that had

haunted her since leaving the Captain's camp. "Oscar, you're Irish."

"Born Irish. I arrived at Oxford with the heaviest of brogues. People actually laughed. Well, I could see at once that a gentleman sports no such impediments, and I set out at once to lose it. I daresay I'm more English than you by now."

"How do you feel about Ireland?"

"As a poet, I naturally embrace my roots. Rhyme, the basis of modern poetry, is entirely of Irish invention. But with the coming of the English, art in Ireland came to an end, and it has had no existence for over seven hundred years. I am glad it has not, for art could not live and flourish under a tyrant. Yet the artistic impulse in Ireland is not dead; it persists in every running brook and in the pervasive esteem for great Irishmen of the past. When Ireland regains her independence, her schools of art will revive."

"But what of her politics?"

He considered this, turning his walking stick between his palms. "My mother, as you know, is quite the Irish patriot. She manifests this not only in her poetry, but in her actions as well. In fact, she once sponsored a revolution. I must confess that, as her son, I am eager to free my country from the yoke of the English favor for which I have a personal need. As with everything in my complicated life, it seems a paradox. Often, I've been criticized for not using my popularity to better aid my country's cause. Left to me, *The Bandit Bride* would have glorified the bandit's patriotism." He paused a moment. "Of course, I couldn't talk democratic principles to our friend the Prince of Wales."

"But isn't there a limit as to how one aids a cause? The price one is willing to pay?"

"Ah, darling, nothing is good in moderation. You cannot know the good in anything till you have torn the heart out of it by excess."

"That's easily said. But having aided those excesses—"

She stopped abruptly as the coachman drew up to her house. In the stillness, Oscar reached over and took her hand. "Come. Whatever it is, simply tell me and be done with it. I've had riddles enough for one evening, thank you."

It took her a moment to decide. When she did, her relief was enormous. To have someone to talk to! To discuss her fears, her stricken conscience, her confusion . . . It seemed like the greatest luxury imaginable.

"Wait here a moment," she told him before running into the house. When she returned several minutes later, she thrust her journal into his hands.

"A bit of fiction," she told him. "I've played critic to your play tonight—however ungraciously. Do me the same honor and critique my scribblings. Only, I shall swear you to secrecy on threats worse than death. The secrets of my soul are not for publication."

"I shall keep your confidence and read your scribblings with pleasure."

"Come to breakfast and tell me what you think."

He kissed her hand and called to the coachman to be off.

She stood in the night air before her majestic gates and watched the coach disappear. She'd felt euphoric on giving it to him. Oscar was the only one who'd ever read her secret writings, for while tough in his criticisms, he'd offered invaluable advice and lavish encouragement over the years. Oh, she'd let the now-dead Michael read her scribblings at the camp, but those had been highly censored and mostly for their amusement. But these writings were of a more sensitive nature. She'd been working on the journal late at night since her return to London. In its pages, cloaked in a third-person narrative, were all the secrets of her days and nights with the Captain. She'd spared nothing in the telling of her tale, and would trust no one but Oscar with the results. His reading it would mean the end of her self-imposed emotional isolation. But now that he was gone and she was alone in the silent night, the relief was seeping out of her to be replaced by dread. She hoped to God she hadn't misjudged her friend. For a mistake in this instance could cost Richard his life.

CHAPTER 26

OSCAR CAME TO breakfast in his favorite olive green coat, a flowing lavender tie, and a wide-brimmed hat that looked suspiciously like the one worn by the Brighton Bandit.

At her raised eyebrow, he said, "I was enchanted with such *chapeaux* on my tour of the Leadville mines," referring to his speaking tour of America, which included the mining towns of Colorado. But Christina knew better. She knew her lover had inspired the new style of hatwear for men, and that Oscar was doing his part to establish it as a fixed staple of English fashion. It was just the sort of flaunting of convention that Oscar loved.

But she didn't contradict him. Oscar was late, and she was nervous enough as it was.

Apparently, he was in no mood to quickly put her mind at ease. He carried the deep blue leather journal in his hand, but cruelly disregarding her impatience, used it to gesture expansively about the enormous, Greek-inspired salon.

"I feel, dearest, like a weary traveler coming home to roost at last. Your absence was intolerable if for nothing save the denial of my person to your home. I always relish my visits here. Your abode is to me such a pagan delight."

"As you well know, it's the Duke's taste, not mine. And I hardly think he'd agree with your assessment of his pagan leanings. Wynterbrooke was staunch in his pursuit of Christian virtues."

He tossed his hat, gloves, and walking stick to a nearby table. "Nevertheless, my visits here are most refreshing. I find myself growing weary of modern life. Modern jewelry is vulgar because the individual craftsmanship is ignored; modern wallpaper is so bad that a boy brought up under its influence could allege it as a justification for turning to a life of crime."

She gave him a sharp look. He was toying with her, and she knew it.

"Perhaps that's the reason for your fictional criminal's departure from society. A mother with vulgar taste."

"If you're hoping to amuse me, you will be sadly disappointed. I find your avoidance to be little more than annoying. Come, Oscar, do put me out of my misery and give forth a verdict."

"What an interesting choice of words, Christina. A verdict. As if you were expecting to be found guilty."

She sighed her exasperation, but followed as he went into the spacious dining hall with its frescoed ceiling and long, stately table. Two places were set close together at the head of that table, making a cozy little nook in an otherwise massively proportioned room. Before them, on Sevres china, was set a breakfast of salmon, deviled kidneys, kippers, scones, and an abundance of fresh peaches and strawberries.

Oscar, popping a berry into his mouth, seated himself and faced her surly look. "Very well. If you want my opinion, I shall comply. A pretty bit of fiction, I must say."

"Is that *all* you have to say?"

He struck what he called his critic's pose. "A fiery pulse of sin, a splendid shame."

"You don't find it a bit—murky?"

"If by murky you mean decadent, I find it to be most engagingly so. I've discovered that where once I was taken by renaissance alone, I'm now every bit as captivated by decadence. Life for me is a bit too sunny. To engage my whole mind, I feel the need for shadows."

"But do you not find it shocking?"

"In its passions, you mean? Poets know how useful

passion is for publication. Nowadays a broken heart will run to many editions."

She sat down, put her napkin in her lap, and took a sip of champagne. "I wasn't referring to the passion, but rather the emotional dilemma. You always talk of art for art's sake, beauty for beauty's sake . . . what of crime for crime's sake? You say often that art should have no morality, should exist for its own sake. But what of life? I seem to have confused the two."

"Ah, it's your conscience that bothers you. In that case, I'm very much afraid you're asking the wrong person. I myself have had my own struggles with my feelings regarding morality. Some nobler self speaks for it, but always loses in the end. To me, life is not about morality. Life serves to teach us to accept existence, to multiply emotions, to heighten and intensify the quality of sensations."

In her frustration, she dropped a strawberry into her champagne and watched the riot of bubbles. Oscar often spoke in lofty terms when what she sought was a straightforward opinion.

Seeing her feelings, he amended his tone. "What I mean, of course, is that the supreme object of life is to live. Few people live. It is true life only to realize one's own perfection, to make one's every dream a reality."

"Even if that dream destroys others?"

"You're speaking now of your bandit."

"Yes. What of the criminal? Are we to forgive him his dreams?"

"Society often forgives the criminal. It never forgives the dreamer."

"In theory, I believe all you say. But suddenly, it has turned on me. Suddenly, I question ideas I've always taken for granted. Oh, what difference does it make *what* you think of my scribbling? It's all rubbish, really."

"It wants polish, perhaps. But it has upon it the imprint of your soul."

She met his keen gaze. "That in itself is terrifying enough. I didn't even have the good sense to make it up."

"Posh. We live in an age when men treat art as if it

were meant to be a form of autobiography. It is only the unimaginative who ever invent. The true artist is known by the use he makes of what he annexes—and he annexes everything."

" 'Stealing from thieves' was how Le Gallienne put it."

"Well, he would."

"And what of glorifying the criminal? What of making a legend of him, as you and Mother are doing with your wretched play?"

"What is true in a man's life is not what he does, but the legend that grows up around him. You must never destroy legends. Through them, we are given an inkling of the true physiognomy of a man."

She looked down at the table.

"I do find it interesting, however, that in spite of your heroine's chagrin at the eleventh hour when she discovers her highwayman's true motives, you *choose* to glorify this particular criminal."

"I suppose it's because I continue to love him in spite of everything. That's what makes it all so ghastly. I can't stop thinking about him, or longing for him. But I don't understand him, and I can't bring myself to sympathize with his ruthless killing of people for his cause. Matthew Arnold speaks of wandering between two worlds: one dead, the other powerless to be born. That's what I feel like. And I don't know what to do."

He left his chair and came round to give her a consoling hug. "Christina, darling, you break my heart. How can I help?"

She gave a small, wry smile. "I suppose you could make love to me. Passion has always been my opiate in the past."

He rose to his full height with a jerk. "My dear girl!"

"Come now! Surely I haven't insulted you?"

"Insulted? On the contrary, I'm complimented. To be offered such a gift? A woman such as you, with a delicate fair body made for love and pain . . ."

"But then," she amended, "I suppose at this point I should feel profane. Even though I know I shall never see him again."

She looked up to find an odd, disgruntled look on his

face that made her laugh. "You actually look disappointed!"

"Well, I don't doubt that making love to a woman such as yourself would require a Herculean effort on my part. But now that I seem to have lost what I never had, yes, I do find that my heart sinks like a drooping lily."

"And you not married a month and telling everyone— much to my amazement—how divine marriage is!"

"It has its amusements for the time. But back to your aborted offer, I applaud you for your immoral thoughts at such a time."

She slumped back in her chair. "Oscar, I'm so dreadfully confused."

He reached into his pocket and withdrew a cigarette, which he lit before speaking. "I take it your bandit is, indeed, the purportedly late Lord Wycliffe."

She hesitated. Then, realizing how deeply she'd already entrenched herself, she gave a short, reluctant nod.

"Working on such an assumption, I took the liberty of fishing out what information I could. His father, Edward Wycliffe, married a young Irish girl of extraordinary beauty. The loveliest woman in Ireland, by all accounts. A peasant girl, no less. The marriage wasn't happy. Bridget—your bandit's mother—never adjusted to the English life. She was, they say, as silent as she was beautiful. She died under mysterious circumstances while living in London. The son, Richard, came down from Oxford to join the guard, and he and Edward went off to Ireland to help squelch the revolution. Years later, Edward turned up dead. Murdered, that is, in a rain-drenched ditch. They say—"

He gave her a piercing look, and she braced herself.

"They say his son Richard killed him."

It was many moments before she could speak. When she did, her throat was so dry that her voice cracked. "Killed his own father? I don't believe it."

"It's common knowledge, apparently. Not long after that, the Prince of Wales was said to have killed your Richard in a duel—hushed up, naturally, by everyone including the Queen herself. Lord Wembly was there, and the story was let out that it was Wembly who killed him. The scandal ruined him. Of course, Wembly's long since in his grave, so there's no help for us there."

She stood and walked about the room on shaking legs. "It's too awful. I don't believe it, yet—I've seen a coldness in him that I can't comprehend. If he went with his father to fight off the revolution, how did he turn on his father and come to fight *for* Ireland instead? There's so much I don't understand. If anything, your information confuses me the more. Oscar, what am I to do?"

"Do you wish my advice?"

"I've asked you, haven't I?"

He stood with his hands deep within his pockets, the cigarette dangling from his mouth. As he spoke, it bobbed with the movement of his lips. "As I see it, you love the man but don't understand his motives. If you love him as you claim, I'd say you should find out the truth about him so that at the very least you can understand why it's not possible to be with him. As to whether or not you *choose* to be with him, you're on your own. I hesitate to advise in such a hazardous situation, as my counsel may very well lead you astray. As you know, I have rather an affinity for criminals—particularly artistic ones. Your bandit seems a man of wit—highly satisfactory to my point of view."

"Oscar, you're right!"

"Am I? What have I said?"

"I owe it to him at least to learn the truth. The things you've said are too awful to contemplate. Maybe if I can find the reason behind his actions . . ."

"Oh, dear, I don't like that look in your eye. What are you planning?"

"What I should have done long before this. I'm going to Ireland, and I'm going to find out the truth—whether he wants me to or not. I've killed a man for him. I have the right to understand why."

CHAPTER 27

*C*HRISTINA STOOD BEFORE the shack, hoping against hope that finally she'd find the answers to her questions. It was little more than a peat hut, crumbling and leaning to one side. In back, a dozen or more children played a rambunctious game of tag, their squeals piercing the country air. When they spotted her, they stopped and came in a group to stand before her and stare. They were little different from the thousands of children she'd been seeing for the last fortnight—fresh-faced cherubs with light titian hair, smudged faces, and clothes that were scarcely more than rags. Ireland, it seemed, was a country of young people. The children outnumbered adults by a wide margin. In fact, it seemed to Christina—raised in the strict English tradition of "Children should be seen and not heard"—that Ireland was a country overrun by noisy, malnourished, wayward red-haired children.

It had begun on the ferry from Holyhead, North Wales. There on the platform, going home from some long-awaited holiday, were what seemed to her a thousand children accompanied by three or four adults. Waiting in line to board the ferry to Dublin, she was shoved, pushed, hit in the back of her knees, and almost knocked down by a host of the most unruly children she'd ever encountered. They ran about, stealing caps from one another, wrestling on the sidewalk, and calling foul names to each other over Christina's head while their chaperones talked amongst themselves, oblivious to the chaos around them. Christina had been a rebellious child, but never so flagrantly, and never—ever—in public. She couldn't imagine why the adults in the group, seeing the disturbance their children were causing the other passengers, didn't say something to make them stop. Had she behaved in such a fashion, her mother would have dragged her by the ear to the nearest private corner and thrashed her soundly. It was just the sort of strict upbringing that she'd detested and rebelled against all her life. Yet, standing there with her grieving heart, feeling like the battered center of this jumble of commotion, Christina had never felt so English in all her life.

It shamed her to feel this way. Normally, she loved children. It was the secret sorrow of her life that she was incapable of having any of her own. And she'd always prided herself on being an exemplary traveler, one who absorbed other cultures with an open mind and an eager willingness to learn. Yet it was just this lack of understanding of Richard's feeling for his Irish countrymen that was standing between them. She felt an aching pressure to like these people, to understand them. Knowing that they represented such a threat to her, though, she felt the barriers even more keenly.

The journey by ferry offered little relief. Although she sat with fellow Englishmen in the first-class compartment, she could hear the ceaseless chants of the children coming from the stairwell outside. "Oiy, oiy, oiy," they howled. "Stick it up your—"

Halfway across the Irish Sea, she left the compartment to find the washroom. Outside, children hung from the stairwell like so many monkeys in a zoo. Trash was everywhere, the residue of their paltry lunches. Discomforted, feeling that the trip had been a dreadful mistake, she went outside to seek a quiet space on the rail. There, she let the crisp sea air sting her face and tried to concentrate on the mission ahead.

To her surprise, she found Dublin to be a charming and magical city. Straddling the River Liffey, it seemed not to have changed in a hundred years. Stately Georgian homes with colored doorways lined the narrow streets. She stood on Ha'penny Bridge and watched the sun cast a delicate rosy glow over the city, wondering if Richard had done the same in days gone by.

If she was beginning to feel more hopeful, it wasn't long before she was once again made aware of her alien status. While she'd expected a city of this size and age to be dirty, she was stunned to find men urinating openly in doorways. Her hotel, the Clarence, was next door to a pub. That night, hoping to sleep off her growing feeling of despair, she was kept awake until four in the morning by the boisterous music and cheers that floated up from the alley. When she complained to the management, they blithely promised to "have a word with the gents next door," but shortly thereafter the noise increased. She suspected the renewed disturbance was a minor act of rebellion. Apparently, they didn't care to have an English aristocrat ordering them about. So she buried her head beneath her pillow and did her best to sleep.

It soon became apparent that her nationality was a stumbling block she would have to overcome. Any questions she asked about the Earl of Wycliffe were met with a stubborn silence. No one knew anything, it seemed. Undaunted, she purchased a set of peasant clothes from a market and took to wearing them about town. If she kept quiet, she could mingle with the crowds and listen in on their conversations in a way that an English duchess could not.

She learned soon enough that not only was Richard Wycliffe known to the Irish to be very much alive, he was thought of as a national hero. Everywhere she went, she heard snippets of news about him. How he'd successfully delivered another shipment of guns "right under the blimeys' noses." How there was an army forming in the craggy west of Galway, made up of dedicated Irish Americans he'd been collecting over the years. How he'd bombed the Bank of England and set another blow for Home Rule. He may have been called traitor in England, but in Ireland he was one of the brave defenders working for a sacred cause.

Once, Christina dressed as a man and sneaked into a nearby pub. Here, talk of Captain Wycliffe flowed as freely as the ale. She felt an odd tug of pride, hearing such unabashed boasting of his deeds. But soon, she began to sense a surprising apathy. From all she'd heard in England, she'd imagined the Irish to be rebels one and all. It didn't take a no-nonsense Englishwoman long to realize that, while they praised their heroes' deeds and cheered them on, few if any of these men were willing to help in the campaign. Rather, they were content to sit in their pubs and rant about English tyranny and let others do the work that was necessary for change.

It angered Christina to think they would so shamelessly drain all her lover's energies, that they'd happily allow him to risk his life for their cause, when they were unwilling to do the same. Still, she couldn't bring herself to understand why he would do it. What made *him* willing to sacrifice his happiness, his identity, his very life for this cause when his fellow countrymen were not?

It was the most frustrating period of her life. She couldn't even obtain the name of someone who might know where to send her for answers. Her explanations were met with suspicious silence. Richard Wycliffe, patriot, must be protected from the English at all costs. Two weeks of covert observation and frantic questioning had led to no further information when a letter from Oscar offered her a final hope.

"It seems," he wrote, "that while we've been searching for the key, it was right under our very noses all the time. Mother, wonder that she is, was an acquaintance of Bridget Wycliffe's during her stay in London. How she met her is anyone's guess. Mother, as you know, has the most remarkable knack for meeting everyone worth knowing. Bridget, lonely in London and desirous of an Irish friend, took to confiding in Mother for a time, before Edward discovered the friendship and broke it off. According to Mother, he was staunch in his insistence that she relinquish all ties to Ireland. Mother, I suppose, represented too great a temptation in his eyes, with her talk of republics and revolution. In any case, Mother seems to recall that Bridget had family in Galway. She did me the favor of wiring her contacts in Dublin and acquiring the name and address of one Patrick—wouldn't you know it?—O'Dell. How distantly he's related is for you to ascertain. I've done my part happily for the sake of friendship, but I'm afraid you will be forever in Mother's debt."

The letter, aside from offering the first hope she'd had, gave her a measure of comfort. After a fortnight of cool rejection, it was a relief to read Oscar's warm and friendly words.

She took the train for Galway at once. Along the way, the rugged, rustic beauty of Ireland was lost to her as she pondered her dilemma. In her short life, she'd traveled more than most of the people she knew. Everywhere she'd been in the world, her status first as the daughter of a marquis and later as a duchess in her own right had opened doors for her that would have been firmly closed to anyone else. Anything she wanted was willingly given. Yet in Ireland, for the first time, her rank was a detriment. It caused fear and suspicion in normally friendly people. As the miles of pastures flashed by her window, she sat and tried to think of a way around it. She couldn't leave without finding what she'd come for. How could she live the rest of her life not knowing the truth?

Now she stood before Patrick O'Dell's dilapidated home in the fierce green country outside of Galway. Dark clouds threatened rain. She could feel the thick moisture in the air. Across her arm was a large wicker basket filled with food. As the children stared, she shifted the linen napkin aside and took out an orange. She held it out to the nearest child, a girl with a snub nose and so many freckles that she could barely see the pallor of her face underneath. As if she'd been burnt, the girl leapt back. Christina held it out to another, who also moved away.

"It's just an orange," she said. At the cultured tone of her voice, the children gawked at her face. Yet it wasn't long before they were once again eyeing the orange as if they'd never seen one in their lives. Their desire for it blazed in their eyes, but so did their fear. One boy actually began to drool.

"Here," Christina said, tossing it to him. Startled, he caught it, then turned red. But he held on to it, so she took another orange and pitched it to another child. Soon, four children were holding the fruit, still staring at her with wide eyes as if afraid she might change her mind and take it away. "Go on," she prompted. "Split them amongst yourselves. It's perfectly all right."

They looked at each other, then, taking her at her word, ran away without thanking her. A hundred paces off, they huddled together, tearing off the peels and shoving the fruit into their mouths. As juice dribbled down the chin of one little girl, they all laughed.

"And just what is it yer offerin' me grandchildren?"

Christina looked up to see an old man standing in the doorway. He was short and squat with a florid face and straight white hair. She'd seen so many men who looked like him on her journey that she felt the features must be a national stamp.

"Mr. O'Dell?" When he nodded, she continued. "I'm Christina Wentworth-Gibbons. I've come from London to ask you some questions."

Instinctively, he closed the door a bit.

"Please don't send me away. I've gone to a great deal of trouble to find you. It's terribly important that I speak with you. May I come in please?"

Reluctantly, he opened the door to her, and she stepped inside. There was a table in the center of the room and some rolled-up pallets on the dirt floor. Looking about, Christina wondered how people lived like this. Her heart ached for the old man with a dozen grandchildren and not even a hearth to warm them. The sight did little to encourage her. Surely if the O'Dells were related to Richard, he would see to it they lived better than this.

"I brought some food. I hope you don't mind." She put the basket on the table. As she spoke, she unpacked the basket. "Some meat, bread, fruit. And some whiskey. I thought—"

"This information yer wantin' must be mighty important for ye to bribe an old man with the bottle." He picked it up and raised a brow. "And sech a bottle."

"Mr. O'Dell, are you related to Bridget Wycliffe?"

The old man froze. Slowly, he lowered his arm and put the bottle back on the table. "Yer wastin' yer time, miss. I'll not have the name of Wycliffe spoke in me own house."

"But she was a relative?"

"A cousin, aye. But that's all I'll be sayin'. Ye can take yer food and yer whiskey and—"

"Please, Mr. O'Dell. It's so important. I'm a friend of Richard's. I have to know."

His watery eyes narrowed on her face. "A friend of Richard's ye say?" He turned his head and spat upon the dirt floor. "Well, 'tis not surprised I am to find him takin' up with the likes of an English skirt. The earldom dies hard, for all his prattle."

She was shocked to hear the bitterness in his tone. "Why, I thought Richard was a hero to your people. He's risked his life to—"

"Hah! Too late, I say. He's come round here with his charity, same as you, tryin' to buy us food and clothing and a new place to live. Do ye know what I said to his high-handed ideas? I spit in his eye, is what."

"But surely he only wants to help. You are his family, after all."

"Family! A good lot it did us to be kin to the Wycliffes. We've done with him, I tell ye. I'll not speak of him again."

She took his arm. "Please, Mr. O'Dell. You have to help me. I love him desperately. You have to help me understand."

He jerked his arm away. "Love him, do ye? Then I'm sorry for ye. The Wycliffes kill what they should love. His father killed our Bridget, just as the son will destroy you."

"How did Edward kill Bridget?"

"By rippin' the very heart from her, that's how. But it ain't the worst he done. He destroyed us all. Him and his son, your precious Richard."

She took a deep breath, trying to remain calm. "Mr. O'Dell, if you want me to beg, I will. It's so terribly important that I know. Please, can't you find it in your heart to tell me the truth?"

He studied her. "Aye, I believe yer sincere. Perhaps 'tis best ye know the truth. Then ye'll know to steer a wide berth round the Wycliffes." He took a couple of cans from a small shelf and poured some of the whiskey into each. Then he handed one to her and she sat down with him to sip the fiery liquid. "Now, lass, what is it ye'd like to know?"

"Did Richard kill his father?"

"That I don't know. It wouldn't make up for it if he did."

"Make up for what? I know he came here with his father to help put down a revolution."

Hatred crept into O'Dell's eyes. "Aye. Edward was in charge of the troops, and he made his good son Richard his number-one boy. Relentless, they were. First Edward used his family connections to wheedle information out of people who trusted him because of Bridget. They figured he was mournin' the poor lass, and told him what he wanted to know. Cursed day it was when the Wycliffes returned. They turned the countryside upside down in the worst bloodbath these parts have seen in many a year. Never mind proof. Anyone even *thought* to be aidin' the rebels was executed on the spot. It was as if Edward had a personal need to kill off his memories as he killed off the countryfolk. But make no mistake. While Edward was givin' the fearsome orders, 'twas his good son Richard that was doin' the deeds. In the name of the Crown, they murdered more innocent people than I'd care to count."

She felt sick, but she persisted. "But war casualties—"

"It wasn't war! It was murder hidin' behind the face of war. Half the poor victims were his kinfolk—some his father's bastards, some family to his own mother, Bridget."

"I—I don't believe it!"

"I care not what ye believe. 'Tis God's own truth I'm speakin' and nothin' else. Ye see, whilst Edward was here before marryin' our Bridget, he played the hell-bent earl to the hilt. Every pretty Irish lass was fair game for the lordly Earl of Wycliffe. He fathered a dozen or more brats, even after bein' married to Bridget. The county was dotted with them. And don't think he didn't know it. We made certain of it. But did he care? Enough to come back and have them murdered by his own legitimate son. One of your Richard's victims was a fifteen-year-old girl named Maureen. His half-sister."

"But surely he didn't know it."

"No. 'Twas Maureen's pa on his deathbed that told the news."

She recalled what the Captain had said to her before she'd left. *I was taught to kill at my father's knee.*

"Poor Richard. He must have been devastated."

"Devastated or no, does it change matters?"

"But he didn't know. Surely he's made up for it since. Surely there can be some forgiveness, after all he's done to atone."

The old man put his whiskey on the table and stood up with a slow and deliberate dignity. "There can be no forgiveness for any Earl of Wycliffe. Not in this house. Not in this family. Related to Bridget as I might be, Richard Wycliffe is no kin to me. He destroyed any love we might have had for him when he murdered his own people. And take me word for it, lass. If ye know what's good for ye, put a wide distance between ye—before he destroys ye as well."

CHAPTER 28

IT WAS INTOLERABLE, listening to the priest drone on. Christina sat surrounded by the golden, spacious splendor of St. Paul's Cathedral, in the midst of her family and friends, and all she could think of was Patrick O'Dell's horrific tale. How much of it was truth, and how much the rambling ruminations of a resentful old man?

Even if she'd wanted to forget, it was impossible. The priest had chosen the Brighton Bandit's sins against God and man as the topic of his sermon. Oscar had told her on her return that after the bombing of the bank, the Captain had been blasted from every pulpit in the nation. The papers were crammed with stories relating his deeds, with editorials decrying his vicious purposes. But the priest didn't-stop with the Captain. He denounced the Irish gypsy Fiaran as the epitome of the femme fatale—as a woman who not only aided an outlaw in his crimes, but who used her female charms to lure him on to wanton and shameless acts. The Salome of Britain.

Home from her travels, Christina had been surprised to see accounts of the bandit's accomplice played prominently in the press. It gave her an odd sensation, reading about her participation in his crimes when she knew she'd done nothing to warrant the publicity. At first, it hurt her as she suspected the Captain had so quickly replaced her with another. But Oscar, laughing, was quick to set her straight.

"I planted the stories myself," he told her with a smirk.

"But they aren't true!"

He waved his arm in the air. "What matter? Do you desire that some sharp dowager should put together the rather obvious fact that this gypsy seems to strike only when the Duchess of Wynterbrooke is conveniently out of town?"

"I hadn't thought much about it."

"That, dearest, is what you have me for. Besides, to give an accurate description of what has never occurred is not merely the proper occupation of the historian, but the inalienable privilege of any man of arts and culture."

Christina smiled, thinking of the time at a party when Oscar, with hand on his heart, had sworn to an acquaintance, "You don't believe me, Miss Nellie. I *assure* you . . . well, it's as good as true."

"You're incorrigible."

"Nonsense. To have done it is nothing. But to make people *think* one has done it is a triumph."

So Oscar, ever the dramatist, had written a scene of her life while she was away.

It was St. Paul's Christina loved more than the religion, more than the conspicuous display of faith. When the ordeal of the sermon was over, she mingled as was expected while the congregation, in their glittering Sunday best, filed out onto the great, columned portico. Once they'd gone, she stealthily made her way to a small side doorway. Climbing a twisted, immeasurable flight of stairs, she came out into a dark hall, and from there onto the gallery about a hundred feet up the center of the cathedral's magnificent dome. From here, she had not only a sweeping view of the church below, but a dizzying look at the painted dome that swept ever upward toward heaven. This balcony circling the widest part of the dome was called the Whispering Gallery. Ever since she was a child, Christina had scurried up after services and spent her own private time talking to God.

When Oscar had first come to London, this had been the first place she'd taken him. She'd been little more than a child then. She'd made him stand just where she was now and had circled to the opposite end of the gallery, across the expanse of the dome, to show him the miracle. If she put her lips close to the wall and whispered something, he could hear it where he stood.

No one understood this freak of architecture. Yet Christina, always restless during the official sermon, felt the presence of her God more deeply as she stood high above, alone in the cool, hushed corridor, where such a sweet little miracle was possible.

This morning, she inevitably thought of Richard as she drank in the solitude. At the camp, she'd told him of her feeling for this place, and of her habit of stealing up here after everyone had gone home. He'd laughed and accused her of being such a romantic that she even romanticized God. Well, maybe it was true. Certainly, her romantic illusions had robbed Richard of something precious—of the right to be himself. If only she could go back and, knowing what she knew now, do it all again. But of course she couldn't. After the way she'd hurt him, he couldn't possibly want her now.

She was lost in wistful thoughts when she heard the whisper. "Christina."

Startled, she looked about. No one was there. For a moment, she thought she was losing her mind. Then it came again. "Christina."

Suddenly, she knew. Her heart pounding, she looked across the great expanse of dome and saw him standing behind the rail. He was dressed in a gentleman's Sunday clothes, with top hat and walking stick, but he was unmistakable. Richard.

He turned his mouth to the wall and said, "Come to me."

With a small cry, she gathered her skirts in her hands and ran round the circumference of the dome. She didn't care that her heels clicked loudly in the reverential hush. All she cared about was flinging herself into his waiting arms.

She kissed him, fondled his arms, his shoulders, his neck. She couldn't stop touching him. His body, so lean and hard and warm with a vitality all his own, felt to her like the home she'd never known.

Even as he kissed her madly, he had the presence of mind to swing her back against the wall, into the shadows. He held her fast against him, strong as a lion, and equally fierce.

"Oh, Richard," she whispered, kissing his face. "I'm so terribly sorry. Can you ever forgive me?"

"Only if you'll do the same."

His voice, so deep and stirring, filled her with an exquisite joy. She hadn't realized how much she'd missed him until that moment. "How did you know I was here?"

"I've kept track of every move you've made since leaving my camp. Did you imagine I'd simply allow you to slip from my fingers like so much sand?"

"Then you know about Ireland."

She caught the flick of pain in his eyes. "Aye, love. I know it all."

"We've so much to talk about. But not here. Reverend Thomas knows I come up here, though he pretends not to. You're in too much danger here."

"Can you get away?"

She tried to think. Her mind was a jumble. All she wanted was to look at him, to drink in the sight of his handsome face, to touch him and make up for all the senseless lost time. "I don't know. I've only just returned. I need time to think. Come to Wynterbrooke Hall tonight. I shall dismiss the servants and assure that you'll be safe." She smiled because the thought of having him all to herself thrilled her beyond reason. "You've entertained me at your home, allow me to return the favor. In my own fashion."

He looked into her eyes. "I don't know that I can wait until tonight."

She touched his cheek lovingly with her fingertips. "Darling Richard. It will be the last time you ever have to wait. I don't know how, but some way, I shall arrange things so that I never have to leave you again."

He came at midnight, when the streets of St. James's were quiet and the lights of the mansions dimmed. Not knowing exactly what time he would arrive, she'd arranged a light supper of caviar and crackers, truffles, cold venison, cheese, fruit, and chocolates—anything the servants could leave on the sideboard that required no further attention from her. She had champagne cooling and brandy at the ready. When everything was set, she sent the servants off with instructions not to return at all the next day, and set about preparing herself for her lover's visit.

As she bathed, washed her hair, dried it before the fire, powdered, perfumed and coiffed herself, she felt as nervous as a schoolgirl. She tried on several gowns, not satisfied with any. White was too virginal, red too obvious. Pink? Too girlish. She had gowns of velvet and lace, satin and lace, brocade, silk voile and tulle. What would he like? Would he even notice? She laughed to herself, thinking what fun it was after living with him night and day to be preparing herself for a romantic tryst.

In the end, she decided on the same black gown with the gold embroidery that she'd worn the night she'd met him. It had brought her luck on that occasion—perhaps it would do the same again. She considered wearing the Wentworth pearls, but at the last minute concluded that the expanse of bosom revealed by the plunging neckline was more dramatic without jewelry. Satisfied, she bundled up the discarded dresses and shoved them hastily into the armoire for Gladys to straighten out when she returned.

Then she had only to pace the floor and wait for his knock upon the door.

She was tending the fire in the salon when she heard a step on the tiles. Whirling with the poker still in her hand, she saw him at the French doors. Apparently, he'd approached the evening with the same attention, for he wore rich black evening clothes, a white silk scarf about his neck, and white gloves. His hair was brushed back, showing off the strong, aristocratic angles of his face. If it was the Brighton Bandit who'd come to this house months before to carry her away, it was the Earl of Wycliffe who stood before her now. He looked so handsome, so utterly elegant in his innate virility, that he took her breath away. She felt frozen by the hearth, unable to move, unable to speak.

He closed the windows, yanked the drapes closed, and moved toward her with a lazy, feline grace. Taking the poker from her, he raised her hand to his lips and, turning it over, kissed her palm. A shock swept through her at the contact. Her knees went weak.

"I thought you deserved at least one evening with a gentleman for all your pains."

It was those pains—her trip to Ireland and the subsequent discoveries—that must be addressed. But suddenly it seemed too weighty a topic to broach after such a long separation. Seeing him in her house, so unexpectedly and unabashedly charming, she felt a little shy. Everything had changed for her: the way she thought, the way she felt, the way she looked at a once dreary world. But she didn't know if he felt it, too. She couldn't discern what was on his mind. Still, she sensed and shared his reluctance to delve into the past or speak of the future. Those issues would wait. For now, it was an unimaginable joy just to be with him.

In her suspended state, she glanced down at her bosom, deeply conscious all at once of the noticeable swell of her exposed breasts. Covered, however meagerly, she felt more naked than she had in all her life. She thought that he must feel the heat of her body from where he stood. Searching her mind for something to say, she spoke softly, her voice sounding thin and distant to her ears.

"I wore no jewelry to tempt you tonight."

"Yet you tempt me with something far more dear."

She met his heated gaze and felt the jolt of undisguised desire. "Even as a gentleman, you remain a thief."

"What have I stolen, Duchess?"

"My breath. My heart. My will." She laughed nervously. "Once again, you've caught me off guard. It's quite unlike me, but I can't think what to do or say."

"What would you do if any other gentleman came to call?"

Thief he might be, but he possessed the wisdom of

the ages. If she was skittish, then she, like her mother, could lose herself in the comfort of playing a role. She'd been born and bred to play the hostess, and the words came fluidly to her tongue.

"I should offer him a brandy, first off. Would my lord care to partake?"

He gave her a courtly bow. "Indeed."

She brought him a snifter and poured champagne for herself. She was watching him closely, arrested by his mood. He was performing faultlessly, yet there was a feral energy about him that his manner and grooming couldn't disguise. Playing the gentleman, he seemed more dangerous than ever.

He tasted the brandy, then raised the glass in tribute. "Napoleon. I'm impressed."

"The Duke's taste was exquisite."

His eyes flicked to her bosom. "In everything."

She took a healthy gulp of champagne.

Beneath the stark brows, a gentle amusement touched his eyes. "I suppose if we're to carry through with it, we should do so with decorum. What would be next on the agenda?"

"A bit of small talk by the fire, I should think."

"Ah. Let's see, then. The weather's unseasonably pleasant. The night is chill and moonless—perfect, I might add, for a bit of mischief on the road. And I trust it rained in Ireland. That, I suppose, should suffice— unless, of course, you've something to add?"

She laughed. "No, my lord. You're handling it beautifully. Do carry on."

"Then we shall consider the small talk behind us. What might you offer next for the amusement of your guest?"

"Supper! I've had the servants lay out a lovely cold repast, if you're hungry."

"My hunger isn't for food." His voice had taken on the coolly deceptive timber of menace that never failed to thrill her. He took a sip of brandy, then, remembering his role, added, "Thank you all the same."

"A pity," she teased, enjoying the game. "Gladys worked so hard. She'll be disappointed."

"I didn't come to please your maid."

"I see. If you're not hungry—"

"Did I say I wasn't hungry?"

She reddened. "Well then, if you don't care to eat, pray my lord, follow me."

She led him out through the columned hallway and up the marble stairs. Following with his brandy in hand, he raised a brow and crooked a little grin. "Upstairs so soon, Duchess? Little wonder your praises as a hostess are flung far and wide across the land."

"My gentlemen callers usually suppress their wicked comments," she tossed back over her shoulder.

"Their manners are impeccable, no doubt, yet I question their measure—or at the very least, their sense. Particularly if you lead them so readily to your bed—"

They walked down a long gallery hung with portentous portraits of the succession of Dukes of Wynterbrooke and their prim-faced wives. He recognized a Van Dyck and a Gainsborough along the way.

Presently, they stopped before a doorway as she turned up the gaslight. Before them was a glorious mirrored ballroom, ornate with gilt. The mirrors lined every wall, creating an impression of endless depth. The ceiling, similarly mirrored, captured the sparkle of the Venetian chandelier and reflected it like a thousand stars. At the far end of the room was a platform for musicians. Christina crossed the gleaming wood floor to a table on which sat a box with a small protruding horn. She put a foil disk upon the box which, when it was in place, looked like a sewing bobbin turned sideways. Then she swung a large arm over the disk and cranked the machine by a handle on its side. She placed the stylus on the edge of the disk, and the machine began to turn, emitting a tinny waltz from the horn.

Turning, she laughed at the shocked look on his face. Clearly, this was the last thing he'd expected. "It's a cylinder phonograph. The sound leaves a bit to be desired, but imagine! Music at the crank of a handle!"

"Quite a toy. The trinket of the idle rich."

"Perhaps. But just the thing for lovers meeting on the sly—with no desire, I might add, for musicians with wagging tongues." She went to him, took the brandy from his hand, and placed it on the polished floor. Then she put his arm about her waist and took his hand in hers.

"What are you doing?" he asked, still glaring at the phonograph.

She began to move to the music. Looking up into his face, she gave him a glowing smile. "Dancing with destiny. Come, Lord Wycliffe. Surely you haven't forsaken your role? Can you not, for one night, lay to rest the torment of the martyr and meet me on my own terms? Tomorrow, if it pleases you, I shall give all my trinkets to the poor."

He had the grace to smile. "Asked so prettily, a gentleman could hardly refuse." Relaxed again, he took the lead and glided her expertly about the dance floor. He crushed her to him as though treasuring the feel of her body against his, so closely she thought he must be able to feel the thudding of her heart against his chest.

As they danced, their image reflected in the mirrored walls, giving the illusion from certain angles that there were twenty, fifty, even a hundred identical dancers on the floor. They made a stunning couple, both dressed in black, black-haired, swirling beneath the flickering lights of the crystal chandelier. Swept away by the beauty of it, she nonetheless became aware of something jingling in his coat pocket. "What's that?" she asked, feeling for it.

He caught her hand and moved it away. "Do you always ask your gentlemen callers impertinent questions?"

The music stopped. He stepped back, bowed low, and once again kissed her hand. His lips sent such a rush through her that she felt the need to abandon the charade.

Looking into her eyes, he saw her impatience. He gave a sardonic grin and stooped to pick up his glass. Swirling the brandy about its rim, he wandered out of the ballroom, opening doors and poking his head casually inside the numerous rooms along the way. All too aware of what he was searching for, Christina felt her breath leave her lungs in little gasps.

He found the stairs and ascended them to the third

floor. There, after several tries, he found her bedroom and stepped inside. Sipping his brandy, he studied the richness of the room with a criminal's eye. He perused her jewelry boxes, then moved to the armoire, which he opened. Spotting the jumble of dresses, he cast her a penetrating look.

"You shouldn't have taken such pains to dress for me. Not when we both know the futility of it."

"Richard—" She stepped forward, wanting him now too badly to wait.

He raised a hand, restraining her. Then he reached into his pocket and withdrew something in his fist. "As I recall, a gentleman always brings the lady of his heart some token of his affections. Turn around, Duchess."

She turned her back to him and he placed something around her neck. As his sure fingers worked at the back, they brushed her skin, sending flickers of desire coursing through her.

When he'd finished, she went to the silver mirror and gasped. About her neck was a magnificent necklace of carved oval turquoise that depicted miniature mythological figures in mid-action. There were eighteen stones in all circling the neck, each so beautifully carved that she could feel the flow of the Grecian robes. Each scene was different, with some figures clothed, some naked, some riding horses or mythological beasts, some picking fruit from a tree, some simply tending to everyday activities. The framework of the necklace was made of gold, box-mounted with reeding and ornamental scrolling, with the cameos linked on either side by dangling loops of gold chain. It was obviously ancient, and worth a small fortune. She fingered it, hardly knowing what to say.

"I'm told it was excavated from the Isle of Crete." He caught the hesitancy in her eyes and added, "Calm yourself, Duchess. I didn't steal it. I won it from another thief. If it's any consolation. Although, I'd caution you not to wear it in the vicinity of Brittany."

She turned, letting her hand drop to her side. "I care not if you did steal it," she told him seriously. "Nothing matters to me anymore but you. If I hesitate, it's because you don't have to give me jewelry. You've given me more than you know already."

He smiled. "Shall I take it back?"

Startled by his suggestion, she whirled back to the mirror to see how lovely it looked on her throat. "Don't you dare!" Touching it again, she added, "I shall treasure it all my life."

Putting his brandy aside, he came up behind her and smoothed his hands along her shoulders. "Such a pity it doesn't match your attire."

She stilled. Moving away from Richard, she faced him and quickly unfastened the back of her gown. She let it slip to the floor, stepped out of it, then let her petticoats, her stockings, her corset follow suit. Soon she was standing naked before him, wearing nothing but the necklace.

"Now it does," she said.

He took the pins from her hair, dropped them to the floor, and let the thick mass tumble to her shoulders. With unhurried deliberation, he ran his fingers through the length of it, caressed its silky dark tresses, and finally settled it about her breasts. "Do all the Duchess's gentlemen callers find her this irresistible?"

"I daresay. Though they shall henceforth be thwarted in their desires. Gentlemen become bores after a time. There are moments when a duchess craves a brigand's hands on her flesh."

She stretched up and kissed him. His lips tasted sweetly of brandy. His rough hands on her silken skin ignited a flame in her that she desperately longed to quench. Restlessly, she took his hand and went to sit down on the edge of the bed, already ahead of herself as images of twined limbs flashed across her mind. When she looked up at him, she was surprised to see him gazing beyond her at the midnight blue velvet drapings that sported the silver Wynterbrooke seal. He met her gaze and curled the corner of his lip into a hard little smile.

"In the Duke's bed? I think not, Duchess."

She stood and he ripped the embroidered silk bedcovering from its place. Then, wrapping it around her, he swung her into his arms and carried her from the room.

CHAPTER 29

HE TOOK HER down a flight of stairs as easily as if he were carting nothing but the coverlet. At the doorway to the ballroom, she gave him a questioning glance.

"A gentleman, no doubt, prefers the dark," he explained. "But this brigand fancies mirrors."

With her still in his arms, he turned up the gas just enough so that the room was bathed in a soft muted light from the chandelier. He slid her to her feet, then, taking the covering, spread it with showman-like execution onto the floor. Christina's unclad body was reflected a dozen times in all its delicate symmetry, radiantly pale and gleaming like Persian pearls.

His task completed, he came up behind and cupped her breasts in his hands. His fingers played with the nipples until they stood erect, and her breasts began to throb. She leaned back into him, feeling that she was sinking into a warm, welcome current of seductive delights. She'd never known a man like him before. Just the slightest touch drove her to madness. She watched in the mirror as his hand explored her skin, brushing her waist, kneading her belly, burying itself between her legs. His mouth nibbled at her ear, but still he watched in the mirror as her eyes blazed like emeralds and her mouth grew slack, losing its control.

She turned and kissed him fiercely, shoving the jacket back from his shoulders. He continued to kiss her as he shrugged out of his clothes. She helped where she could, ripping studs from their holes and letting them drop and bounce on the floor.

Even as she frantically sought to disrobe him, to feel his sleek skin against the satin of her own, she sensed in him a steely control that was more exciting than any rush to possess her could have been. Where she was hurried, he was deliberate, where she was breathless, he controlled his breath with the will of a warrior. Her rash attempts to hurry his pace were met with a composure that shook her as nothing else had ever done.

"I love you, Richard. God in heaven, how I've missed you! How I've longed for you . . ."

She pulled him down into the plush velvet spread and found him with her hands. Wanting to give to him some measure of the exultation he'd imparted to her, she used her mouth, her fingers, the cup of her palm to bring him to life. She wanted to ignite in him the same joyous lust that consumed her when she breathed his masculine scent, heard the irony in his voice, or glimpsed the way-ward waves of hair at the back of his neck. Yet through it all, he regarded her with a serenity that was devastating. It was as if he was holding himself back, waiting for something he hoped would come in time.

"You've played the gentleman too long, Captain. You've forgotten how to play at love."

She straddled him, preparing to slip down upon him and take control until, driven to the brink of his restraint, he would take over and master her with his strength. But before she had him barely in hand, Richard slid his hands beneath her arms and, giving a mighty jerk, pulled her forward so that she lay flat against his chest. He held her pinned against him, panting her surprise as his words wove their way into her spell.

"While you were away, I came to realize my need for you. And I came to understand that need as not being confined to the craving of the flesh. When I heard what you had done—that you'd gone to Ireland to learn the truth—you crossed a barrier no woman has ever crossed before. I want more from you than a hurried coupling beneath a mirrored sky."

He held her so tightly, the breath seemed cramped in her lungs. "What do you want?" she gasped.

"I want . . . what we always could have been, if only we had known. One body, one mind, one soul. I want all of you, Christina. That part of you that you've given no other man."

His eyes caught the starry light of the chandelier. She could see herself reflected deep inside, just a glint of her face as he must see her. She'd never looked happier, more radiant, more unspeakably beautiful. Her eyes softened on his face, and she gave him a loving smile.

"You have that, Richard. You have the love I've kept inside where no one else could see. I believe in you now as never before. But mistake me not. I love you now for who you are. You shut me out of your heart because you didn't trust me, and rightly so. Had you told me, I might not have understood. But finding out the way I did, I felt your pain and made it mine." She put a finger to his lips, loving the feel of them, reveling in her right to caress him. "I don't understand your cause— perhaps I never will. But I understand your motives. You have what I've never given another soul: my devotion, and at last—at last!—my trust. One body, one mind, one soul. It's all that I desire. The future will take care of itself."

As if his spirit had broken free with her words, he gave her a devilish grin. He rolled so that he lay atop her and brushed the hair from her face. "Then slowly, love. You must learn to savor your pleasures."

With the lingering sensuality of the connoisseur, he taught her to do just that. In the midst of the grand mirrored hall, locked away on their velvet wrap like survivors on an island at sea, they explored the physical expressions of their love as if the world and its cares had disappeared, and the day of reckoning been deferred. Beneath his hands, she discovered that love slowly kindled and stretched out over time had a momentum all its own, so that graduating in pitch, it took on a quality of intensity and a depth of feeling hitherto unknown. Any rush for completion was gentled by his infinite care so that she learned the exhilaration of the journey as an indulgence in itself. In motions so slow and languorous that they defied the drift of time, she stretched, she arched, she mewed her pleasure in a myriad of responses. Her body, cherished, coaxed to delight by his fathomless gifts of touch and sight and sound, was freed with the successive unleashing of his love from the wretched bonds of the past. Bathed in gaslight, refracted by mirrors, they reveled in the luxury of celebrating the beauty of their union. The sheen of their bodies glittering off the walls was fuel to their passion. It was a different dance they performed, their bodies exploring and perfecting the rhythm along the way. No feeding of desire was beyond their contemplation. On her hands and knees, she watched as he used his tongue—slowly, slowly—to bring pleasure to every ready crevice of her lustrous form. He worshiped her with his hands, with his lips, with his body, and for the first time in her weary life, he taught her what love could be.

Her pleasure heightened beyond anything she'd imagined, she felt herself soaring in a whirlwind, seared by the wildfire of his devotions, until she crossed a barrier and was reborn.

It was morning before they'd had their fill. Even that, in the end, seemed little enough to seal the betrothal of their no longer restless souls. They lay, wrapped in each other's arms, resplendent in velvet folds, and spoke in lovers' tones of all that was on their minds, all they hadn't dared to risk before. Safe in their new intimacy, the pain of the past seemed necessary if it could bring them, at last, to this.

CHAPTER 30

*E*VENTUALLY, THEY GREW hungry and went down to eat. The Captain eschewed the dining room as being too grand. There was a table in the kitchen where the servants took their meals, and it was there, under the gleam of a single gas lamp, that they ate from the banquet. Christina had wrapped herself in her dark green-and-gold robe, and the Captain wore his breeches and hastily buttoned shirt. She watched him with a tender smile as he devoured the venison, his hair tousled and crisp about his face, his gentleman's manners foresaken. It seemed to her the most wonderfully cozy sight in all the world.

"This is the first time I've been in here," she confessed, looking about the kitchen.

He paused mid-bite and stared. "You're joking."

"Not at all. I haven't lived here long—just a few months, really. Of course, Wynterbrooke took me on a tour when I first arrived. But I'm not one of those wives who fusses over menus and counts the silver. I leave it entirely up to the housekeeper, Mrs. Craven."

"I daresay you'll visit a kitchen or two during your life with me. Can you manage it? Or will the Duchess pine for servants to bring her tea?"

"I think you know the answer to that."

He looked at her seriously. "I do. I suppose I was always afraid you'd run back to the life of ease you'd left behind. When you left me, my prophecy seemed fulfilled. But when you went to Ireland in search of ugly truths, I knew one of two things would occur. Either you'd curse the day you ever met me, or you'd be mine forevermore. I'll confess I feared the former . . . but I'm more than a little content to have you with me."

She sat back in her chair and nibbled on a fig. "You do seem content. That fierce anger has drained from you. Always, it was there between us, like some unspoken barrier. I see no defenses now. In fact, you look rather innocent, with your ruffled hair, shoving food into your mouth as if you hadn't eaten in a week."

He gave her a wicked look. "I've expended enough energy for a week or more. Would you deny me nourishment?"

"Heavens no, darling. Eat. You shall need your strength before this day is through."

They laughed, and the sound of it was so glorious that they leaned over and touched their lips together.

"I shan't deny you anything again," she promised more seriously. "From this day forth, nothing shall keep us apart. Not even ourselves."

He looked thoughtful as she spoke. "Nice to think the anger could be a thing of the past. You're right, you know. I don't feel it now—with you. This night has purged me of a number of demons. I'm not sure I know why."

"Perhaps because you know that what we feel for each other is more pure than anything the outside world can offer. I meant it when I said I trusted you. I didn't before, because I kept hearing those unconscionable accusations that made you seem a person I couldn't love. Or—if love, certainly not support. But the moment Patrick O'Dell began to speak, I knew we were alike. The sorrows of our souls are so similar, Richard, they might have been cast from the same mold. I never did physical harm to my sister, but I was blamed for her death, nonetheless. My very existence—that I lived when their favorite had died—was a blight to my parents' sensibilities. I remember well my shock and devastation. I feel it still. I can only imagine what it was like for you."

"Patrick hates me still."

"Then I rejoice in that hatred, for it made me understand what you never could. Only . . ."

She paused.

He took her hand. "Come, love. We're beyond that now. Ask what you will."

"Did you kill your father, Richard?"

"Aye—the bastard! I'd kill him again, given half the chance."

"Your own father?"

"My father, who took a lovely young girl from an occupied country and forced her into marriage. Who wrested her from her home, her family, all she'd ever known. Who took her to a foreign land where they hated her kind, and forbade her to speak of the past or her Irish ways. Who shut her up like a caged hawk to die by inches in a house that was never her own. Who beat her into submission until she became so fearful, she rarely uttered a word."

Her hand tightened on his. The ring he wore on his small finger bit into her, and she cradled his palm to look at it.

"It was hers," he told her. "He took from her all her Irish things. She wasn't to teach me anything about her people, yet she was burdened with a round-the-clock set of lessons devised to turn her into an English lady worthy of the title Countess. This penny he didn't find, so she had it mounted behind his back and hid it as her private treasure. I found it after her death—although at the time I didn't know the significance."

"How awful for you, growing up in such a household."

"Not at the time. As soon as I was old enough to know things weren't right, I was shipped off to boarding school. Then to Eton, then up to Oxford—the expected route for an English gentleman and future earl. After her death, my father returned to Ireland to carry on with the mission that had taken him there in the first place—the submission of the rebels. Fighting was particularly fierce in those days. Fisheries were being pilfered, acts of sabotage were rampant. The English in the region began to fear for their lives. We had orders to put an end to it any way we could. Carte blanche, you might say. So Father took the natural course for a civilized Englishman—he slaughtered half the countryside."

His eyes found her troubled face.

"Well, I suppose you know all that. Father was so bitter, so obsessed. He kept at me night and day about how it was our sworn duty to put down the dissident forces. He painted them with an evil brush and I—in my grief over losing a mother I'd never really known, was swept into his madness. Wanting to please him, to ease his suffering, I did his dirty work. It has haunted me ever since."

"How did you find out . . . ?"

"That some of the people we killed were my own family? Did Patrick tell you about Maureen?"

"He mentioned her."

"She was the worst of it. It was an accident, for all that matters now. We had proof her brothers had set off an explosion in town. I'd tracked them to their farm and warned them to come out of hiding. They refused, firing at me from behind some bales of hay. I fired back but didn't see Maureen running to them to convince them to give up their arms. She was caught in the crossfire, and died instantly. Her brothers went wild, naturally. In the struggle, the boys were killed and their father wounded. He was close to death when he told me the awful truth—that I'd killed my half-sister."

"Oh, Richard."

"I wanted no more of Ireland and her fight. I had more Irish blood on my hands than I cared to remember. So I sailed for England and became quite a champion of the London pubs. It was then that I met our friend the Prince of Wales. I spent several years on the fringes of Marlborough House trying to drown my memories. Then—well, I discovered something that unleashed whatever anger I had bottled up inside. Suffice to say I learned for the first time about what my father had inflicted on my mother. I went mad. Ran off to Ireland in a fit and killed the old bastard. Then I came back and took care of the Prince so that his only alternative was to challenge me to a duel."

"Bertie has something to do with all this?"

"He does. It was ludicrous, really. He considers himself quite the sportsman, but he wasn't a good enough shot to better me. As I've told you, I learned warfare at my father's knee. I've always suspected that your Bertie cheated in our duel. I shall have my answer one day."

"I don't understand. How does Bertie—"

He took her hand and kissed it, cutting her off. "That, love, is another story for another time."

"So he shot you."

"Without a doubt. I nearly died of the wound. I prayed I would. But a kind friend hid me out and nursed me back to health."

"A woman?"

"Duchess, what a question."

"If it was, I envy her. I wish it had been me."

"I, for one, am glad you never saw me in that state."

"So from there you went to America?"

"At first I felt the need to get away. Then I ran across some latter-day Fenians, and suddenly I knew how to turn it around so it all made sense. I've done what I could, but it's not enough for the family, of course. And it's never been enough for me. Until this night. I have you to thank for that." When he looked at her, she once again saw the peace that lay in the depths of his eyes.

She was quiet for a time before making a confession of her own. "I know something of what your mother must have felt, locked away in that house. My parents used to beat me. Badly, so I'd have welts for a fortnight. Once, when I'd stooped to retrieve something, my father kicked me in the back so hard, I thought it might break. And if we had guests, they'd lock me in a dark closet for hours on end."

"They should be horsewhipped," he growled.

She smiled, enjoying the feeling of protection he gave her. "Oh, there was always an excuse. It was always over some infraction of the rules. But in my heart, I knew better. I knew it was because I could never be what they wanted."

"Forgive me, but I find it difficult to imagine anyone not wanting you."

"I knew in my heart that it wasn't my fault—that it killed them to see me looking so like Elisabeth and then to realize I wasn't. If I hadn't been her twin, I suppose my life would have been different. But it didn't help to know that. When the frustration was too much for them, they released it the only way they knew how—by hurting me. It's why I can't have children," she added softly.

Her lip trembled when she said it, but when she looked at him, she saw the empathy in his eyes, and it gave her the courage to finally voice the words.

"Elisabeth had been dead only a short time when it happened. Father had been drinking heavily, which he did often after her death. He arrived home late one night, came to my room, woke me, and started talking to me as if I were my sister. I tried to tell him I wasn't, but he was too absorbed in his imaginings to hear what I was saying. And then, in the most bizarre and unimaginable way, I grew grateful for his mistake. He was so happy. He took me on his lap and petted me and said all the sweet words I'd so longed to hear from him. In my desperation for his love, it didn't even matter that he thought he was speaking to Elisabeth. Alone with him in the dark, I could pretend it was me. But soon it turned—"

She strangled on the words. "It was so ugly. He began to—"

She put her face in her hands to hide her shame from his eyes. "It became clear to me that while he'd been beating me for minor infractions of the rules, he'd at the same time been loving my sister in an uncommon way. I don't know how advanced it was. But I remembered her telling me once that being the favorite wasn't as happy a circumstance as I might think. I saw then that while he'd been coveting my sister, he'd in his saner moments been punishing me for his deformity—me, the child who looked so like Elisabeth but wasn't. Because, of course, in his own twisted thinking, he could never hurt *her*."

The Captain, listening quietly, took her hand from her face and pulled her into his lap. For a moment, the contact embarrassed her and made her draw away. She didn't want to be touched. But he held her patiently, offering his comfort but not demanding that she take it. Soon she was able to swallow the old terror and relax in his arms. She laid her head on his chest and gratefully allowed the protective strength of his arms to warm her as she continued.

"I began to struggle. He was insistent, and I had to fight him off. Seeing again the girl he took to be Elisabeth created such a fever in him that he was unstoppable."

"Sweet Christ," he said into her hair.

"The only thing that stopped him was that Mother came into the room. She saw at once what was happening and flew into a rage. Began to throw things and scream obscenities—not at Father, but at *me*! And it dawned on me that she knew nothing of Father's obsession for Elisabeth. Or if she'd suspected, she'd never acknowledged it. All she knew was that she'd caught me in an unspeakable act with her husband. I don't remember all that happened then, but after what seemed ages, they left and all was quiet. Then suddenly there he was again, standing at my bed. Only this time he knew it was my bed and not Elisabeth's. And he began to beat and kick me until I was bleeding from inside."

His arms tightened convulsively around her, but still he said nothing, allowing her an anonymous silence in which to speak.

"I called for Mother, but in her rage, she ignored me. He left me there, senseless in the dark. I couldn't move. I spent the entire night bleeding on the floor, praying for death. In the morning, my maid, Patricia, found me and informed Mother. She refused to call a physician. She knew the questions that would be asked, and the scandal that would follow. I was put to bed and fed broth and laudanum as my bruises healed. But I never healed inside. I developed an infection that went untreated for more than three weeks. By the time the physician was allowed in, it was too late. My infection was cured, but I could never have children." She paused a moment then added, "Two months later, I married Mortimer and left home for good."

"And your father?"

"He never remembered that night. At least, he claimed not to. Of course, with actors, one never knows if they're telling the truth. He might have decided the most expedient thing was to pretend to have been too drunk to remember. I do know that he stopped drinking and gave me the Wentworth pearls as a wedding gift. Mother believed him, but she never forgave me. Every time she sees the pearls on my throat, I know she remembers that night and thinks she knows why he really gave them to me. His giving them to me was the final insult. She began to truly hate me, and hasn't stopped for a moment since."

"Surely she can't hate you. Surely she'd see it wasn't your fault?"

"She sees nothing. She thinks I'm a trollop who set out to seduce my own father. She won't allow me even to explain. Better to hate me, I suppose, than her husband—which she'd be forced to do if she heard the truth. Besides, what could I say to her? Poor Elisabeth. When I think what she suffered at that man's hands . . . how could I besmirch her name now, when she isn't here to defend herself? Isn't it enough that she died?"

She was quiet for a moment. "I've never told that story to a soul. I suppose I thought no one would believe me."

"If I'd known you then, I would have killed *your* father as well as mine."

"If I'd known you then, I might have let you."

They sought each other's eyes and knew in that moment that nothing could ever come between them again.

"Listen to me," he said, holding her protectively. "For some time now, I've agonized over the importance I've allowed you to assume in my life. I had an orderly life, and lonely as it was, it was nonetheless—comfortable. I never wanted the responsibility of a love like ours. Then, when it was clear that it was out of my hands, that I would care for you no matter what, I was afraid to tell you all I feel. As if voicing it aloud would hex it. I feared that, just as I'd stolen from others, this most treasured of all gifts might be snatched from me. I knew not how to say what I felt for you inside."

"I suppose I felt the same at times. As if it was too good to be true. As if I didn't deserve it."

"But that's over, just as your conflict with your parents must become a thing of the past. I love you, Christina, as I've loved no other in my life. As I never thought myself capable of loving. As long as I live, you have nothing to fear ever again. For I shall protect you to my dying breath. Should anyone seek to harm you again, they'll have to slay me first. This I give you, on this night of nights, as my most solemn vow."

"Oh, Richard." She put her hand cherishingly to his face. "You've suffered as much as I. I'd like more than anything to make it up to you. To both of us. If only we could put it all behind us. If only together we could find some justice with the past, so that it would cease to haunt us. The circumstances are different, but we're plagued for the same reasons. Patrick O'Dell will no more praise you for your efforts than my mother shall ever commend me. You said it once, that family is the last to acknowledge what you've done. Or how you've changed. It seems such a waste of a life to be so tormented all the time over something that should be dead and buried all in a grave. Do you think it's possible for us?"

"What did Patrick say of our chances?"

"He said—No, Richard. I can't."

"I'm not your parent, Christina. You need have no fear of me."

It was so lovingly said that it made her want to weep. "He said you'd destroy me in the end."

"Then you should listen to him now, before it's too late. I may very well. I've done everything I can to destroy myself."

"It's too late already," she told him forcefully. "You may well destroy me—that I don't know. But I do know this with all my heart: if I be destroyed at your hands, at least I shall have lived."

"Why, woman, you almost give me hope!"

She clutched his hand. "Do you think we can do it, Richard? Do you think that together we can heal ourselves of these awful pains and learn to forget? I'd do anything—*give up* anything—if only we could!"

He put a truffle in his mouth and chewed thoughtfully. "I have an idea of how we might try."

He was about to tell her when the sound of a door slamming made them jump in their chairs.

"Christina," came a woman's voice from the front hall. "Oh, Christiiiina!"

Christina shot to her feet, clutching the throat of her gown. "Dear God, it's my mother!"

CHAPTER 31

*H*E WAS ON his feet swiftly, moving to the door to peer round the corner. "Didn't you lock the front door?"

She thought frantically. "No. I left it open for you."

"Some outlaw woman you'll make. I shall have to teach you better."

"Don't worry. I shall send her packing in nothing flat. Wait here. And pray God she's not in one of her moods."

As she moved past him, he caught her arm and pulled her to him to give her a swift kiss. "Remember that I'm here with you. Nothing else matters. One body, one mind, one soul."

She nodded gratefully, feeling his strength seep into her. Suddenly, she felt that she could face anything now—even Sasha Wentworth.

She fastened her robe more tightly, squared her shoulders, then went out into the hall, assuming her most regal air. "Mother. How dare you barge into my house unmindful of the proprieties?"

Sasha was dressed in evening finery of copper and gold. "One would imagine the formalities might be forsaken between mother and child."

"Nonetheless."

Grudgingly, Sasha extended her arms out to her sides so that her wrap draped gracefully to the floor as she dipped in an exaggerated curtsy. More than anything, it was the reason Christina had married the Duke—so that her mother, suddenly a rank below her, would have to bow in her presence. It gave her an enormous satisfaction to see Sasha swallow her pride and concede.

She was painfully aware of the need to be rid of her mother as soon as possible, yet she knew any hasty motions toward that end would alert Sasha to trouble. As casually as she could, she meandered into the grand salon and away from the direction of the kitchen, where the Captain hid.

"Up so early, Mother? How unlike you."

"Up? I haven't been to bed since the performance. What a night! We took *twenty* curtain calls, can you imagine? Poor Derk is quite worn to a frazzle, but I'm simply reeling so that I can't contemplate sleep for hours yet. I was passing by and saw your lights blazing away."

"You'll regret it tonight, when you stumble out of bed just hours before the performance."

The comment was automatic. She'd grown so accustomed over the years to seeing to such things for her parents—that they had enough sleep, that their costumes were in order, that they were afforded the necessary privacy before a performance so they could prepare their minds for their roles—that it came naturally for her to voice her concern. Yet strangely, Sasha's eyes lit with satisfaction on hearing it.

"Speaking of the play," she said with a studiedly careless air, "you never told me what you thought of our efforts. You pop in and out of town so much, I can hardly keep it straight that I *have* a daughter at all."

Christina was enough the actors' daughter to keep her opinions of the play to herself. It was bred in her not to criticize a performance once the play was in production. Nothing, she'd found, could set her parents off like undue criticism of their art. Instead, she addressed the issue of her absences.

"What would you have me do? Spend Wynterbrooke's money entertaining friends for the duration of my days?"

"You could come back to the theater and dress me once again. I fear the costumes in this production aren't quite what I'd hoped. What do you think?"

Costumes, because they were the work of someone

else, were fair game. "They're atrocious, frankly. You ride to mischief as if bedecked for a ball."

"Well, we can't all have your discriminating way with a needle. Perhaps you'd like to alter the costumes. I have no qualms about switching mid-season. The publicity might even further the run of the play."

"You astound me, Mother. Surely you're not complimenting my stitchery?"

"Have I ever been niggardly in my appreciation?" At Christina's sharp look, she laughed. "Well, the truth is my dresser's in hospital. Consumption, or some dreadful thing. I'm quite beside myself."

"Over her health or your predicament?"

"Well, both naturally. I'm not heartless."

"Aren't you?"

"Christina, really. You may well be a duchess, but I am still your mother. And the play must go on, after all."

"It will have to go on without me, I'm afraid. Is that why you came uninvited to my house at five in the morning? To entice me into refitting your costumes?"

"Well, as I said, I was restless and haven't been to bed." She looked at her daughter closely, for the first time. Now that she'd broached the subject of her mission, she had the leisure to make more careful observations. "Nor, from the looks of it, have you. Your mouth is positively swollen, Christina. What *have* you been doing?"

Christina put her hand to her mouth in a guilty gesture, still feeling the Captain's all-consuming kisses. "I can't think why that would be any of your business. Now, if you'll excuse me, Mother, I don't mean to be rude, but I *am* busy."

"Busy. I don't doubt it." She glanced about the room and spotted the Captain's cloak and gloves on a chair. Her heart stalled, Christina cursed her carelessness. It had never occurred to her that, having dismissed the servants, anyone would be about to see them.

Sasha picked up the cloak and shook it out. "Come, come, who is this new lover? Not the Prince, certainly. I should imagine this garment would remind him too much of the bandit." Christina paled as Sasha put the cloak to her nose and sniffed its fragrance. "Mmmm. A man's man. No fussing with perfumes. If anything, I imagine he should smell of horses and brandy and the English countryside. A sportsman, perhaps?"

"Mother, that's quite enough." She snatched the cloak from her mother's hands and held it possessively to her.

Sasha's eyes, diverted, came to rest on her daughter's throat. Christina had forgotten the necklace, but the light in her mother's eyes reminded her at once.

"My! Whoever your lover is, he has exquisite taste. In jewelry, at least."

"Mother, if you please—"

"I shall leave. But not without your promise to dress me."

"I told you, I'm occupied. I have no time for the theater."

Without warning, Sasha reached up and slapped her face. "Wretched child! You have time to play the whore to your numerous lovers, but not to aid your own mother when she's in need."

Christina clutched the cloak in her hands as tightly as she could, refusing to give Sasha the satisfaction of seeing her rub the stinging cheek. After the most beautiful night of her life, it was a mortifying blow to have the cold wind of her mother's derision intrude. "I want no part of your play, Mother—not now, not ever. I'm a grown woman. You can no longer beat me into submission of your selfish desires."

"When," asked Sasha in a furious voice, "did you ever submit to me? I live for the day when I see you do so!"

"Then you will live forever. Now, please go."

"I shall go with pleasure. But don't think you're fooling me, my sly puss. I know your moods, and I most certainly can detect when you're hiding something. It's none of my business why you're too busy for me? We shall see about that. But I warn you to be on your guard, daughter. Don't be fool enough to think you can keep secrets from me!"

•   •   •

When the Captain came up behind her, she snapped, "Don't tell me I don't have to provoke her. The very sight of her provokes me."

"I'd planned to tell you nothing of the sort. Come." He took his cloak from her and flung it to a chair. Then, her hand in his, he guided her to a long, flat settee and sat her down.

"How," she raged, "while she and I both live, can I put this bitterness to rest?"

"How would you like to leave England?"

"With you?"

He nodded.

She brightened. "I should love it."

"Then maybe we shall. It's becoming too dangerous for me here, and I know better than to underestimate your mother. A woman scorned is bad enough, but a mother scorned is trouble. Before we go, however, there are two more things we must do. After that, we can decide on the future."

"Two things?"

"Don't forget I have a score to settle with the Prince of Wales." He caught the flash of worry in her eyes, and added, "Are you with me? If not, now is the time to say no."

"Of course I'm with you. As you know, I've my own score to settle with the Prince. But you said two things?"

"I've been thinking that we must put the past to rights. But just as I can no more fathom the thought of leaving without my just rewards, neither can you forget your cares without a similar satisfaction."

"I should certainly love to see mother put in her place, if that's what you mean."

"That is precisely what I mean. But subtly, carefully, with great planning. Would it be enough to know you'd done the deed without her knowing it was you?"

Her breath was beginning to come fast. "Yes. I swear it, yes."

"Then listen to my plan. Your parents are performing a play that abuses my achievements, am I right?"

She laughed. "That's one way to put it."

"And one that makes use of my female companion's obvious charms?"

"Precious little use, if you ask me."

"What if we were to break in on that production and rob the theater in the midst of the performance? Show the audience what the Captain and his lady are really about."

Her breath left her completely. "My God! It's the most daring thing I've ever heard!"

"Then you approve?"

"Approve?" She shifted her legs so that she could rise up on her knees before him, too excited now to sit still. "It's absolutely brilliant! I should love it! Oh, Richard!"

She threw herself into his arms, and he fell with her backward into the pristine pillows. Overwhelmed, feeling her desire for him swell once again like a torrent, she suffocated him with kisses. When at last he would come up for air, he gave her a solemn look. "I shall be honest with you. It has worried me in the past that you like this life of crime too much. It feeds your rebellion."

"Is it a crime," she teased, "for a woman to enjoy her lover's work?"

He smiled, but spoke evenly. "If we do these things, they will be the most dangerous stunts we shall ever pull. We shall be dealing with people we know. People who could easily recognize us, given the chance. The Prince we can take care of. At best, he'll be surrounded by bootlickers of his own class with little skill with a pistol. But if we take the theater, there's a very grave chance of being caught. Even with men to guard every entrance, one of them could be overpowered by the crowd. Our best weapon will be surprise. But we must do the deed with as much speed as possible and exit as swiftly as we can. We can't chance some country huntsman with noble ideas taking it into his head to make one of us his prey."

"We can do it. I know every inch of that theater as intimately as I know my jewels."

"Your information will be invaluable to me in the planning. But once we're in, your primary job will be to keep your parents from recognizing you. Do you understand? I shan't risk your life with any undue theatrics."

"I shall be careful, I promise."

"I'll warn you, nonetheless. The impulse to reveal yourself will be almost more than you can bear. Know beforehand that if you do, you may well be sending us to our graves."

"If you're thinking to dampen my enthusiasm, you can't. I know the dangers, I'm aware of the risks. I shall pledge my unburdened soul that I shall take every precaution to see that we succeed. But I know in my heart that I can't leave without doing this deed. It's so perfect, so utterly worthy of the two of us, I can't think how I didn't come up with it myself."

He touched the turquoise collar on her neck. "The necklace is but a trinket. This is my real gift to you."

"To us," she corrected.

"Yes. From now, we work together. As one."

"Oh, Richard, I can't wait. To be done with this . . . to be free to be together the rest of our lives . . . it's too much to hope for. It's more than I have the right to ask."

"It won't do for you to disappear again so soon. Your mother would only suspect. Let's think for a time how to go about this. And when we're done . . ."

"When we're done?"

"Would you go to Ireland with me, until we can plan what to do? Would you allow me time to make my peace?"

She nodded with shining eyes. "Anything, my love. Even that."

CHAPTER 32

❧

OSCAR SHOWED UP unexpectedly the next afternoon to take her to tea. While it hadn't been her intention to go out in public until hearing from the Captain again, she could immediately see the usefulness of conversation with her friend.

"Not tea, though. Tea houses have ears, and I crave a bit of private discourse. Let's take a walk, shall we? I fancy a bit of exercise."

"Exercise!" he balked. "The only possible exercise is to talk, not to walk."

"If you're that lazy, at least let's take a ride in the park."

"Too much trouble. I've only just risen from my bed."

"Croquet, then?" she asked with sarcasm. "You can handle that, I trust?"

He brushed an imaginary piece of lint from his sunflower yellow jacket. "I am afraid I play no outdoor games at all. Except dominoes. I have sometimes played dominoes outside French cafes. To my way of thinking, the most perfect way of life is pure vegetation."

"No wonder you're running to fat. And the lines in your face, Oscar. Really! If you took a walk once in a while, it would keep you young." It was a wicked blow, and she knew it. Oscar was sensitive about his age—being all of twenty-nine—and he knocked off a year or two more often than not. "You can sit on a park bench, at least. Come, we'll stroll slowly lest we wind you."

He relented, however grudgingly, and they made for

the door. As they departed, he put his bandit-inspired hat upon his head and said, "To win back my youth, there is nothing I wouldn't do—except take exercise, get up early, or be a useful member of the community."

They walked to St. James's Park arm in arm and strolled about the Serpentine. There, they found a park bench and as promised, sat down to watch the ducks splash about in the water. It was cool in the shadows of the trees, with a breeze that made her snuggle up to him for his warmth. She didn't stop to think what his bride might say if she should happen by. Oscar, by now, was like a brother to her, and everyone in London knew it.

"Let's see if we can spot the bawdies," Oscar suggested. It was a well-known fact that prostitutes regularly congregated in St. James's Park.

"Not today, Oscar. I have other things on my mind."

Because she didn't broach the subject, Oscar did. "How did you find Ireland?" he asked with his customary tact.

"As a duchess, appalling as you'd expect. But dressed as one of them, I think I learned something of their real flavor. They're an exceedingly friendly people, but not polite. Funny, isn't it? It's the first time it ever occurred to me that there was a difference."

"And the information you sought? Did you find it?"

"Yes—thanks to you."

"Well, do tell. I should think this a private enough confessional."

"What I learned about Richard is between the two of us. You understand."

"I shall have to, I suppose."

"What if I told you a secret I would divulge to no one else? Would that make up for it?"

"Tell me, and we shall see."

She looked about to make certain no one was in hearing distance. Up the way, governesses pushed babies in prams while older children rolled tins or balls with sticks. One venturesome gentleman rode a bicycle, swaying to and fro so precariously that he seemed destined to fall.

"We're going away together," she whispered. "Richard and I."

"Are you! Where to, pray tell?"

"To Ireland first. From there, we'll decide. Who knows where we shall end up? America perhaps."

"Well, this *is* news. You must allow me a moment to catch my breath. I take it your intention is to leave permanently?"

"Naturally, with such a price on his head. I can't envision us making bi-yearly visits to Mother."

"Neither can I imagine your bandit, from all you've told me, settling down to a life of leisure. Nor you, for that matter. Have you addressed what you might do should he choose to continue his life of crime? And his fight for Ireland—a cause for which you have no empathy."

"It doesn't matter. All that's important now is that we're together. Oscar, do be happy for me. It's more than I'd dared hope for."

He answered with a pout. "It's romantic, I shall grant you that. And I can't say I'm surprised. I never did entertain the notion of you settling for some dull country swain with yet another title and more millions to your name. Still, you can't expect me to be overjoyed at the prospect of losing you to this felon. Where once I rather esteemed the fellow, I find that I must now denounce him as a thief. For he has stolen from me one who is more than dear."

"Oscar!" She pulled him to her and stroked his curls. "Darling, no one can abduct what I feel for you. Mark me truly, Oscar, I shall love you till the day I die. And wherever I am in the world, I shall be here for you should you need me. You've only to summon me."

"I know, pet. My mind knows it's true. It's simply my heart that grieves." He sniffed, then patted her knee with resolve. "In any case, I know you well enough to realize that once you've made up your mind, nothing anyone can say will stop you. You may have my lodge at Illaunroe, if you need it. I shall make such a fuss over the ruffian's outrages that no one will think to look for him there."

"Oscar, you're a dear. But I need something else."

"Very well. You might as well ask away. I spend half my life living vicariously through you as it is."

"I need information on Bertie's whereabouts. What his plans are, if Alix is in town, that sort of thing. Anything that might be helpful for—" She stopped, not sure how much to divulge.

"For a bit of tomfoolery? Well, I love you more dearly than I love the Prince, and I'm Irish enough not to despair over making a fool of the Crown. Have no fear, I shan't ask your plans. The less I know the better, if I'm to cover for you when the time is right."

"I knew there was a reason I love you so."

He examined her for a moment through his poet's eyes. To his mind, she'd never been more ravishing, or more serene. Gone was the restlessness that had marked her since her short-lived marriage to the Duke.

"Odd," he commented. "I've known you for a long time, Christina. I've seen you through a goodly number of scrapes. I can't be certain, but I believe I've seen you at your worst. Yet now, on the eve of your elopement with a notorious bandit, you seem less the girl bent on trouble and more the woman than you ever have before. I sense in you a tranquility I wouldn't have thought possible three months ago."

"It's about time, wouldn't you say?"

"I would indeed. If it were anyone but you, I might be envious. I myself have spent most of the years of my life searching for the equanimity I see now radiating from your never-so-lovely face. The closest I've come to such a feeling emanates from the flirting I do with the Catholic church."

Christina laughed aloud. "What I'm feeling now is hardly pious, I assure you. I feel, in fact, wildly happy. Each night, I can't wait to wake up and meet the new day. The day that will bring me closer to him."

" 'Happy' is a paltry word to describe what I see in your eyes. I must say, though, I'm amazed to find you in such a state. From what Sasha said, I had imagined you pining away."

Christina froze. "Mother! What about her?"

"I can hardly venture a guess. She came to call—woke me from slumber, I might add—to tell me I was needed and should hie myself to your abode and take you out for a soothing day on the town. Given your state of mind, I can't help but fear the poor woman has finally lost her mind."

As he'd spoken, Christina's mind was turning over all the reasons why her mother should want her out of the house. Sasha's words came back to her: *Don't be fool enough to think you can keep secrets from me!*

"Why didn't you tell me this sooner?" she cried.

"I didn't give it a thought."

"Oscar, think! Since when did Mother give a hang about my welfare?" Alarmed, she shot to her feet. "I have to go. I only hope I'm not too late."

She ran all the way home. Her lungs and legs were strong, but by the time she arrived home, her corset was cutting into her ribs and she could feel the perspiration trickling down her spine. She ignored it. She knew with certainty what she would find on her arrival. Rushing into the house, she almost knocked Gladys over in the hall.

"Is Lady Northampton here?" she gasped.

"Why, yes, your grace, upstairs—"

"You let her in? How could you!"

"Well—she told me it was your wish, mum. It was never my intention to—"

Christina raced up one then another of the flights of stairs. She burst into her bedroom to find her mother calmly turning a page in her journal.

For an instant, everything inside her died. She saw her future with the Captain for the illusion it was.

"How much did you read?"

Sasha looked up as nonchalantly as if her daughter had just joined her for tea. "Enough to have my suspicions."

Christina cautioned her wildly beating heart. If ever a situation required calm, it was this. With as much composure as she could muster, she crossed the room and took the journal from her mother's hands.

"Suspicions of what, pray tell? That I might have some talents after all, as a writer of romantic fiction?"

"Talents?" Sasha scoffed. "I could hardly judge from what I read. A more estimable piece of sentimentality I've never read."

Unbidden, Christina lost her temper. "A fine critique, coming from a woman who doesn't even read the other actors' parts in a play!"

Sasha raised her patrician brows. "I know truth when I read it. *However* muddled it might be by sentiment."

"Truth? You've never bothered to *look* at me, except to criticize. How can you possibly understand what's true about me? You never even knew me."

"I knew all that was required when you were two years old. You were a devil then, and grew to maturity destined to make my life a living hell. What would the Prince of Wales think, should he read your piece of fiction, is it?"

"What do I care what he thinks? A person can't be hanged for invention."

"I wonder. I should wager the Prince might agree with me that you have a rather—how shall we put it?— *intimate* knowledge of the bandit's activities."

"Or I might simply be the possessor of an overactive imagination. It won't be the first time I've been accused of such."

"How, then, do you explain these?"

Sasha, smug in her assertions, opened the bottom drawer of one of Christina's jewel boxes. A moment later, she held up the triple strand of black Wentworth pearls with thumb and forefinger—as though by touching them, she might acquire some disease.

Christina endeavored to control her shaking. "The bandit returned them to me before he put me on the train. Unbeknownst to me, he'd slipped them into my bag. I can't say why, except perhaps in a tender moment, he took pity on a woman whose parents wouldn't even ransom her return."

"You seem healthy enough to me. What ransom did *you* pay for your release?"

A white anger blinded her for an instant. She had to clench her teeth to keep from saying something she might regret. "I shall forget you asked me that, Mother."

"Very well. Let's assume, as you contend, that the bandit returned your jewels. Why did you not inform your father of the fact when you returned? I distinctly recall his asking you about them that weekend in Norfolk."

"Perhaps I was angered that he showed more concern for his precious pearls than he did for his own daughter."

"Oh, Christina, posh. You always did crave to be the center of attention. When you weren't given the adoration you felt due you, you ran and pouted and cried that you were misused."

"I can't think," came a voice from the doorway, "where she got it."

The women turned as one to see Oscar hanging on to the doorjamb as if the very life were seeping from him. Sweat streamed down his face in rivulets, and he spoke with a panting breath. Touched, Christina realized that he must have run all the way after her.

"Really," Sasha was saying, "one has no time for such nonsense—particularly from a grown woman who ought to know better."

"The same, my dear woman, might be said of you."

Tired as he was, Oscar had lost none of his wit. He was clearly there to protect Christina—perhaps from herself—and she took full advantage of it, relying on his galloping mind to come up with a solution to her dilemma.

"Mother found my journal, and has taken off with the notion that it's an autobiography. Because I deny what isn't true, I'm yet again a thankless child."

Oscar gazed at Sasha with a look of astonishment lighting his poet's eyes. "My dear woman, you can't be serious! I know as well as you that we've had a time with our girl, but to give her credit for the sort of brinkmanship you're implying—forgive me, but I chuckle to think of it."

Hearing it put that way, Sasha frowned in doubt.

Oscar stumbled into the room and put a companionable arm about the actress's shoulders. "I assure you there is nothing to your suspicions, dearest lady. If there were, wouldn't I come to you, bent on saving the poor girl's soul?"

"I should hardly think so, after the scrapes the two of you have perpetrated behind my back."

"Child's play! Mere pranks, compared to this. Think of it logically for a moment. Should our darling child leave hearth and home to marry—God forbid!—an outlaw, what has she to gain? A life of poverty. Fear. Obscurity. One eye over her shoulder at all times. The very comforts one takes for granted would be a thing of the past. The theater, for example. She may deny it, but you and I both know the theater is every bit as much a part of Christina's blood as it is yours and Derk's."

Sasha dropped the pearls to the dresser as Oscar continued.

"Think, if you will, what she should be giving up to pursue her life of crime. Her duchy, for one. Tell me truly, dear. Do you see, in any conceivable situation, Christina becoming less than the Duchess of Wynterbrooke? After she worked so hard to acquire the position? Not to *mention* the money. In a pinch, I can fend for myself. But let's face it, shall we? Your daughter couldn't pour herself a glass of wine."

"Who ever said she'd have to marry the beast? Christina's had lovers enough, without endangering her title."

"I tell you, Sasha, there is nothing to this. If there were, wouldn't I know? She's let me read her work. It isn't the first time—nor, do I imagine will it be the last—that Christina has conjured up dark heroes to fuel her imagination. It comes from her love of the Bröntes, I daresay. But the truth is, though I know you'll disbelieve me, that Christina was hoping to make things up to you. She hoped a novella about the Brighton Bandit might feed proceeds for your play. There, fanciful woman. You've caused me to ruin the surprise."

Christina was appalled by his explanation. She'd be damned if she'd allow the public to amuse themselves with details of her lover. But she had to play along. Once she and Richard were gone, it wouldn't matter that no novella had come to light. It would be too late.

"Actually," she said, scowling at her friend, "I can hardly take the credit. It was Oscar's idea."

"There! What did I tell you?"

Sasha was casting doubtful looks between the two of them. "If you're thinking to mislead me——"

"What could we possibly gain? Christina may have been wayward in the past, but she's hardly stupid. Come, dear lady, surely there must be a way to make amends. What can Christina give to pacify your wounded sentiments?"

Sasha gave her daughter a direct, commanding look. "She can resume her friendship with the Prince of Wales."

Christina closed her eyes.

"To what end, dearest?" Oscar asked.

"When she was—shall we say *friendly* with the Prince, nothing was too good for us. His Highness made certain Derk and I were on all the best guest lists, and that everyone who counted came to our productions. Now, he seems displeased because of this new play. Derk and I can ill afford the disfavor of the Prince of Wales. If I can present him with that which, for some reason, he so relentlessly desires, I should think that should cause him to look more favorably upon us in the future."

"Perhaps," snapped Christina, "you should just deliver my head on a plate!"

Oscar interceded. "Surely, ladies, we can come to terms."

"My terms," said Sasha in a hard tone, "require that Christina go back to the Prince. Lacking that, I intend to inform him of what I've learned this day."

Looking to Christina, Oscar gave a little jerk of his

head as if to say, "Do humor the old bag so we might shoo her on her way."

Swallowing her indignation at being bartered to the Prince by her own mother, Christina forced herself to answer pleasantly. "I have nothing to fear from any disclosure you might make. Still, I don't suppose it would hurt to hear what he has to say. I can make no promises, but if it makes you happy, Mother, put your mind at ease. I shall see Bertie."

Behind the barrel of a pistol, she added to herself.

"Very well. But if you think to fool me with your acting skills—or lack thereof—I should think again. As you know, I can spot a performance at first glance."

She left, but not before casting a last contemptuous look at the coveted Wentworth pearls.

The moment she heard her mother's step on the stairs, Christina closed her bedroom door. "I don't know what I'd have done without you," she told Oscar, allowing herself the luxury of leaning back against the door and trembling. "Killed her, I suppose."

"I won't have you say such things. Murder is always a mistake. One should never do anything one cannot discuss after dinner."

"You must have read my journal haphazardly, then. I have already killed a man."

"That was an accident. Killing your mother would be cold-blooded murder. However justifiable."

"I'd love to strangle her for what she's done. She has the audacity to call me a whore, then to turn round and sell me to the highest bidder. Not to benefit me, mind you. To ensure her bloody place in society!"

"Careful, pet. The walls have ears, as you've said. Now, tell me what I can do."

"Just get me the information we seek. And do hurry, Oscar. Time is of the essence. In light of Mother's suspicions, Richard and I must accomplish our missions, then flee the country as swiftly as we can. But first, I shall throw my beloved mother's words back in her face."

"How do you intend doing that?"

"By showing her she isn't the only actress in this family!"

CHAPTER 33

CHRISTINA MET THE Prince after midnight at St. Katherine's Church just on the northeastern side of Regent's Park. When he arrived, having been summoned from a party, he was disgruntled.

"Deuced nuisance, coming all the way out here. Could we not at least have met in some civilized place? You were invited to the Bakerlys'—I saw to that."

The full moon shone brightly under a cloudless sky, spilling streams of silver moonlight onto the terrain. Christina stepped out of the shadows of the church into the shimmering light, and heard him gasp. She was wearing his favorite dress, a sleeveless black velvet-and-lace ball gown with elegant folds of black lace draped enticingly about the swell of her breasts. A smattering of white roses formed a flowing vertical line down the right side of the skirt. Another rose graced her shoulder. But it wasn't the gown that caused the sharp intake of his breath. It was the three-feathered diamond necklace, the emblem of the Prince of Wales, that caught the moonlight in a single sparkling flash.

"It was my understanding," she said softly, "that you wished to talk of renewing our acquaintance. Would you have me arrange such an assignation at Mott's? You should know by now that I am more discreet."

He stepped up to her and took the necklace in his hand. As he did so, his arm brushed her soft breast. He sought her eyes with his.

"Are you asking me to believe you've brought me on this mission to ignite my tender passions?"

She snatched the necklace from him. "Tender! When were you ever tender with me?"

"I find, to my amazement, that I harbor the most *tender* of feelings for you. My fondness for you has blossomed with the passage of time, Christina. No woman has ever incited in me such a desire to possess her. You must believe me, surely, by now."

She turned her back to him, taking her face out of the moonlight.

"But then," he added in a hardening tone, "the issue seems not to be your level of confidence. Correct me, dear, if I'm mistaken, but did you not just now imply a certain willingness to discover what tender feelings I might now possess?"

She began to walk in the direction of the park so that he had no choice but to follow. "I never promised to do so. Only that I should think about it."

"Surely, you didn't call me away from the Bakerlys' at this hour of the night to once again throw your rejection in my face?"

"Actually, it was Mother's idea that I meet you. You seem to have exerted just the proper pressure. As is your custom."

"Only when my hand is forced."

"You prefer force, as I recall."

He took hold of her arm and jerked her about to face him. "No, Christina," he said, his fingers digging into her flesh. "You're the only woman who ever made me force her into anything. I used to look at you and want you so badly, I thought I might lose my mind. I could think of nothing save you, even in the comfort of my own bed. Do you think I wanted to be your slave, to play the harlequin when time and again you turned your back to me?"

"I think you wanted me *because* I turned my back to you."

"I wanted you because no man in his right mind could look at you and *not* want you. There's something about you—that come-hither taunt in your eyes even as you hold yourself aloof. Even when you don't intend it, there's a look of slumbering passion in your eyes. *Any* man would want to break through your damnable independence and possess you for himself. Am I any less a man because I was born a prince?"

Once again, she stalked away. He followed her through the entrance to the park and along the grassy pasture. Moonbeams lit the earth, seeming to form a path before their marching feet.

"You're less of a man because you never saw me as a woman, but rather a plaything you could use to feed your masculine pride. You wanted to possess me, did you? What of caring, Bertie? What of kindness? You used me like some animal on a chain," she accused.

"And even then," he railed, "even as you submitted to my vilest desires—even as you drove me to the very brink of maddened joy—even then, you held yourself from me. Why do you think I did those terrible things to you? To capture your attention, damn you! Just once, I wanted to see if I could elicit a reaction. Just once, I wanted to see you pant in my arms and cry out my name!"

"Then I pity you. Perhaps if you'd cared less about possessing me and more about what would make me happy—"

"But I do! Christina, as God in heaven is my witness, I've spent a lifetime in the pursuit of pleasing women. I swear to you, in all my philandering, only one other woman has driven me to such madness, and that was years ago. I'm known far and wide as a kind and generous lover. You know that to be true."

"I've heard such rumors, I'll admit. I thought perhaps you'd drugged your victims, to leave them with such misguided impressions."

Above his bulk, his shoulders slumped. When he spoke, it was in a quiet, pleading tone. "Christina. Dearest. Could you not grace me with another chance? I shall make it up to you as only a future monarch can. It will be different this time, I swear. No chains, no other men. Just us, learning to love again. I'd never have had to manacle you in the first place if you'd come to my bed more willingly. Surely your memories can't be *all* bad? There were times when I felt, had your pride not held you back, you might have enjoyed our little romps."

"I didn't dislike what we did," she admitted heatedly, "so much as your brutal intention to crush my spirit. My own mother couldn't conquer me—how did you imagine you could?"

This perplexed him. He remembered their depraved matings with sudden longing. Never had he met a woman more capable of keeping pace with his rampant sexual desires. Was she saying that she was willing to give it another go, this time on different terms?

"Then perhaps we can discuss a new arrangement," he suggested, struggling to keep the excitement from his tone. "One more agreeable to your disposition."

"I made an agreement to hear you out. I shall keep my bargain, if you care to state your case."

They were walking through the remote, northern section of Regent's Park. Even in the daylight, few people ventured this far north. It felt desolate and empty, strangely hushed. His Highness looked around as he sought to organize his thoughts, suddenly noting his surroundings. "Hey now! Where are we off to?"

Christina continued to walk. "I crave privacy. I've had the feeling all day that I was being followed."

"You're growing fanciful," he scoffed.

"Perhaps. Although, Mother had me followed once, before I married Wynterbrooke. I wouldn't put it past her to do so again, just to see if I'd kept my word."

He looked around at the deserted stillness. "I can't say I like the idea of being watched. Gives me the most *uncomfortable* feeling."

"Relax, Bertie. If someone's watching, it's me he's interested in, not you." She cast him a sly look. "If I were being followed, would you protect me?"

He was still searching the surrounding grassland nervously. He happened to glance at her, catching sight of her beauty in the silvery glow, and immediately forgot the implied threat. "I should walk to China and back for you, Christina. I swear it before God."

She took his arm and began to walk toward the trees.

"Tell me, Bertie, since you insist on discussing this. What can you offer me that I don't already have?"

He increased his pace to keep up with her, stumbling a bit over some rough terrain.

"Position, for one. You know yourself that my mistresses have always maintained the highest social position of all the ladies in the land."

"I've position enough as Wynterbrooke's widow. Now if you'd married me, that would have been another story. The prospect of being Queen might have made even *your* bed look appealing."

This wasn't going as he'd planned. He made a weak attempt at humor as a way of thawing her. "Except that you were all of three months old when I married. Did you expect that I should wait?"

She wasn't amused, but continued as before. "You can't offer me money. Until the day you ascend the throne, I have more wealth than you. And love—well, we've already established our differences in that department. Security is laughable. The moment I gave you my heart, you'd lose interest and go chasing about after some French demimondaine. So, logically speaking, Bertie, what have you to offer?"

As he pondered this query, they passed through a dense cluster of pines and out into a clearing. In the conspicuous moon, the trees cast elongated shadows across the meadow, like ghostly sentinels in the night. Abruptly, the Prince came to a halt.

"Bertie, what is it? Do you hear something?"

Genuine panic was reflected in his eyes. "Why did you bring me here?" he gasped.

"What do you mean? To discuss our future, as promised. What ails you?"

He began to mumble in a crazed way. "I didn't realize till this minute where we were. I haven't been here since that night. How could you know? The only ones who knew are dead."

"What night?"

"The night of the duel. It was here—this very place— that I killed Lord Wycliffe." He was darting about, searching in all directions as if expecting an apparition.

"It seems like a lifetime ago. It was not a night unlike this, with the blasted moonlight everywhere, making things seem unreal . . ."

He clutched her arm. "Let us be off at once from this cursed place. I have no desire to dredge up the buried past."

There was a rustle in the bushes, and a low, feral voice came from behind. "Desire or no, Highness, the past has a way of dredging itself up. It comes like a thief in the night to haunt those with guilty souls."

Bertie froze. The Captain and two men stepped from the shelter of the trees to walk slowly forward. Twenty paces away, they stopped and stood looking at the Prince's rigid back. Behind them, a masked woman came up with a small box in her hands.

Slowly, as if the cold hand of death had him in its grasp, the Prince turned to face the apparition. "Richard," he whispered on the shocked expulsion of his breath. "It can't be you."

The Captain reached up with a gloved hand and pulled off his mask, exposing his face to the moon. Then he took his hat from his head and tossed it aside. The woman scurried forth to retrieve it.

"Can't it, Highness?" the Captain challenged.

"Yet it looks like you," Bertie went on, reeling back a step or two. "Just as you were that night, with your cloak about you—A ghost! You can't be real. Surely I'm behexed!"

There was a desperate whine to his voice.

"Do you mean to tell me, Highness, that seeing a ghost on a moonlit night would be preferable to having your old friend return to life?"

The Captain's words were smoothly uttered in a silkily deceptive, pleasant tone.

"I killed you!" cried the Prince so that his voice rang out into the night.

"Did you?" The outlaw put his hand to his chest. "My beating heart says nay. But I can be as cricket as the next fellow. What say you to a rematch? Effected here, in the very place where your luck held so dear?"

The Prince was sweating noticeably now. When he

glanced at Christina, as if entertaining some desperate hope that she could stop this, she could see the fear in his darting eyes. "I've a lady present. You wouldn't be so ungallant as to insist under such circumstances."

The Captain looked to Christina, his eyes flicking over her with chilling disinterest. "Ah, yes. Duchess, you're lovelier than ever, I see. A pity we're forced to meet like this again so soon. But you've brought it on yourself, I fear. Did no one warn you of the dangers of toying with a married man?"

"I won't have you speak to her in that impertinent manner!"

"You tempt me to do more than speak. You took from me and mine once before—what more appropriate theft, I ask myself, to help settle the score?"

"If you touch one hair on the lady's head—"

"Calm yourself. I'm distracted this night by other pursuits. I can't think, though, why the lady's presence should affect our plans. Word on the streets is you desire the Brighton Bandit hurried to his grave. He stands before you, Highness, in all his mortal vulnerability. Why take the chance that he might yet again slip away? Kill me now, as you once so nearly did, and be done with the thing. For I shall confess to you a deep and painful truth." He strode forward, coming to rest just inches before the Prince's face. His voice hardened as he ground the words out through his teeth. "Never again will you find me so assailable. Never again, my old mistrustful friend, will I be so blinded by the rage that tonight afflicts my brain—a rage that, as I see your face before me, roars through my body like thunder and makes my insufficient fist hunger for your throat. If hate blinds a man, then I be blinded beyond reason on this of all unlucky nights. I would caution you to strike now, while my impediment might misdirect my aim."

Christina, who'd been a part of the plan until this moment, listened with growing agitation to the wrath in her lover's voice. They had meant only to scare the Prince, but she could see that, faced with the reality of his enemy's presence, the Captain was quickly losing sight of his equitable intentions.

"In fact, Duchess," he continued, "you might favor us with your assistance. I had hoped to give the pleasure to my own lady, but under the circumstances, I could hardly deprive you of the honor."

He left them to cross the distance to the masked woman. Taking the box from her, he brought it back and placed it in Christina's hands. Then he lifted the lid to display a brace of pistols nestled in velvet.

Christina caught her breath. "You don't intend to go through with it!"

"That," he said, giving her a stern look, "is exactly what I intend. Care to choose, Highness? No? Then you won't mind if I do the honors."

He chose a pistol and handed it to the Prince, who took it as if he were in a daze. Then the Captain retrieved the box from Christina and turned to take it back. As he did so, he tossed over his shoulder, "Take care, Duchess, lest your paramour shoot me in the back. My men—not to mention my lady—may not look kindly on such treachery."

When he was partway back to his men, Christina ran after him and touched his arm. "You can't be serious!" she whispered urgently. "This isn't what we planned."

"Even master planners alter their schemes as circumstances warrant. The mark of the true artist is to leave oneself open to the unexpected."

"Richard, you can't. You'll kill him."

He grinned, flashing his white teeth. "Aye, Duchess. I may at that."

He turned, and she followed once again, softening her voice for his ears alone. "I hate him, too, God knows. But you can't kill him. He's the future King of England!"

His voice lashed out at her like a whip. "Did he behave like a king when he raped my mother and turned her to his dogs?"

He looked beyond her to the Prince, who was watching them with great round eyes.

"You remember that, don't you Highness?" He shoved the box into Christina's hands and stormed back to the Prince.

The masked woman rushed up to take the box from

her. "I don't like the looks of him," Bobby's voice said from behind the mask.

Christina was too stunned by Richard's last words to speak.

Whatever control the Captain had maintained until that point was rapidly vanishing as he spat out a barrage of spiteful accusations, all the while bearing down on the Prince.

"Do you deny it, Highness? Speak up, sweet Prince. We wait breathlessly to hear you explain. Were there not enough strumpets strewn about to fill your bed? Did you have to force yourself on an innocent woman—and destroy her in the process—just to carve another notch on your belt? Was she so lovely that the cry of your filthy loins superseded your sense?"

"She was more than lovely. She was an angel."

"An angel you saw fit to send back to heaven, no doubt." He turned to Christina. "Tell me, Duchess. Was the Prince tender in your bed? Because he wasn't in my mother's. A man who was there at the time, participating in this—*deed* told me of the fun they'd had one auspicious eve. How they tied her, naked, to the royal bed and made her do unspeakable acts. She who was so beaten down by life that she rarely spoke a word."

"You know so much, do you?" cried the Prince with his first show of spirit. "Did you know, perchance, that your father gave me leave? That he was happy to trade the favors of his wife for the advancement of his career?"

For a whole minute, the night was deathly still. When the bandit finally answered, his voice was so low, it could barely be heard. "Why do you think I killed him and left him lying in the road?"

"That's a confession! The Duchess heard it. She'll testify at your trial."

"My trial be damned. If I'm to swing from some English tree, then better I hang for killing you." He shoved the Prince toward the center of the field, then followed and shoved again. "Come, you bloody royal bastard. Let us see if once again your purity gifts you with a superhuman aim."

"You're a madman!" wailed the Prince. "I'll not subsidize your lunacy."

"Please yourself. It will be murder, then, and no sorrow to me. For mark me well, Highness. At the count of ten, I swear to you before God that I shall pull the trigger."

Christina jerked as she felt his gaze rake over her.

"Duchess, you're wanted for the count."

She stood where she was, unable to move. Again, she saw that ruthless quality in him that had so frightened her before. It was no less terrifying now. She had no wish to witness the awful outcome. "I can't," she said helplessly.

"You will, or I shall be forced to shoot in cold blood. Would you have it on your conscience?"

"My conscience is burdened enough as it is. I can be no party to this. Please, I beg of you, don't do this thing."

He cut her off with a look. At the jerk of his head, one of his men came up behind her. It was Toby, limping badly and clearly worried by this turn of events, but otherwise well. He took her arm and urged her to move with him. "Do what he says, my lady. There's no arguin' when he's like this."

He led her like a sleepwalker to the duelers.

"I trust," said the Captain conversationally to the Prince, "that you recall the routine. As you have no second, I forfeit my right as well. Unless you'd prefer to use the ladies. You give little care, I'm told, to the sensibilities of women."

Bertie said nothing. He was trembling so badly, he could barely stand. Christina, in her sleeveless dress, was shivering with equal measure, but not, she knew, from the chill.

The Captain swung his cloak from about his shoulders and heaved it to Toby, then removed his gloves and did the same. Standing straight and tall, he fastened his back to the Prince's and angled a look at Christina. "You may start whenever you're ready, Duchess. All that's required is a slow, measured count to ten."

Toby steered her back, out of the line of fire, then

nudged her to begin the count. Everything inside her screamed at her to defy her lover's wishes. Was this what he'd meant when he spoke of putting the past to rest?

He gave her one last look, holding her gaze with such sinister command that she felt the strength to revolt drain out of her. Against her will, she began the count.

"One."

The two men stepped out, the Captain vigorously, the Prince as though pulled unwillingly by a rope.

"Two."

With each successive number, the men moved further apart. Each step seemed an agony to His Highness, whose legs wobbled as if he were walking on hot sand.

"Six."

Christina's heart seemed to roar in her ears.

"Seven."

Suddenly, a strangled sound escaped the Prince as he fell heavily to his knees. There, dropping the pistol to the ground, he began to weep. "I can't go through with it. I haven't the skill. God help me, I cheated the last time. I knew I could never best you. It was Wembly who shot you, from behind a tree."

Sobbing, he fell forward until his head touched the ground.

The Captain had turned at the first sound. Now he stood, glaring with blazing eyes at the broken mound of a man. Slowly, he raised his arm and aimed the pistol. The look in his eyes spoke of the thirst for murder on his tongue.

"If I could take it back, I would," the Prince was blubbering. "She drove me mad. She was so unattainable, so ethereal. So beautiful. She never wanted me, so I had to make her pay. But in the end, she was just another woman." He raised his head and cried out his defiance. "Kill me if you must. But you do so for naught. I cared nothing for Bridget. I only wanted what she wouldn't freely give."

Just like me, Christina thought bitterly. Her anger strangled her. She looked at her lover as he cocked the hammer with his thumb. *Do it,* she willed him, for one mad moment. *Just pull the trigger!*

It seemed that he would. Then, quite suddenly, he dropped his arm to his side. She heard the hammer click back into place.

"It's enough for me to have what can never be yours," the Captain said in a tone of astonishing calm. "Having taken from you more than the blood I sought to shed, I hereby forfeit my claim to your life. You're free to go, Highness. You need have no more fear of me."

Her shock receded as a similar peace took possession of Christina. Casting a glance at Bertie to see his face pressed with relief into the ground, she moved quickly to the Captain's side and stealthily took his hand. As his gaze found her face in the moonlight, she smiled and gave his hand a squeeze.

Then she crossed the clearing and stood above the Prince of Wales, allowing her contempt to show on her face.

"Some manner of man is this future king. You seduce every woman who catches your eye, yet you can't even fight your own duels."

At her words, the Prince crumpled into a ball, his sobs racking his massive body like a boy's.

The Captain hadn't moved. Christina stood for a few moments, gazing at the man at her feet. "Come, Bertie," she said more gently than she'd intended. "I shall take you home."

CHAPTER 34

HE PRINCE WAS stewing. He paced the floor of his vast salon as Inspector Worthington struggled to make sense of his story. Christina, sitting quietly, played with an ivory fan.

She'd been summoned to Marlborough House first thing in the morning to add weight to Bertie's testimony. The residence was an imposing structure with countless bedrooms, one of the loveliest ballrooms in London, and beautifully manicured lawns adjoining the Mall. It was one of the few London homes that rivaled Christina's for elegance and grandeur.

That beauty was lost on Worthington, who, although he was conducting this investigation, couldn't escape the feeling that it was *he* who was being called on the carpet. It was a feeling that had plagued him all his life. He'd been born the son of Bruno Worthington, a prison guard at Newgate in the old days, when the gaol was the most dreaded of prisons. Bruno the Fist they'd called him. He was notorious in all of England for the undetectable harm he could cause with his fists. Those brought before Bruno knew they'd be made to talk in the end—or they'd die silent. Bruno hated crime the way priests despise sin. From the age of five, he took his impressionable son to the cold, forbidding corridors of the dungeon to witness the treatment of men who refused to bend to the law. The sight of his father inflicting such pain on his fellow man haunted Worthington's youth. Even worse was the disproportionate punishment his father meted out for any imagined violation of the rules. It didn't matter to Bruno that the offender was his own son. The message was loud and clear: you break the rules, you pay the price. There was a time when, wishing to rebel, Worthington had even considered a career in crime. But he knew if he was caught, his father would surely kill him as easily as he extinguished the lives of strangers. Bruno made no distinctions. A criminal was a criminal.

There were times, even now, when Worthington secretly envied the criminals their lives of freedom. He had never been free. His earliest memories were of people boasting of his father's success. "We know you'll grow up just like him," they'd said. And he had. But for different reasons. He'd grown to become an enforcer of the law because he hated criminals as much as his father had. He hated the fact that he'd borne the palm of his father's superiority, that the fear of crime had been beaten into him while it had not in the men he captured. In its own way, it made him as adamant about the law as his father had been.

Then his father died, and the pressures on him to live up to his image eased over time. People stopped comparing them. They began to see Worthington as a peacemaker in his own right. Things were progressing nicely in his career—until this Brighton Bandit came along and made him the laughingstock of all England. Often, in his most inconsolable moments, he wondered what his father would say of his inability to bring the ruffian to heel. Wondered, and was glad his father was in his grave, where he couldn't see.

Though they'd been at it for hours by this time, it seemed to Worthington that they were no further along than when they'd started. For their own reasons, neither Christina nor the Prince cared to make a full disclosure of the events of the night before.

"But, Your Highness," the Inspector moaned, "I merely want details that might lead to the capture of this ruffian. Forgive me, sir, but your story is vague at best. I have yet to determine what you were doing in such a remote part of the park at that hour of the night."

"And I have told you repeatedly, that is none of your business. Must a gentleman besmirch a lady's reputation, even to the police?"

Worthington's already flushed face reddened. He cast an embarrassed look at Christina, who caught the flash of comprehension in his eyes. "Ah, I see . . . well . . ."

Christina snapped her fan shut. It maddened her to think of the Prince's furthering his reputation as a lady's man at her expense. Particularly after last night. She stood and said in her most superior tone, "Really, Highness, if this is the reason you insisted on my presence—"

Bertie waved her to silence. His humiliation in her eyes the night before brought to light a defensive brusqueness of manner that was quite unlike him. He seemed to be endeavoring to prove to her that he bore no relation to the spineless craven she'd taken sniveling from Regent's Park.

"But how did he know you were there?"

"How the deuce should I know?"

The Inspector forced a note of patience into his tone. "Could he have followed you, perhaps?"

Bertie's face brightened. "Why, yes, now I think of it, the Duchess *said* she thought she was being followed."

"I had that feeling most of the day."

The Inspector turned to her. "But why would he care to follow you?"

"I haven't the slightest notion. Perhaps he read a notice of my parents' play."

Worthington gave a blank look. "Why would that necessitate his following *you*? If he wanted revenge, I'd think he'd seek out your father."

She gave him a scathing look. "I was jesting, Inspector. I had thought that apparent."

The Inspector seethed inside. This was just the sort of overbearing treatment he always received at the hands of the aristocracy. They expected him to solve their troubles—instantly, no less—and then treated him with the lack of respect and amused tolerance they might show a frolicsome child. Their bloody horses were deferred to more than the Chief Inspector of Scotland Yard!

He felt his frustration like a growing tumor in his

brain. It made him want to lash out at someone—the Prince, even this infernal duchess, who was to his mind obviously the Prince's lover. But that would never do. He'd been taught to respect and even fear authority. The Prince might be known to be dull-witted and over-indulgent in his appetites, but he never hesitated to crush those who crossed him.

Worthington's only answer was to find the bandit. The Prince would be so grateful to have the nuisance finally disposed of that he wouldn't care what condition he was in when he arrived. If only Worthington could capture the bandit who was making his life such hell and vent his outrage once and for all!

Meanwhile, he must keep his frustrations to himself and deal with these ruddy aristocrats.

"I hardly find this a matter worthy of jest," he answered stiffly. "Better use our time to determine what the bandit might want of you."

"Your questions are immaterial," the Prince exploded, losing his patience with Worthington's stodgy justification of his incompetence. "The point is we now know the fiend to be Lord Wycliffe. Now, what I want to know is what are you going to do about it, man? Must I shake in my sheets for fear that he might come in the night and finish the job?"

There was a subtle rap on the door, and the major-domo came in, bowed, and announced, "The Marchioness of Northampton is here with Mr. Wilde, Your Highness. Do you wish me to send them away?"

"No, no, we're nearly done here. Bring them along." Then, to Worthington, "Well, sir?"

"Well, naturally," Worthington blustered, "we shall have every available man on the job. Knowing his identity may help. Although I can't think why the Duchess didn't realize it sooner, when last I asked her."

Christina bore the Inspector's sharp look with a raise of her chin. "Perhaps because the bandit didn't see fit to confide in me while I was a guest in his camp. Also, as I explained before, we know him to be a master of disguise. Really, Inspector, this grows tiresome."

The Prince cut in. "Every available man is not good

enough. I want men taken off other posts with instructions to shoot to kill. I want this man found, Inspector, or the Crown will have not only your job, but your head as well. Do I make myself understood?"

"Perfectly, Your Highness. We shall capture the bandit if it's the last thing we do. You have my word."

"Let's hope the caliber of your word has improved since the last unfulfilled promise you made."

Worthington bowed and left with a stilted gait.

In the ensuing hush, Christina said, "You want the bandit killed so he won't tell what he knows. Tell me, Bertie, do you plan to have me silenced as well?"

The rustle of satin in the doorway heralded Sasha's entrance, rendering a retort impossible. "My darling girl, I came as soon as I heard!" She rushed forth with extended arms and took Christina's head in her hands to give each cheek a kiss. So convincing was her display, no one but Christina knew that her lips missed her daughter's cheeks by a wide margin and her kisses were given to the air. Only then did Sasha turn to the Prince with the required curtsy. "You'll forgive my rudeness, Your Highness, but a mother's thoughts are with her offspring first. Particularly when she came so close to death the night before."

Oscar, leaning against the doorway, gave Christina a droll look. He came into the room at a more leisurely pace and bowed to the Prince. "We heard from the Duchess's servants what had happened. I trust you're well, Highness?"

"Perfectly, now that the ordeal is behind us."

"But pray what happened?" asked Sasha. "The servants were distressingly taciturn, as only servants can be. They only gossip when it will embarrass their employers. Am I not right, Oscar?"

"As always, dear lady, you express your singular dogma with the conviction of a prophet. But do continue, Highness. The suspense has kept us dallying long enough."

"There's not much to tell. The Duchess and I were robbed by the bandit in Regent's Park."

"Regent's Park. Correct me if I'm wrong, but wasn't that the site of the famous duel?"

Angrily, the Prince ignored him. "Suffice to say we have proof the bandit is Lord Wycliffe."

Oscar flashed a look at Christina. "Indeed?"

"I spoke to him myself," Bertie answered gruffly.

"Oh, to be a fly on the wall," murmured Oscar.

"But he won't be loose for long. I've given Worthington what-for. It's his last chance to come up with the beast, and he knows it."

Sasha, who'd caught Oscar's look at her daughter, rose to her full height and assumed a simpering look. "I don't suppose the woman was with him? This Fiaran?"

"She was indeed."

"Really!" This obviously unsettled Sasha, for she began to move restlessly about the room. "Tell me—for the sake of my performance, mind you. Was she all they say of her?"

Bertie thought a moment as if the question took him by surprise. "Why, yes, I should say so. She seemed to me an exceptional beauty, though she was cloaked in shadows."

Christina thought of Bobby stuffed into her hastily altered costume and lowered her eyes.

"And was she as fierce as they say?"

"I believe she was. She handed the fiend the pistols— when he sought to rob us, that is," he amended hastily.

"You don't say," Sasha murmured, clearly disappointed. "Well, it seems I owe you an apology." She cast a resentful look to Christina.

"You can be proud of your daughter," the Prince said, remembering for the moment what he chose of the encounter. "She was quite the heroine. Begged for my life most prettily, as I recall."

"Did she indeed!" cried Oscar. When the Prince shot him an indignant look, he added, "And rightfully so. The Duchess has confessed to me her abominable treatment at the hands of the blackguard. I can't say it endeared him to me. I do hope Worthington conquers the odds and brings him to justice. I, for one, shall even forgo my morning sleep to be at his hanging. Unless, of course, the Crown might find it in their hearts to accommodate me with an evening affair . . ."

That afternoon, when Gladys came back from the market, she announced that there was a man standing up the square watching the house. She and Christina went to the window and peered out together. A man in a brown suit and bowler hat leaned against the lamppost, reading a newspaper. Every few moments, he glanced up in the direction of the house.

"I wasn't sure at first," Gladys whispered, as if the man could hear. "But what with all the excitement lately, I thought it best to keep my eyes and ears open. You never know what might 'appen these days, even in a neighborhood like this here one."

"You were good to spot it," Christina told her. "Of course, we could be mistaken. Suppose I go out for a stroll and see for myself just what the gentleman is up to."

She put on a smart hat and went out as though for a leisurely walk toward the park. Casting a quick glance over her shoulder, she saw that the man was following. She stopped, bending as though to admire a group of pansies and marigolds, and saw that he paused as well. All at once, she knew who he was. The Captain must have sent him to keep an eye on her until they could finish their final job and leave.

If that was true, then this man could get a message to the Captain for her. She dropped the facade of a walk and headed straight for him. Nonplussed, he dropped onto a bench and shook out his paper.

She sat down beside him and took a deep breath as if enjoying the air. "Lovely day, isn't it?" she asked.

He glanced up at her as if he hadn't seen her sit down. He was very young, with curly sandy hair and a long waxed mustache. "Mum?" He cleared his throat and hastily returned to his paper. "Oh, yes, lovely, quite."

"Tell me, good sir. Is it my imagination, or have you been following me?"

"Following? Your grace, I've done no such—"

"Then how do you know who I am?" He flushed. She leaned toward him in a conspiratorial fashion. "Come, you may admit it. I know who you are. There can be no more pretense between us."

He let the paper fall, crumpled to his lap. "I told 'im I wasn't up to this. It's my first time, you see. But everyone else was needed for the lookout, so here I am."

"I'm very glad you're here. It saves me a bit of trouble. I should like you to deliver a message of the utmost importance."

She caught the doubt that crept into his eyes. "Deliver—? I don't know that I can. My orders were to watch your every move. If I abandon my post—"

"I doubt he'll mind, when you tell him I instructed you."

"I don't know, mum. I 'ave me orders. The Inspector's likely to 'ave me head if I disobey."

Christina stilled in horror. "The Inspector?"

"Certainly. I got me orders straight from 'im. I'm to stay with you every second, whether you like it or not. I do 'ope you don't mind too much, mum. I wouldn't care to upset you."

She slumped into the wrought-iron back of the bench. Her near blunder left her feeling chilled. She could so easily have blurted out something that might have helped the Inspector. She didn't even want to think about the possibilities. The fact that she was being watched was clue enough that she and the Captain were in more danger than she'd even suspected.

"Did the Inspector say why he wished to have me watched?"

"Indeed 'e did. For your protection, 'e said. What with the bandit on the loose. 'E said something about you 'aving been followed."

It would be a comfort to believe this was for her protection, but she knew she couldn't afford the luxury. If Inspector Worthington had gone to the trouble to have her followed, she must assume the worst—that he suspected her involvement and meant to have her lead him to the Captain.

"So you can see why delivering a message would get

me in a spot," the lad was saying. "I was told not to let you know I was following. Though, as I said, it's me first time. I'm embarrassed to think 'ow easily you caught on. If the Inspector knew, 'e'd 'ave me 'ead, so 'e would."

She gave him a reassuring smile. "Rest your cares, my good man. I have no intention of telling the Inspector anything that might have you replaced with another man."

Oscar returned to her after ten that night, dressed for the theater. Earlier, she'd sent Gladys to him with a message to come by. When he'd answered her call, she'd sent him out to keep her rendezvous with the Captain. No one would suspect Oscar, as he had a habit of dropping in on Wynterbrooke Hall at all hours of the day and night.

"Did you see him?" she asked anxiously when the front door was barely closed.

"I did, although it was difficult at best. He was loath to show his face when you didn't appear. I had to stand like an idiot, whispering into the night, 'It's Oscar Wilde. I've a message from the lady.' " She laughed. "It was sloppy melodrama at best."

"I seem to recall that you've written a sloppy melodrama or two in your time. But come, what did he say?"

"He says the threat is taken care of. You've only to step out the door to see."

She puckered her brow. "Did you tell him what I said?"

"Naturally. I told him you feel the climate is too dangerous to go on with what you'd planned. As you instructed me, I said you were grateful to him for the thought, but under the present circumstances, you feel it best to leave at once, without completing the task."

"And what did he say?"

"I gather the danger doesn't disturb him. Although he agrees that you should be protected if you feel inadequate to the situation."

"Exactly what does that mean?"

"I took it to mean that you should bloody well stay home if you're so scared."

"Oscar! Did you explain that I'm not afraid for myself, but for him? With the police crawling over every inch of London with orders to shoot to kill—"

"I believe he understands that, dearest. And I should add that he seems to be possessed of a good notion of the risks. I gather he feels it adds to the challenge. He asked me what would make me happier: a job easily completed or a job successfully completed at great risk and hardship. I, naturally, prefer the lazier route, but I have enough imagination to concede his point."

"Did he say anything else?"

"Just that you should go talk to your watchdog."

"Whatever for?"

He shrugged expansively. "How should I know, darling? I'm just your message-boy."

"You're a dear to do it."

"Nonsense. What are friends for? Charming man, by the way. I do believe he cares for you a great deal. He remembered my sally the night of our robbery about dueling with wits, and offered a future match to repay my kindness tonight. I should enjoy that, if I thought the two of you would be around long enough."

"And Mother?"

"Sasha is well convinced that she was mistaken in her assumptions. Fumingly so, I might add. I told her she always was theatrical to the point of lunacy—which, I don't have to tell you, hardly went over well. Suffice to say she has turned her thoughts in other directions."

"How can I thank you?"

"Don't be silly. I've enjoyed my role in your little intrigues," he teased. Then he added, "No. Now that I think of it, there *is* something you can do."

"And that is?"

"Be careful, won't you?"

She gave him a hug. "I shall be well protected, have no fear."

· · ·

When he'd gone, she went outside to the Inspector's man and was surprised to see that he'd been replaced. Bobby, beneath a sandy wig and phony waxed mustache, winked at her.

"Evenin' yer grace. Nice night we're havin', ain't it?"

"How did you get here?"

"We clubbed the bobby on top the head. Never saw us comin', he didn't."

"You didn't hurt him?"

"Naw. He's trussed up. We'll let him go after the job. How do you like me English accent?"

"It's passable. Just remember to drop your *h*'s. If anyone on the force should try and engage you in conversation, I'd advise you to speak as little as possible."

"Aye. The Cap'n sent me to keep an eye on you. He says there's no need for you to come, if you've a mind to stay home. We've hired on a number of extra men sent from Dublin just for the job. You're not to feel ashamed. You've only to pass on the information through me that he needs."

She looked at him closely beneath the gaslight. "Do you have no qualms about my participation? Do you not feel that I'm leading him astray?"

He had the grace to flush. "It was wrong of me to say those things, my lady. I hope ye can forgive me in time. Ye saved me life—'tis me privilege to return the favor, if ever I can."

She smiled. "Thank you, Bobby. I shall be there as planned. Only, I do wish he'd reconsider. I have a bad feeling about this. I walked past the theater this afternoon, just to test the waters. There are police everywhere. I've never seen such a spectacle."

"Then we'll have to be more careful, is all. Now, if you're comin', listen to me closely, my lady. This is the plan . . ."

CHAPTER 35

*R*IDING TO THE THEATER the next evening, Christina shivered as if the cold north winds were blowing off the Thames. She wore a black brocade cloak with the onyx buttons fastened from neck to foot, yet still she could scarcely contain the trembling of her limbs. For beneath her cloak she wore the costume of Fiaran, the Irish gypsy. And beside her in the closed coach was not only Bobby in his bodyguard disguise, but the Captain himself.

It was the most daring escapade they had ever contrived. Looking out the windows of the coach, they could see policemen everywhere. It seemed there was a bobby on every street corner. Not knowing where else to search, the police were concentrating their efforts in and about London. If the bandit had been so recently in Regent's Park, mightn't he return to London to strike again? Hadn't he shown a wanton disregard for the forces of the law? In fact, it seemed the more precarious the situation, the more chance there was of being caught in the act, the more likely the bandit was to challenge the odds and chance an attack. He'd shown that he thrived on the danger of slipping in under the noses of the authorities, then flinging his triumph in their embarrassed faces. Inspector Worthington was gambling heavily that if he increased security about town, the bandit would prove true to character and try to outwit him once again. But this time, Scotland Yard was prepared. This time, it would be a fight to the death.

In spite of the odds against him, the Captain had decided to oblige. In the midst of the tightest security London had known for many a year, the Brighton Bandit was doing what Inspector Worthington would least expect: walking into the trap openly and undisguised.

Christina flashed him a nervous look. He, too, was perusing the army of uniformed men beyond the window, but as he felt her gaze, he looked at her. Her fears for him had engulfed her to the exclusion of all else, so that she was surprised to see the animated sparkle of his eyes. He grinned at her like a boy bent on a prank, sat back in the cushions, and brought his booted foot to rest on the edge of the seat across the coach. Then he clasped his hands behind his head and stretched.

"You're enjoying this!" she cried, astonished. Her heart had been in her throat for hours.

"And why shouldn't I enjoy it?" he asked. "Tell me. What could be more engaging than outwitting the mighty London police force by beating them at their own game?"

"As long as we do outwit them."

"Do you doubt we will?"

"I don't know. I should prefer not to."

"Surely my outlaw woman doesn't suffer from cold feet?" he teased gently.

"I have premonitions of doom. I'm afraid we've overlooked something. There will be so many people. It would be so easy for one brave person in the audience to pull a pistol and—" She couldn't finish it. "I don't care if anything happens to me. Even if this be my last night on earth, I should die with the knowledge that at least I've lived. That I had true happiness and joy once in my life. That I was loved and understood. But you—if anything should happen to you—" She averted her gaze. "I couldn't bear it. I should *want* to die."

He leaned toward her and took her hand. "Nerves," he told her, "nothing more. Do you trust me?"

"Yes."

"Do you believe in me?"

"You know I do."

"Then know that I would never attempt it if I thought

we could not succeed. It's dangerous, yes, but not impossible. I have looked ahead to every foreseeable situation, and have taken the necessary precautions. So cease your fretting, woman, and set your mind on the adventure ahead. The time for trepidation is behind us."

"It's not the foreseeable situations I fear. It's the unforeseeable."

"Those we shall deal with when the time comes. Think of it this way: the future is uncertain. We don't know when we might have such an opportunity for mischief again. Think of it as a highwayman's last bit of sport."

She raised a questioning brow. "Highwayman? So the leopard *does* change his spots."

He flashed a sheepish grin. "Well . . . if a man can't give his lady memories for her old age, what's he good for?"

"I hope you'll be good for more than memories!"

Bobby, his ears flushing, made a great show of looking out the window and ignoring what they were saying.

"Feeling better?"

"Not especially."

He took her chin in his hand and brought her face close to his. "Then think, my love, of the look on your mother's face when the bandit at her side is not the bandit she expected, after all."

She felt his courage stream into her through his touch. "Yes," she admitted, smiling. "It will be a thing to remember, and to cherish, when we are old and grey."

He winked at her, and she caught the white flash of his teeth. Suddenly, for no explicable reason, she felt lighthearted and happier than she'd ever been. She feasted on his exhilaration and made it her own. Catching the surge of confidence in her eyes, and in her smile of anticipation, he leaned over and gave her a quick kiss on the mouth.

"We're nearly there," said Bobby.

The Captain caught her eye. "All right now?"

She nodded. "I am more than all right. I shall make you proud."

•   •   •

The stage-door manager smiled at her from behind his little desk. "We've seen a lot of you lately, Duchess. It's beginning to feel like old times."

"You know what they say, Garrett. Once the theater is in the blood . . ."

"Aye, it's in your blood, I know. I still can't get used to calling you 'Duchess.' Not when I used to scold you for making too much noise backstage as a little girl." He eyed her companions. One, the shorter of the two, stood with an out-thrust chest as if assuming an air of importance. The other's face was obscured by the stack of large boxes he was carrying. "What's this, now?"

Christina cast a quick glance at the two policemen who'd been stationed backstage and were standing in the corner, whispering to each other as they watched the proceedings. "I'm delivering some costumes. You recall my bodyguard Constable Miller from yesterday. It seems Inspector Worthington continues to worry for my safety."

"And well he should, with that bandit still about. Though why they've stationed so many bobbies here at the theater, I can't figure. The actors are complaining it hurts their concentration. Might I help you with those boxes? Your man looks like he might drop them any minute."

"No, thank you. You're busy enough. We shall manage. If worst comes to worst, I shall put the constable to a more useful endeavor, and requisition his help. With all these police swarming about, I doubt I shall need much protection tonight."

She waved cheerily and led the way backstage. It was close to curtain, and there was commotion everywhere. Actors rushed to and fro in search of items of clothing or hairpieces while the stagehands adjusted the scenery and moved the props into place. Already, the audience was taking seats out front. Below, the orchestra was tuning up in short spurts from the tuba, French horn, or strings.

Christina moved through the swarm with the ease and familiarity of someone born to the boards. She knew well the panic that ensued the half hour before curtain call, and knew that this was the time when strangers would least likely be noticed. So she walked right through the bedlam as if she and her two male followers were invisible, straight back to the darkest recesses of the backstage.

There, in the blackness, she gestured toward a series of wooden bars against the far wall that served as a ladder. "There's a scaffolding up top where you can see everything without being observed," she whispered, taking all but the bottom box and handing them to Bobby. "Everything you'll need is in that box. Change at once so the noise covers your motions, and fix everything in place as quickly as you can. Once the curtain rises, the slightest creak will be heard."

The Captain nodded his understanding, gave her a last mischievous grin, and swiftly scaled the wall with the box tucked under his arm. As she watched, her heart began to pound again in her breast. Suddenly, it seemed real. She motioned to Bobby, and he followed her once again. As they passed more police, she took a deep breath to steady her shaking knees.

She led him to a corner deep in the blackness of the back theater. There they waited, unseen but with a perfect view of the side of the stage. People came and went. It seemed the minutes dragged into eternity. Then suddenly, she saw her parents coming out to await their cue. Sasha, dressed in a bawdy imitation of gypsy attire, peered out at the audience from behind the curtain. "How's the house?" she asked.

"Sold out," said the stage manager, passing by.

"Well, that's something. Are those *policemen* standing out in the audience?"

"That's what they are."

"Whatever for?"

The stage manager shrugged. "Some ploy of Scotland Yard's apparently. They're stationing officers at every public place the bandit's victims are known to frequent. So they tell me."

Sasha put her hands on her hips. "Whoever ordered this? Is Worthington out of his mind? He should have his men combing the countryside for the wretch, not disrupting my performance!" She cast a quick glance at her husband, standing beside her. "*Our* performance," she amended sweetly.

Derk gave her one of his famous grins. "A ploy of Scotland Yard's, is it? Most likely a ploy to see the play for free."

Christina put her face in her hands. She told herself that things would be all right, in spite of the insurmountable odds. She thought again of all the Captain had told her in the coach, and of the cool, even reckless way he'd said it, as if he hadn't a care in the world.

I have looked ahead to every foreseeable situation, and have taken the necessary precautions.

And she recalled her own response.

It's not the foreseeable situations I fear.

All at once, the orchestra struck a note, and the buzz of the audience stilled. There was a moment of breathless anticipation before the overture began, fast and free, easing to a note of tragedy before the curtain rose. Safe in their corner, Bobby and Christina could hear the projected voices of the bit players setting up the scene. A coach on the high road to London, in the black of night. Derk dashed from the wings, and his booming voice filled the theater. "Halt, driver, if you value your life!"

Bobby, listening, turned to Christina and made a face.

The fictional robbery proceeded. There was much clumping of boots upon the stage. The victim, an accosted aristocrat trying to soothe his frantic wife, wailed while shaking in his boots, "What manner of man is it that would scare an old woman with such vile threats?"

Suddenly, as if a flame had been set to a candle, Sasha Wentworth came alive. Throwing back her head, she let her clear, wicked laughter fill the rafters. Then, still in the wings, she cried in a bantering tone, "How come you, sir, to assume 'tis only a man who haunts the shadows?" And with that, she made her appearance on stage.

As her mother's voice continued to ring out, Christina slipped back down the hall and through the maze of doorways to Sasha's dressing room. It was large and gaily decorated with flowered wallpaper and pink chintz chairs. Her costumes were tossed about the furniture, lined up in sequence. Fingering one, a pink-and-copper gauzy thing that was virtually transparent, Christina turned her nose up at the inferior workmanship. To anyone else, they would have seemed fine costumes indeed. But they were paltry in comparison to the masterpieces Christina had created.

She looked about at the mess in distaste, thinking that when she'd dressed her mother, everything had been hanging on padded hangers, ready but organized, not this jumbled heap of clothing piled about the room. Well, it was her problem no longer. Just her thinking about those days caused a knot to form in the pit of her stomach—days and nights spent obeying her mother's high-handed orders and catering to her nonsensical whims like a servant girl eager for promotion. Trying to make up for the fact that she wasn't her poor, beloved sister Elisabeth, and could never be what they desired. Trying to prove she was worthy of her parents' love and their forgiveness. Humiliating herself over something that would never be. Tonight, she reminded herself, none of that mattered. Tonight, she would have her revenge at last.

She must work quickly. She knew just how long her mother would be onstage, and she must be out of the dressing room and hidden again before her return. Swiftly, she unbuttoned her cape. Discarding it, she took a quick look at her costume in the large mirror, scrutinizing it carefully for flaws. Painfully aware that any similarity to her own clothing might give her away, she'd taken great care to disguise herself. She'd padded her figure so that her breasts, her waist, her hips looked twice their normal size, forming a voluptuous hourglass figure to mask her slender curves. To contrast her mother's low-cut, transparent costumes, she'd cut her own simply with a high neck and long fitted sleeves. Then she'd ripped open a feather mattress and painstakingly sewn hundreds of feathers in layers about the dress so that from a distance she looked like a swan. "A swan dress," she'd quipped to the Captain, "for our swan song." Of course, she'd never dream of wearing such an impractical costume to rob a train or stop a coach at night upon the road, but she'd wanted something that would be remarked upon so that it would distract from her person. There would be too many people in the audience who knew her well—even intimately—and she would be under the glaring lights of the stage, at that.

Satisfied, she fixed a snow-white wig on her head, a similarly feathered mask about her eyes, then pinned on the hat with its ostrich feather soaring into the air to arch and dip gracefully over her right eye.

Suddenly, there was a noise at the door. A woman's voice called out, and the knob began to turn. Frantically, Christina grabbed her cape and the box she'd brought in and dashed behind the changing screen. She knelt down as low as she could, but the feathers made the gown stiff, and she could gather it in only so far. She held her breath as someone came into the room and closed the door behind.

"Bothersome constables," a woman's voice grumbled to herself. "Wink at me, will he? We'll just see to that."

There were noises on the other side of the screen that sounded like the tidying of the dresser and the shifting of clothes. All the while, the maid continued muttering to herself. "Why we need all these bobbies, I'll never know. This'd be the *last* place to pinch that bandit. He ain't got the nerve to show his face here. If you ask me, he's long gone to Ireland, *he* is. If he's any sense, that is."

There was a moment of silence, then she said with renewed passion, "I didn't know them bobbies was so fresh. I've a good mind to give him a piece of me mind. In fact . . . whyever not? Wink at me, and see what happens . . ."

The door opened and closed again, and she was gone. Peering around the screen, Christina released a sigh of relief. That was too close. She must get out of here and hide before the maid thought better of it and returned.

Suddenly, a gunshot rang out from the stage.

CHATER 36

CHAPTER 36

$\mathcal{I}$N THE ENSUING panic backstage, Christina rushed through the bedlam to see the Captain swing down from the rafters on a rope and land, standing, at Derk Wentworth's feet. The audience, assuming the feat to be part of the show, burst into applause. When the bandit turned from the gawking actor to swirl his cape about him with a flourish and offer a deep bow, the applause swelled, echoing through the three tiers of the theater. Only when the newcomer calmly put a pistol to Derk's head did the audience begin to sense that something was amiss.

Gradually, the message became clear and the house quieted into a shocked reverberating hush, with only a few gasps escaping from the front rows. The Captain, with his most charming grin, put up a hand for silence.

"Allow me to introduce myself," he said, projecting his voice as Christina had taught him so he would be heard even in the upper back rows. "For those of you who don't already know me, I am Richard Wycliffe, former Earl of Wycliffe, and currently known—although I loathe the title—as the Brighton Bandit." It was the first time he'd publicly admitted his true identity, and Christina could see the quiet pleasure it afforded him. "I should apologize for the interruption, but some nasty rumors have reached my ears concerning the production you are presently enjoying. The tales I hear about the depiction of my activities are enough to make any self-respecting bandit cower. From what I've seen this night,

I am afraid I must concur. Sad to say, my lord"—he addressed the livid Derk—"had I been so slipshod in my manner as your portrayal would have me, I should have deserved to be captured long before this."

His voice had hardened as he spoke to Derk, and a look of stark anger glinted in his eyes. Christina knew he was thinking of her confession about her father, and suddenly she wondered if this was such a good idea. A man like the Captain was fully capable of using this arena to kill the man for his past misdeeds.

Derk was sputtering long before the bandit's speech was over. "Why—why—this is an—"

"An outrage. I know, Lord Northampton. I've heard the tenor of your dialogue this night. I shall strike a bargain with you. You save me the platitudes, and I shall finish my business without delay, so that you might get on with the production—that is, if you have the gall after I've shown you how it's *really* done!"

By now, people in the audience were beginning to panic as they fully realized for the first time that this was apart from the spectacle they'd paid to see. They stood in their seats and began to dash for the doors. As they did, the policemen moved with swift efficiency down the aisles. Derk, noting this, threw the bandit a supercilious look. "It seems you're to be foiled in your attempts to chastise us, Lord Wycliffe."

The Captain gave his impostor a secret smile. "Alas, my lord, but you've misjudged me once again."

Soon enough, it became apparent what he meant. The police, instead of rushing for the stage to take the scoundrel into custody, stopped the flow of patrons with pistols pointed at their ribs and escorted them, grudging and grumbling, back to their seats. Backstage, Bobby and the two policemen held the actors and crew together with a similar show of arms.

"You see," the Captain explained, "for this night only, the police work for me. Did it not strike you as odd that our old friend Worthington would so heavily guard these hallowed halls? I should dearly love to see the Inspector's face when he discovers that they were my men merely costumed for their roles—but alas I shall forgo that particular pleasure." He turned to the audience. "As you can see, my friends, the doors are blocked on all levels. The theater staff is in the custody of my men, in case any of you harbor hopes of escape. As my men pass among you, you'll be good enough to hand over any valuables in your possession. Should anyone wish to play the hero, I fear I must admonish that you do so at great risk. Not only will you be happily shot by one of my men for your pains, you will also ensure that the performing Wentworths play their swan song this very night."

To emphasize his words, he raised the pistol to Derk's head so that all could see. Lowering his voice, he goaded, "Feel free to ignore my warning, my lord. Given provocation, I should dearly love to end the life of such a miserable excuse for a man."

Derk, not understanding the source of the bandit's sentiments, but sensing the truth behind the words, grew very still.

The Captain's men moved along the seats with dispatch, taking jewels, cigar cases, cuff links, gold and jeweled hair ornaments, and depositing them into black velvet bags. Once or twice there was a comment from one of the braver men in the audience, but when the bandit offered them a platform for their views center stage, the hecklers desisted at once.

All this time, Sasha was watching the proceedings with her eagle eye. Certain her mother would be the first to try to upstage the Captain, Christina stayed out of the way and kept her gaze fixed firmly on the actress. When Sasha saw that the outlaws backstage were occupied with the other actors and looking away from the stage, she saw her chance and broke for stage left. But before she could cross the wings, Christina stepped in front and put a pistol to her face.

"I wouldn't be so bold, my lady," she said, careful to disguise her voice in a whispery Irish brogue. "You might find that my outrage over your portrayal of me makes my finger itch upon the trigger."

Sasha backed up onto the stage, and for the first time, Christina came out into the lights. Those who saw her gasped, for with the lights glinting off the feathers she did, indeed, look as graceful as a swan.

The bandit saw her then and motioned to Bobby to take his place. When Bobby had put his own gun to Derk's head, the Captain moved between the ladies, took each of their hands, and swept them with him to the footlights.

"I realize you're occupied, good friends," he called to the audience, "and far be it from me to disturb you at such a time. But I beg your indulgence to introduce my lady. I ask you fair-minded patrons, gazing at the real and the impostor, can there be any comparsion?"

Sasha angrily snatched her hand from his, but Christina looked at him with all of her love for him shining in her eyes. Then, determined to keep her head, she went to Sasha and, taking in her hands the elaborate necklace she wore, ripped it from her mother's neck.

This amused Sasha greatly. She gathered herself together, rising up to look taller than she was, and contemptuously spat out the words, "It's paste!"

It was the very reason Christina had taken it. The Duchess of Wynterbrooke would certainly know the necklace was a fake. An Irish gypsy might not. She shrugged as if learning the news for the first time. "In that case, it will make a pretty souvenir."

"You shan't get away with this," Sasha warned. "I shall see that you're caught for this travesty if it's the last thing I ever do. If I have to spend the rest of my life making sure of it, I shall see that you suffer."

The Captain looked at his lady and caught her radiant, confident smile. Taking her hand, he quietly said to Sasha, "I doubt, madam, that after tonight you will have the power to harm either one of us."

Christina, feeling that it was true, that this night her mother had lost the power to wound her ever again, turned and gave Sasha a victorious, pitying look.

They waited for the men on all three levels to finish making their way through the audience. Then, as the uniform-clad men began to retreat, the Captain gave a jaunty salute and cried out, "Many thanks for your generosity, my fine English ladies and gents. My lady and I bid you good-night. We're leaving England and vow before God never to trouble you again."

With that, still holding hands, the Captain and Christina raced backstage and disappeared out the stage door, onto the waiting horses, and off, laughing, into the night.

CHAPTER 37

*T*HEY RODE WEST surrounded by a contingent of fraudulent police. The first challenge was to get out of town as quickly as possible before Inspector Worthington picked up their trail. It wasn't too difficult, as a group of galloping men costumed as police was virtually indistinguishable from a legitimate force pounding through town on their way to track down a criminal. Yet, they hadn't ridden long before they encountered the first of their troubles.

Christina's swan gown, so painstakingly stitched in the midnight hours, was shedding. At first it was just a feather or two that flew free to waft into the faces of the men riding behind. Soon enough, however, the feathers were drifting in ever-increasing numbers, until they began to cling like new-fallen snow to the men's clothes.

Laughing, Christina pulled up outside of town and called for them to stop. "I'm sorry, men, this just won't do."

"Bloody Christ," cried one of the men she'd never seen before in a heavy Irish brogue. "She's leavin' a bleedin' trail."

The disdain in his voice reminded her of the days when Bobby, Michael, and Toby resented riding with a woman. She looked back down the road to see that she had, indeed, left a trail of feathers that Inspector Worthington would find little difficulty in following.

"Not to worry," she assured them cheerfully, still soaring from the experience of robbing the theater, still wanting to crow her exultation to all who might hear. "I shall change in an instant."

She maneuvered her horse to the side of Richard's so that the men were on her right, dismounted, and pulled a plain black riding habit from the saddlebag. Without wasting the time it would take to find cover, she hastily stripped off her gown of feathers, ripping it in her haste, and stepped into the split skirt she'd brought for this very purpose. The men, restless at first, casting worried glances back down the London road, were arrested by the movements of a woman dressing just the other side of a horse from them. Their muttering stopped, and they sat transfixed, staring covertly into the dark in her direction, fascinated by the unexpectedly scandalous phenomenon, yet loath to look lest the Captain give them grief. The Captain, more accustomed by now to Christina's impulsiveness, put a gloved hand to his mouth to hide his smile.

"This will have to go," she said, holding the white gown up so that the moonlight gleamed along her naked arm.

The Captain took it, tossed it to Bobby, and jerked his head. As Christina swiftly buttoned her jacket, Bobby steered his horse to the side of the road and pitched the vexatious costume into a ditch.

"There," Christina said, satisfied. "That didn't take long." She took the white feathered gloves and flung them off into the night, in the direction of the dress.

As the men regained their composure and at a gesture from the Captain rode off once again into the night, Christina mounted, tore the mask from her face, and threw it to the winds. "I've done with masks," she said joyously to her lover. "Fiaran has served her purpose and is needed no more. Lovely, adventurous Fiaran. May she rest in peace."

"Fiaran is dead," he quipped with a grin. "Long live the Duchess."

She stood in her stirrups and leaned over to kiss him. "God, how I love you. If you only knew what you've done for me tonight!"

Her horse skitted away, and she put her hand on Richard's shoulder to keep her balance. He took her hand and kissed it tenderly. "Come. It may all be for naught if we fail to escape England with our lives."

It was a gentle reminder, but it served its purpose. She nodded and kicked her horse into a gallop and set off with him up the road to catch up with the men. In her euphoria, she had no idea that she'd just sealed her own—and her lover's—fate.

They had intended to use the "police" escort as far as the closest town where they could safely board a train for the west coast of Wales. At each town along the northwesterly road, the majority reined in on the outskirts of town, careful to keep to the woods, while two of the "policemen" rode in to the station to check out the situation. It was hardly surprising that Windsor, Maidenhead, and Goring would be heavily guarded, given their proximity to London, but when they reached Dorchester to find no letup in the defenses, it became obvious that a reevaluation was needed.

"It would seem to be assumed that we shall take to the trains," the Captain calculated swiftly. "If that's the case, my guess is that every station in England is being fiercely guarded against the possibility of our using that avenue of escape. We'll have to thwart their plans by taking to the roads. As it happens, we shall make better time than we have. It will free us to take the back roads and avoid the risk of too much exposure."

So they decided to head for Wales on horseback, assuming that with the trains closely watched, the roads would be clear. It wasn't to be. They ran into soldiers on every road they took, no matter how small or out of the way. At each juncture, it was always the same. Bobby and the men claimed to be looking for the Captain, pumped the soldiers for information regarding their opinions on where he might be, and gave them clues that would indicate they were heading in the wrong direction. While the voices droned on, the Captain and Christina hid in the woods and prayed their horses wouldn't choose just such a time to give their where-abouts away.

After several such encounters in the matter of an hour, and having made little headway, the Captain called a halt. He spoke thoughtfully, but the air of command in his tone held everyone at rapt attention. "If what the soldiers say is true, Inspector Worthington has wired ahead to be on the lookout. It's clear they expect us to flee from the southwest—most probably from Wales. There are only two ways to Ireland from that route, out of Swansea Bay and Goodwick. They may assume we'll board a ferry in disguise. Or since they know we've a hideout somewhere in the vicinity, and that we've sent ships of our own to Ireland, they may expect us to lie low in the south for a time, then make a dash for it in a boat of our own. We're hampered by their knowledge of our destination. My fault, I fear, but nothing we can remedy at this point in time. While I never said we were going to Ireland, it's the natural assumption."

"What do you suggest, Cap'n?" Bobby asked. "We can't keep this up. I'm beginnin' to feel like a trapped chicken. Likely someone'll ask one too many questions and find us out. And then where'll we be?"

"Where, indeed?" the Captain mused. He pursed his lips, concentrating. Then he sat up straight in his saddle, animated as if the very energy of life were shooting through his veins. "Let's gamble, shall we?" he asked with a grin. "Since we've never been known to plague the north, I say we head north instead. Bobby, go into town and take a train for Fleetwood. Pay off the men, take the ferry to the Isle of Man, and arrange for a boat that can get us to Dublin. No one knows what you look like, so you should travel unimpeded. The lady and I shall hole up for a few days to let things settle down. By then the authorities will either have assumed we've gone and given up the chase, or will be doubling their efforts to comb the southern regions. If we can find a place to hide in the north, we may very well be able to don light disguises and step onto the ferry at Fleetwood in a few days' time with no trouble at all."

"But where will you be, Cap'n?" Toby asked. "We've no connections up north."

"Haworth!" Christina gasped, echoing the Captain's enthusiasm. "I've a cottage at Haworth. Very small, delightfully isolated, the perfect hideout up on the moors."

The Captain grinned. "Haworth it is." He held her gaze a moment, and a spark passed between them. It was as if the same thought had registered itself in both their minds at once: several days alone in Haworth with nothing to do but wait! Excited now, Christina returned his grin.

She didn't even hear the rest of his crisply stated orders. All she could think of was the heady anticipation of having him all to herself in her favorite of all places on earth.

There was a chorus of "Aye, Captains," and the men were off, riding stealthily into the night to do his bidding. Quite suddenly, the two of them were alone on the open road. The night was cool, the breeze faint, the moonlight touching their faces.

"What shall it be?" he asked in a hushed, intimate voice that promised more intimacies to come. "Chance the trains by ourselves, or stick to the roads?"

"Oh, the roads are more romantic by far. I seem to recall hearing a story of Dick Turpin once when I was a child. Of how he and his horse Black Bess escaped the law by riding at breakneck speed from London to York in only nine hours. If Dick Turpin could manage the feat, surely we can do the same."

He studied her glowing face in the moonlight. "So the lady still covets the romance of highwaymen?"

"Can you blame me? When you look so wretchedly dashing, sitting atop your steed with your cloak lifting in the breeze?" She laughed at herself, then grew serious, and her eyes softened on his moon-shadowed face. "That's how I first saw you. I think, evermore when I look back on these days, I shall remember you just so— cloaked in the black of night, alert and dangerous, taking what you want and prepared to flee into the darkness once you've accomplished your goal. Yes, you're right. Just once more before we leave this life of crime for good, I should like to ride by your side with the wind in my face and the dogs at my heels."

"I don't suppose there's any room in that romantic picture for the image of those dogs ripping at our throats. If we're captured, what becomes of your windmills then?"

She was quiet for a moment, and when she spoke, her voice was as delicate as the breeze. "Richard, I'm no Don Quixote. I know the windmills for what they are. It's just that . . ." She sought the words. "It's just that this time in our lives is something I shall treasure all my days. I want to remember every sensation. I want to impress each moment on my mind, to keep my memories like dried flowers that I can take out and fondle through the years. Always, I want to remember you just as you are tonight, just as you look now. I want to do it all one last time so that I *will* remember. So that nothing, neither time, nor distance—*nothing* anyone can do to us, will erase this magical image from my mind. Surely you can grant me that?"

He could hear the inflection of fear that crept, unbidden, into her voice. The look they exchanged was like a flash of premonition. A whisper on the wind seemed to moan, *Remember this. It's all you'll have.*

He shook the mood away as if slamming the door on the fates. "If the lady wants adventure, she shall have it," he said decisively. "As long as she marches into the noose with her eyes open."

"My eyes were opened the night I first saw you on the road. Fear not, my darling. I stand before you humbly willing to take any consequences that my rash behavior warrants."

Suddenly, he threw back his head and laughed aloud.

"What *ever* are you laughing at?" she demanded in her duchess tone.

"At the image of you being humble. Come, then, my adventuress. Let's go see if we can't find some dogs to plague our heels."

They both laughed then as they rode off. It was good to laugh, Christina thought. To laugh in the face of impending doom. To ride in the moonlight with the wind in her hair. To feel the power of the horse beneath her, and the triumph surging through her veins at the thought of the night's deeds. It was romance, it was adventure, it was the life-enhancing thrill of danger. And in some unaccountable way, it was a blessed comfort. It was life pared down to its simplest and purest form. In this complex world, there was suddenly only one choice to be made—to live or to die. In the action of choosing, it served to keep the fear at bay.

CHAPTER 38

---

*I*T WAS TWILIGHT of the next day before they reached Haworth. Several times, it had been necessary to hide along the road, sometimes for hours at a time. Once, in the dead of night, when they'd been pursued for a quarter hour by particularly persistent soldiers, Christina's horse tripped in a pothole and fell to its knees, pitching Christina over its head and onto the hard ground. The soldiers weren't far behind. They had only time for Christina to leap onto the Captain's stallion and for them to dash into the woods before the soldiers stumbled onto the injured horse they'd left behind. There, just yards away, they listened with heaving breath as the soldiers decided to send someone back with the horse and to send the rest of the company in pursuit of the criminals. It shouldn't be difficult, the leader pointed out, as they were now riding a single horse, which would slow them down considerably.

All through the duration of this discussion, Christina leaned back into the Captain with her head resting back on his shoulder. As her fear of discovery threatened to choke her, her hand wandered down to his, then took it and placed it on her breast. The feel of it was distracting enough to banish the fear that she would somehow give their presence away. But by the time the men had galloped off, her tension had been heightened by the fondling of his hand, and all at once, in the aftermath of anxiety, she needed a release. As before, the danger was an aphrodisiac, but the fear that she'd once relished seemed almost too real. In her lust, she felt the added need of the comfort of his body to convince her they were safe. Ignoring his rational arguments about the necessity of finding another horse and resuming their journey, she flung up her skirts, lowered her drawers, leaned forward over the horse's neck, and coaxed him into making love to her right there on the steed, clamping his hands over her breasts with her own so he could find the purchase he needed to bring about a shattering climax. She was then left with a renewed confidence in their venture, and could guide him to a nearby farm, where they had little difficulty in pilfering a horse and tack.

Once they reached the north, they were plagued no more, and they began to assume a more leisurely pace. Now, as they passed through Yorkshire, the lush green countryside began to change, growing wild and austere. The scenery tumbled before them, as reckless as the Bröntes' imagination, which had lured Christina to the region. It was a vastly changeable land—slick with ice and sleet in winter under a forbidding grey sky, wet with rain and fearsome with lightning in the unrelenting spring—yet a land that, in its haunting isolation and its mood of restless discontent, remained throughout the centuries curiously unchanged. Now, in the bounty of late summer, the gentle air softened the harsh terrain, beckoning to the lovers as a haven from harm. The clouds were puffs and streaks tinged with copper in the twilight sky. As the sun set, it cast a magical rosy mist upon the land, creating about the moors and bogs and rocks a feeling of magic.

They rode through Haworth just as the sun was slipping behind the moors. The tiny village was deserted, the people supping by their hearths. Together, they rode through the steep, narrow, empty streets and out into the open hills. The coppery pink lights deepened to lavender and gold as they rode, and everywhere there was a quiet and expectancy that was thrilling.

It was two miles to the cottage up a narrow dirt road.

Beyond the possible prying eyes of the villagers, they dismounted and walked the rest of the way, holding hands as they did, dangling the reins loosely in their other hands so the horses followed behind, drinking in the cool country air. They meandered past black stone fences steeped upon rugged slopes, the crumbling stones tumbling down through the tufts of rough grass. In the distance, streams flashed like quicksilver through the valleys. A lone tree topped a rise near a seemingly abandoned farmhouse. All about them, there was an air of a place passed over by the forward-marching insistence of time. The air was filled with the sound of wild birds as hawks and falcon soared in the mystical sky. Stark, dirt roads cut into the hills, rutted with potholes. Wooden posts from long-forgotten fences tipped to their sides, as if tired of the effort of standing up against an abandoned land. Beyond them, like a valley of barbarous kings, stretched the moors—wreathed in heather, lonely and compelling under the darkening sky. In spite of the wildness, there was a deep serenity about the place, an aura of splendor and decay.

Presently, they came to a clump of trees that secreted in its midst a small unkempt cottage with an arched green door and rosebushes blooming in unrestrained disarray at the back. Evening had stolen with a hush upon the moors, but there was still enough light with which to see. The sight of the dilapidated bungalow seemed so incongruous, belonging as it did to the elegant Duchess of Wynterbrooke, that the Captain turned to her and arched a curious brow.

"And what are you punishing *your*self for?" he asked.

She caught the intimate hush of his voice in the mystic stillness. With key in hand, she looked at him, tall and achingly handsome in the evening light. He raked a hand through his black hair so that it tumbled onto his forehead. He'd slung his cloak over his arm so that he wore only snug black breeches, a loose white shirt open at the throat, and his sleek riding boots, which hugged his muscular calves like a second skin. He fit into the wild surroundings as surely as if he'd been born amongst the fells. Outlined against the great expanse of the moors, he looked once again like the image she'd first had of him, the image from her dreams. A dark, feral, brooding hero out of the pages of the Brontës. A Heathcliff or Rochester, who in his madness and passion could tear the heart from a woman and brand her soul as his for all time. A romantic, desperate figure from another time. A thief of the night—a highwayman. Suddenly, she knew why she'd bought the cottage on a whim. All along, in some strange and inexplicable premonition of her fate, she'd known she would bring someone here one day—someone worthy of the honor of sharing her dreams—someone like him.

"What am I punishing myself for?" she repeated. "After last night, nothing. This place—being here with you—is hardly my punishment. It's my reward."

He studied her face seriously for a moment. "Your reward—my salvation." He pulled her to him with a soul-searing kiss. "Christ, what did I do to deserve this moment?" Tearing his eyes away, he took the key from her, unlocked the door, and lifted her into his arms. Opening the door with his boot, he carried her inside.

The ceiling was low and hung with wooden beams, the hearth made from the same black stones that dotted the hillsides. The overstuffed furniture was draped with dusty sheets. The cottage was small and cramped, and smelled of disuse, but to Christina, it looked like paradise.

"We shall open the doors and let in the light and air," she announced, wiggling out of his arms. "No more barred windows. No more running. No more hiding. For a few days, with you, this cottage will be home. The only real home I have ever known."

CHAPTER 39

TOBY SHOWED UP as planned the next morning, coming in from Fleetwood on the train. His presence was necessary as a cover. Haworth was such a small, isolated village that any newcomers would be noticed. He would prove useful in going for food and gathering the latest news regarding Worthington's fruitless chase. Should anyone ask, he was the new caretaker of the cottage sent by the Duchess of Wynterbrooke to ready it for a possible autumn visit. He was also to look out in case anyone drifted by out of curiosity, and was to steer them immediately in another direction. It was imperative to their plans that no one suspect their presence here. Still, the matter of privacy was a small enough worry. Christina had chosen the place for its segregation, wanting simple quarters where she could escape the social obligations that were part and parcel of her title and be left completely alone.

The first order of business was the cleaning of the filthy cottage, which, since Christina had bought it, had lain fallow, locked up against inquisitive villagers' eyes.

"I had always intended to spend time here," she explained, "but somehow I never did. I was waiting for you, I suppose."

The Captain sat at the crude but charmingly carved wooden table in the cozy kitchen, sipping strong black coffee that Toby had conducted from the village and recently brewed. A shaft of sunlight spilled onto his shoulder, warming him and giving him a sleepy look that she found enormously appealing. It gave Christina a snug, homey feeling to while away the morning breakfasting with him in the kitchen and chatting about their day. In neither of her two marriages had she felt this degree of comfort, this lack of a need for conversation, this un-questioned pleasure in gazing drowsily at a beloved face. Still, the morning was half gone, and there were things to do. She couldn't bear the dust and grime any longer, so she popped up from the table and set about the task.

He brought his boot up to rest on the bench beside him then leaned his forearm onto his bent knee. There was a lazy, appreciative look of amusement in his eyes as he watched her open cupboards, then close them again in frustration. "You're very busy suddenly," he commented.

She put her hands on her hips and glanced with a puckered brow about the room. "I am doing my best to discern where there might be some cleaning utensils. I haven't the foggiest notion where to look."

His eyes, looking in the morning light like splintered green glass, flicked over the room. At the back was a minuscule scullery leading to a back door. Setting down his cup, he stood, crossed to it, found a tall, narrow closet, and withdrew a mop and pail. "Might this be what you're looking for?"

He held it up for her to see, a mockingly derisive look flitting across his dark features. When she gave him a where-did-you-find-*that* look, he let out a laugh. "You don't seriously mean to tell me you intend to spend this fine day scrubbing this hut? Is this the same Duchess of Wynterbrooke who only a few short weeks ago had never set foot in her own kitchen?"

"The Duke's kitchen," she corrected. "Mock me if you will. I intend to show you what a helpmate I shall be in our new life together. You've warned me that we may be forced to live roughly for a time. Who knows? I might even learn to cook!"

"That I should like to see." Putting down the mop and pail, he closed the distance between them and took her in his arms, looking down into her upturned face. "You have nothing to prove to me, Christina. I knew of your lack of domesticity when I fell in love with you. My men have cared for me these many years, and I imagine we shall survive whatever domestic crises that may crop up."

"It's not that I'm stupid, or even inordinately lazy," she defended herself. "It's just that while my female peers were learning about such things as how to run a proper English household efficiently, I was dressing my parents in the theater. There was never enough time for—or to be honest, interest in—domestic lessons. Mother, who was rarely home in any case, never saw the need. Having been possessed of competent housekeepers all my life, and having trusted the running of my numerous houses to them, I never gave it a thought. But that doesn't mean I'm incapable of learning. I'm an intelligent and highly imaginative woman. I shall simply teach myself by trial and error."

His smile was tender but disbelieving. "Nonetheless, I didn't ask you to come with me so you could cook and scrub while I sit by the hearth and take up the pipe."

She gave him a wicked grin. "Oh, I have no intention of waiting on the lord and master hand and foot. I may be willing, but I haven't entirely lost my mind! I shall attend to the dust. Toby may scrub the floors and clean out the hearth." She picked up the mop and pail and handed them to him. "And you, Captain, will doubtless be happy to take the windows and the walls."

With that, she left him holding the mop and pail with a dumbfounded look on his face.

She tied his black kerchief over her hair and set to work, dragging the dusty sheets outside and shaking them out. By the time she was finished—having mistakenly shaken them into the wind so that the dust flew back in her face—she was covered in grime from head to foot and coughing continually. Undaunted, she tore one of the sheets into rags so she could remove the dust from the rest of the furniture, then swept the floors clean. During this process, she threw the doors open to let in the sun and air, then went out to cut her favorite white roses from the back to distribute in glasses of water throughout the cottage. She'd bought the cottage for its abundance of white rosebushes, which, untended, were now growing wild.

Coming in with her arms full of flowers, she heard Toby muttering. "We'll only be here a day or two," he grumbled. "And if yer askin' me opinion, that's a day or two too long. All this friggin' scrubbin' for naught."

She paused in the doorway to give them an affectionate smile. Toby, stripped to the waist with his wrinkled flesh sagging over his waistband, was on one knee, scrubbing the old wooden floor with a stiff brush, dragging his bad leg behind him. The Captain was busy wiping at the window with such vigor, she feared the pane might break.

"Shut up," he snapped, not seeing her. " 'Tis for the lady's pleasure. Would you have her sleep in a filthy hovel?"

"I've slept in worse than this in me day."

"You're not a lady, so I'll thank you to keep your opinions to yourself."

"Time was when sleepin' in a stick hut in the woods was good enough for m'lady, duchess or no."

"Time was when my men respected my authority without a lot of guff."

"That was before ye 'ad us swabbin' bleedin' floors."

The Captain put his rag into the pail of soapy water at his feet, then scoured the window more irritably than before. As he reached for the top sill, a stream of water slid down his arm, wetting him from arm to chest.

"Bloody hell," he swore, shaking out his arm so the rag flung water around the room. Some of it hit Toby in the face, and he jerked up with an oath.

"Christ Almighty God, Cap'n. Watch where yer flingin' yer suds!" As an afterthought he amended sulkily, "Sir."

Christina laughed aloud. "Never have I seen such a helpless couple of ruffians in all my life. Here. Let a newfound expert do it."

She dropped her roses into a chair, took the rag from the Captain, submerged it in water, then reached up for the same sill. As before, water streamed down her arm. She looked at the dark wet stain on her dress, then up at the Captain. As one, they burst into hysterical laughter, falling into each others' arms. Christina brought her arms round his neck, and the rag dripped soapy water down his back, causing them to howl louder than before.

"We're useless," she gasped.

"Enough of this," the Captain said, assuming his natural air of command. He took the rag from her and rubbed at the exposed dusty skin of her throat, which the water was turning to mud. In doing so, he soaked her bodice and caused her to squeal. Narrowing his eyes on her bosom, he added with a playful growl, "I would much rather scrub you."

"Is that so, Captain?" she teased. "Do you suppose you could do a better job of scrubbing me than you have my windows?"

Spanning her waist with his two hands, he lifted her easily and threw her over his shoulder so that her face flopped into the folds of his shirt at his back. "Let's give it a try, shall we?" He carried her toward the narrow flight of stairs leading to the upstairs bedroom above. Bending his head to keep from hitting it on the low landing, he called back to Toby, "Fetch us some water for a bath. And when you've done that, be a good man and clean up this mess."

Christina giggled, kicking her legs mirthfully all the way up the stairs until the door to the bedroom was slammed shut and the sounds of their laughter was muffled.

Toby threw his rag into the pail, sloshing water on his newly scrubbed floor. "Swab the floor, fetch the water, clean up the mess," he mimicked. "I've become a bloody chambermaid is wot I 'ave."

CHAPTER 40

"I'M AS STIFF and sore as a work-weary dog," Christina announced that evening. "Aren't you?"

The Captain, lounging back in an overstuffed chair with his boots propped up on a low table, raised a derisive brow. "From washing a few windows? Not likely."

"Then I envy you your fortitude. Every muscle in my body is clutched tighter than a fist." She reached back and rubbed her knotted shoulders. "Even my feet hurt. Had I known this was what housekeeping was about, I should have given Mrs. Craven a raise in salary long before this."

The Captain looked at her thoughtfully a moment, then called over his shoulder. "Toby. Put the kettle on to boil."

"Why not?" Toby muttered. " 'Tis nothin' but a bleedin' slave I am this day." When he'd done as his master had requested, he announced huffily, "I'm goin' for a walk to clear me head. Her Highness can get her own tea, if it's all the same to you."

When he was gone, Christina burst out laughing. "Such insubordination!"

"I shall have to speak to him," the Captain said with a mock frown.

"Never mind. I don't care for any tea."

"You'll care for this."

When the kettle boiled, he stood, stretched his arms to the ceiling, then went into the kitchen, calling behind him, "Take off your shoes and stockings."

"I beg your pardon?"

"You heard me."

She did so, then wandered curiously into the kitchen behind him, feeling the cool, rough wood beneath her toes. He'd stoppered the small sink, poured the boiling water into it, pumped in some cold, and was testing the temperature when she entered. "Come along," he urged.

She went to him slowly, wondering what on earth he could be up to. He gave her little chance for questions. Instead, he picked her up and sat her on the small counter by the sink. "Pull up your skirts," he ordered.

"My lord, you shock me!" she laughed.

"Here."

He shoved her skirts up over her knees, then turned her so that her feet slid into the sink. Instantly, she could feel a jolt of relaxation as her bare feet sank into the hot water. It was as if her entire body let go a sigh of relief.

He rolled up his sleeves, then thrust his hands into the water. Taking one foot in his hands, he began to massage it. His firm fingers rubbed the top of her foot, working between the delicate bones. They rounded the foot, kneading the tender back of her heel. With each stroke, she could feel the tension seeping from her body. She threw her head back and let out a sigh.

"Oh, Richard. That's heavenly!"

He took the other foot and performed the same procedure. She watched, fascinated, as his wrists moved in and out of the water as he worked, the hair on his forearms clinging to his damp skin. His fingers were so strong, so sure, working with such masterful strokes, that she closed her eyes and surrendered herself to him completely. Her mind began to float like petals in a pond, forgetting all but the moment, and the exquisite pleasure of his touch. The warm water lapped at her ankles and mixed with the pressure of his fingers to create in her a drifting feeling of languor. Nothing she had experienced in her short but varied life had ever felt so good.

Then he brought his thumbs around and drew them in firm strokes from heel to toe on the underside of her foot. A shock of desire swept through her, so unexpected in contrast to the somnolent spell that had stolen over her senses. His thumbs moved in small circles at the base of her foot, causing flickers of fire to shoot up her legs and to leap across her spine.

Her eyes flew open, and she looked down at him from her perch with the passion he'd incited smoldering like embers in her eyes. She pulled her foot from his grasp, took his broad shoulders in her hands, swung herself around and leapt onto him, wrapping her legs around his waist. Tightening her arms about his neck, she kissed him deeply, moving her hands up to tunnel through his hair, clutching his head and devouring him as though there could never be enough of him to savor in a lifetime of such moments.

When he could, he eased his mouth from hers with a smile. "It was my intention to relax you."

"Relaxation be damned. I want you. Now."

"Ah, the Duchess of Wynterbrooke rears her head. Let's take care of that tension, shall we? Before we discuss other options."

"I'm beginning to wish I'd never mentioned it, if it delays the inevitable."

"Patience, Duchess. What did I tell you? You must learn to enjoy the process, not merely the end result."

"I'm an impatient woman, Captain. It's a difficult concept for me to learn."

"In that case, you need another lesson."

He carried her up the narrow stairs to the bedroom. It was a cramped, slope-ceilinged chamber with room for little else save the mahogany bed, an armoire, and a small side table. He laid her on the bed and stripped her clothes from her in a leisurely fashion, patiently pushing aside her hands when she tried to touch him, shoving her back into the bed when she attempted to reach up and kiss his face.

"Turn over," he commanded.

She did so, lying flat on her stomach, still wondering what he was up to.

"By the time I'm done with you," he told her, "your aching muscles will be the very last thing on your mind."

"You're a little late, I'm afraid. They've faded into distant memory even now."

"You only think so. Now be quiet and let a master work."

He began to rub her back with virile fingers, finding a slow, lulling rhythm. When she realized what he was about, she moaned her delight. As his fingers worked, she could feel her muscles let loose their punishing hold. Her satiny skin stretched and coiled, glorying in the manly feel of his hands, in the cajoling power of his touch. Slowly, in silence, as though he could happily spend the night luxuriating in his task, he worked on the small of her back, circled his thumbs upward toward her shoulders, massaged the length of her arms and one by one took her small hands in his and released from her fingers tensions she didn't know she had.

Presently, he kicked off his boots and straddled her, sitting lightly on her naked buttocks, his long legs bent on either side of her. Starting with his hands flat at her waist, he pushed his palms into her with a single steady motion, moving indomitably up her back, over her shoulders and down her arms. She sank lower into the feather mattress, feeling her body slump and the last resistance of her muscles give way.

"My God, that's wonderful," she sighed into the pillows. "But tell me, highwayman. Did you favor all your former-captives/present-lovers with such splendors?"

In reply, he reached back and playfully slapped her backside. "Hush, woman," he admonished, then proceeded with his massage.

Minutes passed, and time ceased to exist. He moved lower, massaging the back of her thighs, kneading his thumbs along the graceful line of her calves. Again, she felt unexpected stirrings of desire. She was feeling so relaxed by now that her mind felt numb, incapable of thought, her body unable to move. She felt as if she had molten lava flowing sluggishly through her veins. Every transit of his fingers brought new pleasure, and sank her deeper into the refuge of the bed. The silence, broken only by their breathing, seemed the sweetest of sounds.

Raising himself up, he spread her legs apart and moved down between them. His hands worked at the muscles in the inner thigh, sending a thrill through her so sharp that she lifted her head off the pillows and gasped out loud. His thumbs came close to brushing the hot, sensitive flesh between her thighs, but always at the last moment shied away. The torture was exquisite.

He took her buttocks in his hands and squeezed them between his fingers, then parted them so that she felt exposed and open to his eyes. As he continued to press into her, she glanced back over her shoulder to see his eyes fixed on the gentle curve of her behind. Her pulse tapped a frantic drumbeat in her throat. The appreciation of his eyes, the sumptuous, decadent indolence of her limbs, made her feel naughty in a slumberous sort of way. Smiling into the pillows, she spread her legs further apart and moved her hips with the graceful sensuality of a cat, offering him a more enticing view.

With a soft chuckle, he lowered himself onto his elbows and stretched out over the edge of the bed. Trailing his fingers along her inner thighs until she felt her loins ignite, he found her at last on the throbbing bud of desire between her legs. He rubbed as she purred in voluptuous appreciation, then spread her cheeks further and with unhurried relish, replaced his fingers with his tongue.

She was moaning audibly now as waves of yearning engulfed her. He slid a finger inside her, moving it so she could feel him deep within. By now, her body was on fire. She wanted him so badly that any semblance of rational thought was driven from her brain. With her toes, she found his erection through the tight fabric of his breeches and rubbed, hearing his growl of acknowledgment. Then she felt his tongue, hot as a wet and searing flame, blaze a fevered path along her cheeks and to the small of her back. He worshiped her with his tongue as she clutched the sheets and twisted them in her hands. His hand tangled in her soft hair, arousing her so that she spread her legs wider still and thrust up against his hand, urging him inside. With his other hand, he caressed her in front, and inserted his fingers in her until her body felt impossibly full. At the same time his thumb brushed against her bud and sent jolts of unrestrainable longings through her body with the velocity of an electrical storm. His mouth nuzzled her buttocks, his tongue gliding over the skin one moment, his teeth nipping at the flesh the next.

As he stimulated every part of her, the sensation was so intense, she could hardly tell where the pleasure came from, or where it began or ended. She felt herself swirling, rising and falling, so hot, so hungry, she felt the need to bite the pillow in two.

She wanted it never to end. Some last vestige of sanity told her this was what he'd meant when he said to savor the process, without thought to the final result. The enjoyment was so sweet, so feverishly delicious, that she could have spent the rest of her life, suspended in time, building to a climax that was just beyond reach. Too soon, she felt the first signs of her release, the building of pressure between her legs, the concentration of cravings, then the gradual ripples of pleasure that tumbled, one over the other over the other, in an ever-expanding roar. Sensing it, his fingers moved more insistently inside her while his thumb continued to graze her. Feeling thoroughly depraved, totally open to his penetrations and his eyes, feeling herself blossom beneath his agonizingly skillful ministrations, she suddenly felt the need to be a part of it, to participate and not simply be administered to. Just as her climax shook her, she reached beneath herself and replaced his thumb with her own fingers, leaving his free to roam at will. The combination of sensations—his strong fingers inside her, pushing her to the brink, moving with a superb, instinctual force, and her own soft fingers on her flesh, wet with her own juices, bringing her over the edge of raw delight—was enough to do her in. She heard her own voice, hoarse and low, whispering words of encouragement, words of love, words of lust that expressed her unbridled longings in no uncertain terms. As she exploded, ensnared by sensations that at moments seemed too rapturous to bear, she thrashed her head back and forth, biting the sheets and sucking them into her mouth, then throwing back her head and again and again crying out his name.

When her breathing had slowed and her body relaxed, he lay atop her, still dressed, and kissed her steaming temple. He took the backs of her hands in his, twining his fingers through hers, and put his mouth to her ear.

"Feeling better?"

She could hear the self-satisfied grin in his voice. Pulling free her hands, she struggled beneath him to turn onto her back without pushing him off. Then, pinned beneath him, she gave him a long and loving kiss. "The truth?" she murmured, marveling that it was so. "I've never felt more cared for in all my life."

CHAPTER 41

$\mathcal{T}$HEY SPENT THREE blissful days in Haworth, reveling in each other's company, and in their freedom from fear of capture or pain from the past. Weary of life as they'd been, and as close to losing each other as they'd come, this time together, this promise of a future, seemed to both of them too wondrous to be true. That they had time on their hands to laugh, to love, to explore each other's every whim and desire, seemed the supreme luxury. They knew in the backs of their minds that there was one more hurdle to come, that of their escape from England. They knew nothing was certain. But by mutual and silent agreement, they chose to take their happiness while it was at hand.

Yet, while the cottage was filled with their love and laughter, Toby's spirits continued to plunge. He was none too happy about his enforced isolation.

"I should be with Bobby and the lads, so I should, arrangin' for the transportation home. Why we have to roost in this God-forsaken place is beyond me understandin'."

To keep him occupied once they'd cleaned the place, Christina gave him a treasured copy of her favorite *Wuthering Heights*, inscribing it to him and signing "Fiaran" with a happy flourish.

"It was written in the nearby priory by the lonely and secluded Emily," she told him in a storyteller's voice meant to coax his interest. "The only time she ever left the sanctuary of her family was once for a short time when her father sent her off to school. But she was so miserable and sick that he brought her back, and she spent the remainder of her days in the priory, dreaming and writing about the moors. She never had a lover, had no friends save her brother and sisters, yet she wrote a book of such passion and such understanding of the human heart and soul that you'd think her the most experienced and worldly of women."

Apparently, her ideas of romance were not enough to entice him. He remained sulky and restless, worried because he could find no news in the papers of Worthington's activities.

"Likely the Inspector's not willing to admit defeat publicly once again," soothed the Captain. But as Toby's restiveness became more apparent, and the air seemed to grow blue with his complaints, he decided to send him back to Fleetwood to check on Bobby's progress and await their arrival in two days.

It was blessed relief when he was gone. The place was too small for three people, one of whom was so vocally discontented with the quarters. Christina saw after Toby had gone that he'd left behind the book she'd given him. She held it up to her lover with a wry smile. "He never cracked it open. Even after poor Michael read it and raved."

"Toby prefers penny dreadfuls." He came and took her in his arms, holding her so tightly that the forgotten book fell with a thud to the floor. "What do you say we take advantage of his absence?"

They did just that. For once, Christina brushed but didn't dress her hair, allowing it to flow freely in thick dark waves down her back. This was something that, since she was a child, she'd never allowed herself to do. It was one of her few rigid rules. Even in camp with the men—even wearing her oldest dress, she'd always been meticulous about fixing her hair. Now, she ignored the guilt that her lack of grooming inspired. She wore no jewelry, didn't care how she was dressed. She'd never felt so relaxed, so shamelessly and harmoniously oblivious to the trappings of the everyday world.

They spent the day walking along the moors, chasing

after butterflies, climbing the hills, and lying on the grass with their arms spread wide and their faces to the sun.

"Do you know who we're like?" she asked with her eyes closed, watching the orange and yellow patterns of sun at the back of her lids. "Like Cathy and Heathcliff before tragedy struck and they were forced apart. I think I bought this place because I wished so desperately that someday I might find my own Heathcliff to run with me along the moors."

She could almost hear him grinning. "Ever the romantic. Tell me, did a black-hearted bandit ever enter into your fantasies?"

She opened her eyes and looked at him. He leaned on his side, propped up on one elbow, and he had a long blade of grass in his teeth. His black hair shone in the sun like a raven's wing, spilling over his forehead. His loose white shirt, tucked negligently into his breeches, was open at the throat, falling to one side to reveal the muscular curve of his shoulder. As he reached up and dragged his hand through his hair, the fabric shifted, covering the taut flesh from her view. "The moment I saw you," she told him honestly.

With a slight smile, he reached over and ran his thumb along the line of her jaw. "Why were they separated— your Heathcliff and Cathy?"

"Because she thought she wanted money and position more than she wanted him. He was a ruffian, a scoundrel. She was ashamed of him, so she married a wealthy and socially acceptable man. But Heathcliff's and Cathy's souls were like one, and even though she kept pushing him away, they couldn't deny the fierceness of their love. She died in his arms, looking out at the moors, realizing too late what she'd lost. Years later, after he'd lived a miserable and lonely life without her, he died with her name on his lips. People said they saw their ghosts after that, his and Cathy's, wandering hand in hand along the moors." She rose up, looking earnestly into his face. "But you and I shall never be separated after this. Because I would gladly relinquish every scrap of position and money and anything else I have in the world to spend my life with you."

He gave a small smile. "Pity we can't stay longer, if you love it so."

"I don't love it. Not the place. Not *any* place. Only what it represents." She looked out over the moors and breathed in the sweet scent of them, wanting to remember this moment all the days of her life. "Maybe we'll come back someday. Maybe after we're gone, our souls will come back, like Heathcliff's and Cathy's, and haunt these lonely moors. And people will say, 'I saw that bandit the other day. He and his lady. They were walking hand in hand through eternity.' "

Their eyes met and, unbidden, caught a flash of fear. She closed her eyes against the naked truth in his. The white light behind her lids melted to a soft apricot beneath the sun, deepened to peach, then shimmered a brilliant orange and expanded in undulating waves to an angry red ball of fire that, in her imagination, widened and engulfed her, and threatened to consume all the happy, tender feelings of the moment. She recognized it for what it was: the old fear coming back to assault her. The fear that somehow, her mother would win out again, would hurt her as she used to, would destroy her once and for all. Now, as she stood on the threshold of happiness, the fear assumed more power than ever before.

As a child, she'd locked herself away in the private and confining hell of her own mind, telling herself it didn't matter if her mother hurt her, telling herself that the fortress of her body and her beliefs could protect her from the bombardment of emotional pain. It wasn't true. On the brink of finally realizing the life she'd always sought, the love she'd always craved, the old terror had the power to paralyze her body and waste her resolve.

Her rational mind told her she was beyond harm now. She'd left her mother behind in a world that she'd rejected, that was no longer a part of the Christina who, under the tutelage of an outlaw, had been born anew. But her heart still skipped with the quick, light, fearful rhythm of the child she'd been. The child who had craved love and never found it. The child who, not yet a woman, had married a man she didn't love in a desperate attempt to find the attention she needed. Out of her defenses, she'd grown biting and sophisticated, worldly and self-sufficient, throwing her self-sufficiency in the face of every man who crossed her path. As if to say, "I'm not dependent on you, as I was on her." All the while searching for the one man who had what it took to care for her needs. The one man who could stand up to her mother as her father never had. Now she understood that only by loving another and giving to another could she fill the void that lack of love in her life had left.

She only hoped it wasn't too late.

"Hold me, Richard," she whispered. "Hold me and don't ever let me go. Tell me this isn't just another fantasy, or some romantic dream. Tell me I'm not foolish to believe there *is* a happy ending for us, after all."

He told her with his touch. Casting the grass blade from his teeth, he slid his arms beneath her and pulled her to him with such ferocity that her breath was forced from her lungs. He kissed her, driving her head back with brutal force, so that she felt her own desperation reverberate through him. His lips moved on hers, his tongue raking through her mouth so that she made a strangled sound in the back of her throat. When he pulled back, she wrenched her mouth from his and cried, "No! Don't stop! If I were to die kissing you, I should do so with an inexpressible joy in my heart."

He kissed her again, with all the unleashed passion of a storm, plunging his hands into her flowing hair. She reached up and unbuttoned his shirt with trembling hands, parting it and letting her cool hands spread out against the hot flesh of his chest. Her blood was rushing through her head, forcing out the haunting thoughts, making her dizzy beneath the unrelenting onslaught of his kiss.

"I've known many men," she panted when he moved his mouth to her throat. "But never—ever—did I know it could be like this."

"That's because you didn't love them," he said, trailing hot kisses along her neck, her collarbone, the curve of her shoulder, shoving her dress aside as his lips explored her skin.

"No, I didn't. Not for a moment. Not one." She moved her hands to his face and gripped him tight, running her thumbs along the prominent bones of his cheeks.

"And none of them loved you. Not as I do. Not as you deserve to be loved."

His words calmed her and, for a time, made her feel whole. "Thank God you came along when you did. I couldn't have stood one more man's hot hands on my flesh. One more man desperate for a love I couldn't give him."

"Then I must disappoint you. For I am yet another man desperate for your love. And I intend to put my hot hands *all over* your flesh."

To illustrate his point, he slid his hand up under her skirts, thrust aside the layers of petticoats and lace, and found her in the moist recesses between her thighs. His fingers parted the lips and moved inside, thrusting against the slick, wet walls as his mouth found her nipple and made it hard. Memories of the night before fluttered through her mind, making her pulse race.

"The only way you could disappoint me," she gasped, "is if you *didn't* want me."

"Then you should be a very happy woman, indeed."

Impatient now with the confines of her clothes, he yanked at the bodice of her dress. The buttons in back gave way, and he rent the material to her waist, where he could feast on her full breasts with his eyes, his hands, his mouth. The warmth of the sun beating down on her mixed with her hot, consuming passion and the heat and sweat of his body burning into her flesh. Her heart raced, her blood pumped, and the wild, demanding fire between her legs begged to be quenched. Thrusting her hands above her head, she gripped the long grass, pulled it up by its roots, and arched herself against him with a pleading cry. She could feel him hard and swollen against her, fanning the flames of her desire until she could lie still no longer.

Disengaging her hands from the tufts of grass, she reached for his breeches, pulling them so the buttons snapped free, parting the material to see the thick black hair inside. She urged his pants down over his narrow hips and saw him then, long and thick, hard as a staff, standing proud and free. He was so beautiful, so unabashedly masculine, from the breadth of his shoulders to the flat of his stomach to the stiff, curling hair on his horseman's thighs. All at once, she couldn't stand it. She had to pay homage to him, had to show him the euphoria that bubbled through her at the thought that he was hers.

Shifting, she took him between her hands and kissed him with her soft lips, then slid him into her mouth in one slow, tight, worshipful motion that consumed every inch of him. As she drew back, she sucked greedily, feeling him swell and bulge beneath her tongue. She smiled as he caught his breath and took her loose hair into his fist. Again, she took all of him, cupping her hand beneath him and, as she withdrew, using her other hand to stroke and pump him with a gentle rhythm. His hand tightened in her hair as his breath came now in audible groans.

When he spoke, his voice was graveled with passion. "Do you think your heroine served her Heathcliff so up here, overlooking the same moors?"

She withdrew her mouth, maintained the rhythm of her hand, and looked up at him. "Emily Brönte, most distressingly, neglected to say. But if I were Cathy, I most certainly would have."

"Well, we know *that*," he quipped.

Their eyes met, and they both laughed, easing the earlier desperation. Her mouth was damp. He reached down and ran one strong finger along her lips, then put it to his tongue. "Never forget," he told her, "how much I love you, or how happy you've made me. Promise me."

She ran the flat of her tongue up the length of his shaft as he shivered in response. "Only if you promise never to allow me to forget."

He flattened himself on her, lowering her by his weight to the ground. Shoving aside her skirts, he entered her with a single thrust, bringing her legs to his shoulders and watching the desire cloud her eyes, flick over her face, as he thrust mercilessly into her and caused her to cry out loud. "As long as I am with you," he promised.

She pulled him closer over her so that his thrusts penetrated her so deeply that her pleasure bordered on pain. With her hands clutching his shoulders, her breath coming in short gasps, she told him, "Until we leave these moors, I want to do every naughty, wicked, and wonderfully lusty thing we can think of. I want to love you in every conceivable fashion, from now until dawn, until we're so spent, so utterly wrung out with satisfaction, that we haven't even the strength to *contemplate* another go. Let these, our last nights in our homeland, be spent in bliss."

"Ah, Duchess."

"I warn you, Captain. It's no easy task you take upon yourself. Right now, I'm not certain I can get enough of you in a hundred years."

"If there's one thing I appreciate, it's a challenge."

And, rising to it, he carried her with him beyond the lonely moors to a world of their own making.

CHAPTER 42

*F*URIOUSLY, SASHA WENTWORTH paced the floor of her elaborate salon as her husband, Derk, read aloud from a play. She was dressed in a brocade dressing gown in her favorite autumn hues, and in spite of her agitated state, she looked stunning. No crisis in her life had ever prevented Sasha from presenting her best face, even to her husband.

Not one to be outdone by his wife, Derk was attired in a maroon-and-black velvet smoking jacket that set off his salt-and-pepper hair to perfection. Stretched out in a negligent posture on the settee, he flipped the pages with an actor's flair as he read, missing the ashtray as he flicked his cigarette ash onto the priceless Indian carpet that had been in Sasha's family for generations.

"It's not bad," he expostulated. "With a little work, it might even be a success."

"We *had* a success," Sasha raged, moving like a tiny whirlwind to brush the ash from the rug. "When I think of all we've lost because of that infernal—*knave!*" she concluded, unable to think—without a script—of anything bad enough to call the bandit.

The aftermath of the robbery had been a nightmare for them. The theater patrons had angrily demanded their money back and were none too pleased when it was discovered that one of the bandit's men had taken the proceeds from the play, and they were told they would have to call for their refunds at another time. The whole fiasco was enough to ruin Derk and Sasha. Not only must they refund the night's proceeds, but they were experienced enough in the theater to know the subsequent performances would be canceled. It was one thing to come to see such a play out of curiosity—quite another to come knowing the bandit himself could pop in at any time. They'd been counting on at least another six months' run to make a profit on their investment. Now, in spite of the success so far, they would lose an incalculable amount of money. Not to mention the stigma of superstition that lingered, with everyone afraid to come to see them, lest the bandit might have a personal vendetta against them. It was really quite disastrous!

Then there was the damnable investigation during which Inspector Worthington questioned the cast and crew in his droning, laborious way. The same questions asked of the same people, with nothing resolved. Who was the bandit's accomplice? Where might they be heading? Which way did they go? An hour of speculation that led back to the same questions but no insight.

Once again, Sasha picked up the Irish dictionary Oscar Wilde had left behind when working on the play. She'd borrowed it to look up some of the Irish phrases in the dialogue to better understand her role. Now, idly skimming through it, she came upon the *F*'s and out of curiosity searched the columns. "How odd," she said aloud.

"What's that, darling?"

"This word. *Fiaran*. The name of my part in the play. It seems to be a verb. Here; have a listen. 'To leave home in a huff; to go awandering.' "

Derk gave a snort as he turned another page. "Sounds like our Christina."

There was a knock on the door, and the majordomo announced the arrival of Inspector Worthington. The Inspector was shown in, hat in hand, looking—as he always did in the presence of the aristocracy—as if he were on the verge of a perpetual bow.

"Well!" Sasha greeted. "I do hope you have more encouraging news! We are at our wits' end here, trying to make a decision as to the future, whilst waiting for you to do the job you were hired to do."

The Inspector flushed. Derk, feeling sorry for the man under the lash of his wife's tongue, rose to his full height and came forward to shake hands. "You mustn't mind the Marchioness, you know. She's the eternal optimist where her career's concerned. She harbors hopes that you will apprehend the fiend in time for us to rewrite the third act and save ourselves from ruin." After the briefest of pauses, he added, "I have to admit, old man, I rather hope for the same thing."

The Inspector squirmed. If he'd hoped for the camaraderie of a gentleman's sympathy against the irrationality of a slighted woman, he could see that he'd miscalculated. Derk Wentworth might know the publicity value of a good romp in public with his wife, but he always backed her in the end.

"We haven't caught the fiend, if that's what you mean." He held up a hand against the combined tirade that followed his words. "Came bloody close. Almost had him on the road a time or two. But we seem to have lost the blackguard. He doesn't seem to be anywhere that we expected him. I fear he may be halfway to Ireland by this time. In which case, we can only hope he keeps his word and never bothers us again."

"Mark my words carefully, Inspector," Sasha said in a clearly enunciated, menacing tone. "We have no interest in seeing the brute vanish into thin air, never to return. It may make a fine, romantic ending to a play, but we've been victimized by this man, and we intend to see him hang for his pains. Do I make myself *quite* clear?"

The Inspector sighed. He'd come from a similar conversation with the Prince of Wales not a half hour before.

"Have you *no* clues?" asked Derk in a more reasonable tone. "Perhaps he's hiding out somewhere, ridiculing your attempts to pursue him. Were I he—and I feel I have the right to say so, having lived inside his skin for as long as I have—I should have no intention of scuttling off to Ireland. I should, however, have a fine time allowing everyone to think that I had."

"We have only one clue," the Inspector admitted

grudgingly. "The woman seems to have discarded her costume along the road. I've just taken it along to the Prince of Wales to see what he might tell us. His interest in clothing is well known, after all."

"Bah!" cried Sasha. "Bertie is interested only in how his tailor might disguise his growing bulk. Bring the wretched thing in to us. We, after all, are more familiar with costumes, having spent the majority of our lives costumed in one form or other."

"Well, I hadn't thought—"

"Of course you hadn't. Isn't that why this criminal is still prowling about? Because you lack the ability to think as he does?"

By this time, the Inspector was fuming inside. It was bad enough to have such a thankless job. But to be continually treated by the aristocracy as if he were less than the dirt beneath their feet—

"Very well, madam," he said in a clipped tone.

He poked his head out the door and spoke to his man in the hall.

"You've hurt his feelings," Derk hissed at his wife.

"And what, pray tell," Sasha demanded, "do I care for a simpleton's feelings when our lives are in the very *throes* of catastrophe?"

The Inspector returned a moment later with the discarded swan gown, mask, and gloves. They were torn and dirty now, having been trampled in the road. Sasha snatched the dress from him impatiently and held it up to her. It was too large, but she felt a haunting sense of familiarity with the richness of the material, and the impeccable workmanship. She slipped one of the gloves on her hand. It fit her small hand perfectly. How, she wondered, looking again at the costume, could such an apparently large woman have such tiny hands?

So this was the costume of the notorious Fiaran. The actress in her thrilled at the opportunity to study her firsthand. *What I could have done with such a costume!* she thought. Instinctually, she studied it, looking for clues to the character of the woman in what she chose to wear.

Fiaran. To leave home in a huff. It sounds like our Christina.

Suddenly, she froze. The phrase kept repeating itself in her head. *Like our Christina. Like Christina.*

"Once, when I was a lad," the Inspector mused, cutting into her thoughts, "I borrowed my father's saw without his permission to make him a surprise. What it was doesn't matter. When I forgot to put the saw back, he thought I'd stolen it. Found it beneath my bed. To teach me never to steal, he put my thumb in a vise and tightened it till I thought he'd split my thumb in two. To this day, I can't move it, but it taught me never to take what wasn't mine." He demonstrated his thumb's lack of mobility, then added in a tortured tone, "I'd like to do that and worse to this bloody bandit. God Almighty, how I long to make him pay!"

Slowly, Sasha turned up the hem and examined the seams of the skirt. She looked carefully at the stitches. She'd seen her daughter's workmanship often enough to recognize its finer points. Chilled, she dropped the costume as if by her touching it, some of its evil might rub off onto her.

It was several moments before she could collect herself. She recalled the Irish gypsy's look of victorious pity behind the mask—a look that until now, she had failed to understand. It all made sense now. How the outlaws had been able to sneak into the theater under their very noses. How the bandit's men had pulled off their disguises. Christina—her own daughter!—had supplied them with costumes she'd stolen from the theater. Easy enough to check.

Even in the face of her earlier suspicions, she was stunned to sickness by her discovery. The worst of it was her own naivete. If she hadn't let Christina—and Oscar, damn him!—talk her out of her suspicions, she could have avoided this disaster. As it was, it was as much Sasha's fault that they were ruined as it was Christina's. How could she face Derk with the knowledge that she'd had it in her hands to avoid these hideous consequences, that she'd stupidly turned her back on all the clues?

Her dropping of the costume and subsequent silence held the men's attention. They searched her face with interest, expecting nothing, but succumbing to that quality Sasha had of garnering the attention of those around her by virtue of being present in the room. She turned her back to give herself a private moment, practicing the air of a bereaved and worried mother until she had it perfected. Once again, she thought of the smug look on her daughter's masked face. How clever she must think herself! So, she thought she'd won, did she? Well, her ungrateful daughter was going to be surprised!

When she was ready, she turned back to them with believably tearful eyes. "Inspector," she whispered with her hand at her heart, "I fear I've some distressing news."

CHAPTER 43

*I*T DIDN'T MATTER that Christina knew it was a dream. In that suspended state in which the dreamer looks down upon the horror of the vision she's seeing, she was nonetheless encircled by the spiraling emotions of an incident long since buried in time. She hadn't consciously recalled the episode since childhood, which was why, all these years later, the humiliation was still fresh, and her anguish quite real.

She was thirteen years old. Little more than two months had passed since her father, mistaking her for Elisabeth, had molested her in her bed. Once her bruises had healed, she'd gone to the country to her friend Cynthia's to complete the recuperation that had begun with the healing of her body. She'd taken long walks in the woods in an attempt to soothe her soul. So consumed was she by her recovery, so free did she feel away from the ugly restrictive silence that had since permeated her parents' home, that she abandoned all the little disciplines that had been beaten into her at the end of a cane. She washed only when necessary. She rarely gave a thought to the condition of her hair. And she wore the same dress for days at a time before realizing that she did. In the country, these things that had once seemed so essential had become unnecessary. What *had* been necessary was to drink in the solace of the pastureland, the song of the birds, the healing warmth of the sun. Everything else seemed superfluous.

It was a badly needed time of mending that allowed

her once again to face her unhappy London life with the dignity that had become her mainstay and protection from anyone guessing at her secrets. But upon her return, she found to her dismay that she couldn't get a comb through her tangled hair. Any other girl might have gone to her mother for help. But Christina knew that, so soon after witnessing the horror with her father, her mother would use this innocent oversight as an excuse for more abuse. So she brushed the outer layers to cover the rat's nest at the base of her neck and prayed Sasha would never look closely enough to be the wiser. Soon enough, she'd be back to school, she told herself, and out of her mother's reach.

Of course, Sasha found out. She grabbed Christina by her matted hair, dragged her screaming to the small, stuffy laundry room—Christina could see every steamy detail in her dream—and took hold of a pair of long-bladed shears. As Christina cried out repeatedly and begged her mother's forgiveness, Sasha took swipes at her hair with the shears, all the while berating her for her scandalous behavior. "If you can't take care of it, you shan't have it," Sasha screamed at the top of her lungs.

And even as she was experiencing the terror of it, a part of her mind told her this was not about her hair. It was about her mother's jealousy. Misreading Christina's intentions with her father, Sasha sought to defeminize her daughter in the time-honored way—to deprive her of the crowning glory of her hair.

Christina fought as well as she could. When she resisted, her mother began landing blows on her face and, as she covered her head with her arms, on her head and shoulders. She would be bruised for days as a result of those blows, so savage and hurtful, coming as they did from such a small woman. In her dream, Christina relived the raw humiliation. Begging her mother's forgiveness. Promising never to do it again if only she'd spare her hair. Fighting not to cry against the hateful words that spilled from her mother's mouth. "You're an ungrateful wretch of a daughter. I deplore the day I had you. You've been nothing but trouble to me since the day of your miserable birth!" Never once mentioning the incident with Derk, even as the memory of it hung between them in the air.

And soon Christina's shame was replaced, inevitably, by anger. By a rage that her mother would believe the worst of her daughter and not her husband. That she should have the power to belittle her so. That she would allow herself to care what her mother thought. But she did care. All she'd wanted was her mother's love and care. Some tenderness. Some hint of feeling. In her most despairing moments, she longed for her mother's protection from her father, for always in those early days, there was the fear that it might happen again. Instead, her mother hated her. She hated everything about her—her flawless complexion, her luxuriant black hair, her vivacious spirits. She wanted to crush everything that made Christina what she was, to show it forth as meaningless to her world.

It had happened too many times to count. But this time, the rage was like a blinding red light in her brain. This time, she couldn't just cower against the blows like a trapped beast. This time, she'd had enough. As her mother chopped the hair haphazardly off at the neck, she hurled herself up and hit her mother back.

She bolted up in her bed. It was black in the room in Haworth, but still she could see in her mind's eye the shocked expression on her mother's face all those years ago. Christina had paid for that blow. Not only was she whipped by her mother in retaliation, but her father had added his own blows when he'd returned. She could still remember her hatred of him: for not standing up to his unreasonable wife, for not admitting what this fuss was all about, for not accepting responsibility for his actions, for allowing his daughter to take the blame. She could feel her embarrassment at being packed off to boarding school with the whacked-off hair, at having to go to the headmistress for the care and solace she required. At pretending, with a proud uplift of her chin, that she didn't need comfort or maternal tenderness, that she was just fine, thank you, on her own.

It was only in her dreams that Christina ever blamed

her father. The impulse to protect him was strongly in-grained. For, like her mother, if she didn't admit it, didn't think about it, she could pretend it had never happened. Then she could face her father in a civilized way without wanting to rail at him—or kill him—for what he'd done. For, although she feared no man alive, she knew in her heart that she could never confront her father with this. She would never challenge his unspoken contention that he didn't remember. Because if she found out that he did, something would be lost to her forever. Perhaps it was the ability to dream.

Sometimes she thought she'd imagined the whole thing. Sometimes she thought *that* was the dream.

She was shaking, and her gown was soaked with per-spiration. Beside her, the Captain slept with deep, rhyth-mic breaths. All was quiet. All was peaceful. Then why, she asked herself, was she so terrified inside?

She'd gone to bed that night determined that tomor-row would be the beginning of her new life. That she would never again allow her parents to hurt her. That she would seize from her mother whatever power she'd had over her life and her feelings. But deciding it and feeling it were two entirely different matters. Deciding it, no matter how resolvedly, didn't take away the fright that had long been ingrained in her child's heart. It made her *want* to be free of her mother's reign of terror—it didn't break the chains.

She lay back down in her damp bed, trying to relax. The feel of the man beside her was a comfort. Where, she wondered, had this come from? Did her mother have such power over her that even now, she could ruin the best time of her life? First yesterday out on the moors, and now in her dreams. What did it take to be rid of her haunting presence? She'd thought robbing the theater would be enough. But if it was, why was she so afraid that her mother would somehow find a way to ruin her happiness? That she'd somehow win out in the end? And even as she thought this, she realized that she'd always—always!—blamed Sasha for what Derk had done.

The Captain must have sensed her turmoil, for he

rolled over and reached for her. "You all right?" he murmured sleepily.

"Fine," she whispered, cautioning her voice to remain calm. "I just had a bad dream."

He gathered her in his arms, then, touching her, woke up completely. "You're soaking wet. What did you dream?"

She didn't want to tell him. She'd never told anyone the details of her confrontations with her mother, because it shamed her even now to remember those days. But somehow the words spilled out of her as he held her quietly in his arms.

"I used to write stories as a way of escaping," she said when she'd told him the dream. "All alone in my room, I used to pretend to be anything but what I was. I couldn't act, that was clear, but I still had the family gift for losing myself in a character—except that I was creating the character. They were silly fantasies, really. I never wanted to write about reality. Reality was all too real for me. So I created bandits and ladies fair who fell in love with them."

"And then you met me. And began to live it."

She snuggled closer against him. "Sometimes I wonder if you really exist, or if I just created you in my dreams."

He kissed her forehead and brushed away the damp hair. "One day, when we're out of this, you can write about us. About our adventures. About how we had the last laugh on them all."

The thought didn't cheer her. The dream had left her with a deep sense of doom. In the wake of it, she could only hope that they survived to tell the tale.

"You're safe now," he reminded her. "Don't forget what I told you. I shall die before I let anyone harm you again."

She was shivering—from cold or trepidation, she couldn't be sure. "I'm so afraid Mother's going to spoil it somehow. I know it's irrational. But I can't seem to let go of this feeling. Tell me it's going to be all right. Tell me we're going to find everything we're looking for. Tell me you won't *have* to die protecting me."

There was a long pause before he spoke. He wouldn't lie to her, and even though she almost wished he would, she loved him even more because he wouldn't. "God willing," he said at last, and held her closer to him to absorb his warmth.

They spent their last day peacefully on the moors, appreciating their freedom more for the shared anxiety of the morning, and then, when reality threatened their composure, finding respite once again in each other's arms.

They talked for hours. Christina told him how she had dreamed of this place as a child, how she'd seen it all in her mind's eye, and how once she'd come on her own, it had proven a more enchanting and reckless a place than she'd even imagined. A place after her own secret heart. They spoke of the past, painting for each other pictures of their childhoods with brushes colored with their pain, their loneliness, their despair. As he spoke, the Captain continually twisted the ring on his small finger. Once, she reached over and took his hand, halting the motion.

"It's over now," she reminded him, hoping it was true.

After a brief hesitation, he smiled into her eyes. As always, they were left with a feeling of being bonded together by the similarity of their feelings and their pasts.

They returned to the cottage that night full of sun and wind and joy in each other's company, feeling that nothing on earth could touch or harm them ever again.

They took a supper of cold chicken and wine up the narrow flight of stairs and fed each other lounging in bed. The room was so small, so confining with its low, sloping ceiling that it might have been a cave, yet, dropping bits of chicken into her lover's mouth, Christina couldn't imagine ever wanting to be anywhere else.

"I can't remember ever being so content," she told him, taking a sip of wine. "Right this minute, I feel as if I need nothing but you to give me peace."

"You're an easy woman to please."

"It isn't true. Never before you. I wanted so much

from life that there never seemed time enough to taste everything it had to offer. Yet, all my varied experiences have left me feeling empty and quite alone. I suppose it's true what they say about love. I never quite believed it before, but it *must* be true. I've never felt so complete before."

"Nor I."

She propped herself up on an elbow, and her long hair fell over her shoulder. "Do you?"

"Aye, love. For the first time."

"That's why I'm so afraid of losing it. I've enjoyed our time here more than I can say. But I have to admit I shall be deeply relieved when we're out of England and certain that we're safe."

"It's your fear of the past that makes you feel unsafe. Not your fear of the future."

She took his hand and rubbed the coin in his golden ring. "Then let's be done with the past. No memories. No pain. Just us, and now. I don't know what the future holds, and I don't care." She worked at the ring until she'd pried it off his finger, and tossed it to the end of the bed. Then, straddling him with her naked legs, she leaned down so that her hair fell forward and formed a curtain around them both. "Tonight, I want you all to myself."

As always, he obliged her willingly. Eventually, the urgency for each other that was born from fear subsided, to be replaced by a spent languor that was so peaceful, so like floating in a tranquil pool, that they continually bubbled with laughter deep in their throats.

Exhausted as they were, they found no will to sleep. Their last night in England was a time to savor. All through the night and into the early morning hours they alternated loving with feasting on chicken and wine, speaking the instinctual language of lovers that no other human, if he heard, would understand.

They were wrapped in each other's arms with the sweaty sheets tossed aside, her slim white limbs draped over his hairy legs, when they heard the thunder of horses' hooves descending on the house. Depleted by the day's expenditures, the Captain rose up, casting his glance automatically about the room. For once, he was unprepared. There wasn't so much as a pistol in sight. Christina lay frozen in his arms, her breath gone, her heart stilled, as a fist banged with repeated insistence upon the door.

CHAPTER 44

*T*HE CAPTAIN SHOVED her from the bed with a curse. "Get dressed," he ordered distractedly, pulling on his pants and looking about the chamber. It was clear they were trapped. There was no window in the room, and the only exit was down the stairs and through either the front or back door.

"Perhaps it's one of your men," Christina offered hopefully as she pulled on a white silk robe, the only garment at hand. But even as she said it, the door was burst open and the familiar, ominous sounds of booted feet could be heard bounding through the cottage.

It happened too quickly for thought. Before they knew it, a band of armed men were taking the stairs two at a time and were bursting into the room. The Captain threw a pillow at them to distract them, then lunged into them, fighting three men at once like a fury. But his strength had been sapped, and Christina, feeling the guilt of it choke her even as her panic grew, threw herself at one of the men and tugged on his arm, trying to pry or shove him loose. More footsteps were heard on the stairs, and the narrow hall was suddenly overfilled with struggling bodies. Christina was pushed back into another soldier as a familiar voice was heard booming up the stairwell. In the confusion of flailing bodies, a gun went off, blasting their eardrums in the enclosed space. Everything seemed to freeze for a moment as she felt something slicing through the back of her left shoulder.

"Fool!" cried Inspector Worthington, shrugging his way through his men. "I promised the Marchioness that she would go unharmed!"

In a haze, Christina realized the significance of his words. Mother. Her mother had sent them after her. She looked up through a veil of hair to see the Captain, bare-footed and bare-chested, pinned spread-eagle between the guards, the fight drained from him, staring at her with a look of horror on his face. She thought for a moment that he blamed her, maybe thought she'd arranged this perfidy, until a long lock of hair fell from behind her shoulder, and she saw the blood that stained it. Only then did she realize she'd been shot.

She felt no pain. Only a sick weak feeling as her senses began to slip away. She fought to remain conscious, feeling behind her with her right hand so that it came bloodied before her eyes. Someone was bending over her, but time was passing now as in a dream. It had no meaning. All she could see was the harsh reality of the look in her lover's eyes as he stared down at her, never taking his tortured eyes from her, even as the Inspector's men dragged him away.

She must have passed out then, for the next thing she knew, she was flopping over a horse's mane with someone behind to steady her. She thought at once that it was Richard, that he'd broken free and carried her, sick and bleeding, in his arms to thrust her before him on his horse and cart her away to safety. As she struggled to rise from off the horse's neck, she felt the pain in her back that ripped through her and robbed her of strength. Slowly, as she regained consciousness, she became aware of the droning voice of the Inspector, sounding cold and hard and full of hatred.

"Thought you could make a fool of me, did you?" She heard a thud and a soft groan. "Make me look the simpleton in front of God and countrymen, eh?" Another thud. "Not to mention the Prince of Wales, and the Queen herself. I imagine you had a fine time, laughing in your beer thinking yourself well rid of me."

Another whack, harder than the rest, reached her ears, and belatedly Christina realized they were beating the

Captain. With her last ounce of energy, she swiveled her head on the horse's neck and found him through the mist of pain before her eyes. They'd tied his hands behind his back and were holding him with a chain around his neck in the small clearing. The light from the open doorway spilled out into the night, highlighting the ghoulish, angry, bloodthirsty features of the soldiers. Inspector Worthington, outwardly calm but seething in tone, paced before him, flipping his billy club into the palm of his other hand.

One of the guards took hold of the Captain's hair, jerked back his head, and kicked him savagely in the back. As he did so, Christina caught sight of the blood trickling from his mouth and dripping onto the bare, out-thrust muscles of his chest. "Answer the Inspector, brute!"

Beneath the kick, the Captain lunged forward, and the Inspector smiled a cruel smile. "I do believe he's trying to escape, men." One by one, the soldiers hit him gleefully with fists, with nightsticks, until he fell to his knees on the ground. "What?" cried the Inspector in mock surprise. "Haven't learned your lesson yet? Still trying to escape?" He pulled back his foot and kicked the Captain squarely in the face.

The Captain slumped beneath the blow, falling to the ground, shaking the blood and sweat from his eyes, barely able to keep his hold on consciousness.

Christina could look no longer. The sight of her commanding lover being brutally tortured, kicked and beaten like a dog on a chain, was too much for her to bear. It brought back memories of horror, but even those paled in the wake of her lover's suffering. If she'd had the strength, she would have begged them to whip her instead. For once, she would have taken it gladly. She was going to die anyway, she felt. Better that she die saving him.

"I've waited for this," the Inspector was saying again in that deceptively smooth yet furious tone. "I've longed to have you just so, *Lord* Wycliffe, at my mercy. Perhaps you'd like to beg for your life? The Prince wouldn't care, you know, if I brought your head in on a pike."

In reply, the Captain spit savagely at Worthington's feet. He was rewarded with a round of clubbings from the irate guards.

As the Inspector's voice droned on, Christina felt the helpless reproach resounding in her head, wounding her more than the bullet in her flesh. *It's all your fault,* it blasted in her brain. *Just minutes before, you were so happy, so hopeful that you had a future. Yet, it was that very happiness that made him careless. You caused him to let down his guard, to forget about weapons and the need for vigilance. You sapped his energy with your demands—energies he might have used to free the two of you tonight.* Reason told her that even at full powers, he couldn't have triumphed before so many men. But she cast out her reason along with her optimism as her self-condemnation echoed like a wrathful lament in the depths of her paralyzed mind. It was hopeless, she thought before the blackness mercifully came to claim her. Now that they had him, they'd kill him, and she'd never see him again.

CHAPTER 45

SHE AWOKE IN a haze of dull, throbbing pain. Vague memories flitted through her consciousness of being put in a bed and made to drink something vile. It seemed to her that she'd drunk from the same cup numerous times. Each time, she'd wanted to spit out the liquid, and each time, a voice had urged her to drink. She had a sense of people hovering over her, but the memories were so hazy, they might have been dreams.

She stirred in bed and felt the fire in her shoulder. It was better if she didn't move. She kept her eyes closed, waiting for the nausea to subside. It seemed to her that there was something she had to do—something urgent—but her brain was so fuzzy, she couldn't think what it could be. She felt so weak, she wasn't sure if she could sit up, much less rise from the bed.

Without opening her eyes, she knew she was in her old room at Northampton House. She couldn't be sure how she knew. The unforgotten feel of the bed, perhaps, or some elusive scent. Even the act of opening her eyes was torture, but she pried them open and looked around. The light of dawn softened the artistic lines of the room—the silk hangings depicting Japanese mountains, trees, and flowers on a background of white, deep blue, and green; the bed curtains done in a similar Oriental flowered design; the cherrywood furnishings, elegant and understated so as not to detract attention from the expensive wall hangings, which were the focus of the room. It was all distantly familiar in the way of an often-visited museum, but not with the intimacy of home. She couldn't think clearly, but being here in her mother's house made her break out in a cold sweat. There was something threatening here, something to run from. Or was it something to run to?

She had an eerie sense of reliving the past. For it was here, in this very room, that she'd been put to bed after her father's beating that horrible night. Here where she was kept a virtual prisoner, not allowed to see a doctor, until her telltale bruises healed. For one confused moment, she thought she was still thirteen, and it had just happened.

The door opened, and her old maid Patricia came in with a golden goblet on a tray. "Ah, yer awake, yer grace. Yer shoulder must be painin' ye, aye? Here, I've somethin' for you to ease the pain."

Christina's mind protested, but she didn't have the strength to speak. As before, she relented and drank the vile stuff. Soon, the pain receded and she began to drift into a more pleasant and free-floating place.

She didn't know how long she drifted in her drugged state of alternating pain and near-awareness before they forced the medicine upon her again. She thought at times that she saw her mother, but she closed her eyes, hoping it was a dream, and when she opened them again, Sasha was gone. She came awake with a start one morning to the sound of birds singing outside her window and the singsong of hawkers in the square below. "Strawberries! Who'll buy me strawberries?" "Bread for sale. Fresh bread for sale." When she opened her eyes, she could see the bright yellow sun streaming in through the window. She was aware that the pain was better. Reaching beneath her silk nightgown, she felt the restraint of a bandage running across her shoulder and under her arm. Her back was stiff, but she could move it a little easier than before.

Suddenly she remembered. Why she was here. Why her shoulder was so painful. What had happened that awful night in Haworth. She struggled up in bed, looking about the room for some signs of how much time had passed. She caught her breath with a gasp as she saw her mother sitting in the corner, her amber eyes coolly assessing her.

"I was wondering when you would awaken," Sasha began in her impersonal tone.

A rush of memories flooded Christina's mind. The roar of a gun. Inspector Worthington's sneering voice. *Fool! I promised the Marchioness she would go unharmed.*

Christina swallowed hard, looking about for some escape. Her mouth was dry, and her head ached mercilessly. She cautioned herself to think in spite of her discomfort. There were things she had to know. She must be careful. Her mother had the advantage over her, in her weakened state.

"How long have I been here?" she croaked in a voice that sounded oddly unlike her own.

"Long enough for your lover to have been tried and sentenced to hang." The satisfaction of her mother's tone was inescapable.

Christina jerked so abruptly that she wrenched her shoulder. She reached back with her right hand, trying to breathe deeply and ease the pain when all she really wanted to do was scream. After what seemed an interminable time, she asked, "When?"

"Will he hang? Day after tomorrow, I believe." As if she didn't know the exact time and place it would occur.

"I thought they didn't hang people anymore," Christina said groggily.

"Not for robbery, gracious no. But for murder—that's quite a *different* story, isn't it? And they have the death-bed confession of that guard in the armory that your lover was the one who killed him. It was all quite simple, really. He's to hang at dawn, just as we predicted in our play. Frankly, I can hardly wait. Once the wretched affair is over, we shall be able to reopen our production. We should see quite a return on our investment, after all, with the publicity of his hanging. I must admit that in some oblique way, we have you to thank for it. For being your own predictable self, and leading to the capture of the brute."

Christina flashed a venomous look. "You told the Inspector to look at Haworth."

"Naturally."

"You'd do that to your own daughter?"

"Well, really, Christina, what did you expect? That you could make utter fools of your father and me—in *public*, no less—and just waltz away scot-free? But come now. I shouldn't feel too remiss if I were you. You simply made the same mistake you have always made—you underestimated me dreadfully. Perhaps this will teach you once and for all that I shall always have the upper hand where you're concerned."

It was useless to answer. "Why was I not allowed in the courtroom?"

"Why, you're so terribly ill, dear." At her daughter's doubtful stare, she added more truthfully, "Besides, I struck a bargain with the Inspector. He would have his bandit, and in return you would not be implicated. No one knows that you were the notorious Fiaran save the Inspector, your father and myself, and the soldiers present that night. And they have been sworn to secrecy. No one is to know, not even the Prince of Wales. It was the only way I could think to salvage your reputation."

"My reputation!"

She could no longer lie back in bed, feeling open and vulnerable to the weapon of her mother's words. It hurt to move, but she forced herself to push aside the covers and swing her legs over the side of the bed, then carefully feel her way around it, supporting herself with her hand on the mattress, until she came to lean before Sasha.

"Mother, listen to me. Whatever has passed between us, let it end here. Let it be enough. Haven't we hurt each other enough?"

"I should certainly agree that *you*—"

"Mother, I need your help. I have to see him. You can arrange it for me."

"*Me?*"

"It's so dreadfully important. Surely you can see that? Please."

"Important!" Sasha stood up rigidly. "I did not go to

the lengths I did to have you visit the ruffian in *prison* and pour your bleeding heart out in front of guards who will spread the gossip all across London—"

"What do I care for gossip?" Christina cried. "I have to see him. Mother, please, if you ever had one shred of love for me, you have to help me now. I beg of you—"

"Help? As you helped me when I asked it?"

Christina gave her a blank look. Her strength was draining fast. Nausea threatened her. The arm that supported her shook visibly. She couldn't think what her mother meant. "Help you? When?"

"When I asked your help with my costumes for the play, naturally. As I recall, you all but spat in my face."

She couldn't believe what she was hearing. "Mother! This is my *life* we're speaking of. You asked me to help with a play!"

Sasha drew herself up to her full height and assumed an injured air of dignity. "The theater," she said, enunciating every word, " *is* my life."

A clammy perspiration dotted Christina's face. Her strength drained, she sank to the carpet and took her mother's skirt in her hand. "Mother, please." She put the skirt to her forehead. "Please. I've never begged you for anything. I shall never ask anything again. I shall do anything you ask of me. If you only help me now."

"I have helped you, Christina, by keeping your name from being dragged through the mud."

Christina looked up bitterly. "You've kept *your* name from being dragged through the mud. You don't give a farthing what happens to me!"

"As long as our names are the same, and as long as I can still be disgraced by your actions, I shall endeavor to keep your scandals from the public eye. Even if I have to keep you locked in your room for the rest of your miserable life!"

With that, she left. A moment after the door closed, Christina heard the lock turn. She slumped to the floor, wanting to weep, but finding no tears to shed. It had been so long since she'd cried, she wondered if she was even capable of it.

CHAPTER 46

$\mathscr{E}$ACH TIME CHRISTINA tried the door, it was locked. It soon became obvious that her mother meant what she said and intended to keep her safely barricaded until after the hanging.

At lunch, when Patricia brought her broth to eat, she requested that Oscar Wilde be sent to her. Patricia informed her that Mr. Wilde had been here, but had been sent away by the Marchioness, who explained that her daughter was too ill to see anyone.

"Please tell my mother that I am feeling better and wish to see him this afternoon."

Patricia bobbed a curtsy and went to deliver the message. When the lock turned again, Christina was surprised to find her mother at the door.

"If you think I am stupid enough not to realize that you and your precious Oscar conspired behind my back to avert my attention from your scandalous behavior"— she took a breath—"you have another thing coming. Oscar Wilde is no longer a welcome guest in this house. Not, at least," she added smugly, "until the hanging."

Later, when Patricia came to take the tray and give her the laudanum, Christina made certain no one else was at the door before whispering, "I have something I want you to do for me, Patricia. For old time's sake."

Patricia cast a sly glance at the door. "If I can, yer grace."

"I shall write out a note to Mr. Wilde. At the first opportune time, I want you to deliver it for me."

"Oh, mum! I couldn't do that! Her ladyship'd 'ave me 'ead, so she would."

"I shall make you a promise never to tell her if you don't. It's imperative that I get a message to Mr. Wilde this afternoon."

"I'm apprised of yer delimma, yer grace, but her ladyship always finds out what goes on beneath 'er nose. If I was to defy 'er, I'd be out of me job. I've a sick husband to care for, and seven daughters too young to work—"

"Yes, yes. I understand."

"If only I could, yer grace. But you 'ave to understand me position."

When she was gone, Christina leaned back in her pillows and listened to the lock click behind. The swell of frustration tasted like vomit in her throat. There must be a way, she thought. She had to get out of here and see the Captain. If there was any way to help him escape, she had to take the chance. She couldn't just lie back in her sickbed and allow him to hang . . .

There had to be a way!

She thought of Richard as she had seen him that last night, beaten and bleeding, yet defiantly spitting on Worthington's shoes. She thought of him rotting away in Newgate, while she languished as a prisoner in her mother's house. What must he feel? What must he be thinking? Did he assume she'd deserted him because she wasn't at the trial? Was he all right? Or were they torturing him even now? The image of Toby, beaten to near death within those same walls, rose fresh in her mind.

She shook her head to chase the thoughts away. She couldn't think of that. If she did, she'd lose her will to act. It was likely that he was depending on her to help him. She owed it to both of them to keep her head, to not allow her mother to rattle her to the point that she couldn't function where she was needed.

If only she could think of a way to get to him!

The opportunity presented itself that very evening in the most unexpected way she could have imagined.

$\bullet$ $\bullet$ $\bullet$

It was almost dusk when Sasha let herself into the room with the bustling air of a woman in a hurry. Patricia followed her with a tub of steaming water and some towels.

"What's this?" Christina asked, eyeing with suspicion her mother's nervous actions as she rifled through her wardrobe for just the right gown. Apparently, a selection of Christina's clothes had been sent from Wynterbrooke Hall.

"The Prince of Wales has sent a messenger to announce that he intends visiting you in a half hour's time. We must have you properly prepared in enough time that we don't keep him waiting."

"I thought you were denying me visitors," Christina mumbled sarcastically, wishing to see anyone except Bertie, of all people.

"I can hardly deny the Prince of Wales, can I? But I warn you—he knows nothing of your involvement. He thinks you were kidnapped by those ruffians the night of the robbery. I expect you to comply with my story, if you know what's good for you. I won't have my position with the Prince ruined because you feel some fatalistic urge toward confession."

Her mother's bowing and scraping before royalty had always sickened Christina. She suffered the indignity of being bathed, perfumed, and dressed in her most feminine pink silk gown and robe—"Pink will bring color to your cheeks," said her mother—because she understood the futility of arguing. But she couldn't help feeling she was being fattened up in preparation of being offered to the butcher.

Bertie arrived on the dot and filled her room with his enormous bulk. His light hair had been freshly washed, his beard trimmed and mustache newly waxed, and he was dressed in the very height of evening fashion. Apparently, he'd taken pains for this meeting. Christina pondered him silently from her propped-up position on the bed, allowing him to set the tone of the visit.

He cleared his throat. "You're looking disarmingly beautiful, Duchess, for one who has been so ill."

His air was one of unusual formality. She followed his lead with a slight bow of her head. "Thank you, Highness."

"I—" He looked about the elegant room, running his hands along the shimmer of his waistcoat, as if wondering what to do with them.

"Are you nervous, Highness?"

"Nervous? Hrumph! Nervous, good heavens no, not nervous in the slightest. I merely wanted to tell you—"

"Yes?"

"Well, damn it all, I'm told you suffered indignities at the hands of that pirate. I feel it's my fault."

"Your fault, Highness?" She wondered what indignities he meant.

"Well, after all, it was me he meant to harm. If he hadn't known how—close we've been, he might never have absconded with you, and he'd never have had the opportunity to pull that blasted trigger."

"To pull—?" Suddenly it all made sense. She realized he thought the bandit had shot her. Doubtless, her mother was spreading the story far and wide. Of course, they couldn't let it be known that one of the brave defenders of the Crown had accidentally shot a woman in the scuffle. Had they accused Richard at the trial? Dear God! What must he think of her?

Her anger must have shown in her eyes, for his own flashed unexpected fire. "When I think of the brute manhandling you that way—well, the hanging can't be too soon for me, that's all I can say."

It was then that the answer presented itself to her. She lowered her eyes so that he wouldn't see her thinking. "Bertie," she said softly, breaking the stilted air of formality that they'd never maintained for long. "I should like to see the—bandit one more time, just to tell him what I think of his—manhandling me. It all happened so quickly. I never had a chance to express the depth of my feelings."

The room was silent for some time. When she dared to look up, she found his eyes on her, glowing like coals.

"I knew it," he said in a fevered voice. "I knew you could never do the things they said. There were rumors, you know. Some had the audacity to accuse *you* of being that infernal woman, that Irish peasant what's-her-name. But I knew you could never do such things. I knew you couldn't betray me in the end. I always knew you'd come back to me eventually."

He moved to sit beside her on the bed. He took her small hand in his portly one and stroked the back of it with reverential awe. "You must realize, my dearest girl, what your mother would think should I arrange such a visit. To Newgate, no less. Hardly the place for a woman of quality. I daresay our dear Sasha should never forgive me, were I to risk your health in such an irresponsible manner."

"You know yourself that Mother would never object to anything you saw fit to do. She wouldn't dare. Besides, she doesn't have to know, Bertie. Since when have I kept my mother apprised of everything that passes between us? All she need know is that I am accompanying you somewhere. She won't question your designs. I hate to say you owe me this, but haven't I kept the secret of what happened that night of your duel with the bandit? Surely one secret in exchange for another is not too much to ask?"

"You ask a great deal from one you have so recently professed to loathe. Perhaps you might see fit to tell me why I should grant favors to one who is as—ungrateful as you have been?"

She knew then from the look in his eyes what the price of her visit would be. It sickened her, but in some strange way, it also fueled her resolve. Suddenly, her weakness didn't matter. She knew what she had to do, and she knew she had the strength to do it.

"I should be—*most* grateful to you for any assistance you might offer. I should hate to live the rest of my life knowing I had the chance to tell the bandit what I thought of his behavior and didn't take it. It should haunt me for the rest of my days. I should have nightmares, dreaming of all I might have said."

"I wouldn't want to be the cause of your nightmares," he said carefully. "But what you ask is difficult."

"Very well, Bertie. Let's have it, shall we? What is it worth to you?"

"The question more precisely, dearest Christina, is what is it worth to you?"

She met his eyes evenly. "Anything I might have to pay."

A look passed between them that she couldn't fully discern, but it had in it the raw light of truth. If he guessed her real intentions or feelings in that moment, he didn't let her know. He merely licked his thick lips and allowed his gaze to wander, as he had wanted since the moment he'd entered the room, to the tantalizing swell of her bosom.

Then, without another word, he stood, walked to the door, opened it, and popped his head out into the hall. "You, girl, we don't wish to be disturbed. Run along, and I shall call if you're needed."

He took the key from the outer lock and used it to lock the door from the inside. Then he turned back to her with his eyes gleaming anew.

She felt a momentary panic. "Not here, surely, Bertie. In my mother's house!"

"Your mother, as you have so aptly reminded me, is not about to question my orders. No, Christina, she won't disturb us. Even if she guesses what we're about, I shouldn't think she'd object, would you? In fact, I should imagine she would applaud your belated good sense."

What he said was true. Her mother, once again, would be no source of refuge.

He walked to the bed, pulled back the covers, and looked at her silk-clad body appreciatively. "I shall be careful not to hurt your shoulder," he promised.

"It doesn't matter, Bertie," she said as he lowered his lips to her neck. "You shan't hurt me."

She gave herself to him, gritting her teeth against the wracking pain in her shoulder as he worked his massive body over hers. It was all she could do to keep from gagging and allowing him to see how sickened she was. She'd vowed never to do this again. But she reminded herself that it was for a worthy cause. Just this once. What could it hurt? If it would save Richard's life . . .

He eased off her, his body slick with sweat, and lay beside her for many minutes with his eyes closed, silently stroking her naked flesh. She bit her lip to keep from recoiling beneath his touch, thinking it would be over soon, and she'd be on her way. But she knew when he looked up at her that she wasn't to have it so easy.

"It's not enough to have you merely submit to me, my angel," he said as the glow of lust returned to his eyes. "I would have you willingly beneath me. Shall we try again?"

With a sinking heart, she closed her eyes for a brief moment. She thought of Richard, of him counting on her to help him escape the noose. She thought of the life they would share once this living nightmare was over. The thought of the future they'd nearly lost gave her strength. She reached for the Prince and gently pulled him to her, kissing him with convincing enthusiasm. Without taking his lips from hers, he lowered himself onto her and she could feel him hard and swollen beneath his bulging belly. Her skin crawled as he ran his hand along her with the possessive certainty of a man who knows the woman beneath him is his for the taking.

"How I've dreamed of your lush body," he gasped as he entered her again, sounding feverish as he rocked, planting crazed kisses about her face. "You can't imagine how I've wanted you, night after night dreaming of you while in another woman's arms. No one satisfied me the way you do, Christina. No one has ever made me want her as you make me need to possess you." He rocked harder, hurting her. "Talk to me, sweet. Talk to me the way you used to. No woman alive can talk in bed like you."

Swallowing her disgust, she obliged him in a soft voice, whipping him to a fevered frenzy with her words. All the while he cried into her ear, "Yes, yes . . . God Almighty, yes . . ."

It went on that way for some time. Just when she thought he might be satisfied, he would take her again, insisting on her willingness, insisting that she service him with the same wanton abandon that she'd displayed in earlier days, when she'd played the more willing mistress. When she thought her strength was sapped completely, he rose from the bed, and she breathed a sigh of relief. It was over. She'd paid her price, and victory would now be hers. But when she looked up, she saw that he had taken a jar of cream and was smearing it along his hand. He smiled at her in that same crazed, lusty way and murmured, "Now, Christina, give me your arse."

For a moment, she knew she couldn't do it. But then she thought again of Richard, of how he would die if she didn't oblige. Resignedly, she rolled over on the bed, safeguarded her shoulder in a pile of soft pillows, and raised her backside to his view. As he smeared the grease into her, he spoke in colorful words of all he wanted to do to her while he had her in his power. As he entered her with a lusty gasp, she reflected, with a detached part of her brain, that the only time Bertie had ever been the articulate man he thought himself, was when he felt himself the master in bed.

Finally, it was over. In spite of his attempts at care, she felt bruised inside and out. Her body was so stiff, she could barely move. She wanted nothing more than to sink into the bed and sleep for a week. To forget her degradation. To forget the price she'd had to pay. To forget the look of contempt on Richard's face as he'd described what his mother had suffered at the hands of this same man. But he rose almost at once and dressed with resolute efficiency. Once his need for her had been sated, he assumed an official tone.

"Get dressed," he ordered, obviously feeling the upper hand now that he'd used her in his own fashion.

"Surely you don't suggest we go now?" she cried. "This minute?"

"If you want to see your bandit, you will do so now." He took paper and pen from her desk and began to write while still standing.

"But Bertie, I must bathe and—"

He turned and gave her a firm stare. "I repeat, Christina. If you go, you go now. This instant. Or you don't go at all."

He finished writing while she continued to stare at him. She wondered again if he guessed the truth. Why else would he insist that she rise from his bed and go to her lover with the seed of her betrayal still smeared upon her thighs?

"This paper will grant you entrance to Newgate," he explained, still officially. "With my signature, they won't question the orders. I've requested that you be left alone with the prisoner. I assume that's what you desire."

He gave her a keen look.

"Thank you, Bertie. You're very—kind."

"He's the only prisoner in residence at the moment. I shouldn't imagine you'll have any trouble. I, of course, will decline to accompany you. But I have a guard out front, whom you may use as escort. You may let me off at Mott's and take my coach." He waved the paper to dry the ink, then handed it to her. When she moved to take it, he held it fast a moment, still looking into her eyes as if trying to discover the truth. "You must want to see him awfully, to go to such lengths."

She ignored this. "You won't tell Mother? Remember, you promised."

"If it pleases you, Christina. After all, you have more than pleased me." He gave her a small, grateful smile, the first sign of his continued weakness for her. "I shall send in your maid to help you dress, and shall go down to attend to the Marchioness. Mind, dearest, you have three minutes, or I shall leave without you and not look back. I should like to see you escape the hawk eyes of your mother without my assistance."

When he'd left, she felt her way to the chamber pot and vomited into it. Then she splashed water on her face and grabbed the first dress she could find. She had no doubt that Bertie meant what he said. If she wasn't downstairs in three minutes, he would leave without her. And all of this would have been for nothing.

CHAPTER 47

*I*T WAS SUFFOCATING in the prison—dark and tomb-like, smelling foul and stale, a throwback to the uncivilized days when prisoners were treated like rabid animals in cages. She'd never been inside a gaol before. Walking down the dark, dank halls, she felt the stone walls closing in on her. With her natural fear of being too confined—by people, by commitments, by anything—prisons represented the incarnation of her nightmares. Poor Richard. How could he bear it? Probably the way she was—by telling himself it wouldn't be for long.

" 'Ere we go, yer grace," the guard said, stopping in front of a heavy, barred oak door. " 'Is 'Ighness says privacy, and that's what it'll be. But if y'need 'elp, give an 'oller, eh? We'll take care of the brute, sure enough." He raised his voice. "You 'ear that, Lord Bandit?"

The door creaked open, and she went inside, her eyes still adjusting to the absence of light. The Captain was sitting on the ratty cot, his elbows resting on his knees. He looked up when she came in, and she could sense rather than see his surprise. As her eyes focused, she could see the bruises on his face, the cut and swollen lip. Yet, she could feel his innate vitality flowing through the room. She longed to borrow it and make it her own. She waited until the door slammed behind and the sound of the guard's footsteps echoed down the long stone hall.

"I'm sorry I wasn't at the trial," she said, her voice sounding as stiltedly civil as it had the first minutes with the Prince. "I've been kept a virtual prisoner in my mother's house. I only just found out what they've been saying—that you shot me—" She couldn't go on. All of her strength was concentrated in keeping on her feet.

He rose quickly and crossed the awful cell to take her in his arms. "Did you think I'd blame you?"

He caught a quick flash of something like guilt in her eyes before she turned away to rest her forehead on the cool bars. "Oh, Richard."

There was a moment of deep, resounding silence. Then his voice, sounding hard, asked, "What have you done?"

She shook her head helplessly.

He grabbed her arm and turned her around, hurting her shoulder so that she cried out softly. Her eyes were used to the darkness now, and she could see the old fearsome look in his eyes as he stared down at her.

"If your mother was keeping you prisoner," he asked slowly, carefully, as if struggling to control his voice, "what did you do to gain admittance to see me?"

She couldn't look him in the eye. Shamefully, she tried not to tell him, but he shook her, and she knew it was useless. She couldn't lie to him. "I gave Bertie something he wanted badly in exchange for an opportunity to see you."

It was a moment before the meaning registered. "Jesus God." He dropped his hand from her and left her standing there against the door, feeling more alone than she'd ever felt in her life.

"It doesn't matter," she said softly. "I'd do anything for an opportunity to save your life. This was the only way."

"Only way?" He lunged at her and took her throat in his hands, frightening her so that she instinctively cowered from him. "Did you think it wouldn't matter to me? That my woman—that my love—was forced to sell herself for the sake of my miserable hide? Did you think I could hold you in my arms again without remembering what you'd done? Christ in heaven, I could wring your sorry neck!"

He nearly choked her. Then, realizing what he was doing, seeing the terror in her eyes, he loosened his hold. With his hands still lying at the base of her throat, he said in a defeated tone, "I imagine that's the way you looked at your mother, once upon a time."

She looked up at him pleadingly. "Richard, forgive me."

He gathered her to him and held her against the solid wall of his chest.

"I don't care what happens to me," she told him. "It's because of my mother that you're here, awaiting the rope. I should do anything, Richard—I should sleep with the devil himself—for a chance to set you free."

"Do you love me as much as all that?" he asked quietly.

"You know I do."

"Well . . . You're young. You have a long life ahead of you. You'll get over me."

It was a lie. He knew she'd love him till the day she died.

She looked at him now with genuine fear stinging her eyes. "What are you saying?"

He turned his back on her. "I am saying that I have felt shame this night that I never felt when robbing a train, or accosting an old woman on the road, or even killing the rutting bastard that passed for my father. That a woman like you should be forced into degrading herself with the man she most loathes in all the world—"

"I wasn't forced. I chose to. I should do it again—now—here, in front of you—if it would save your life."

"—that you'd do that for me—" he continued as if she hadn't spoken.

"I did it for us."

"For us." The bitterness in his tone made her quiver. He went to touch her face, and her skin seemed to leap at the contact. "Tell me, Duchess. What *is* us exactly? A desperate man whose woman is forced for his sake into desperate acts. I was mad to think it could work when I knew all along—"

"Don't say it."

"I will say it. A dying man must say what's on his mind once and for all."

"I didn't bespoil myself so you might die. You'd be

better off to spend your precious time offering me a plan of escape."

He looked at her coldly. "Very well. Send me an armed friend whom I might use as a hostage. I shall take it from there."

She nodded. "And after that?"

"After that I shan't see you again."

"Richard! You can't mean it!" She saw by the sadness in his eyes that he did. She clutched his arm. "Don't you see what you'll be doing if you push me away? They'll have won. My parents. Worthington. Bertie. All of them. Even if you escape with your life, they'll have beaten us. Is that what you want for yourself? For me? The knowledge that after all we've been through, they've bested us at last?" He turned away. "What about our future?"

"Future," he scoffed. "I wouldn't be so quick to count on a future. This brilliant plan of escape might very well backfire. I could be shot. Your friend could be killed. Even if it works, they could track us down again. If you're found with me once more, God only knows what they'll do to you. You've already been shot because of me. You could have been killed—"

"I don't want to hear this."

"You have to hear it! Christina, there is no future for us. I've seen this night a truth I refused to look at because it was convenient to look the other way. I thought I could change our destiny by the sheer force of my will. But I see now it's impossible. I swore to protect you, and I failed."

"That wasn't your fault."

"No? Then tell me. What kind of life can I offer you? What else might you be forced into for my sake? What further degradation of the soul to save a desperate love?"

"Degradation of the soul!" she cried, her voice ringing out through the halls. He moved to her swiftly and clamped a hand on her mouth. When she'd calmed down, she pushed his hand away and spoke more softly. "I had no soul till I met you. Richard, you can't mean this! The morning after tomorrow, when you're free—"

She stopped. She saw in his eyes the old cold ruthless

glare that shut her out of his thoughts and his life as completely as the bars of his cell shut him away from the world. Beneath that glare she realized she was babbling like a silly fool. She'd never begged anyone for anything in her life, yet today she'd begged three people almost on her knees for things she was afraid in her heart couldn't be. His words now only confirmed that belief. For the first time in her life, she didn't want to hear the truth.

But pride, at this juncture, was as futile as her words. "Richard, please," she whispered. "I love you. I've never loved anyone else. I never shall. I don't care what happens to us. Let us have what happiness we might find. Do you think I could live the rest of my days without you? Longing for you every awful, empty day of my life?" When he didn't answer she cried, "Richard—!"

He went to her then and took her face in his hands. She closed her eyes against the look of torment she saw buried in his cold eyes and simply relished the feel of his strong fingers on her cheeks. Once again, something whispered, "Remember this." She began, for the first time in many years, to cry.

He laid his head against hers. "Christina. I never thought I could love a woman the way I love you. You have brought more joy, more love, more meaning to my miserable life than I ever hoped to find. You have given me more than I can ever repay. Whether I die at dawn or live to be eighty, I shall never forget your saucy mouth or your wicked laugh—or the way you feel as if you were made for my arms."

Tears flowed down her cheeks as if, once started, they might never stop. He raised his head and used the pad of his thumb to brush away the tears. "There. I've made you cry when even your mother couldn't." Still, her eyes were closed against his face, his words. The truth.

"Look at me, love." She did so reluctantly, opening her tear-filled eyes a bit at a time as though afraid of what she might see. What she saw was an unbearable tenderness in his eyes that hurt her more deeply than his coldness ever had. "I, too, love you enough to sacrifice what I must so you might live. Do you think I relish a life without you by my side? Do you think I won't look out at the stormy sea and see your face in the darkness? I shall treasure the memory of you till my dying day. But one of us must be strong and do what we know is right."

"I *don't* know it's right," she sobbed. "I know in my heart, Richard, that pushing me away is the only truly wrong thing you've ever done."

"If it is, then I shall live with it. But I won't take you where I'm going. I won't demand of you the sort of life that being with me requires. I have nothing to offer you but danger and a desperate love. I'll not burden you with that. I shall hurt you no longer. You were made for finer things."

She turned from him slowly, wiping her eyes with her fingertips. Finer things. She thought of the life she'd led before him. Of the endless round of pranks and men and travel, bent on filling the emptiness of her heart. She thought of her parents, of Bertie. How could she go back to it now, knowing what she'd known with him? They'd had so much! And now, because of her mother . . .

"Where will you go?" she managed to ask. "After Ireland, I mean?"

"I'd hardly tell you, given all I've said."

She clutched her heart, which ached so deeply, she thought she could feel it break. "I shall find you. I shall search the world until one day you change your mind and come back to me. I shall make a spectacle of myself everywhere I go so you'll know I'm there."

She turned and looked at him and saw the anguish in his eyes.

"I shan't give up on you," she warned. "Not ever."

"Then you will waste your life. I won't come for you."

"We shall see." She straightened her shoulders, ignoring the pain that gripped her, and wiped the remaining traces of tears from her cheeks. "I shall send Oscar to you the morning after tomorrow, shortly before dawn." She touched the hard planes of his cheeks with her fingers, wanting terribly to remember the feel of him. "Do me a favor, Richard, for all we've meant to each other."

He just looked at her.

"Tonight and tomorrow, as you wait for dawn, think long and hard. Imagine the endless stretch of your life without me at your side. Imagine the faceless women who will fill my place in your bed—but never in your heart. And if you can bear it, then I shall go off without a fight. But if you can't—if all you can see is the same empty road ahead that I see—"

He clutched her to him suddenly and crushed her mouth under his, halting the terrible flow of words. As she kissed him, deeply and hungrily, she began again to cry. "I knew it," she whispered brokenly against his lips. "I knew you couldn't mean it. I shall go with you, come what may, and we'll be happy, darling, just as we were in Haworth—"

His hands tightened on her arms, then abruptly he pushed her away.

"Guard," he called, banging his fist on the door. When the guard's face appeared in the barred window, the Captain said, "The lady is ready to leave."

She left, looking back once to see his back turned resolutely. She accepted the pass from the guard and walked up the hall with leaden steps. At the end of the aisle, a man stood waiting. She looked up, expecting to see the guard Bertie had sent, and saw instead, with a heavy heart, that it was the Prince himself who stood waiting for her.

"I changed my mind," he said sheepishly, "and came instead. Thought you might need moral support, and all that."

She gazed down the long corridor at the Prince, seeing a past that held no tender memories. A future without a future. Looking at him, she saw the reality of the years stretching ahead of her. It took every ounce of courage she possessed to walk down the long aisle and accept Bertie's offered arm.

If he guessed the truth, he had no intention of letting on. "I hope you gave him what-for," he said. "I hope you told him how despicable he's been."

She looked back once more at the long, dark corridor of barred doors that separated her from her love. "Yes, Bertie," she said tonelessly. "I told him."

CHAPTER 48

*S*HE AWOKE EARLY the next morning feeling devastated. Her body was wracked with pain, and her breast felt dull and heavy with the inescapable numbness of one who has lost her heart's desire. But in spite of it all—in spite of her body's protests, in spite of her mind's craving for rest—her first thought was nonetheless of how to go about getting in touch with Oscar.

For one mad moment the night before, she'd considered asking the Prince to take a note to her friend. But no sooner had it occurred to her than she realized it wouldn't do. Even Bertie, dull-witted as he could be, would find little difficulty in putting the facts together and realizing that she had maneuvered the Captain's escape with his aid. No. No one must know. No one must even suspect that she was up to anything except resting from her ordeal the day before with the Prince.

All this flitted through her mind before she was even fully awake. She could hear the sounds of stirring in the square below. Some children were squealing as they ran from the governess. A dog yapped. The hawkers called out their wares as they moved from house to house, hoping for a sale.

Suddenly, she had it. As a woman's voice sounded up the square, "Fresh fruit for sale. Berries, apples, peaches, and pears. Fresh fruit for pies," she eased herself out of bed as quickly as she could in her stiff condition, pushed aside the curtains, and looked out on the square. Even at this hour, the sky was overcast, heavy with the thick, moist feel of threatened rain. She saw the old woman two houses away, dressed in brown homespun with a limp apron, carrying fruit in a wicker basket that bowed her back and gave her a perpetual stoop. Forgetting her injury, she pushed on the window to open it and felt the pain rip through her. Cursing, she had to lean against the window with her face against the glass, waiting for the dizziness to subside. As her head gradually cleared, she watched her breath make puffs of steam upon the pane.

As she stood wondering what to do, she had a stroke of luck. The key turned in the door, and Patricia, carrying in her breakfast tray, gasped and cried, "Yer grace! What are ye doin'?"

"I wanted a breath of fresh air. It's so dreadfully stuffy in this room. Open the window for me, Patricia, there's a dear."

"Well, mum, if you think yer health won't suffer—"

"Fresh fruit," called the hawker, passing below the house. "Who'll buy me wares?"

"With a little fresh air," Christina added, careful not to show her anxiety, "I should think my health would improve immensely. But do hurry, girl. I feel I shall faint if I have to breathe this thick air any longer."

Patricia shook her head but obeyed the order. It was a well-known fact among the servants that the Duchess's wants were often unconventional and defied understanding.

"There now," she said, having opened the window. "You get back in yer bed and eat yer breakfast and drink yer laudanum, and I don't doubt ye'll be feelin' much better before too much longer. I'll be back when yer finished."

Christina waited until the maid was gone, poured the laudanum into the chamber pot, then stuck her head out the window and called down to the old woman, who had just passed by the house. The woman looked back over her shoulder and gave a toothless grin.

"Are ye wantin' some fruit, deary?"

"Fruit? No, no. I want you to deliver a message for me."

The woman looked at her as if she were daft.

"I shall pay you a great deal more than I would for a piece of fruit."

When the woman continued to peer up at her doubtfully, Christina said, "Wait here." She went back into the room and looked about hurriedly. She had no money, but there were no end of valuable things in the room. She grabbed her sterling comb and went back to the window. "Here. Catch this."

The woman dropped the comb, but hastened to retrieve it. Looking at it critically, she peered up at Christina once again. " 'Ow do I know this 'ere's real?"

Christina sighed her impatience. She cast a quick glance back at the door to make certain no one was coming. "My good woman, do take a look at the seal imprinted on the comb."

The old woman did so. "Wynterbrooke!" she breathed, impressed at last.

"And do you consider that Wynterbrooke would have given me anything but the very best?"

"Why, no, mum, I didn't mean to imply—"

"Then shall I assume that it's sufficient payment for your services?"

The hawker considered the comb in her hand, then frowned up at the strange lady in the window. "What if they thinks I stole it?"

"If it will make you feel any better, I shall write you out a note saying I gave it to you."

"Then I'll do it, mum."

"Thank you. Wait there. And don't tell anyone what you're doing. I shall be but a minute."

She took up paper and pen with a shaking hand, and scrawled out a note to Oscar entreating him to come to her window immediately and to keep it secret from everyone, even his wife. Then she wrapped it around the crystal paperweight and tossed it down to the woman.

"That's to go to Mr. Oscar Wilde at 9 Charles Street near Grosvenor Square and no one else. Not a servant, not his wife, no one but Mr. Wilde himself. That is crucial. If you have to wait for him, do. When you've returned to tell me that he's received the note and will do as I request, I shall give you the letter stating that the comb was a gift. But I warn you, if you don't return to me with news, I shall report the comb stolen this very afternoon."

The woman was bobbing her head, excited now as she realized the profit she would make this day. "I'll be back, mum, count on it."

"Another thing. You're not to mention this to a soul. I don't care who asks you, this conversation did not take place. Do you understand?"

"Aye, mum."

"Then go. And bring me word soon. Throw pebbles at my window to let me know you're here. But only if no one is about to see you."

"I've got it, mum. You can count on me."

It was a full three hours before the woman came back to say Mr. Wilde accepted her invitation with great pleasure and curiosity. No, she assured Christina, he wouldn't tell a soul. Christina wrote the promised note and, feeling giddy with gratitude, included a small matching crystal-and-sterling box as the woman's payment. Then it was simply a matter of waiting—while appearing not to wait—until Oscar appeared.

She was looking out for him when he rode up less than an hour later. It was raining, and the sky was nearly black, keeping people off the streets. Oscar looked none too happy about his soaked condition as he climbed down from his horse, struggling with a bulky umbrella. When she called to him, he looked up at her window and called softly, "Am I to serenade you in this downpour, after being so unceremoniously banished from your side?"

"Hush," she warned. "They'll hear you. Climb up the trellis."

"Do what?"

"Tether your horse and climb up the trellis. Only do hurry, before you're spotted."

He did so, after some hesitation, and climbed into her window puffing and wheezing. "Good God, the things I do for you." He put his hand to his chest and struggled to catch his breath. He was shivering, and he dripped water on the rug. But he took one look at her pale face and forgot to wheeze.

"Darling, you're as pale as a ghost. Here. Let me help you to your bed."

"Bertie says I'm more beautiful than ever in my distress."

"And so you are. But white as a sheet. Do sit down. You'll have me fainting dead away at the sight of you."

"I'm all right. It's not your solicitude that I require."

"Nevertheless, you shall have it. Although I will admit to being more than a little peeved at being banished from your bedside. I should think that I, of all people, had earned the right to hold your hand while you convalesce."

"It was Mother who sent you away. She knows about Richard and me, and she knows you lied to protect my secret. She has me locked away like Rapunzel in her tower, lest I breathe the truth."

"Ah! The clouds part. But I'm still a bit fuzzy on details. I heard your Richard shot you—"

"It's a lie. One of the soldiers shot me in the scuffle."

"Well, then, that explains it, doesn't it? I went to the trial, by the way. You'd be proud of your bandit. He conducted himself with a great deal of dignity and restrained contempt. Quite a heroic performance, I must say. Perhaps I shall put it in a play one day. Unless, of course, you care to. The story does, after all, belong to you."

"Oscar, please, not now!"

"You're right. Here I am babbling away while you languish in your grief. Do forgive me. Come, let's have a look at your wound. If I'm to write about it, I should see it firsthand."

"I suppose you'll hound me until I do."

"But, darling, of course."

He pushed aside her nightgown with the air of a man whose interest in women is artistic rather than physical. She'd been given a smaller bandage by the doctor that morning, and it was no problem for him to lift it off the back of her shoulder and take a look. "You're lucky. It's a clean enough hole. I predict that once it's healed, what scar you have will resemble a rather charming dimple."

"I don't care about that. I called you here because you're going to help me break Richard out of prison."

His fingers stilled on her back. "*I'm* going to *what*? My dear girl, have you finally lost your mind?"

"I will if you refuse to help."

"Refuse to—Christina, precious, I hardly know what you're talking about, let alone refuse you anything. But, dearest, your wound must have gone to your head. Your Richard is set to hang at dawn. Surely you must have heard."

"I've heard. I've seen him."

"Well, that *is* a feat. With the wicked witch imprisoning you like a fairy princess, how *ever* did you manage it?"

She lowered her lashes. "I slept with Bertie so he'd take me to the prison."

"Oh." It was more an expulsion of breath than a statement. He sank down on the bed beside her and took her hand in his. "My poor pet."

"It doesn't matter. All I care about is that Richard go free. He said to send him an armed friend whom he could take hostage. I told him I'd send you." She turned to him. "It's his only hope, Oscar. Tell me please that you won't let me down."

His look was tender. "How could I? You surprised me, that's all. So it's Oscar to the rescue, is it? Well . . . I suppose I shall have more to write about from this than I'd imagined."

"No, you won't. If we come out of this, I shall write about it someday and sing your praises, and glorify your name. I shall do it more splendidly than you, through enforced modesty, ever could."

He laughed. "Picture me, being modest. Write to your heart's content, dear. You've earned the story, after all. But disguise my name, won't you? I shall give up my penchant for living vicariously for your sake, but I don't relish the consequences. I shall play the hero for you and then retire into cowardly silence."

She kissed his cheek. "I knew I could count on you. Now, this is what you're to do." She reached into her bedside drawer and withdrew a piece of paper, suddenly all efficiency. "This is the pass Bertie wrote out to get me into Newgate. I've pondered the problem of how to remove my name and have yours inserted, and there's no way to do so without the tampering being detected. You will have to find a forger to copy it over exactly, except using your name instead of mine. Present it to the guard, and you should have no trouble. You'll need to acquire a pistol and ammunition. Hide it on your person. No satchels, nothing suspicious. If anyone at the prison questions you about weapons, put on your most indignant sneer. You're there on the orders of the Prince of Wales, say. How dare they imply such an impertinence?"

"I shall enjoy it. One thing I excel at is giving my intellectual inferiors a good rounding down."

"There's not a moment to lose," she warned. "You have only this afternoon to acquire what you need and find a forger to get the job done."

"Not to worry, sweet. I know a goodly number of unsavory characters here and about. I shan't fail you."

"One last thing. Before going to the prison, bring a saddled horse with my own groom to keep him quiet. Put them on this side of the house—that way, my parents won't hear. It will mean rising at two or three in the morning, I'm afraid, to accomplish all this and be at the prison well before dawn."

"Pshaw. I shall stay up all night. I can sleep after, and dream of my heroic deeds."

"Do what you must," she agreed. "So long as you don't fall asleep on the job."

CHAPTER 49

*I*T WAS STILL dark the next morning when she left. She'd packed a small valise, which she threw down to the groom, then she climbed with difficulty down the unsteady lattice. It proved more taxing than she'd imagined. Running on nerves and virtually no sleep, she felt her shoulder throb with every stretch of her arm. She had to stop several times to push down the wave of nausea that threatened to impede her. But she thought of Oscar riding even now to Newgate, bravely stepping out of his role of epigrammatic observer to help her in her hour of need. The image, imponderable as it might be, gave her the courage she needed to gather her strength and continue.

At her whispered orders, the groom strapped the valise to her saddle, then helped her mount. Sworn to secrecy by the promise of a hefty bonus, he watched as she rode off toward Newgate with a pounding heart to meet her future and get her answer once and for all.

It never occurred to the guards at Newgate to search the flamboyant Mr. Wilde. Aroused from slumber so that their brains were functioning more slowly than usual, they were confronted by a poetically robust man with long curls framing his head, dressed in jacket and tails that were stitched to look like a cello. He'd worn the suit to the opening of an art gallery years ago and had caused a sensation. This morning he figured that anyone caught unaware by the attire would forget to search the contents. He couldn't have calculated more correctly. As soon as his back was turned, one guard looked at the Prince of Wales's signature on the paper in his hand and rolled his eyes at the other guard as if to say, "Only a friend of the Prince could dress like that and get away with it."

Before entering the cell, Oscar held out a gloved hand and told the guard, "I shall take the pass as a souvenir."

His tone left no room for argument. The pass was handed back to him, and the door thrown wide.

"You'll 'ave to wake him," the guard said. " 'E's a cool one, sleepin' afore 'is 'angin'."

The Captain did, indeed, appear to be asleep. But as soon as the guard had shuffled off yawning down the hall, he was up with the unleashed power of a tiger, casting a quick glance out the bars of the door before turning back to Oscar.

"It was good of you to come," he said, ignoring the outrageous costume. "What have you for me?"

Oscar removed the pistol from his breast pocket, and handed it forth. "I'm glad to be rid of it, if you must know. I swear it burned my breast the whole way over."

The Captain flipped open the barrel of the gun, checked the loading, then shut it and put the extra bullets Oscar handed him in his breeches pocket. Then he took his cloak and fastened it about his neck, readying himself for departure.

"How fares the Duchess?" he asked in a carefully casual voice.

"The Duchess suffers for you—no surprise. I've known her longer and better than anyone, I daresay, and I've never seen her passionate about anyone except you. I don't know what quality you possess, but whatever it is, I wager half the men in London would pay handsomely for the secret."

The Captain said nothing but scowled at him intently.

"What I'm trying to say in a rather uncharacteristically bumbling way is that I hope you haven't decided to leave her behind."

"Did she say so?"

"Good heavens, no, man. She doesn't tell me your secrets. But I should hate to see you make such a grim mistake. Simply put, it would break her heart."

Suddenly, as if he'd had enough of the conversation, the Captain grabbed Oscar, pulled his back to him, and put the pistol to his head. "Better a broken heart than a broken head. I thank you once again for your assistance, Mr. Wilde, but not for your advice. Now, call the guard."

He was holding a restraining arm about Oscar's neck and shoulders. When Oscar hesitated, gathering his courage, the Captain shook him roughly as incentive.

"My good man," Oscar cried, "I care not what you do to my person. But *do* mind the suit!"

Then he took a breath and bellowed for the guard.

Christina had been waiting for some time on the road to Newgate in the gathering pink of dawn. She'd tried not to think of the moments to come, of what he might do or say, of how her life hung in the balance. She tried only to remain aware, to be ready for whatever happened.

Way up the road, she heard gunshots. She stiffened her back, determined to be brave, even as her heart slammed like a sledgehammer in her chest. Then, before her, came the clattering of hooves. He'd escaped! Her pain, her worry, her anguish were all gone at the sound of those joyously fleeing hooves. He was free. Nothing else mattered.

She saw him before he saw her. He was on a stolen horse, galloping for all he was worth. She kicked her horse into the road so that he would have to stop. When he came upon her, he drew rein and pivoted his mount to face her. The steed, whipped to a frenzy only a moment before, tossed his head and pranced impatiently beneath him. The Captain cast a quick glance behind. She could hear hoofbeats in the distance, in hot pursuit.

Christina moved toward him. His anxiety communicated itself to the horse, and it shied away, turning and bunching its haunches for the chase. Only the Captain's firm hand on the reins held the beast at bay.

"Take me with you," she called to him.

He met her gaze, his eyes a deep, excited green, sparkling with the old thrill of the chase. His black hair was wild from the wind, his cloak tossed over his shoulder at a rakish slant. He personified, in that moment, everything she'd loved about him from the beginning. But as he looked at her, his expression was closed, and she knew he was leaving her behind.

"I shall wait for you," she told him. "I'll be at the hideout tomorrow at dawn. Get a boat and come for me. We'll sail to Ireland as we planned."

He moved his horse closer and took her chin in his hand. She could feel the electricity flowing through him, and his impatience to be off. But she could see in the flash of his eyes all the love and feeling he carried for her in his heart. He squeezed her chin hard, as if to emphasize his words. "Take up with no more highwaymen when I'm gone."

She shook her head. "You're my last highwayman. I shall have no need of them, once I'm by your side. I shall count on you. I shall wait for you, Richard, until you come. I shan't give up."

The sounds of pursuit were closer now. "Don't forget all you've meant to me." He leaned over and gave her a last, hard kiss. That same prophetic voice inside told her it was the last time she'd ever see him. She clutched at his hand, afraid she wouldn't have the courage to let him go.

"I shall be waiting," she repeated.

Too quickly, he was gone. He jerked the reins and took off in a shower of flung mud down the road. She watched him disappear, as mysterious a figure in that moment as ever he had been in the beginning. Then the guards rounded the corner and nearly stumbled over her horse. She did everything she could to remain in their way and give her lover more of a head start. But they brushed her aside with curses and set out with their guns drawn to track him down.

CHAPTER 50

*E*XHAUSTED AND WEAKENED by the exertions of the morning, Christina waited at Victoria Station most of the morning, then took the afternoon train to Sussex. Oscar accompanied her, explaining that he had no wish to remain in town and be questioned with undue haste regarding the convenient visit paid the bandit just as he escaped.

"Besides which, traveling alone in your weakened state, you might arouse suspicion. With a man by your side, no one will question your purpose."

"And what a man," she said, taking his hand tenderly. "How can I ever repay what you've done for me?"

"Oh, give me time, darling. I shall think of something."

It took most of the afternoon to reach the station and the better part of another hour for the coach to rumble along the rain-softened roads. Christina was finally able to sleep in Oscar's arms and awakened at the inn feeling as thick-witted as if her brain had been simmered in mush. They had decided earlier that they'd take a room at the closest inn to the turnoff for the hideout, and from there, Christina would hire a horse as if she were going for an afternoon ride. Oscar insisted on going with her, but she couldn't bear for him to go along. She wanted to be alone to await Richard's return, in the place where they'd spent so many happy months.

The room was little more than functional, but it was clean, with two overstuffed chairs by the cold grate. Oscar ordered wine to fortify them, and Christina drank it to please him, eager to be off. He could see that she was endeavoring to sip the wine slowly when all she really wanted was to gulp it down and be on her way.

Finally, he laughed and rose from his chair. "Very well. I can see that my scintillating company is no longer your prime concern. I shall go down and order your horse. You're all right to ride, I take it?"

She nodded. She still felt weaker than she cared to admit, but all she could think about was getting to the hideout to be there when Richard came for her. It was the one thought that burned in her mind and kept her body going.

As if reading her thoughts, he took her hand and asked gently, "What will you do if he doesn't come?"

She was silent for many moments. "I don't know, Oscar," she said at last. "What would you suggest?"

She dressed in her riding habit while he was downstairs. She couldn't think of "what-ifs" now. She had to stay focused. She had to stay strong. She had to keep from thinking so she could keep from going insane. Hope was the only thing she had left to her now, and she hung on to it as if her life depended on it.

She was so absorbed in her own thoughts that she scarcely noticed the rumble of hooves in the courtyard below. She heard the tramping of boots and raised voices, but assumed a new group of travelers had just arrived. Oscar returned, closing the door quietly behind him, as if afraid to make a sound.

"I'm quite ready. Did you arrange for the horse?" When he didn't answer she prodded, "Oscar?"

She looked at him then. The blood had drained from his face, and his poet's eyes looked droopier and sadder than she'd ever seen them. An air of defeat permeated his stance.

"What is it?"

"There are some men below. Local villagers, I think. They came bearing news."

"What news?" Even as she asked, she didn't want to hear.

"They say he's dead."

She said nothing, but stood frozen by the dresser.

"They say the guards found his horse lying broken among the rocks below a cliff. The fog was so thick along the coast, they assume he rode over the edge without realizing—"

"No."

"The tide was high, so they haven't found his body. But they say they have his cloak."

"No."

"The guards are on their way back now with the news that he's dead."

"I don't believe it."

"Let's wait and see what proof they have," he soothed, although she could see, even in her shock, that he assumed it was true.

The guards came by within the hour, a horrible hour in which Christina paced the room feverishly, repeating the phrase in her mind, "It isn't true. It isn't true. It can't be true." Oscar went down to greet them and came back minutes later with a grim face.

"It's his cloak. I recognized it. I saw him put it on this morning."

"No!" She rushed past him to go see for herself.

He caught her and warned, "Don't give yourself away. If they think you're too concerned, they may guess at the truth. I won't see you imprisoned. It's bad enough that he's—"

She wouldn't let him finish. She went downstairs, where the guards were emptying tankards of ale and boasting of the death of one of the most notorious criminals in recent memory.

Heeding Oscar's warning, and aided by her sense of shock, Christina went down the stairs with a deadly calm and asked to see the cloak. The guards exchanged amused glances, feeling full of themselves. This news would relieve them of the responsibility of allowing the bandit to get away.

One of the guards, chewing on a tough piece of mutton, handed the cloak forth. "Bet you've never touched the cloth of a criminal before, eh, lady?"

Christina resisted the urge to hug the cloak to her breast and handed it back with a small, sad smile. "Never like this," she said, before turning and just as calmly leaving the room.

"Was it his?" Oscar asked.

She nodded. He'd known all along.

"I'm sorry," he said.

"It doesn't matter. I don't believe it."

She received a stunned silence. "Darling, really—"

"Don't condescend to me, Oscar, as if I'd lost my mind. Do you think Richard isn't clever enough to run his horse off a cliff and leave his cloak behind so they'll assume he's dead?"

"Well . . . I suppose it's possible."

"It is more than possible. It's brilliant. It's just the sort of thing he loves to plan. With the guards turning back under the assumption that he's dead, he can hire a boat and come for me tomorrow. . . ."

Oscar gave her a pitying look. She turned from him in annoyance. "Don't look at me like that. You don't know him as I do. I have to believe it's true. Don't you see, Oscar?"

She swayed on her feet, and he caught her, holding her close. "Yes, pet, I see."

"Then fetch my horse. I'm going as planned. And with any luck, you shall never see me again."

It was nearly dark when she arrived. The hideout, though little changed, had the feel of desertion about it. The bluebells were gone. The waterwheel had rusted again and merely squeaked in its efforts to turn. Dusk hung about the place with a feeling of gloom. She did her best to shake it away.

She tied her horse in the forge that had served as a barn. There, on a cool spring night that seemed an eternity ago, Captain Wycliffe had held a knife to her throat and whispered the words, *I've never raped a woman in my life. I have no intention of starting now.*

She shivered, remembering the revelation that his lovemaking had been. Wandering idly, she found her way along the path to the stick shelter they'd shared out in the woods. Here, they'd made love under the light of the stars. They'd planned capers and read of their successes in the papers and laughed at the authorities' failure at pursuit. What innocent times those seemed now. Times when the consequences of their actions had never entered their minds. Now, Richard could be dead, and she—

No, she wouldn't allow herself to think it. One more night. All she had to live through was one more night before she knew the truth. She stood in their deserted love nest and offered up a prayer. *Let this night pass quickly. And if he doesn't come, then for God's sake strike me dead!*

She couldn't bear to be there. It was too intimate. If she dwelled too long on what she might lose by never again touching him or kissing him or loving him through the nights, she knew she wouldn't make it until morning. She must keep herself focused. To pass these interminable hours, she must find something to do.

She went back to the mill. The millworks rose through the center of the floor as before. There were small reminders scattered about the place of their stay—one man's pipe, another's worn-out boot, the Captain's knife stuck into the table. She couldn't look at the knife. There were too many memories that, unexpectedly, seemed too fresh and raw to abide. The way he'd held it to her throat that night of her seduction, then, when he'd seen that he wouldn't need it, had tossed it up into the rafters and used his hands as weapons instead. The way he'd flung it to her with his insufferable orders to clean the fish. She smiled, thinking back on it now. But even as she smiled, she ached inside. What if it was never to be again?

It was in the basement that she found her solace. The basement that had once been piled high with booty.

Now, only a tumbled-down pile of books remained. The books the Captain had once given her to read, to while away the time before he'd taken her with them on their raids. She picked up a handful and looked at the colorful covers. It made her feel close to him, to hold the source of his inspiration in her hands. It was a closeness she could tolerate. Not the caustic, sharp, intimate pain of memories in his bed. But the more remote memories of the essence of the man. What he stood for. What he hoped to accomplish. What he was willing to give up for her sake.

It was important to remember the last, for if he'd been willing to give his life for her once, she could only hope . . .

She took the books upstairs and made a fire, then settled down to read. Penny dreadfuls. Odd that they should come to symbolize to her the spirit of the man she loved—a man whose wit and intellect were as sharp as any she'd ever known. She looked at the covers once again and smiled to think that one day she might hold such a book in her hands that was written by her own pen. *The Last Highwayman,* she would call it, by Christina Went—No. By the Duchess of Wynterbrooke. Better yet. And in it, she would tell all the wonders she'd discovered while riding by her bandit's side.

She slept feeling him close to her. Sometimes, in her feverish slumber, she imagined he was in the room, watching over her. She was tempted to look, even in her sleep, but something, that same little voice that warned her well, told her it was better to savor the sensation while she could. So she slept with a smile on her face, with the knowledge that he was with her and that she would see him when she opened her eyes at last.

Of course, she didn't. But her conscious mind hadn't anticipated that he'd be there. Her conscious mind told her that her salvation lay in the sight of sails on the horizon. Her conscious mind told her she had only to wait.

She packed the books in her valise, then walked out to the cliffs in the chill silence before dawn. She sat on the cliff, dangling her legs over the edge, thinking of how she'd sat just so upon hearing the news that her parents had denied her ransom. She'd been devastated, and he'd come and given her a comfort and an understanding she'd never before expected or received. He'd kept his word and had taken her with him on the next raid, and in doing so, had given her the gift of a new life.

Now, she sat on the same cliff hoping for the same miraculous gift. A new life at his side. She looked out at the sea. The horizon was a gunmetal grey. She could see nothing yet. But it didn't matter. She could wait. She had all the time in the world.

He can't be dead, her conscious mind cried. He'll be here. *He'll be here!* She had to believe.

She watched with enforced calm as the sky lightened in the east. The breeze toyed with her hair. Perfect sailing weather, her conscious mind said. What a day they would have at sea!

Only when she saw the sun, red as fire, did she begin to despair. Still, she was torn in her grief. She could believe he wouldn't come—the finality in his eyes had hinted at that—but not that he was dead. Never that he was dead. For while he lived, there was always hope. Hope that someday, somewhere, he would find her and claim her as his. If he didn't come, she could almost bear it if she didn't think he was dead.

But he had to come! If he didn't show up, where would she go? What would she do? She was twenty years old. She had a lifetime to fill without him. If he didn't come, what would she do with the rest of her life?

All at once, it was morning. A bright, clear morning, red with the sun's rays. A perfect morning, if only she could look up and see the clean white sails of a ship. If only she could see him standing on the deck in the distance, with that mischievous, insolent grin on his face. If only she could dive into the water and swim the sea and meet him halfway, each of them planting wet and joyous kisses on the other's dripping face. If only . . . If only . . .

She looked out at the horizon and saw nothing but the empty sea.

EPILOGUE

*T*HERE WAS NOTHING left for her but to go home.
Home? It was a deplorable word, signifying nothing. It
had meant little enough to her in her life, and it meant
less than nothing to her now. Home meant an empty
mausoleum without Richard by her side.

She rose laboriously, finding it difficult to breathe. Her
body, already ravaged, was stiff from sitting on the damp
ground far longer than even her dogged optimism
should have allowed. Her legs shook so they could
scarcely hold her. Her stomach heaved. Cold perspiration beaded on her brow. She thought she might be sick.

But what did it matter? He hadn't come for her. After
all was said and done, she, apparently, meant less than
nothing to *him*.

She heard a twig snap behind her. Terrified, she
wheeled around, expecting the authorities to have followed her. Instead, Richard stood there with a purposely
broken twig in his hands.

His hair was slightly ruffled. He wore a crisp white
shirt open at the throat, and black breeches tucked into
gleaming knee-high boots. In spite of his yellowing
bruises, he looked sleek and handsome—and altogether
distant.

The sight of him was such a shock that her breath left
her in a strangled gasp. For a moment, her throat burnt.
He tossed the twig negligently away.

When at last she could speak, she said, "How did you
get here? I expected . . ."

"Would you have a highwayman reveal *all* his secrets?"

In spite of the twinkle in his eyes, there was a hard, sardonic look to his features. He looked as if he were asking himself why he'd come.

"You bloody bastard!"

He raised a startled brow. "Hardly the welcome I'd anticipated."

"You made me think you weren't coming. You made me *pray* you were dead. Because knowing you cold in your watery grave, I wouldn't have to ask myself the same nagging question for eternity: Why didn't he come?"

"Ah," he said softly. "But he *has* come."

"But not with open arms, I see. He comes with the knowledge of what I've done in his eyes. Once again, it seems, the Prince has come between us."

"He comes knowing you loved him enough to sacrifice anything for him—even to pay the highest price. Thinking it over, I found that I couldn't stay away."

"How romantic of you. The epitome of romance, I suppose, to the unimaginative. I, however, had a different sort of reunion in mind."

"What was that, Duchess?"

The title, softly uttered, was like a caress. She turned her back, unable to look at him. "I had thought to see your sail on the horizon, crisp and white in the morning sun. I imagined the moment of seeing one another would be such unutterable joy that we should fling ourselves into the sea in our haste to touch one another and know we were real. That the past wouldn't matter in the face of our love for one another and the prospect of a future." She paused, her eyes closed. "Well. You always said I was too much the romantic. The trouble with having a writer's imagination is you can write a better scene in your head than the one life provides. For the reality is, I can't seem to bring myself to look you properly in the face."

"I see. So it was a baptism you fancied."

"Of sorts, I suppose I did."

"A washing clean of our sins and our ugly past. Rebirth, as it were."

"Rebirth, yes."

"To rise cleansed from the water and start anew."

"Oh, yes." Her voice was but a sigh on the breeze.

Even then, her mind dared to hope. That he'd come up behind her and put his hands gently on her shoulders. That he'd turn her around and kiss her and make her forget the guilt that plagued her heavy heart. That she could forget the anguish of the look in his eyes when he'd discovered what she'd done.

There was nothing but silence for a moment. Her shoulders slumped. So he would deny her even that.

Then she did feel him behind her. But instead of the tender contact she'd foreseen, he unceremoniously threw her over his shoulder and carted her across the meadow.

"Put me down this instant! What do you think you're—"

Before she could finish the sentence, he tossed her into the stream.

The icy shock of it caused her to scream, which caused her mouth and lungs to fill with water. She almost drowned in her attempts to right herself, weighed down by her heavy skirts as she was. When she finally ascended from the water with a mighty, gulping thrust, he asked her coolly, from the safety of dry land, "Not drowned, are you?"

She flung her hair out of her eyes. "No bloody thanks to you."

"Good. Consider yourself baptized." He plunged in after her, boots and all, put his hand to the top of her head and shoved hard, dunking her below the surface once again. When she finally loomed up out of the water, she was spewing wrathfully.

"Yes," he murmured appreciatively. "I want you spitting fire. Do you think I came back for a woman who cowers at the sight of me? Who can't look me in the face for shame of what she's done? How dare you malign me so, Duchess! Has it not occurred to you that what you did for me touched the hidden corners of my heart? Not once in my life has anyone thought so much of me that they would sacrifice themselves for me. Not till you. Did you think I'd take that lightly, Duchess? Did you imagine I'd hold it against you that you soiled your precious body for the sake of my miserable life?"

"Yes," she screamed. She was dripping wet. Her shoulder throbbed, and she shivered and coughed. But she felt alive! "Yes. Yes, you bastard! *Yes.*"

"Then I demand an apology."

" *You?* Demand an apology from *me?* After dunking me in the drink?"

"I demand an apology for misjudging me so completely."

"Do you blame me for misjudging you, when you keep all your wretched thoughts to yourself?"

"My thoughts, when directed at you, are hardly wretched."

"And how am I to know? You keep your blasted secrets like a virgin guards her chastity. You plot and plan, holed up in the sanctity of your own mind. And when you're ready"—she shoved at his chest with the flat of her palms—"you *condescend* to let me know what you've decided."

She pushed him again, her anger strong and deep-rooted, and fueled by her frustration. To keep her still, he grabbed her arms and yanked her to him.

"And just what have I decided that displeases you so?"

"That we'd never marry, for one. That you'd sail away without me, and leave me with my broken heart—"

"But I haven't sailed away. And who says we shan't marry?"

"You haven't *asked* me, you bloody—"

He wrenched her around with him, threw her back on the bank of the stream, fell atop her, and pinned her hands to the ground on either side of her head. "Call me a bastard one more time—" he raged.

"And what?"

"You're the most infuriating woman! I came thinking you'd be happy—"

"Happy? That you've granted me this favor?"

"—happy to put the past behind us. If I *have* made all

the decisions—and I beg leave to argue that point at another time—it's most likely because you've behaved as pigheadedly—"

"Pigheaded!"

"—as you're doing now. If you won't listen to what I came to say, I shall have to show you my tender sentiments in another way."

There was nothing tender about him. Her shoulder stung mercilessly beneath his weight. For all she knew, she was bleeding again. Her teeth were chattering from the cold of the frigid stream. But she was so incensed by his rough treatment that she fought to get her hands free so she could rake them across his smug, superior face.

Sensing this, he held her fast. After a brief moment of peering into her face as if pondering the possibilities, he leaned over and took the top button of her riding habit in his teeth. He jerked his head, then turned it to spit the button into the stream.

"Did you think I wouldn't touch you after what you did?" he demanded.

"Yes," she hissed.

He used his teeth to wrench another button. "That I couldn't kiss you"—and another—"or lie with you"—and another—"or love you without remembering you in the Prince's bed?"

She turned her face away. "Yes," she whimpered. "That's exactly what I thought. It's what I saw in your eyes when you first saw me."

"What you saw in my eyes," he corrected, "was my own realization of what a fortunate cur I am. When I saw you there, so breathtaking, so tragic, and yet so hopeful at the sight of me, I had a moment to ask myself one last time: Do you really deserve this gift from the gods?"

She looked at him then. "And what did you answer?"

He gave her an insolent grin, as of old. "I decided I do."

All at once, her anger was gone. "Oh, Richard. You forgive me, then? Truly?"

"Forgive you?" He grew serious. "Christina, listen to what I say and remember it. I've had precious little to love in my life. A father who betrayed me, a friend who thought he'd killed me, a mother I never knew. I've been turned out by the only family I have left. In this whole world, the only one who's ever truly loved me has been you. I'm not accustomed to loving someone. Because of that, I'm rather bumbling at times. I haven't always told you how I felt, and I haven't trusted you with all my plans, it's true. I suppose it's because I kept waiting for you to leave me like everyone else had."

"I told you I'd never leave you."

"How was I to know? When you went to Ireland, I knew I could trust you. But when you were shot, I didn't know that I could trust myself. To keep you safe. To give you all you deserved. What does a wretch like me know of love, anyway?"

"You're not a wretch."

"That's right. I'm a bastard, as I recall."

There were tears in her eyes. "Richard, stop—"

He leaned over her and rubbed his face against her cheek. "Since the day I realized I loved you, I've been afraid of losing you one way or another. Either by your own choice to leave, or by the circumstances of my life that made protecting you an impossibility. When you sacrificed yourself for me—to Bertie, of all people—I admit it shook me. I could see nothing ahead for you but misery at my side."

"Yes, yes, I know all that. Do proceed to the happy ending, won't you?"

He looked up and found her eyes with his. "I meant to leave you. To make the same sort of sacrifice you had for me."

"Richard, for God's sake, do get on with it."

"But I couldn't."

She began to smile. "Yes?"

"Your absence left such a hole in my life, that I didn't see how I could fill it. It occurred to me then that the worst had happened. All my fears had come to pass. And there you were, still willing—"

"More than willing."

"—to run off with me to God knew where and live any life I chose."

"So long as I have my say."

"Do you want to hear this?"

"Naturally, darling. What do you think I've been waiting for?"

"I realized the worst had happened and you were still mine. And suddenly it occurred to me that—"

"—there was nothing left to fear."

"You've heard this tale before."

"No. I felt the same. That it didn't matter what happened from here on in. That it was enough to be together."

"I've been a coward."

"You?"

"I made decisions based on fear. You were right to revile me."

"When have I ever reviled you wrongly?"

"We shan't go into that. The point is, I love you. I've never loved anyone else, and fight it though I have, there's nothing to be done for it. I love you—"

"Say it again."

"*I—love—you*. And knowing that—"

"— at long last!"

"—I find I can face the future unafraid."

"Reborn."

"Renewed."

"Alive."

They smiled into each others' eyes.

"What do we do now?" she asked. He still held her pinned to the grassy bank, with her legs dangling beneath him in the stream.

"Are you asking me to make a decision?"

"Just this once, for old time's sake, I'd say yes—since you seem, by virtue of positioning, to be in charge."

Still looking into her eyes, he considered. "Have I leave, then, to do anything I like?"

"Within reason."

He grinned. "Oh, I have *good* reason." Then he lowered his head and bit the last button from her bodice.

He spit it out and asked, "If I release you, will you behave?"

"I shall behave abominably."

He freed her hands and undressed her warily, expecting resistance, or at least another vengeful shove. She was too complying. But she allowed him to strip her habit from her. Then she leaned back, elbows on the bank, to thrust her gloriously naked breasts out at him, tempting him as he hastily shed his clothes.

"You're a wicked woman."

"Lucky for you."

He had horrible bruises and gashes on his torso from the beating the soldiers had given him. She had only an instant to wonder how much it pained him before he was against her, his flesh feeling warm against her tingling skin as he lowered his mouth to hers. On contact, her blood began to sing. She arched against him, feeling every taut contour of him pressed into her. With a rapid sly movement, she flipped him around so that she was on top, her legs straddling him as she kissed him with all the rampant passion she'd feared never to expend again.

"I thought I was in charge," he said with a laugh, when he could breathe.

"I said you could do what you wanted. I never promised to be *meek*."

"Am I to take it, then, that you still want me?"

"*Want* you?" She flung herself at him with such force that they fell over, rolling in the water as she covered his face with a flurry of ecstatic kisses. They came up sputtering, but she wouldn't stop. "With all my heart and soul."

He grabbed her and kissed her so hard that they drifted under the water once again. They hardly seemed to notice, as they ran their hands along limbs slick with water. When it was finally necessary to draw a breath, he heaved her out of the water and flung her back against the bank, half in the stream and half out. As he gasped for breath, he covered her flat belly with heartfelt kisses. Dipping into the stream, he came up with a mouthful of water and dribbled it all along her breasts.

"My body seems to want you, as well," she informed him as her nipples hardened beneath his tongue.

"No more regrets?"

"None."

"No more thinking of the past?"

"I bless the past. It brought you back to me."

He turned her so that her back was to him. Before she could guess what he was about, he'd ripped the bandage from her shoulder. She cried out, but he merely said, "It's best to do it quickly." Then he lowered his mouth and kissed her wound.

"As love is sometimes best done quickly," she prompted in a husky tone.

"Are you impatient, love?"

"I'm ravenous."

He put his hand between her legs and inserted a finger into her. The impact was so sudden and so welcome that she gasped her ecstasy into the open air. Her body felt as if a string of firecrackers had ignited beneath her skin.

He worked with a reckless skill, submerging another and yet another finger, until his hand was filled with her, and she was arching against the hard bone of his thumb. He nipped at her back and neck as she threw her head back to let her flowing hair dangle in the water at her waist.

"It's been too long," he murmured against her skin.

She looked back over her shoulder. "Then come along, highwayman, stop wasting time."

Raising his head, he saw the flagrant invitation in h eyes. Grinning, he removed his hand, turned her to f him, and slid up her body so that his loins covered h His chest was bearing into her breasts, his mouth a fraction of an inch away from hers. She needed no preparation, no coaxing. She was as ready as he, hungry and greedy, and she wasn't ashamed to show it. No feminine wiles, no falsely modest hesitations. He entered her and heard her gasp as they moved together, smiling their delight against each others' mouths.

The pleasure was too great. With panting breath, she tore her mouth from his. "Baptism," she said, "was never so good."

"If you're not careful," he admonished, "you'll roast in hell."

"I've had my hell. It's heaven being here with you."

He let himself go. Thrusting her back against the bank, he drove into her with a force fueled by his gratitude and his love, until she lost control and brought her lips to his shoulder, sinking her teeth into his flesh.

They lay in each others' arms for a long time, unmindful of the world around them, grateful for each others' warmth. Where earlier they'd felt strain and isolation, they enfolded themselves now in the comfort of peace, in renewed confidence, in a sense of having healed. Apart, they'd been malcontents seeking expiation of their demons. Together, at long last, they felt whole.

Eventually he said into her hair, "Christina, you've made me a happy man."

"Oh, Richard. I love you so! I promise from now on—"

He put his fingers to her mouth to hush her. "Make no unrealistic promises. I've no need of them. I love you as you are."

"Very well. Then I promise to love you till eternity, for that's a vow I can easily keep. I promise never again to doubt you, or leave you of my own free will. I promise never to allow the past to come between us, or spoil our happiness again."

"That's all well and good. But do you promise not to call me bastard again?"

She laughed and nipped his chin with her teeth. "Not if you infuriate me. There are, after all, limits to what even I can do!"

Inevitably, they became aware of the water lapping at their hips. With a great deal of reluctance, they left the stream. Christina's hair hung in long tangles. She wrung it out, laughing as he fished out a soaking boot. They laid their clothes out in the sun to dry.

"For all the good it will do me," she scoffed, "as you've ruined yet another of my riding habits."

"Can I help it that you're so impatient? Perhaps you should remain naked and at the ready, if you insist on being so demanding."

"You're the one who demanded the apology," she reminded him, and laughed as he crushed her mouth with his.

It was too chilly to remain naked for long. They ran to the mill and retrieved blankets as their teeth chattered noisily in the still morning. "I shall miss my cloak," he commented idly as he wrapped one of the blankets around her. Then, lifting the corner of his mouth, he tossed the blanket over his own shoulders, careful not to chafe his wounds. "So you think you can write a better ending than I?" he asked mischievously.

She had the grace to smile. "No, darling. It looked for a time as though *my* ending was going to be tragic. I like this one much better."

Wrapped in the blankets, they wandered hand in hand toward the cliffs. There, on the distant horizon, were the crisp white sails she'd hoped earlier to see.

AUTHOR'S NOTE

As a child, I wanted nothing more than to write books. Writers, I believed, wove magic. They enriched peoples' lives. They helped them escape, forget their troubles, envision a more romantic and, perhaps, meaningful existence. They taught people to dream.

This passion never left me. I defined myself, at one time, as a writer first and a person second. As a consequence, I suffered dearly when, after years of struggle, I still couldn't seem to find a way to make my books work. After writing eight to twelve hours a day, I tortured myself with the question, "What am I doing wrong?"

It wasn't until I learned to embrace a more holistic attitude that things finally changed. When I realized there are *many* ways of serving, and writing is only one of those ways, I surrendered my ambitions for success and went back to writing because I loved it.

Out of this, *The Last Highwayman* was born. I decided to try and write a book that would be fun for me to write and hopefully fun for someone else to read. A book about heroes and magic, and the ability of love to transform peoples' lives. And I learned not to expect the fruits of my labors, but to feel grateful for the opportunity and joy of writing. I discovered that sometimes you have to surrender to get what you want. And I found out that suffering has its purpose, because it helps us learn. For that, I'm deeply grateful.

I'd like to thank all the friends and family who never lost faith in me. Specific thanks go to the people who made this lifelong dream come true:

Barbara Alpert, my editor, who discovered the book, loved it for what it was, and made all of this possible.

Her enthusiasm, astute observations, and respect for writers and the writing process, all make her an extraordinary editor. Her warmth, humor, and generosity make her a joy to know. I can never thank her enough. Meg Ruley, my agent, whose exuberance is matched only by her kindness. Her boundless encouragement, sense of the absurd, and general good cheer are such happy additions to my life that I can't think about her without smiling. Like Barbara, she's a godsend. And Nita Taublib, a dynamo who is not only fun and energetic, but who offers support even when she doesn't have to. The editors and authors at Bantam, for making me feel so welcome. Russ Galen for leading me to Barbara. Susan Johnson for recommending Meg. My dearest friend, Mary Cunniffe McKinney, who has done so much for me that expressing it on paper would trivialize it. Neither can I adequately express what the friendship and kindness of Richard Rush and Claude Roberts have meant to me—I hope they know. Katie Kocis, who brought new dimensions to my life. David Pond, who changed my life by telling me a truth I needed to hear. Richard Lloyd, who set me free. Lucy Pond, for her wisdom and support throughout the years. My father James O'Neal, and my mother-in-law Elizabeth Arnold, for helping me with the horses, so I didn't go crazy in the process. Finally, and most importantly, my daughter Janie, who never said "if" in reference to the publication of my work but always "when," and who never complained about having a mom who began every conversation with, "Just let me finish this sentence." No one could ask for a more loving or more beautiful daughter—or friend.

When I asked Barbara Alpert, "How do I thank people for standing by me during the seventeen years it took me to get published?" she answered, "You don't have to tell them it took seventeen years." But I want you to know. It was only by relinquishing my ego that this gift was given to me. And what if I'd given up in the sixteenth year? What if I'd listened to people who said it couldn't be done? Never give up. Abundance is our birthright. If my dreams can come true, anyone's can.

Even yours.

Katherine O'Neal
19 August 1992

I'd love to hear from you. Please write me at:
P.O. Box 2452
Seattle, WA 98111–2452

ABOUT THE AUTHOR

KATHERINE O'NEAL is the daughter of a U.S. Air Force pilot and a fiercely British artist who met in India in the fifties. The family traveled extensively and lived for many years in Asia. Katherine is married to William Arnold, a noted film critic and author of the best selling books *Shadowland* and *China Gate*—a man she feels makes her heroes pale in comparison. It was he who said, "You're a romantic person; why *not* write romantic fiction?" Together, they continue the tradition of travel whenever possible. They also enjoy their dogs, cats, horses, and each other—not necessarily in that order. They have a daughter, Janie, who isn't sure if she wants to write, but who's definite in her love of horses.

Women's Fiction

On Sale in February

TEMPERATURES RISING

56045-X $5.99/6.99 in Canada

☐ **by Sandra Brown**

New York Times bestselling author of
A WHOLE NEW LIGHT and FRENCH SILK

A contemporary tale of love and passion in the South Pacific.

OUTLAW HEARTS

29807-0 $5.99/6.99 in Canada

☐ **by Rosanne Bittner**

Bestselling author of SONG OF THE WOLF,
praised by *Romantic Times* as "a stunning
achievement...that moves the soul and fills the heart."

THE LAST HIGHWAYMAN

56065-4 $5.50/6.50 in Canada

☐ **by Katherine O'Neal**

Fascinating historical fact and sizzling romantic fiction meet
in this sensual tale of a legendary bandit and a scandalous
high-born lady.

CONFIDENCES

56170-7 $4.99/5.99 in Canada

☐ **by Penny Hayden**

"Thirtysomething" meets Danielle Steel—four best friends
are bound by an explosive secret.

Ask for these books at your local bookstore or use this page to order.

☐ Please send me the books I have checked above. I am enclosing $_____ (add $2.50
to cover postage and handling). Send check or money order, no cash or C. O. D.'s please

Name _____

Address _____

City/ State/ Zip _____

Send order to: Bantam Books, Dept. FN95, 2451 S. Wolf Rd., Des Plaines, IL 60018
Allow four to six weeks for delivery.

Prices and availability subject to change without notice.   FN95 3/93